M000207471

THE WAY
THROUGH A FIELD OF STARS

Book one of the
Through a Field of Stars
trilogy

BRIAN JOHN SKILLEN

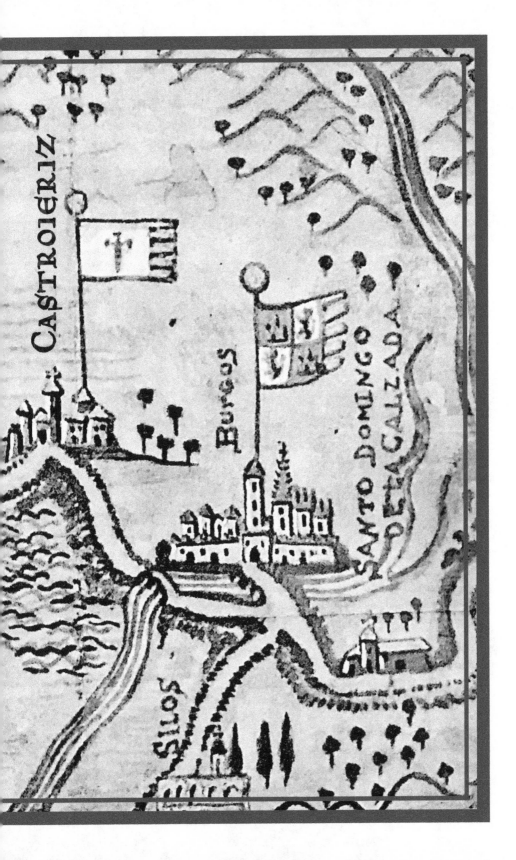

Published by: 1881 Productions
Arvada, Colorado, USA

ISBN 978-1-7353036-1-1

Design and formatting by Valeria Fox
Developmental Edit by Parisa Zolfaghari
Line Edit by Lessa Lamb

Printed in the United States of America

August 2020

www.throughafieldofstars.com
theway@throughafieldofstars.com

This book is dedicated to all the pilgrims from
the Camino de Santiago
who inspired

The Way: Through A Field of Stars,

especially my wife Chelsea.

I hope reading this novel inspires you
to take the adventure of a lifetime.

Buen Camino!

AUTHOR'S NOTES

On April 8, 2017, in the small town of Castrojeriz, I was first told about a secret code of the Knights Templar on the Camino de Santiago. This code inspired me to write *The Way: Through a Field of Stars*. As I hiked the Camino across Spain, the story for this novel played like a movie in my head. The things I saw, the people I met, and the experiences I had all wove together into the perfect narrative. Since that day, I have walked more than a thousand miles doing research for this book series.

The Way: Through a Field of Stars is set in the year 1306, one year before the Knights Templar mysteriously disappeared, along with their treasure. The novel follows Princess Isabella of France on a fictitious pilgrimage along the Camino de Santiago as her father, King Philip, plots to disband the Templars. Join Isabella and her companions as they travel through foreign lands, unlock the Templar's secret codes, avoid immortal Shadows, and discover the wisdom of the Camino de Santiago.

Being a historical fantasy, many of the characters are historical figures, like King Philip IV of France and the Knights Templar. Though these characters are actually historical figures, I've altered certain things about them to fit the narrative, like Isabella's age. To learn more about the factual history of these characters, refer to the appendix in the back of the novel. Being a fantasy, there are also some supernatural entities you can expect along the way.

I have walked the miles my characters have walked and learned the lessons they have learned. All of the characters in the novel that aren't based on historical people were inspired by pilgrims I met on my Caminos. This book is dedicated to them. "Buen Camino!"

FUN FACTS

All the secret codes in the novel are based on symbols, ruins,
and other things I saw on my own Camino. If you walk
the Camino de Santiago yourself, and know where to look,
you can still see all these fascinating markings today.

The title of the novel, *The Way: Through a Field of Stars* has a deep
meaning. The Camino de Santiago is often referred to as
The Way or *The Way of St. James*. The second part of the title comes
from the saying, "There is a star in the Milky Way for every
pilgrim who walks the Camino de Santiago."

TABLE OF CONTENTS

PROLOGUE..1

CHAPTER 1 - THE ARC OF SAN ANTON 3

CHAPTER 2 - CASTROJERIZ...8

CHAPTER 3 - THE BOAT HOUSE 20

CHAPTER 4 - CARRION DE LOS CONDES 35

CHAPTER 5 - THE MESETA 44

CHAPTER 6 - SAHAGUN...52

CHAPTER 7 - PARIS...57

CHAPTER 8 - BENEATH THE STARS...59

CHAPTER 9 - LEON 65

CHAPTER 10 - THE LAKE...78

CHAPTER 11 - HOSPITAL DE ORBIGO 88

CHAPTER 12 - NOTRE DAME...94

CHAPTER 13 - THE SECRET OF THE GREEN MEN 97

CHAPTER 14 - THE ALCHEMIST...102

CHAPTER 15 - BEAUTIFUL LIFE...107

CHAPTER 16 - ASTORGA 112

CHAPTER 17 - SWEET CHARITY 117

CHAPTER 18 - THE PAPAL COURT 129

CHAPTER 19 - RABANAL DEL CAMINO 131

CHAPTER 20 - CRUZ DE FERRO..139

CHAPTER 21 - MOLINASECA 141

CHAPTER 22 - PONFERRADA 146

CHAPTER 23 - TEMPLAR CASTLE 153

CHAPTER 24 - FIRSTS AND LASTS.. 161

CHAPTER 25 - O CEBREIRO 170

CHAPTER 26 - THE TEMPLAR COMPANY 174

CHAPTER 27 - THE TEMPLAR LIBRARY 176

CHAPTER 28 - THE GALICIAN FOREST 184

CHAPTER 29 - OLD ACQUAINTANCES... 186

CHAPTER 30 - THE GUARDIANS OF GALICIA... 193

CHAPTER 31 - THE EMPTY... 199

CHAPTER 32 - PORTOMARIN 204

CHAPTER 33 - PALAIS DE LA CITÉ 213

CHAPTER 34 - THE DARK NIGHT OF THE SOUL 216

CHAPTER 35 - SANTIAGO DE COMPOSTELA 227

CHAPTER 36 - GOOD FORTUNE OR BAD 238

CHAPTER 37 - OLVEIROA 241

CHAPTER 38 - LAST NIGHT...246

CHAPTER 39 - FINISTERRE..248

EPILOGUE 252

APPENDIX..254

PROLOGUE

Spain, 1183

Chisels rang out in the great Cathedral of Santiago de Compostela,[1] as Grand Master Arnold of Torroja[2] inspected the masons' fine work. He traced his fingers over a newly hewn symbol on a massive pillar.

The final code—one last precaution to protect the treasure and bind the evil it has brought into this world.

Arnold's body stiffened as the sound of footsteps echoed toward him. A burly man came into view and Arnold loosened his clenched fists. "Oh, it's just you, Paulo."

Paulo stopped, and put his hand on his stomach in a sign of fidelity. "Grand Master, the work is almost complete. Would you like us to engrave anything else?" Arnold looked past Paulo's shoulder at the other masons. They had worked ceaselessly since their arrival, and every column lining the immense cathedral was now covered in symbols.

"No, that will suffice. You and the others have done good work—God's work."

"Forgive me for saying so, Grand Master, but desecrating a church with these symbols doesn't feel like God's work."

Arnold chuckled and shook his head. He gestured toward the symbols he had been examining. "I hope neither you, nor anyone else, will ever have to understand this."

Paulo nodded. "Forgive me for questioning, Grand Master."

"There is nothing to forgive. You are strong and loyal, my boy. You would have made a fine soldier in the Holy Land..."

Arnold's vision blurred and the smile disappeared from his face. He heard the screams again; they had haunted his waking thoughts since he had left Jerusalem.

He rubbed the stitching of the red cross that adorned his white tunic and muttered, "A Templar's[3] sworn duty is to protect. How many has the evil taken since?"

"Grand Master?"

"Oh, it's nothing. That will be all." Arnold straightened his garments and walked to the pew where his sword lay. He hoped its weight would steady his shaky hands.

Arnold knelt, and the pew groaned, sending its melody to the rafters where it mixed with the beating chisels. He made the sign of the cross and bowed his head.

My Lord Jesus, I pray our actions will protect what you have entrusted to us, and that you will forgive the sins of my predecessor, Odo...[4]

The screams began again. Odo's name triggered the memory of the day Arnold's life, and the world, changed forever. Arnold took a few breaths, but the Battle of Montgisard[5] continued to rage in his head. It was here that Odo used the power of the treasure to enable eighty Knights Templar, and a few thousand soldiers, to decimate an army of twenty-six thousand Saracens. Odo was warned not to use the treasure, but he didn't listen.

A drop of perspiration fell from Arnold's brow and hit his clasped hands. He blinked a few times, unsure how long he had been trapped in that memory. A well of emotion rose inside him as he stared at the cross.

I fear Jerusalem will soon fall.

Arnold's hairs stood on end. His prayer was interrupted not by a sound, but by the unsettling silence. The hammers and chisels of the masons had ceased.

Everyone was gone.

Arnold took the sword from his lap and walked cautiously in the direction he had last seen Paulo. As he approached the final pew, the smell of death hung in the air. Arnold took a putrid breath and rounded the corner, weapon drawn.

At the base of the column lay Paulo's severed head, staring at him. His eyes, which had been so full of life moments earlier, were now transfixed with a look of horror. Tears filled Arnold's wrinkles like Paulo's blood filled the cracks of the floor.

Were those screams...were they...real?

To his left there was movement. An ominous shape crouched in the dark recesses of the church. *A Shadow.*

Arnold closed his eyes. He knew what was coming. He was the last living Templar from the Battle of Montgisard. "My Lord Jesus Christ, have mercy on me. It ends here, today," he whispered through quivering lips. A deafening hiss filled the air, and Arnold felt movement like a winter's wind. He raised his weapon just in time to intercept a curved sword. He opened his eyes, but it made no difference; all he saw was darkness, a giant shadow looming over him.

CHAPTER 1

THE ARC OF SAN ANTON

Spain, 1306

Isabella's hair whipped her in the face as her dappled gray steed tore through the night. She wanted to forget what lay behind, but she needed to know...

Isabella glanced over her shoulder.

Tristan, the captain of her personal guard, followed behind her on his black stallion. *Is that all who's left?* He looked like a horseman of the apocalypse silhouetted by the torchlight from the pursuing army. A chill ran through Isabella's body. She bit her lip and refocused on the Arc of San Anton.[6] Its fortified walls were a beacon of hope in an otherwise dark night.

The massive Commandery of the Knights Templar lay like a slumbering beast. Its time-stained Arc jutted into the air and a fortified gate blocked the passage of the Camino de Santiago,[7] the ancient pilgrimage that had led Isabella from the safety of her father's palace to this desolate land. Now, here she was fleeing murderers into the hands of those she had been taught not to trust.

Isabella was glad she had chosen the fastest horse in her father's kingdom for her pilgrimage. Had it not been for his speed, she would be dead like the others.

She leaned forward and whispered, "Faster." The steed obeyed the direction and thundered ahead.

Isabella cursed her father for sending her on this quest, but she wouldn't have wanted him to give the task to anyone else. She was his favorite; the one he trusted. She would deliver the treasure he needed to save their kingdom and make him proud. Besides, it was her only chance at a life of freedom.

An arrow whistled past Isabella's head, followed by another. She hoped Tristan was still with her, but she didn't dare look.

Her horse's hooves pummeled the ground hard. *Three steps, five steps, ten steps.*

A deep base bell rang from the Arc, accompanied by others. The sound passed through Isabella's body and bounced off the surrounding hills. The ringing was the sound of salvation, the sound of safety. Isabella's whole body sighed in relief.

Following the bells, a large signal-fire burst into flames on the highest point of the Arc. One by one, all the surrounding hilltops burned brightly. The message had been sent; help was coming.

Isabella was now just a hundred yards away from the closed gate. She would not slow her pace even if they crashed into the stone walls. Death was better than being captured by the Moors.[8] In childhood, she had heard stories of the invaders from the south who had devoured this part of the land. Isabella would make it, or die.

The portcullis moaned and raised just enough for them to pass. Isabella exhaled and ducked beneath. On entering the courtyard, she came to a screeching halt; in her path was a line of Knights Templar with their shields raised and swords drawn.

Isabella's horse snorted and reared up. She leaned in close to him and squeezed tightly. "Steady, we made it." Her soothing voice calmed the beast. He circled a few times then came to a halt.

In front of her stood a Templar knight with his hands on his hips, surrounded by guards. *He must be the Commandery Master.* Isabella knew the Arc of San Anton was one of the five Templar Commanderies associated with the town of Castrojeriz. Each had its order of Knights Templar and their respective Master.

"Reveal yourself," the Commandery Master ordered.

Isabella pulled back her white silken hood. Her long hair had loosened from its braid and fell gently over her shoulders. Silence filled the courtyard and all the soldiers stared. Isabella wasn't surprised; she knew the last thing they expected to see was a young woman, barely sixteen.

Next to the Commandery Master, a fierce-looking young man with a dark complexion dropped to one knee. The red Templar cross on his black sergeant's tunic was obscured by his hand covering his heart.

"Your Highness," the sergeant said, bowing his head. Isabella's escort took off his hood, and the sergeant said, "Tristan," in a low clipped tone, just audible over the closing gates.

Isabella's brow furrowed, she glanced from her guard to the man kneeling. *Who would know us here?*

"Reveal yourself!" the Commandery Master ordered once more.

Tristan moved his horse next to hers. "This is Her Highness Princess Isabella,[9] daughter of King Philip the IV of France,[10] and I am Tristan, the captain of her personal guard."

"Can you attest to this?" The Commandery Master asked the kneeling sergeant.

"I can."

"To arms! Deus Vult!"[11] shouted the Commandery Master. The Templar battle cry from the Holy Land electrified the courtyard.

"Deus Vult!" The soldiers thundered back.

"Shoot anything that comes into range!" There was great commotion in the courtyard as the archers and other knights positioned themselves. Soon, only the Commandery Master, Isabella, Tristan, and a few guards remained.

"Welcome, Your Highness," said the Commandery Master. He bowed and all of the remaining soldiers followed suit. On rising, he asked, "Who is following you?"

Isabella dismounted and approached. "It is the Moors," she said softly. "They ambushed our party. We are the only ones to survive..." Isabella bit her lip again. Even though she had suffered a great loss, she wouldn't let her face betray any emotion—especially in the presence of her father's enemies, the Templars. "Thank you for your protection."

"It is a Templar's duty to protect, Your Highness. However, these are strange tidings. The Moors haven't been seen in this region for decades. They must be after something, and it would appear that something is you."

Isabella's body froze. *They are after me?* She inhaled deeply, noticing the sergeant was still kneeling. "Rise. How is it that you know us?"

The sergeant stood. When he lifted his head to look at her, Isabella gasped at his familiar brown eyes. "Etienne?" she whispered, happiness quickly overtaking the shock she felt. "I thought you were dead." She reached out to touch his face, but Etienne turned from her hand sharply.

The excitement drained from Isabella's body and was replaced with a numbness. It was the same numbness that had robbed her of her ability to speak two years ago when she had last seen Etienne. She had replayed the scene many times in her head. The look of helplessness on his face as they dragged him out of the throne room had haunted her. *You died because of me.*

"Master, the Moors are approaching," said Etienne stoically. His voice shaking Isabella free from the memory.

The Commandery Master smiled and pointed to the west. "So are reinforcements from Castrojeriz." In the distance, a line of Knights Templar raced toward them at an amazing clip. "Etienne, accompany the princess and her escort to the Baron of Castrojeriz—war is at our doorstep. God willing, we will meet again."

"Yes, Commandery Master. Your Highness, if you will follow me." Etienne's voice was deeper now, but still his own. Even though great calamity had struck, fortune had also smiled on Isabella. Etienne was alive, and the Moors had forced her into the protection of the Templars—the exact place she needed to be to further her quest. Yesterday, she didn't know how she would infiltrate the Templars undetected, but now, she didn't need to.

Etienne felt like he was being drawn and quartered, his body pulled in one direction and his spirit another. He looked at the Arc of San Anton and gripped the reins tightly, longing to return to the fight.

Isabella caught Etienne's eye, and he quickly turned his head. She had changed and grown just as he had, but her eyes were still the same. An echo of the love he once had for her spread through his body and dissipated as quickly as it had come. It was the first emotion of this nature he had experienced since he took his vow of chastity, poverty, and obedience.

Besides the pounding of hooves and the screams behind them, their ride had been silent. *What is there to say? She's just a memory to me now.*

Etienne had many painful memories, but his last of Isabella had left the deepest scar. She had stood by as he was sentenced to death. She could have told the truth. She could have saved him, but instead she remained silent as he was dragged away.

Etienne had trusted her. He had loved her. They had bonded over being different from the others. The shade of his skin had separated him. He was the only person of color at the palace, and the other squires constantly reminded him of it. They'd isolated him and never accepted him. Isabella had been isolated as well. She was Philip's only daughter. Her brothers hadn't wanted to play with her because she was a girl, and her father had disallowed her from mingling with common folk. This isolation had brought them together, and they'd formed a secret companionship.

However, the day of his sentencing, her actions made it clear that he never actually belonged. He often felt the only reason he was accepted by anyone, including the Templars, was because of his ability to fight.

Etienne distracted his mind by admiring the imposing castle of Castrojeriz. It towered on the hill in the distance like an eagle protecting the walled city. *Soon we will be at the gates, and I can return to the Arc.*

After a mile, the spires of San Maria Del Manzano came into view over the city wall and a delegation of Templars rode to the travelers. Etienne slowed his horse and motioned for the others to do the same.

"Ahh, Brother Etienne, what are you doing here? I have never seen you leave a fight before," said the Provincial Master, leading the pack.

"Provincial Master," Etienne said, lowering his head. "I am under orders from the Commandery Master of the Arc to deliver these pilgrims to the Baron."

The Provincial Master studied the two pilgrims. "And who are they?"

"Her Highness Princess Isabella of France, and the captain of her guard." Etienne purposely didn't name Tristan—that name felt like a foul word in his mouth.

"Thank you for your service. You may return to the Arc now, where you are needed on the front lines. We will escort the princess the rest of the way."

"As you command," Etienne said. Relief should have filled him as he turned his horse, but now that he had the opportunity to be free of Isabella, he was reluctant to move forward.

"Your Highness, if you would follow us," said the Provincial Master.

"No," Isabella answered firmly. "I won't move from this spot unless Etienne accompanies us."

Etienne's body tensed and his mouth gaped. His instincts told him to run, but even after all that had happened, he still felt drawn to Isabella. *Could she feel the same?*

"Your Highness, forgive my bluntness, but this isn't France and you are not the one giving orders here."

Isabella raised an eyebrow and, with a firm tone, said, "You will treat me with the respect my station deserves."

Etienne looked at her with wide eyes. *This isn't happening. Let me stay dead.*

A long moment passed before the Provincial Master answered, "As you wish, Your Highness, I will grant you this request. Sergeant, you will join us to see the Baron."

A knot formed in Etienne's stomach. The reality of Isabella being here had loosened so many repressed emotions. He often looked forward to going into Castrojeriz. He loved exploring its churches and narrow streets; but tonight, he felt like entering the city would change his life forever.

CHAPTER 2

CASTROJERIZ

Two skulls and crossbones were carved into the church of Santo Domingo. Above them was engraved the inscription, "O mors," and "O aeternitas." *Oh death. Oh eternity.* Etienne had always liked these carvings. Every time he passed them, he thought of mortality. Tonight was no different: Etienne's mind was on death.

He thought of all the pilgrims over the centuries who had walked past this spot on their way to Santiago de Compostela—their immortal footprints stamped into the Camino long after their bodies were gone—always leading the next generation of pilgrims to the forgiveness of their sins.

What sin could Isabella have?

Etienne had been stationed on the Camino de Santiago for nearly two years. In that time, he had seen countless pilgrims from around the world pass under the Arc of San Anton. Each had been taking the pilgrimage for a different reason: some to recover from the death of a loved one, some searching for purpose, some hoping for a miracle; but most, to receive an indulgence for the forgiveness of their sins. When a pilgrim reaches Santiago de Compostela, where the bones of Saint James[12] lie, all of their sins are forgiven. The rich could buy their forgiveness, but the poor had to walk their miles. As a Templar, it was Etienne's job to protect them all, both sinners and saints.

After he had escaped death, Etienne had been taken west on the Camino by the Templars to his assignment at the Arc. The journey was life changing. His eyes drank the beauty of the world outside the city walls of Paris. When they'd climbed the Pyrenees, his breath was taken away by the rolling vistas stretched out in front of him. It was the closest he had ever felt to God.

After the mountains, they'd passed through the lush landscape of eastern Spain into the wine country, where they had eaten grapes off of the vine and had their fill of drink. The farmers always left out a portion for pilgrims on the Camino de Santiago. Their journey had ended at the beginning of the Meseta. The landscape changed to a hot dry land with a wind that whipped through you. In the scorching summers, fields of sunflowers would come up, but besides that, not much else would grow. Most didn't like the landscape, but Etienne loved it. It was the perfect place to start anew. It was the perfect place to be forgotten.

"Etienne, ride with me," the Provincial Master ordered as he passed.

Etienne picked up speed to join him. When they were out of earshot from Isabella and Tristan, the Provincial Master asked, "Why did the princess demand you accompany us?"

Etienne looked down. He never spoke about his past, but he also never disobeyed orders from a superior. "She knew me long ago."

"How is that possible? Being a sergeant, clearly you are not of noble birth."

"When I was young, the captain of King Philip's guard took mercy on me and trained me with the other squires."

"Ahh, so you know King Philip as well?"

Etienne clenched his jaw so tightly his temples throbbed. With a glance to his superior, he said, "He tried to kill me once."

The Provincial Master nodded knowingly. "King Philip is capable of terrible things. He has borrowed substantial sums of gold from our order to pay for his wars with England. This is well known. What you may not be aware of is that France has become destitute, and the King has no way of repaying this debt. I have a feeling his daughter being here is no accident. It appears that Isabella trusts you. I want you to accompany her for as long as she will allow it. Discover what her motives are on the Camino, and report back to myself, or another superior officer."

Etienne sat straight in his saddle and furrowed his brow. "Is that an order? If not, I—"

"It is an order, Sergeant," the Provincial Master firmly stated, effectively ending the conversation just as the convoy entered Castrojeriz's main plaza. The townsfolk hustled around the courtyard preparing provisions for the battle happening a mile away at the Arc. Etienne shook his head. This battle wasn't theirs, but they would reap the consequences of it anyway.

"Why is the Arc under attack? Our home will be next," a villager shouted at Etienne and the Provincial Master as they passed. "Does it have to do with these pilgrims?"

All eyes in the plaza turned to the Provincial Master. "Calm yourself. Our city has been under attack many times and we have always prevailed. We can handle any burden this world throws at us."

"If this fight isn't ours, we should give the attackers what they want. We should give them these pilgrims and be left in peace."

The crowd jeered and pressed in. Etienne drew his sword and positioned himself between the mob and Isabella. "It is a Templar's duty to protect pilgrims, and protect them we shall. They are not the enemy, and neither are you." Etienne could sense the other Templars had formed ranks behind him. He knew his brothers would always have his back, even with their biases.

With this show of force, the mob slowly disbanded, but one man stayed, pointing a boney finger at Isabella. "I know it's you they want."

Etienne had never seen the townsfolk act like this before. Even though he didn't trust Isabella, he was worried for her safety.

To Isabella, the castle was just as imposing inside as it was on the outside. It was nothing like the lavishness of her father's palace. The gray stone walls stretched high and had blackened with time. As they walked down a long hall to a busy courtyard, the wind whipped, making the torch flames dance eerily.

A man with an air of aristocracy left his conversation with several Templars and approached the Provincial Master. "Edgar, who joins you? And what is their business here?"

Before he could answer, Isabella stepped forward. "I am Princess Isabella, daughter of King Philip the IV of France. It seems it is my presence that has brought this terror upon you," she gestured at the soldiers nearby preparing for battle. "I am to be married soon..." She paused, shifting her gaze to Etienne. She hoped to see some reaction, but he stared forward with an impenetrable look. "... and was walking the Camino de Santiago as a pilgrim, to purify myself before my holy union. Our party was struck down by the Moors tonight." She gestured to Tristan. "We were the only ones to survive. I thank you for any protection you can offer."

The Baron's whole demeanor changed as she spoke. Isabella could see the gears churning behind his eyes, figuring out how to turn this situation to his advantage. Stepping closer, he kissed her hand. "Your Highness." Isabella's index finger flinched at his wet lips. After a lingering moment, he regained his composure and removed his mouth, but continued to hold her hand. "These walls have never seen a beauty as great as yours." Isabella was no stranger to this switch from indifference to flattery. It was often the way of things once people discovered her station in life.

The saliva began to dry on Isabella's hand as the Baron continued, "Moors haven't been in this region for years. Someone must have informed them of your Camino." Looking at her sympathetically, he said, "As much as I would like to offer you protection...I can't extend our hospitality. I fear that the people will try to turn you over to the Moors. It is best for you to flee the city and continue on the Camino to the Kingdom of Leon: a place the Moors wouldn't dare to venture. I will inform your father. And, if you put in a good word for me, I will provide some supplies for your journey. It is the least I can do."

Isabella immediately withdrew her hand from the Baron's grasp and discreetly wiped it on her cloak. "Thank you for your sage advice. Your generosity *won't* be forgotten." She had dealt with men like him in court. He was an opportunist. He had no interest in her wellbeing. He would pass on the responsibility to the King of Leon in the hopes the Moors would follow. Isabella couldn't wait to be out of his presence.

An elderly Templar who had been speaking with the Baron when they arrived stepped forward. He had white hair and haunting blue eyes.

"Brother Ronan," said the Provincial Master, placing his hand on his stomach in a sign of fidelity. Isabella didn't know too much about Templar hierarchy, but she did know not many Templars outranked a Provincial Master.

Ronan put a hand on the Provincial Master's shoulder. "You will take your men to the frontline, and I will escort them to Leon. My stay here has come to an end as well."

"I feel Brother Etienne will render a greater service to our order if he joins you," said the Provincial Master. Ronan nodded his head in agreement.

"Very well, you may collect your supplies at the Iglesia de San Juan," said the Baron. "Let it be done. Buen Camino."

The small convoy left the castle and descended the hill. Speaking of Edward made Isabella think of her quest. All who had accompanied her from Paris thought she was taking the pilgrimage to purify herself before her marriage—except Tristan; he was too smart for that. He knew Isabella didn't care for Edward, nor marriage.

Tristan was the only one who knew her father had sent her on a quest to find the Templars' greatest treasure. Finding it had become her father's secret obsession. He told her it would save their kingdom, and repay what the Templars had stolen. Most importantly, though, he told her she wouldn't have to marry Edward if she succeeded.

Her search had been in vain until yesterday in the Cathedral of Burgos. Tristan had made inquiries in the dark places she couldn't be seen in, and had returned with an old crone. The crone had led Isabella to a door in the cathedral that had a strange face with a slot for a mouth carved into it.

The Crone had said, *There are seven doors resembling this one hidden on the Camino. They need to be unlocked to free the treasure. The doors have been bound with the blood of many, and it will take blood to unlock them.*

The crone then cut Isabella's finger with her wicked nails, and, with her blood, drew a symbol resembling a z between the eyes of the carving. *If you want to find the treasure, find these doors and unlock them as I have shown you. The task won't be easy. The Templars have hidden the doors well.*

Isabella had thanked the crone and asked what payment she required. The crone had squeezed Isabella's finger and taken more blood. *I have already received my payment.* She'd laughed wickedly and departed.

Isabella didn't mind bleeding if it brought her closer to her goal. *The deaths of those I have lost tonight won't be in vain. I won't fail you, Father.*

When they reached the last stone church before the city wall, Ronan stopped. "We must gather the supplies here," he said, beckoning for them to follow him inside. Isabella was grateful for the torches on the old stone walls. Their warmth helped to brush off the cold night.

"Thank you for your help," said Isabella.

Ronan waved her gratitude away. "It is a Templar's sworn duty to protect pilgrims. You are no exception." Ronan bowed slightly. "You must excuse me; I need to prepare some things for our journey." He walked to the front of the church, accompanied by Etienne.

Isabella couldn't take her eyes off Etienne. Her emotions swirled inside her every time she saw him anew. She had thought he was dead. Now that he wasn't, she had so many questions.

"Your Highness." Tristan pointed to the rear of the church. High on the back wall was a stained glass window twinkling merrily, with a pentagram forged into it. "The sign of the devil. I don't trust these Templars, and what is *he* doing here?"

Isabella made the sign of the cross, not only to ward off the pentagram, but to ask for guidance. Since Etienne had shown up, she had felt lost and distracted from her purpose. Her focus was divided.

"I don't know. I never thought I would see him again," said Isabella, her eyes once again glancing back to him. With a shake of her head, she continued, "Tristan, don't you see. This is the best thing that could have happened to us. Our close proximity to the Templars gives us special access, and a better chance of learning their secrets. Once we reach the Kingdom of Leon, we can send word to my father about the doors the crone told us about. If we find the Templar treasure, our friends' deaths won't have been for nothing. Tristan, I could be free of my marriage to Edward." Taking his hand, she continued, "Thank you for all of your service and diligent protection."

"Your Highness." Tristan's eyes looked past Isabella as he spoke. Behind her, Ronan and Etienne approached with something in their arms.

"Put these on. It will be safer for you to travel dressed like this," said Ronan, handing her a bundle of clothes.

Isabella's fastened the gray cloak and tied the sporran around her waist. Holding the wide-brimmed hat in her hand for a moment, she traced her fingers over the attached scallop shell. *The symbol of the Camino.* Each line of the shell ended in one place, just like the many roads that led to Santiago de Compostela.

These shells served as signposts on the road to Santiago; they marked both the Camino and the pilgrims who walked it. Isabella knew she was never lost when she saw a shell.

To complete the disguise, Ronan handed each one of them a staff with a gourd attached. Now, with their new clothing, they were indistinguishable from the many pilgrims Isabella had passed on her Camino.

Bang! Bang! Bang! Isabella jumped as the old wooden door of the church shook with each thud. "We know you're in there. Give the pilgrims to us. We don't want to fight their war," a voice shouted, followed by a chorus of others.

"Those are the same people from the town square," Isabella said, pulling her cloak around her tightly to shield herself from what lay on the other side of the door. Isabella winced at the thought of being turned over to the Moors. She was so close to escaping. Isabella's eyes frantically searched the church for another exit.

The door shuddered even louder; the force of the sound reverberated through the church, and caused Isabella to take a step back.

"They are ramming the door!" Etienne said, drawing his sword.

Ronan motioned for Etienne to lower his weapon. "No innocent blood will be spilled tonight. I was not planning to leave this way, but as we have no other choice..." Ronan scanned the church from left to right then surveyed the ceiling.

"What? You don't expect us to climb out," Tristan said. Isabella had seen Tristan brave many things, but heights wasn't one of them.

"No, that isn't it at all. We must find the seed." The door rattled as it was rammed again. "Seeds become flowers, and inside every flower lies a tree with deep roots."

"Have you gone mad, old man!" Tristan shouted. "We need a way out, not a flower!"

Etienne grabbed Tristan by the tunic. "You will treat him with respect, or I will—"

"You will what, Etienne?"

"I will do what I should have done years ago."

The door rattled again, this time it was accompanied by the sound of wood splintering. Isabella looked worriedly from the door to Ronan, willing him to hurry and find their escape.

"There's no time for this," said Ronan. "Etienne, extinguish that torch and give it to me."

Once he had the torch, Ronan knelt and drew. A bead of perspiration had formed on Isabella's brow. She wished he would draw faster. A figure of seven conjoining circles soon appeared. The ashen pattern was beautiful. Isabella had never seen anything like it before.

Ronan pointed at the picture. "We must find a cluster of seeds. Together they make the flower we are looking for. It could be anywhere. We must search the whole church."

The door rumbled again, this time little shafts of moonlight pushed through the splintered wood.

Isabella ran toward the back of the church searching the pillars and walls as she went. She'd gotten only as far as the entrance to the cloistered garden when a loud boom filled the air, making her flinch. The church door had flown open, and townsfolk with weapons rushed in.

"To Isabella!" Ronan shouted. Before she knew it, her companions surrounded her and they hurried her into the cloistered garden. Etienne latched and barricaded the door behind them. Immediately the pounding began again.

"This won't hold them for long," said Etienne. "We must fight."

"There is always another way. The mind is stronger than the sword," said Ronan.

Isabella searched the cloistered garden, but there was no hope for escape, nor anyplace to hide. Besides the walkway surrounding the garden, the only thing in the cloister was a lonely dilapidated well covered by a large stone. The walls of the cloister stood tall, and there was only one entrance. She turned her attention to the rafters of the walkway, raising her torch to get a better look. Just beyond the crossbeams, something silver caught her eye. There were several small circular objects on the main beam, spaced evenly. Each one boasted a slightly different design.

"Look." Isabella pointed to the small discs. "The third one in. Is that what we are looking for?"

Ronan rushed past her and held his torch high enough to almost reach the wood.

"You have keen eyes, Your Highness," said Ronan. "Etienne, Tristan, quickly lift me so I can reach it."

"I can climb up," said Etienne.

"No, I must go. I have already revealed too much," Ronan said. "Besides, there is a specific sequence—if it isn't followed, there are dire consequences. It is better for me to take the risk." Isabella's heart pounded, not because of the villagers trying to break in, but because Ronan was about to reveal a Templar secret. Her excitement outpaced her fear.

Etienne and Tristan took Ronan by each leg and hoisted him in the air. Isabella would have found the sight of the old Templar balancing himself with Tristan's head comical in any other circumstance, but the pounding on the door was a constant reminder of the danger they were in. Isabella strained her eyes and memorized the pattern Ronan was tapping on the small circle.

A creaking noise came from the middle of the garden, and the handle of the well spun wildly by itself. Metal gears churned followed by a rumbling noise. Slowly, the stone in front of the well descended, creating a ramp leading down.

"Every tree has deep roots," Isabella mused while the others helped Ronan back to the ground.

"Quickly, let us away," Ronan said as they followed him into the abyss.

Etienne took the rear as they walked down the dimly lit passage. A nervous energy rushed through his body. Ronan was leading them into a place that few had ever seen: the Templars' secret vaults. Etienne had heard a vast network of winding tunnels spread out beneath the city and stretched up to the castle on the hill. But, being a sergeant, Etienne had never entered. That privilege was reserved for Master Templars.

How does he know about these tunnels?

Etienne knew every Templar in the region and many that had passed through the city, but he had never met Ronan. All the Templars in the castle treated him with fidelity, even the Provincial Master. Besides this respect, Etienne didn't see any other sign of his ranking.

The tunnel forked many times, but Ronan was sure of their direction.

"What is that?" Isabella pointed to an ornately decorated door with vines growing in and out of it. In the center was an image of a man with a slot for a mouth.

"It would appear to be a door, Your Highness," said Ronan.

"What is on the other side?"

Ronan laughed, and the sound echoed down the tunnel. "Either the entrance to heaven or hadis, neither of which are for us."

Etienne couldn't tell if Ronan was joking or serious. This old Templar was different than others he had met.

"Ouch," Isabella said.

"Are you alright?" Ronan whirled around with a worried look on his face.

"Yes, I just pricked my finger on the door."

Ronan's gaze narrowed. "I would advise you not to touch anything else."

Etienne examined the door as he passed and saw a small smudge of Isabella's blood between the eyes of the face. Etienne's hairs stood on end. He was last in the group, but he had the distinct feeling something was behind him. He put his free hand on his sword and turned. The tunnel was empty, and there was only darkness.

They walked on for what seemed like hours. It was hard to have any sense of time. They continued forward, but Etienne kept looking behind. He couldn't shake the feeling that they were being followed. They turned a corner and there was a slight breeze.

Ronan held up his hand. "We are approaching the exit." He gave Tristan and Isabella pieces of cloth. "If you will put these over your eyes."

"And if I won't?" Tristan spat.

"Then I will leave you down here to wander the tunnels forever. The choice is yours." Isabella put on her blindfold, and Tristan begrudgingly followed suit. "Sergeant, secure those tightly."

Etienne came behind Isabella and gently fastened her blindfold. The smell of her hair brought back memories of France. Etienne quickly pulled away and moved to Tristan. He tugged tightly on the fabric. "They are secure."

"I shall return," Ronan said, extinguishing the torch. It was completely dark, and the air was moist inside the tunnel. The churning of rocks filled the void, followed by a shaft of moonlight. "This way."

Etienne led Isabella and Tristan out of the tunnel and joined Ronan under a bridge in a small ravine. The entrance to the tunnel closed, and Etienne unfastened Isabella's blindfold.

"Ach, no!" A scream pierced the night air, and footsteps thudded over the bridge.

Etienne halted abruptly and put his finger to his lips.

After the footsteps passed, Etienne hoisted himself out of the small ravine, leaving Isabella and Tristan with Ronan. To the right, three torches danced like fireflies, pursuing a dimmer glow, and gruff voices hollered on the wind.

"We must help immediately," Etienne said.

Tristan tore off his blindfold. "Help? Help who? We need to get the Princess to safety."

"A pilgrim will be dead soon if we do nothing." Etienne's sense of duty was sown deep into his blood. His honor was all he had. He'd sworn an oath to protect pilgrims, and he wouldn't let Tristan stand in the way of that oath.

"The Princess's life is more valuable than the life of any simple pilgrim!"

Etienne was through arguing. He leapt to his feet and ran after the torches. As he neared, he saw three Moors chasing a bald pilgrim whose stomach bounced with every step. The pilgrim's stalky legs were moving fast, but the Moors were moving faster. When they were within striking range, the pilgrim stopped and turned the girth of his body. "Come on then. I'll take the lot of ya!" he bellowed, brandishing a wine bottle wildly.

The Moors laughed and drew their curved swords. The sound gave Etienne cover. He thundered in and pierced a Moor with a scared face. Before he hit the ground, Etienne engaged the other two. The sound of clashing metal rang out. Within minutes, both the Moors lay dead. Etienne tried to wipe the sweat from his brow, but his arms were too exhausted.

"Behind ya!" shouted the pilgrim.

Five feet away from Etienne stood a Moor, a head taller than him, with his sword raised. Etienne hadn't conserved enough energy to fight a man of his size. He felt foolish for not looking behind himself at the bridge. Etienne's desire to prove himself to Isabella and Ronan had made him careless.

As he stepped forward to meet the brute head on, the Moor let out a strangled gurgle, a small trickle of blood flowing from his mouth. He slowly fell to the ground, revealing Isabella with a blood-stained dagger in hand.

Etienne's eyebrows raised. He looked at the pilgrim, who shrugged his shoulders, then back at Isabella. "I didn't know you could—"

"Did you think I only came to the training yard to visit you?" Isabella said as she cleaned the droplets of blood off her dagger. "You are still as good as I remember."

"I take no pride in killing. It is a sin."

The bald pilgrim staggered up to Etienne. "Uh… ah, where did ya come from?"

Before either of them could answer, Tristan jogged up and said, "Your Highness, your father wouldn't—"

"I don't care what my father would think. I can't have anyone else die at my expense tonight."

"Die… Ach, no, Clair!" The pilgrim grabbed Etienne's cloak. "Ya 'ave ta help me." He broke into a run toward a grove of trees.

Etienne and the others followed the pilgrim through low-lying boughs to a clearing. In the middle was a short wiry woman with a frying pan in hand. She stood over two Moors knocked out cold, and was giving them a piece of her mind.

She turned to the pilgrim and exclaimed, "Ach! Wer' ye be'n, y' boggin bampot?"

"What did she say?" Etienne asked.

"Ta be precise, she said, 'Where have ya been, ya foul smelling idiot.'" The pilgrim held up his arms. "Ach, Clair, ya daft woman, I was protecting ya. Come 'ere." They ran to each other and embraced.

"We'd like to thank ya for your help. I'm Andy Sinclair, and this is my sister, Clair. What can we do ta repay ya?"

Etienne smiled at Andy and placed a hand on his shoulder. "There is nothing to repay, it is a Templar's du—"

"Always the same speech, Etienne," Tristan said.

Etienne gripped the hilt of his sword, but looked at Isabella and released his hand. His job wasn't to fight Tristan; it was to deliver Isabella to safety.

Breaking the tension, Andy asked, "Clair, how's our treasure?" Clair picked up a torch and led them deeper into the grove.

"Is that smoke?" Etienne said, rushing past Clair into the clearing.

Ten paces beyond the tree line, a carriage was ablaze; flames licked its sides, and a plume of dark smoke billowed into the sky. Andy gasped, and before Etienne could stop him, the Scotsman dove through the door. Etienne couldn't think of any sane reason a person would dive into a fire. He was a few paces away and had to shield his face from the heat.

Andy reemerged with ash on his face and the corners of his clothes on fire. He ran in circles, yelping, until Etienne grabbed him and extinguished the flames

"Clair, our treasure, she's gone," Andy wailed, collapsing to the ground. Clair put her arms around him and they wept.

"We must move immediately. This smoke will attract the Moors," Ronan said. "Andy, Clair, I am sorry for your loss. But now is not the time to grieve. You can join us as far as the boathouse at Rio Ucieza. You should be able to resupply there."

Andy and Clair didn't budge; overtaken with sorrow, it seemed that nothing else mattered.

Etienne crouched down and put a hand on Andy's shoulder. "Come with us. We will help you." Andy nodded. Compassion overtook Etienne as he helped them both to their feet. He knew what it was like to lose everything.

CHAPTER 3

THE BOAT HOUSE

"Tristan, I did it, and they didn't even notice. I marked the door just as the crone said." Isabella was elated that they had found another door. The success only resolved her conviction to find the other doors. She took in a deep breath of the morning air and looked at the sky.

"Yes, Your Highness, and you almost got us caught. We are deep into enemy territory." Tristan pointed at Ronan and Etienne who were leading the group. "Remember, we don't have escorts; we have prison guards."

"They hardly look like guards to me. It is just an old Templar and Etienne... What, you still can't be jealous of Etienne." Isabella raised an eyebrow. "You know my father always preferred you best."

"I know your father did..." Tristian stared at Isabella.

Isabella cleared her throat. "Come let's catch up with the others." Isabella didn't like Tristan bringing up the subject of her past with Etienne. She knew she would have to face it soon enough. She quickened her pace to join Andy and Clair.

Andy had been talking nonstop to Clair until she elbowed him in the ribs and said, "I canna believe ya can jabber on after we lost..." Clair shook her head.

"Ya ken I canna help myself. 'Tis my way of dealing with the pain. I 'ave ta keep my mind busy ta move forward. Well never mind. What can I tell ya about? Spain's history, mathematics, legends about giants."

"What do you know about the Templars? How did they get so rich?" Isabella asked, catching up to them.

"Why 'ello," Andy said, straightening himself proudly and puffing his chest. "Well, the Templars went ta Jerusalem, nine poor knights. So poor two had ta ride on one horse. For years they dug under Solomon's Temple[13] in the Holy Land, until one day they found a secret treasure."

"What did they find?" asked Isabella. She had heard many accounts of this story as she'd researched for her quest, but she hoped Andy might know something she didn't.

"Some say 'twas the Holy Grail. Others say 'tis the Ark of the Covenant. Still some think 'tis a secret they hold against the church. Whatever 'tis, this treasure gave them great wealth and power. I'm a scholar in my country, an' I think 'tis one of the ultimate mysteries ta figure out. Why, I've even thought 'bout joining the Templars once or twice just ta have a better chance of knowing.

"They didn't get rich because of a secret treasure. They got rich because they're thieves," Tristan's deep voice grumbled. "They exploit the pilgrims and go against the church." Isabella wished Tristan wouldn't have interrupted. She could tell Andy had a keen mind, and she wanted to learn more.

Andy lowered his voice, making sure Etienne and Ronan couldn't hear. "What do ya mean?"

"When you came on this pilgrimage, what did you do with your gold?" asked Tristan.

"I gave it ta my local Templar Commandery and they gave me my credential." Andy pulled a coded piece of paper from his sporran. Isabella had a credential as well, and enjoyed the connivance of not carrying gold with her. Anytime she needed more, she sent Tristan to a Templar Commandery.

"Do you know what happens to that gold if you die on this pilgrimage?" asked Tristan.

"Well, I suppose it would-a go back ta my family."

"Wrong," Tristan said with a snarl. "They would keep it for themselves. Also, beyond that, they go against the church by charging interest, which is a sin."

"Na, they just are charging me a rental fee for the space my gold is takin' up," replied Andy with one eyebrow raised.

"Call it what you like, it's still interest," Tristan said loudly.

Ronan and Etienne stopped. "Is everything all right?" Ronan asked.

"Yes, all is fine," Isabella said quickly, before Tristan or Andy could reply.

It was reaching the midday hour and the sun beat down with its full force. It was only spring, but Etienne could tell the heat was taking a toll on the others. Their march had been hard. After leaving the burning coach, they summited the three-thousand-foot mountain of Alto de Mostelares. They had reached the top of the flat mesa just as dawn broke and sunlight flooded the valley. Etienne had taken one last look back at the Arc—at his home—and was relieved to see the defenses had not failed.

"Let's stop here for a rest," Ronan said as they found a grove of trees. "We will have two watches; I will take the first."

"I'll join you," Etienne said.

"Suit yourself," Andy said as he plopped down on the ground and took his shoes off. The smell of old boots filled the air and everyone moved away, covering their noses. Andy took no notice, and as soon as his head hit the ground, he began to snore.

Etienne watched the others as they followed suit. Each laying out their cloaks on the ground, claiming their own piece of grass to call home until the midday heat passed. Ronan motioned to Etienne and they positioned themselves a small distance away.

Etienne kept watch, as Ronan sat in prayer. He was so curious about this mysterious Templar.

Ronan made the sign of the cross, finishing his prayer, but before Etienne could speak, he asked, "There seems to be some animosity between you and Tristan. Is he someone not to be trusted?"

Etienne pulled some weeds and tossed them away. "I haven't seen him for many years and cannot say whether he is to be trusted or not. The Provincial Master seemed to think that he and Isabella were on the Camino for more than one reason. He ordered me to watch them, since Isabella trusts me."

"How do you know them?" Ronan asked peacefully.

No one at the Arc knew where Etienne came from, nor who he had been before becoming a Templar. Until yesterday, he always changed the subject when the question was asked. He simply said he had no life before the Templars. However, there was something about Ronan that made him feel safe—something that made him want to open up. Maybe it was that his past was sleeping just a few yards away.

"My life changed twice because of Tristan. After my parents died, I lived on the streets of Paris. One day, Tristan and the other squires attacked my only friend and started beating him ruthlessly." Etienne's fists clenched. "I stepped in to protect him, but there were too many of them. The Captain of the Kings Guard intervened and restrained me. He was furious, but after seeing that my friend was dead, and that I'd single-handedly defeated four of his boys, he decided to spare my life, and trained me with the other squires."

"A life for a life," Ronan said, sympathetically. The death of Etienne's friend had shaped his moral compass. He always felt remorse when he had to take a life—even in the defense of others.

Etienne nodded. "I was always an outcast with the squires, partially because of my skin color, and partially because of Tristan. He was jealous that The Captain and Isabella were both fond of me." Etienne paused and shifted some dirt on the ground. He thought of the many summer nights he and Isabella had spent hiding away from the others. She could understand him in a way no one else could because they were both different.

Etienne shook his head. "Tristan and his cronies found Isabella and I together one night. They beat me and dragged me in front of King Philip. Tristan falsely accused me of forcing myself on Isabella. When Philip asked Isabella what happened, she just stood there and said nothing." Etienne picked up a handful of dirt and threw it. "She watched as I was sentenced to death for a crime I didn't commit."

Ronan placed his fingertips together under his chin. "How did you become a Templar?"

"The Captain of the Kings Guard knew I was wrongfully convicted. He arranged for the Templars to take me away before my execution. I owe a great debt to him and the Templars for this."

Ronan's steely eyes pierced Etienne. "I am happy God found you and delivered you to us, my son," he said in his strong, even-toned voice. "It is a testament to the man you are that you have agreed to protect those who persecuted you. Now you must learn to control your anger if you shall ever wish to lead. Templars are a sign of strength and war, but we are also a sign of safety and peace. You must find this peace within yourself and forgive your past."

Etienne glanced away, knowing this might take a lifetime. Instead of responding, he picked up a stick and drew the picture Ronan had drawn in the church.

"Very good," Ronan said, eyeing the image. "The seed of life is a symbol of creation. The seven overlapping circles represent the seven days of creation. Each circle in itself represents a cycle and encompasses a point of the heavens. The overlapping circles mean that each event of creation isn't independent, but is built on the one that precedes it."

Ronan sat next to Etienne and drew several seeds around the first. "If you continue to add circles, the seed of life becomes the flower of life. It builds on the seed and expands outward, like creation. Just as the seed is built of the same building blocks as the flower, so it is with all things in the universe."

"And what was this tree you spoke of?"

Ronan poked some dots inside the flower and drew connecting lines.

"That, my son, is a lesson for another time. You have great potential. Don't waste it on anger and revenge." Ronan cleared the dirt. "Come, the heat of day has passed."

Andy watched the last glow of day disappear as the small company approached the boathouse at Rio Ucieza. The moon had risen in the east behind them, and a few stars were visible. The boathouse, with its jolly light coming from the windows, was the first sign of civilization Andy had seen all day. The roaring river mixing with laughter got louder as they approached. Andy's stomach grumbled at the prospect of a warm meal.

Ronan held up his hand, stopping the company a few yards from the entrance. "Etienne and I will enter first and procure our rooms. The rest of you will wait here for our return. Andy and Clair, we'll secure your rooms as well. It is best if no one sees... our company." All nodded their heads in agreement, except Andy.

After Etienne and Ronan entered, Andy crept a little closer to the boathouse and peered through a window. "Ach, I canna wait to get inside," he said as he saw the glow of a warm fire, food on the table, and most importantly a large bar. The room was filled with pilgrims; a chorus of different languages and laughter entered Andy's ears. He looked longingly at the bottles of wine on the table. "That does it," he said, making his way to the door.

"We're supposed to wait here," Isabella protested.

"I dunna know why. No one is goin' ta notice another fat bald pilgrim amongst the crowd," Andy replied as he turned the knob and entered.

The warmth of the fire and the smell of food greeted him, and he smiled for the first time since Castrojeriz. He grabbed the edges of his cloak and strutted his way to the bar.

Oh, the familiar sounds of a pub. A drink will help me forget all of my troubles and calm my nerves.

When he reached the bar, he was greeted by a barmaid with long black hair and tan skin. "I'll 'ave a red wine," Andy said, with a smile he hoped was charming.

"Que?" she said, leaning closer over the bar.

"I said, 'red wine,'" Andy repeated loudly.

"She can hear you," a smooth voice with a Spanish accent said.

Feeling his cheeks heat with shame, Andy turned his head. To his right was a Spaniard with sun-kissed skin and green eyes. His face was framed with a strong beard, and he had an air of confidence about him.

"She doesn't speak the common tongue," the stranger said. "Un vino tinto, por favor," he said to the barmaid with a coy smile. They locked eyes and held a long gaze, then she readied Andy's drink.

"Thank you," Andy said to the stranger.

"No need to thank me. You are a guest in our land, and we your hosts," the stranger replied with a boyish charisma.

Andy's drink appeared in front of him. He reached for his sporran to pay, but the barmaid stopped his hand and said, "Nada." She turned to the stranger and said something in Spanish.

As she finished, the stranger translated, "Alba says the drink is her gift for a weary pilgrim." With a smile to Alba, the Spaniard took two drinks from the bar in one hand and clasped his other arm over Andy's shoulder. "Come, join us."

When they reached the man's table, he said, "I am Mariano the Mercenary," He motioned to the giant of a man already seated. "And this is Gerhart the Destroyer."

Gerhart stood, and his head nearly reached the ceiling. As he rose, his cape fell off his shoulders to reveal a chiseled body and arms the size of tree trunks. His pecs flexed a few times. Gerhart extended his hand, which was the size of Andy's head.

"Gerhart," he said in a very thick Bavarian accent. His loud booming voice filled the hall, taking up almost as much space as he did.

"Ach, my, you're a tall drink-a-water," Andy said, looking the man up and down.

Gerhart laughed heartily. "And what accent is that?"

"I'm Scottish," Andy said proudly.

Gerhart let out another bellowing laugh that filled the room and looked down at Andy. "I heard your people were giants. Apparently, that was just a rumor."

"Why you…" Andy said, throwing his arms in the air. Mariano put a reassuring hand on Andy's shoulder and guided him to a chair.

"Forgive my friend. He always speaks his mind. We were just in the middle of a game. Have you ever played Thimble-rig?" Mariano asked.

"I canna say that I 'ave."

"Gerhart and I were just playing for drinks. I lost the last round so—here is your drink, sir," said Mariano, handing Gerhart a cup. They toasted, and both drank.

"Let's play again. I like winning," said Gerhart.

Mariano produced three thimbles, two peas, and a peppercorn. He placed each under a thimble and smiled at Andy. "The trick is to remember where the peppercorn is." While Mariano moved the thimbles around swiftly, Andy kept his eyes riveted on the thimble with the peppercorn. "All right, Gerhart, where is it?"

Gerhart brought his massive hand to his face and stroked his chin. "It's on the left."

"Ach, no, 'tis in the center," interjected Andy.

"Let's see which one of you is right." Mariano lifted the thimbles.

"Ha, I told ya so," Andy said, placing both hands on his stomach.

"That was just a practice round." Mariano raised an eyebrow at him. "Do you think you would be able to win again?" Andy looked around the bar for his traveling companions. He found them seated at a table by the window. Clair waved, and he held up a finger indicating that he needed a few more minutes.

Andy turned back to the table. "Absolutely. 'Tis easy."

"Alright then. I might have better luck with you. Let's play for the next round of drinks."

"Deal," Andy said, leaning forward.

Mariano's hands moved faster than any Andy had ever seen. He focused all of his attention on the ballet the little thimbles were performing.

Andy barely noticed Alba clearing a glass of wine from the table. Her hand slipped and the contents spilled out towards Andy. "Ach!" Andy pushed back from the table as the liquid hit his clothing.

"Lo siento. Lo siento," said Alba, as she wiped off the wine.

"Well," said Mariano. "Where is it?"

"Ya canno' expect me to ken after that." He stopped Alba's hands from brushing him off. "'Tis fine. 'Tis fine." She curtsied and hurried back to the bar.

"You're right, that wasn't fair. We will do another round." Mariano's hands danced furiously across the table, the thimbles intersected and wove through each other. But Andy knew where the peppercorn was this time.

"So, where is it?" said Mariano, clapping his hands.

Andy pointed a confident finger to the center thimble. "'Tis there."

"Are you sure?" said Mariano, smiling broadly.

Andy picked up the thimble. It was a pea. *How could I ha' been wrong.* "Ya must 'ave cheated. Lift up the others."

"You lost fairly. You only get to see below one."

"I'll win the next round."

"And our drinks," said Mariano.

Andy muttered to himself as he walked to the bar. *I ken it was under that one.*

Andy held up three fingers. "Vino tinto," he said, remembering the words Mariano had spoken.

Alba appeared with three cups of wine. Andy reached into his sporran and found it empty. *'Twas full a few minutes ago.* He looked at Alba, then at Mariano, who waved grinning.

Andy's eyelid twitched and the vein in his head pulsed. He ran and leapt at Mariano, who turned his body slightly, sending Andy sailing through the air. Gerhart let out a belly laugh and picked up a large ax.

Both men moved toward Andy, but before they took even one step, their heads shot down. Andy stood to get a better view. Behind them was Clair, who had both pinned to the table by their ears.

"Donna touch my broder," she shouted. At this, the whole bar was up in arms. The tension in the air was thick as a lynchpin, ready to spring at any moment.

"What is going on here?" Ronan demanded as he and Etienne approached the table, swords drawn.

Andy pointed at the two men Clair had subdued. "These men cheated me and stole my gold."

"Well, to be more precise, she stole your gold," Isabella said, gesturing to the barmaid. "People run this scam all of the time in Paris."

Mariano loosened himself from Clair's grip and reached for his knives.

"I wouldn't do that if I were you," Ronan said firmly, shifting his pilgrim's cape to show his Templar mantle.

Eyeing the men warily, Mariano said, "I think we got off on the wrong foot. Why don't you all join us. I am sure your friend's gold will be found. Señora, would you mind releasing my friend?"

"'Tis alright, Clair. Let the big oaf go," Andy said. Clair released Gerhart and climbed on top of the table with her hands on her hips. As Gerhart rose to his full height, he and Clair met eye-to-eye. Gerhart gave her a big goofy, school-boy grin.

"I have never seen him look at anyone like that before. I think he likes you," Mariano said.

"Now sit-ye doon, ya bigg ox," Clair demanded, her hands on her hips.

"What?" Gerhart stammered.

"She said, sit down, you big ox,'" Andy translated. Gerhart sat abruptly, and the chair gave way under his massive weight, sending him to the floor. The whole bar broke out in laughter.

Mariano was doubled over. After a moment, he managed the words, "And that's why we call him Gerhart the Destroyer." The whole bar erupted once again. Gerhart paid no attention. He just looked up adoringly at Clair, who was now towering over him.

Isabella sat with her traveling companions, Gerhart, Mariano, and Alba, into the wee hours. *What would my father say? I'm sitting with a Templar, a person he had condemned to death, a pair of drunken Scots, and three thieves.* Isabella smiled and shook her head. Even though her company was sordid, Isabella had to admit, this was the most she had ever laughed. Her cheeks were hurting from smiling so much.

"Mi amore," Mariano said to Alba who was sitting on his lap. "Nueve vino tintos." Alba gave him a scolding look. "Por favor," he said, raising his eyebrows and sticking out his bottom lip. Alba shook her head and smiled. As she left the table, Mariano said, "I love that woman more than life itself. Even the sun pales in comparison to how brightly my love shines for her."

"Well, then why aren't you helping her with the drinks?" Isabella asked with an arched eyebrow. Mariano opened his mouth to speak, but instead, he leapt to his feet and rushed to the bar.

The captain of the ferryboat they would take the next morning sat at the table next to them with a group of Irish pilgrims. He stood and his white hair and beard caught the glow of the fire. He took a breath, causing his broad chest to rise, and all eyes turned to him. "I would like to close out the evening with an Irish toast. 'Tis called the Parting Glass."

Of all the money that e'er I had,
I spent it in good company.
And of all the harm that e'er I've done,
alas was done to none but me.
And all I've done for want of wit,
to memory now I cannot recall.
So, fill me to the parting glass.
Goodnight and joy be with you all.
Of all the comrades that e'er I had,
they're sorry for my going away.
And of all the sweethearts that e'er I had,
they wish me one more day to stay,

Choking back tears he was unable to continue. He sat and an Irish pilgrim put his hand on the captain's shoulder. The captain took his hand and they exchanged a look of compassion. The pilgrim smiled at him and sung.

But since it falls unto my lot
That I should rise while you should not,
I will gently rise and I'll softly call,
"Goodnight and joy be with you all!"
Oh, if I had money enough to spend
and leisure time to sit awhile.
There is a fair maid in this town
That sorely has my heart beguiled.
Her rosy cheeks and ruby lips,
She alone has my heart in thrall.
So fill me to the parting glass.
Goodnight and joy be with you all.

The Irish pilgrim's voice hung in the air after he sang the last note. The song stirred emotions inside of Isabella that she hadn't been facing. She hadn't let herself think of her friends she had lost at the Arc of San Anton. Her lady Jessica had cared for her since she was a child. Now she lay dead on the Camino. Isabella hoped she had been buried. She deserved so much more than that. Jessica had done so much for Isabella. In the excitement of everything, Isabella hadn't thought about how she was going to get by. She had always been waited on and had her needs met. Even here on the Camino, she'd had Jessica to wash her clothes and bathe her.

Not only that, Jessica had always listened to her sympathetically. She would have known what to do about Etienne and Tristan. Isabella felt utterly alone. She was a stranger in a strange land. Her emotions continued to rise to the surface. She could feel them pushing against the back of her eyes. Isabella stood abruptly and pushed back from the table. Everyone looked at her with wide eyes.

"If you will excuse me." She turned and made her way up the stairs to her private sleeping chamber.

The coldest part of the day arrived: that moment right before dawn, when night rules the land. Mariano tucked the blankets around Alba and walked to the window. The world was dark, and all was silent except for the roar of Gerhart's snore coming from the bar downstairs. Mariano peered through the cracked door, past the wrap-around balcony, to see Gerhart passed out on the table with a pint glass in hand. *The beds are too small for him anyway.*

Mariano looked back at Alba. Having been found out, the three of them would have to leave in the morning. They would go to the next town and set up their operation there. Mariano preferred gambling to being a mercenary; it was safer.

We almost have enough money to leave this all behind. You will be my wife soon, and we can have a normal life. With Gerhart, of course.

The sky in the east glowed, sending morning shadows along the road leading to the boathouse. As the minutes passed, the shadows grew longer, and Mariano noticed something strange. Nine of the shadows grew at a great speed—they seemed to be running from the rising sun to the boathouse. It looked like they were trying to escape the light. Soon, these nine figures were upon the house, their blackness finding refuge in the dark places that hung around the building. *I still must be dreaming.* Mariano pinched himself. He was definitely awake.

A cold breeze rushed into the room and Mariano ran to the cracked bedroom door—Gerhart was still head-down on the bar snoring away, but the entrance to the boathouse was now wide open. Like the night that creeps in suddenly, the shadows crept into the cottage.

They made no sound as they entered, and neither did their victims when they came upon them. Mariano watched the creatures enter room after room on the ground floor, and return with their curved swords covered in blood. Mariano couldn't make out exactly what the creatures looked like, but they felt like the origin of fear: that primal feeling that terrorizes you as a child.

"Mi amor," Alba mumbled, as she felt the bed next to her for Mariano.

Seeing her beautiful eyes gazing up at him snapped him out of his stupor. He shook and willed himself to move. He couldn't let anything happen to her. He wouldn't.

Grabbing his knives, Mariano stealthily ran down the stairs as the shadows vanished into the ferryboat captain's room. He shook Gerhart, and the giant opened his sleepy eyes. Mariano put his finger to his lips and pointed to the wide-open door of the captain's room. The shadows raised their swords high above the captain. "Oh God!" he managed to stammer before the blades found their mark.

Gerhart and Mariano lifted a large table and ran full speed to block the door of the bedchamber. The shadows all turned in unison. But it was too late, Mariano and Gerhart reached the door first, blocking them in. Gerhart let out a loud roar and Mariano's muscles strained to hold the table fast. The remaining pilgrims rushed downstairs, weapons drawn, surrounding Gerhart and Mariano.

"What's happening?" Etienne asked as he drew his sword.

Gerhart raised his giant hand and held up three fingers, he slowly lowered them one at a time; it was the countdown to the release of the table and the fight with whatever lay on the other side. As his last finger lowered, he and Mariano discarded the table and everyone rushed in. The room was empty except the captain, who was bleeding out on the floor.

Alba ran to the captain and cradled him in her arms, soaking her clothing in his blood, but he was already dead. She turned to Mariano with tears in her eyes. "Quien hizo esto?"

Mariano shook his head, anger and guilt warring inside him. He should've done something more. "I don't know who did this. Shadows, all I saw were shadows."

"We must run!" Ronan said with the urgency of a person who has just received a death sentence. "Run!" Ronan shouted again.

A white heat hit Mariano hard pushing both him and Alba to the floor. Something caused the casks of wine behind the bar to explode, sending shards of burning wood in all directions. Flames licked each wall around them. The boathouse was now an inferno.

Gerhart lifted Mariano and Alba; together, they followed the others and ran to the shaft of light streaming in from the exit. Mariano's eyes had trouble adjusting to the outside world. He coughed, releasing the smoke trapped in his lungs. All of them had escaped the blast. Mariano turned to the burning structure, and to his horror, saw nine Shadows streaming out of the exit with the black smoke. Looking at the shadowy cloaked figures was like looking at a hole in reality, where nothing replaced the void. However, beneath their black hoods was an amorphous face, always changing. Mariano's hair stood on end.

Mariano blinked and two Shadows stood in front of them. He took Alba's shaking hand and placed her behind him and Gerhart. Mariano threw two knives at the closest Shadow, and they seemed to disappear into the emptiness of the creature. Gerhart let out a battle cry and swung his mighty ax. He made contact with the curved sword and an awful sound rang out. Mariano cringed. The Shadow pushed back and Gerhart toppled over him and Alba.

From the ground, Mariano saw Etienne, frozen, looking at the face of a Shadow above him. The Shadow swung its sword, and Isabella blocked the blow with her dagger. Etienne snapped out of it and rammed the Shadow. The creature stumbled back a few inches into the broad daylight, and it let out an unearthly cry as its exposed hands blistered in the sun.

"Quickly, into the light!" Etienne shouted.

Mariano took Alba and rolled from the shade of the boathouse into the light.

The Shadows did not pursue; they were like caged animals hissing and gnashing their teeth in the darkness.

"To the boat!" Ronan shouted.

The old wooden boards moved under Mariano's feet as he ran to the dock, Alba by his side. Gerhart and Ronan were helping Isabella and Andy into the boat, as Etienne and Clair were untying the knots.

Mariano stopped—he felt Alba's hand release his and the dock shuddered under his feet. He turned to see Alba lying face down with his own knife protruding from her back. "Mi Amore!" Mariano shouted. He lifted her, and her body convulsed as a second knife hit her back. Alba's head slumped, and she gave up her spirit.

"No!" Mariano yelled in anguish. He gently placed Alba down and moved toward the Shadows. Before Mariano had taken two steps, a huge plume of smoke billowed from the cottage, blocking the sun. With this new cover, the shadowy figures were released from their dark prisons and moved to Mariano with the speed of the wind.

"It is too late, my old friend," Gerhart said, as he restrained Mariano and pulled him into the boat.

"Mi amor!" Mariano cried, struggling to get free from Gerhart's tight grip. Mariano watched in horror as the Shadows leaned in to feast.

Mariano slumped into the boat, heartsick and furious, watching the smoke from the carnage that lay behind them. He turned to Ronan. "What were those things?" he demanded. "Well!" he shouted again, hitting his fists on the boat.

Ronan calmed Mariano with his look of compassion. "Peace be with you, Brother. I am not your enemy," Ronan said calmly.

"But you did know we needed to run when I said shadows were in the room. I thought you Templars were supposed to be brave. You lost the lives of several pilgrims today," Mariano spat.

"I know what those things are," Andy said. "I dinna think they actually existed. They are the Immortals."

Ronan nodded. "He is right."

"And what exactly are the Immortals?" Isabella asked.

When Ronan hesitated, Mariano couldn't help himself. "Tell us!" he shouted, fighting back tears.

Ronan looked at him squarely. "Our order first encountered them in the Holy Land. At first, there were just whispers of 'Immortal Shadows' fighting with Saladin's[14] army. Soon it was apparent these whispers were fact, and slowly, these assassins turned the tide of the war. They were indestructible, never slept, never tired; they only killed. It is because of them that we lost the Crusades."

Mariano listened intently as Ronan continued, "The only report of the Shadows outside the Holy Land was here on the Camino de Santiago, one-hundred and twenty-three years ago. There was one survivor amidst the carnage, Grand Master Arnold of Torroja. When he was found, he was in an altered state repeating the words, 'Shadows,' and 'the Alchemist.' The Shadows haven't been seen since. Some say the Grand Master sealed the Shadows into the walls of the Cathedral de Santiago. Others say he just went mad and killed his own men. Either way, we have much to fear."

"This blood is on my hands as well. First the Moors, now this," Isabella said, a vacant stare on her face.

Even though she was wearing pilgrim's clothes, Mariano could tell she was no commoner. Everything about her was refined, the way she spoke, the way she held her silverware, and the confidence she walked with. He glared at her, happy to blame anyone for Alba's murder. "And who are you that you are so important?"

"She is no one, just a pilgrim," Etienne said.

"Things like that don't come after no-ones." Mariano glared at Etienne, pulling back his vest to show his daggers.

"We are just pilgrims," Tristan said, grabbing the hilt of his sword.

Now he knew they were no ordinary pilgrims. Gerhart stood and the whole boat rocked.

"Ach, settle down, settle down," Andy said, waving his arms. "She's a princess. I 'eard Etienne and Tristan call 'er 'Your Highness.' I would guess she's Princess Isabella of France, King Philip's daughter."

Clair elbowed him sharply in the side. "Why d'ya always 'ave ta do tha'? Ya canna keep a secret."

Mariano spun one of his knives by the tip on the wooden bench. "So, *Princess,* why are these things after you?"

"You will call her, Your Highness," Tristan said as he unsheathed his sword.

"Enough! Stop this madness at once," Isabella ordered.

"Yes, Your Highness." Tristan bowed his head, sheathing his sword.

"You all will address me as Isabella. It is safer that way. I do not know why these things are after me, nor why the Moors drove us to this place. But I do know none of you are my enemy."

"She is right. These Shadows are our enemies. We must find their weakness and destroy them for the sins they have committed," Etienne said sternly. "Now, we must be even more careful to cover our tracks."

They reached the other side of the river, and Mariano watched the smoke from the boathouse streaking the sky in the east. Gerhart and Etienne jumped out and pulled the boat ashore. Mariano was the last to leave the vessel. He remained looking longingly at the devastation. "I swear I will destroy these Immortal Shadows for what they have done."

CHAPTER 4

CARRION DE LOS CONDES

Isabella's body ached as they pressed through the hottest part of the day. With each step, the battle of the morning hung around the edges of her thoughts like a bad dream. *Was that real?* She swallowed and tasted the metal tang of blood still inside her mouth.

Her companions had the red dust of the Camino, and a gray haze of ash clinging to their clothing. Their skin was touched by the sun, reddening some and bronzing others: the sign of a pilgrim who has walked their miles. Mariano kept his head down and his face covered by a hat he had found in the boat. But Isabella caught sight of his wet eyes. She could tell by his expression that they weren't tears of sadness, but of rage.

Was Mariano right? Had these Shadows attacked because of her? Was death a consequence of her quest? Isabella shook her head. *I won't take the blame for this.* It was too painful for her to consider the idea. She could see how much Mariano loved Alba and could empathize with his feelings. She'd had a gamut of emotions after Etienne was taken away: anger, sorrow, love, hate—most of all, regret. *I need to talk to Etienne. I need to explain what happened.*

Entering Carrion de los Condes, Isabella noticed the contrast between the well-dressed inhabitants of the city, and her bloodstained, dusty garments. She had never looked this poor before—but clothing didn't make a person. She held her head high and walked through the streets with the same authority she walked through the palace.

"We will stop here," Ronan said, pointing to the convent of Santa Anna.

The convent stood like a fortress built to God with walls stretching high into the sky. The cross that towered above the red-tiled roof was a welcome sight. It was a symbol of refuge, peace, and sanctuary. Isabella's body relaxed slightly; *The Shadows of the morning wouldn't dare to venture into a house of God.*

They entered through large double doors into the courtyard and were greeted by the guest master. "Welcome, pilgrims," he said with a kind smile. "Come, find rest from the heat of day and the many miles you have traveled."

Etienne swayed and steadied himself against a wall. Noticing a steady stream of blood covering his hand, Isabella touched his arm. "Etienne, you are bleeding."

"It's nothing," Etienne said.

"We have a well-equipped infirmary here," said the guest master.

"Aye, laddie, that doesna look so good," Andy said. "I 'ave some bumps and bruises too. I'll go ta the infirmary with ya."

Etienne looked at Isabella. "It's nothing. I will only go after I know you are safely in your room, Isabella." It was the first time he had used her name. Blood rushed to her cheeks and she looked away. He didn't just say her name, he said it the way he used to in Paris. Perhaps Mariano's loss had changed something inside him.

"Then by all means, let me show you to your rooms with haste," said the guest master.

He led them into the albergue de peregrinos, or in the common tongue, the pilgrim's shelter. "Ladies, your chamber is to the left, and gentlemen, yours is to the right." The guest master ushered them into their rooms, then took Andy and Etienne down a long corridor.

Isabella and Clair's chamber was very simple. It contained two single beds, crucifixes, and one window. Clair immediately walked over to the window and opened it.

Isabella closed her eyes; the sound of the nuns' afternoon vespers entered and drifted through the room, their beautiful song ringing off the walls. Isabella put her hands to her chest. *My God, thank you for delivering us from darkness into safety. I am so sorry for all of the lives that were lost at my expense. And now Etienne is injured...I'm sorry.* Isabella's body let go and warm tears streaked her face.

Moments later, she felt the tight embrace of Clair. "'Tis allari', child. 'Tis allari'. We all lost somthin' taday. Were-a safe noo." Isabella's body stiffened. She wasn't used to being touched like this, especially by a commoner. But she felt so utterly alone, she let Clair hold her.

Isabella sniffed again and responded, "I am sorry you lost your treasure in that coach. I hope it can be replaced."

Clair got a distant look on her face. "I didna lose anything tha' can be replaced. I lost ma child. I lost my 'Eather."

Isabella gasped and brought her hands to her mouth. "I am so sorry." She wrapped her arms around Clair and returned her embrace tightly. "I didn—"

"She's 'bout your age. She 'ad the Fire of San Anton.[15] 'Tis why we took the pilgrimage ta the Arc of San Anton. I kenned tha' they coulda healed her. But it doesna matter noo."

"I'm sorry—"

"'Tis the 'ardest thing I 'ave 'ad ta deal with. No parent should outlive their wee-one." Clair's eyes misted and her stare was vacant. Isabella could only imagine the pain she was going through, and wondered how Clair was keeping it together. "But 'Eather 'ad been dyin' for a long time, an' I've been grieving all tha' time already, too. The Fire of San Anton 'twas taken' 'er. I knew it, even if I wanted ta try one last 'ope for savin' 'er by bringing 'er on this journey. The travel alone coulda been 'er undoin', so fragile and delicate a lit'le thing she'd become. I knew the risks when we set oot. It doesna make the pain go awa', but at least I know I did everything I coulda for 'er. 'Tis best she is at peace noo," Clair stated wearily, emotion clogging her voice, even through the words of acceptance.

"Clair, I…"

"Hush noo, lassie. I donna need ta talk about it anymore. 'Eather is with God noo, and there's nothin' more a mother could ask than for God to look after her precious lamb. Ye should rest," Clair said as she stroked Isabella's hair. Isabella struggled to keep her eyes open, but her body gave way to exhaustion and the abyss of sleep overtook her.

Andy was met by the smell of medicinal herbs and smoke as he and Etienne entered the infirmary. Inside, there were a few beds and a long table with many tools for the healing arts.

The guest master cleared his throat. "Hmm, hum, the nuns will be with you shortly." He bowed and left the room.

Andy made his way over to the table and picked up a large sharp metallic corkscrew. "Ach, what da ya think they do with this?"

"If you don't put it down, we will show you," an imposing nun said from the doorway.

"Ooo, what do we have here, Sister Caroline?" asked another nun, poking her head in around the first.

"Well, Sister Fransie, it looks like we have one pilgrim, and a very handsome knight."

"Sister Caroline!"

"Just because I am married to Jesus doesn't mean I can't look."

"They're covered in blood. We will have to mend their wounds immediately," Sister Fransie said, as she rushed into the room. "First, we will have to get you out of those blood-soaked clothes. Thank heavens you made it to us."

Etienne and Andy looked at each other with raised eyebrows. After a moment, Etienne removed his Templar's mantle, revealing his war-hardened body. A gash on his shoulder sent a small stream of blood to his wrist.

"Oh, heavens me, I will definitely have to pray the rosary tonight," Sister Caroline mumbled. "But first, we must tend to this wound." She moved quickly to the table and grabbed thread and a needle, along with a cloth and jug of water to clean the laceration.

"And what about you?" Sister Fransie said, motioning to Andy.

Andy shyly lifted his shirt. As he removed it, he heard Clair laugh from the door. "Let er oot, ye fat-arse." This caused Andy to release his gut, sending it out well over his beltline.

"Where did ye come from?" Andy asked, as he struggled to take his shirt the rest of the way off.

"What did she say?" said Sister Fransie.

Andy turned red as a cherry tomato. "She said, 'let it out you fat a—'"

"Oh, my!" Sister Fransie exclaimed "Would you look at that, just one tiny scratch. We can tell who the better knight was." Andy eased at this remark. Sister Fransie touched his shoulder gently. "God made us all beautiful the way we are, no matter our size. Now give me these dirty clothes."

"And that does it." Sister Caroline took one step back admiring her handiwork. "This will be a good one to add to your collection." She motioned to Etienne's other scars.

Andy's stomach rumbled loudly. He turned bright red again and gave Sister Fransie a sheepish smile.

"You poor pilgrims must be famished," Sister Fransie said. "Since we are finished here, let's go to the kitchen to get you something to eat as we prepare for the evening meal." Andy liked this woman more and more by the moment.

Sister Caroline gave Etienne a simple tunic. "Please, put this on. You keep causing me to sin."

"Sister Caroline!"

The ancient bell reverberated five times through the walls of the convent, and Isabella was awakened by a small hand on her shoulder. She opened her eyes to Clair looking down at her compassionately. "'Tis-a time ta eet."

Isabella squinted, and Clair mimed the actions of eating. Isabella nodded her head in understanding. "Also." Clair motioned to the chair where Isabella's clothing was freshly laundered.

"Thank you so much!" Isabella beamed a smile at Clair. "You will have to teach me how to do that." Isabella felt like there was so much she was going to need to learn now. It scared her, but also gave her a sense of independence she had never felt before.

"Aye," Clair said winking, "bu..." Clair held up Isabella's cape, "...I cudnna get all tha blood oot. I 'ave a surprise though." Isabella jumped out of bed and dressed. Clair took her by the hand and they were out the door.

In the courtyard there was a band of merchants, complete with animals and all of their wares. It was a kaleidoscope of colors, smells, and sounds. There were so many different languages being spoken, Isabella couldn't keep track. Clair took her by the hand and they went from stall to stall examining all of the exotic merchandise.

Clair held a dark green cape up to Isabella. "Don't ya look bonny." Isabella had never had the experience of buying her own clothing. At the palace, her clothing was always chosen for her. It was an exhilarating feeling having the freedom of choice.

Andy walked up to them. "'Tis a mess," he said, crossing his arms.

"Where are the others?" asked Isabella.

"Etienne and Ronan are prayin' in the chapel, and—"

"And I am here, forever at your side," Tristan said from behind.

"What beautiful roses have just appeared in the garden?" said a very charming man, from a booth next to Tristan. He appeared to be from the far east and was dressed in silk from top to bottom. When he moved the fabric shimmered like water. "My name is Katsuji, but you can call me Ethan, and this is my caravan. It is an honor to meet you." He bowed, and the ladies curtsied.

"I prefer Katsuji, if that is your given name," Isabella said.

"As you wish." Katsuji smiled and bowed again.

"I am Isabella, and this is Clair." They walked closer to his stall and examined his fabrics. They were the most beautiful Isabella had seen in the caravan. Some of the fabrics were even silk.

Isabella held up a royal blue silk cape. "How much is this?" Isabella had never said that phrase before. She hoped she wouldn't have to haggle over the price. She had no idea where to begin.

"Only the wealthy can afford that one," Katsuji said, "and I don't see your money purse."

"Tristan," Isabella said. Tristan stepped forward and jingled a sack of gold.

Katsuji's eyes lit up. "Perhaps you can join our caravan tomorrow and examine some of my rarest silks."

"Perhaps," Isabella said. "Oh, I forgot to introduce you. This is Tristan, my... and Andy."

"And I am, Gerhart," said Gerhart, coming up behind Katsuji, clasping his enormous arm around his shoulder. Katsuji popped the sword from his side and pushed the handle into Gerhart's chest.

Gerhart let out a roaring laugh and held out his arms. "And, what do you intend to do with that toy?"

In one swift movement Katsuji spun his sword and re-sheathed it. "My hope is nothing." The moment his sword was back in place, Gerhart's belt split and his trousers dropped to the ground.

"Ach, quit measurin' swords," Clair said, as she pushed between the two men.

Isabella followed Clair into the refractory and sat at one of the four tables that stretched the length of the room. The kitchen doors opened, and the nuns entered with large bowls of soup for the first course. Something about this simplicity felt more real than the life she had left behind. Every day of the Camino, Isabella felt a divide growing inside her. For the first time in her life, she felt like just Isabella, not Princes Isabella. She cherished this moment; she was no one, just another pilgrim. *Is this what freedom feels like?*

The main course was on the table and the smell filled the hall. The nuns had prepared roast chicken and potatoes with rosemary. Isabella was delighted and thankful for the feast. She felt the strength coming back into her body and spirit. *Food made with love heals the body and the soul.*

When the meal finished, the nuns sat with the pilgrims and one of them played the lute. Its haunting sound filled the hall and Isabella felt a sense of peace fall upon her.

After the song, a large nun who looked tough as nails stood, and the room became silent. The nun held the room in suspense for a moment, then she smiled and everyone relaxed.

"Thank you, pilgrims, for joining us tonight. I am Sister Caroline. It is a blessing to have you here."

Isabella looked at her companions solemnly. She knew the hardships that each had experienced in the last twenty-four hours. Isabella felt Clair's arm wrap around her. It was a new sensation for her, but she knew she had to play her part as a commoner. Gerhart put his massive arms around Mariano and Andy. Ronan and Etienne looked in Isabella's direction and nodded, as did Tristan.

It unnerved Isabella how much she liked this feeling of belonging. But, she was here on a quest, not to make friends. Her father had entrusted her with a mission. If she failed, she would be imprisoned in a marriage that she did not want. She had to succeed—but at what cost? Would her mission take the lives of her new friends as well?

The Moors and these Shadows are after me. *They shouldn't have to pay the price for it.* Isabella smiled at the others, but felt the numbness enter her body again. Isabella knew what she had to do. She had to leave with Tristan in the morning, alone. *This burden isn't theirs to carry.*

"We would love to have you share something from your culture," Sister Caroline continued. "You are as diverse as the Milky Way, and each of you is a unique star that has a special light to shine on the world."

Andy stood, a little inebriated. He walked up to Etienne and bowed. "May I borrow your sword, sir?" Etienne smiled and drew his weapon.

"Thank you." Andy walked to the center of the room. He withdrew his own sword and put both down on the ground in an "X." Isabella knew immediately he was going to do the traditional Scottish sword dance, the Ghilie Callum. She had seen it once in her youth and loved it.

Andy stood very proudly and pointed to Clair, who began to sing. Isabella couldn't understand the words, but the rhythm was infectious. Everyone clapped their hands in time as Andy jumped, to and fro, from one quarter of the swords to the next. His large belly rising and falling with each leap was hypnotizing. With a twirling jump that physics would deem impossible for a man of his size, Andy finished the dance and landed on one bended knee. The crowd erupted into applause.

As the night drew to a close, a nun, who introduced herself as Sister Fransie, stood. "We would like to give you something as a gift to help you remember that no matter how hard the road is that lies ahead, you always have someone praying for you. We will pray daily for your safe delivery to Santiago. We will pray that St. James walks every step of the Camino with you, and that he will help to guide, keep, and protect you. We will pray that the Virgin will send her love down on you and feed you when you are hungry, find you shelter when you have none, and hold you when you feel your weakest. We will pray that our Lord Jesus will find your heart and heal any wounds that this world has afflicted on you. May God carry you in his healing hands and shape you into the person you were meant to be."

The nuns presented each traveler a small stone. Isabella smiled as she held hers close to her heart.

When all the pilgrims had a stone, Sister Fransie continued. "May this stone represent the light that shines inside each of you. Just as you follow the path of the stars in the sky to reach your destination, may you also follow the light of your heart to become who God meant you to be. Know that just as there are many stars in the sky to guide you, there are also many hearts to guide you through the dark places on your Camino. May God bless you. Goodnight, my beloved pilgrims."

Isabella shot out of bed. She had overslept. The exhaustion on her body had been too much. She scanned the room and Clair was gone. *That will make things a bit easier.* Isabella hoped to leave before the others. She didn't want to explain why she was leaving, nor say goodbye. She had spoken to Tristan about it the night before. They were supposed to meet in the courtyard before sunrise. Isabella looked out the window; the sun had risen more than an hour ago. Perhaps if she left now the others would be at breakfast. Isabella dressed and left the room.

The courtyard was filled with the sounds of animals and people hard at work packing. The air felt crisp and refreshing. It was the type of air that makes people feel alive, but Isabella felt numb when she saw Tristan in a heated conversation with the others. She'd wanted to avoid saying goodbye, especially to Etienne, but there was no way to avoid it now.

Tristan pointed to Mariano and Gerhart. "We don't need them." He then motioned to Clair, Etienne, and Ronan. "We don't need any of you."

Clair looked up at Isabella with large eyes as she joined the group. "Isabella, is it true? Ya want ta leave withoot us?"

Isabella avoided eye contact with her. "I don't want to put anyone else at risk." Isabella crossed her arms tightly. To reassure herself of her conviction.

Stepping forward, Etienne said, "We are bound to protect you, and will not leave you until we are relieved of our service."

Tristan took a step forward as well. "You are relieved."

This wasn't how Isabella had wanted things to happen. She'd wanted to avoid this situation.

"And what is all this?" Andy asked as he joined the group. "I canna leave you alone for ten minutes."

Ronan turned to Andy. "Mariano and Gerhart have found employment to protect a caravan." He motioned to Katsuji who waved at Andy. "Their employer has invited all of us to join, but Isabella feels her presence will jeopardize the safety of anyone she travels with." Andy looked at Mariano.

Mariano shrugged his shoulders. "We are mercenaries; our service goes to those who pay the highest price. Katsuji offered a handsome sum. Plus, Isabella doesn't want to travel with us."

"Ach, ya ol' coward, ya sold ooot," Clair piped up, full of spit and fire.

"I agree, Clair, they are cowards. Y're too afraid of the Shadows, aren't ya?" Andy crossed his arms. Gerhart looked longingly at Clair, then hung his head, unable to meet her eyes.

Mariano pointed at Isabella. "Death follows this one." Her body had a visceral reaction to his words. Everything tightened up. She could feel his anger directed at her.

Andy stepped between Mariano's finger and Isabella. "My point exactly. If ya want revenge on them Shadows, ya won't find it with this caravan." Andy turned his back to Mariano and faced Isabella. "Clair and I will come with ya, lassie. We have become very fond of ya. Since our Heather died, we decided ta walk the Camino all the way ta Santiago. We couldna' think of better company."

"What about the Moors and the Shadows?" Isabella asked.

Andy chuckled. "I was married te a woman much scarier than those Shadows we met yesterday." Andy winked. "Plus, what better place to hide than in a Caravan?"

Isabella smiled, and all of the tension released in her face. The others were smiling too. Andy knew how to change her mood. This wasn't the first time he had raised her spirits. Isabella didn't know why they were all fighting so hard to remain in her company. There was no benefit for them. No reward.

Katsuji walked up to the group. "It's time to go," he said to Mariano and Gerhart. "I insist that the rest of you join us, at least as far as Calzadilla de la Cueza. It is eleven miles away and there are no towns between here and there. I know your business is urgent, and you must travel with speed, but the Meseta is hot and can be deadly if you don't have the proper provisions. At least accompany us that far. We won't slow you too much," Katsuji said, flourishing his arms and bowing.

He was right, Isabella and Tristan had no provisions for a trek across the Meseta. She hadn't considered that. She looked around at her companions. With a sigh, she reluctantly said, "We will join you."

Katsuji smiled like a salesman and motioned to a scallop shell that marked the path of the Camino de Santiago.

"Shall we?" he said.

Isabella was uncertain about walking on the open road of the Camino again, but if Andy was right, there was no safer place to hide than in a caravan.

CHAPTER 5

THE MESETA

The wheels of the coach kicked up dust as they left the town and commenced on the Camino. Minutes outside of the city they were approached by riders. Isabella could see that some were injured.

"What happened, friend?" Katsuji asked from the wagon.

"We were attacked by a raiding party of Moors early this morning on the Camino. When they saw we didn't have what they were looking for, they continued west. Be careful out there." Isabella's heart skipped a beat. Had she left earlier, she would have been captured. Isabella said a silent prayer of gratitude. She was relieved to be with the safety of the caravan.

"It is a shame Clair decided to walk. She would have enjoyed seeing my garments," Katsuji said.

"She is a very determined woman. Don't take her refusal too harshly. Once she decides something, there is no way to convince her otherwise." Inside, though, Isabella wondered if she didn't ride with them because of her. Had she hurt Clair by wanting to leave without saying goodbye?

Isabella motioned to the many people walking with the caravan. "Where did all of these people come from?"

"All corners of the earth. Some have accompanied me long before the great mountains."

"You mean the Pyrenees?"

"No, those are just foothills compared to the mountains in the east." Great adventure flashed behind his eyes as he spoke. "Those who accompany this caravan are my community; my family. They have joined me on many adventures. There is strength in community. In a land not so far from my own, I was told by an old master that there isn't much difference between heaven and hell. In both there is a giant pot of food on a table with many people sitting around. Each person is given a set of chopsticks that are three feet long."

No idea what he was referring to, Isabella's eyebrows raised. "We will say spoons that are three feet long." He smiled gently. "Each person must hold the spoon by the end of the handle. In the case of hell, people are always starved. No matter how hard they try, they can't get the food into their mouth. However, in heaven they feast, because they each feed the person sitting opposite them.

"Here in my caravan, it is like heaven; we feed each other, help each other, and protect each other. This is why so many people from around the world have joined us."

Katsuji clapped his hands together. "Would you like to see some of my silks?" He held up the finest silk Isabella had ever seen. "This beauty came all the way from my home."

"It is beautiful," she said, admiring the way the light glinted off the fabric. Looking back to him, she tilted her head. "Where is it that you come from?"

"I come from the Land of the Rising Sun. It is the furthest east you can travel before hitting the great waters. Our silk is the finest in the world, especially this one. It is fit for a princess or a queen. Plus, they are the only ones who could afford it." Katsuji winked.

"Oh, have you met many princesses?" Isabella asked with a small smirk.

"I have been in court once or twice in my life. I have even visited the Palais de la Cité in your country. Have you ever been?"

"I can't say that I have." Isabella tried not to laugh. It was wonderful that he had no idea who she was. She was anxious to see what he would say about her home. "Would you tell me about it?"

"Why, of course. It is one of the most impressive places I have seen in all my travels. It sits on an island and almost looks like a massive ship cutting through the Seine River. There is a large wall surrounding the whole palace and turrets with blue roofs reaching to the sky. If it were made of gold, I would swear I was looking at heaven."

"And what about the people of the court? What are they like?"

"Just between you and me, most of them are stuck up."

Isabella laughed. Katsuji really had been to court. Isabella couldn't stand the way people treated each other there. But more importantly, she hated the way they treated people who were different from them, like Etienne.

Katsuji continued, "What I wouldn't give to live in a place like that..."

Katsuji's description made Isabella homesick. She missed the comfort of her father's palace. She missed not having to make decisions. She even missed her schedule. Her lady Jessica and the others had attended to her on the Camino. Even on a dangerous quest, they were her security blanket. Now Tristan was the only thread left tying her back to the palace.

If only I would have never left, they would be alive. Jessica would be preparing my bath about now instead of being dead. But, I had to leave.

With the memories of home came thoughts of her impending marriage to Edward II of England. Her father had arranged the marriage to secure an alliance between France and England. She didn't love him, and she had no idea how she was supposed to marry him, only that her duty required it of her upon her return—if she ever did return. Isabella looked out the window at Etienne and Tristan walking close by.

I have only ever loved one man. Isabella couldn't maintain her polite smile any longer. Her stare was vacant, and she felt a separation from the world.

She could feel Katsuji's watchful eyes on her. "Isabella, why are you walking the Camino?"

Turning back to him, she said, "To purify myself before the marriage my father has arranged." Isabella gave the same story to everyone she met on the Camino. She had told it so many times she almost believed it herself. This may have been one of the reasons, but it definitely wasn't the first or even second.

"You are not happy about this union?" Katsuji said, raising his eyebrows.

She shook her head ruefully. "No, I can't say that I am. I had no choice in the matter."

Stroking the silk garment in his hands, he softly said, "You sound like my Akari." Katsuji's eyes became distant. "She is why I am here now. I left everything behind for love."

A well of compassion rose inside Isabella. She was dealing with her own situation of love and loss. Before when others spoke of love, she'd been jaded and really hadn't cared. But, ever since seeing Etienne, she felt these dormant emotions awaken.

"Who is Akari, and where is she now?"

"Akari is my love. She is more beautiful than all the sakura in the world and more peaceful than the deer in Nara. She awaits me in Kyoto. Since we last met two and a half years ago, I have traveled further than any of my people before."

"If you love her, why are you away from her." Isabella had the same question for Etienne. Why hadn't he let her know he was alive?

"My country is run by many powerful Shoguns. They are warlords, not unlike your kings. Akari is a daughter of Prince Koreyasu,[16] a strong ruler. My family is also of noble lineage, however, I am only the second son. Akari's father did not find me worthy to wed his daughter. He said to me, 'You will only be found worthy if you leave here with nothing and return a rich man holding a jar of sand from the end of the world.'

"That very moment, I renounced my family name and possessions and have been traveling west since. The only thing I have left of my former life is my family's sword, and this silk kimono Akari gave to me. She said its value would allow me passage back home should I ever need it." Katsuji folded the kimono and returned it to its box.

Katsuji's story made her think of her situation again. *Etienne may have left without saying goodbye, but my actions sent him into the world penniless and alone.* Isabella admired that both Katsuji and Etienne had survived. She made a note to tell Etienne this when they spoke.

The caravan stopped for the midday meal when the sun was at its zenith. On either side of the Camino, barren fields stretched for miles. Some would find it desolate, but Etienne found it beautiful. Something about its emptiness made him feel whole. Perhaps it wasn't the scenery, but that for the first time in his life he was surrounded by others who looked like him. There were several people in the caravan who had dark skin just like his.

He had been the only person of color at the palace in France, and at the Arc there were Spaniards, but he was still different. The Templars treated him as a brother and equal, yet even there, he once heard an older Templar say that Etienne reminded him of the enemy.

Etienne moved away from the caravan for his noontime prayers. It was his daily ritual and constant companion on all of the miles he had traveled. For him, the journey inside was much more important than the journey outside.

The other travelers sat in the shade of the coaches with their shoes off, all trying to prevent blisters. Pilgrims dined and laughed in little groups of three or four. Some slept, others drank. The storks were in the fields, always just out of reach; their long slender bodies and expansive wingspan added a certain sort of mystique to the land.

Etienne bowed his head. *My Lord, I pray you will forgive me for the lives I have taken in defense of your pilgrims.* The scared face of the Moor, Etienne had killed in Castrojeriz, flashed into his thoughts. Etienne shook his head. *It couldn't have been him...*

Etienne hadn't told the others why he froze at the boathouse. When he'd seen the Shadow's face, it was the face of this dead Moor staring back at him. *It couldn't have been him? Are these Shadows the souls of the people I have killed? Did they come back to destroy me and those I care for?*

Etienne grabbed the crucifix that hung around his neck tightly, and blood ran down his hand. He ignored the pain; he had taught himself how to numb his senses long ago. A lifetime of violence had caused him to adapt. He focused on his breath.

Forgive me for the lives I have taken.

His meditation was broken by the sound of running water. He opened his eyes to see an old pilgrim close by relieving himself. Etienne loosened his grip on the crucifix and wiped the blood on his garments.

When the pilgrim finished, he turned and laughed. "Ohh, I didn't see you sitting there," he said, laughing again. His long gray beard and wrinkles accentuated his laughter. It seemed that each line etched into his skin held all the smiles the pilgrim had ever smiled. He was tall and slender with powerful muscles that supported his wiry frame. Etienne had never seen eyes like his before, they had a certain brightness and almost seemed to glow.

"Do you mind if I join you?" the old pilgrim asked, reaching for his staff.

"As you wish," Etienne said.

"Why are you on the Camino?" The old man's question reverberated through Etienne. It felt like the question was posed directly to his soul.

"I was ordered here," Etienne said. Trying to make his voice sound confident. However, to him it sounded hollow. "Ahh, I see." The old man stroked his beard. "Some choose this path and others are called. You have been called."

"What does that mean?" He tried to maintain eye contact, but the weight of the stranger's gaze made it impossible.

"There is a saying that the Camino will provide whatever you need. You are needed here. If you didn't choose of your own free will to be here, it means that there is a great need for you on the road."

Gathering his composure, Etienne looked at Isabella and the other pilgrims. It was as if this man could see past his answer to the truth—a truth he was just realizing: he was here for Isabella.

"Why are you here, old man?"

"I have always been here." The stranger extended his arm. "Give me your hand!"

Etienne tried to resist the order, but the pull was too strong. "A wound just like my Lord's," said the old man. "You carry the burden of suffering. Like him, you have taken on a heavy task." The pilgrim clasped Etienne's hand between his own and held it. When he released his grip, Etienne's wound was healed.

Etienne dropped to his knees and bowed his head. He couldn't believe his senses; he had just witnessed a miracle. "My Lord," he whispered. A mixture of gratitude and joy fountained inside him. For the first time in his life he was feeling jubilation.

"Rise, I am not your Lord. I am a servant just like you."

"I cannot," Etienne said, without rising. "I am not worthy."

"Rise!" commanded the old pilgrim. Etienne's body followed orders without his consent once more. The old pilgrim's eyes burned brightly. "I have been ordered to show you something. The Camino always provides."

The pilgrim slammed his large staff on the ground. On impact, a ring of fire burst forth and rippled off to the horizon. As it stretched out, everything slowed in its wake until time came to a standstill. The pilgrims stood motionless. When time had almost stopped, something strange happened: miniature comets appeared, streaking above the ground. The slower time went, the more comets appeared. When time had completely stopped, Etienne looked around and saw thousands of these comets surrounding them. They stretched to the horizon, shooting through anything that stood in their way. Some were gold, others green, and some were brilliantly white or silver. Each was a glowing ball with a tail of light tracing after it. The ones that were the last to appear had the longest tails stretching for hundreds of yards.

"What is this?" Etienne managed. He was in awe of this second miracle he was witnessing.

The old pilgrim let out a laugh that echoed and shook the small comets. Each comet struggled to push forward past the invisible force holding them fast. "These are the prayers of the pilgrims."

He reached down and picked up the closest one. It was only a few inches in length. His long slender fingers pinched the trembling prayer and brought it to Etienne's eye level. He stretched the blazing green prayer apart with both hands. It expanded, making a fiery frame, opening a window into a room with a young man ill in bed. "This pilgrim lies sick in Leon. He is praying for God to heal him, and that this sickness will go away as soon as possible."

"Will God heal him?" Etienne asked in wonder.

"Yes and no. Not quickly, his belief isn't that strong. Prayers travel at different speeds: the more someone believes, the quicker and stronger the prayer moves. There is also a more profound aspect to this man's sickness. It is actually a blessing in disguise."

The pilgrim reached down and plucked a silver prayer from the air that was a yard and a half in length. He expanded it, and Etienne saw a young woman with blond hair kneeling in prayer through the silvery frame. "God has called this woman to the Camino. She is a woman of strong belief and has been praying that she will meet her future husband. The man who lies sick is the one God has set aside for her. Had he not been taken by illness, their paths would have never crossed. For she now travels with this party, and is two days away from Leon." The old pilgrim motioned to the caravan, and there stood the woman who was in the silver prayer. "Sometimes, the things that seem to be our greatest challenges turn into our greatest rewards."

Etienne looked around him in wonder. Not knowing what else to say, he asked, "Are these around us on the Camino at all times?"

"Yes, however, prayers move faster than sight, so they are imperceptible. Remember, there is power in prayer, and the Camino will provide; not always what you want, but exactly what you need to fulfill your life's purpose." With this, the old pilgrim hit his staff on the ground once more, and the prayers were released. They moved at incredible speeds until they disappeared, along with the old man. Once they vanished, the members of the caravan began to move again and Etienne was knocked to the ground. He looked up at the blue sky above him and laughed ecstatically.

When Etienne composed himself, he found Ronan, and told him the incredible story of what he had just experienced. When he finished his tale, Ronan shook his head in amazement, taking it all in. He studied Etienne up and down.

"Describe this pilgrim to me."

"He was tall with a gray beard and wore a hat with a scallop shell. His eyes burned with a brightness like I have never seen before, and he carried a staff with a gourd on it. That is all I can remember."

"Well, I guess even saints need to pee," Ronan said, and started laughing at his own joke. He cleared a tear from one of his eyes.

Etienne's forehead creased in confusion. "What do you mean?"

"You met Santiago—St. James, the apostle of Jesus. Pilgrims travel thousands of miles to pray in front of his remains in Santiago de Compostela. He is the reason the pilgrimage exists. Do you know the story of how the pilgrimage began?"

Etienne shook his head feeling slightly ashamed that he didn't know the story.

"Legend has it that after St. James was martyred in the Holy Land, his followers brought his body to Finisterre, where he had preached when he was alive. Knowing the Romans wanted to find his body and destroy it, his disciples hid his tomb and it was lost to time.

"In the ninth century a farmer saw radiant light coming from the woods by his pasture. He walked over and discovered the tomb where St. James was buried. He then went to his bishop, who confirmed that this was indeed the body of St. James. Soon construction was underway to build a cathedral worthy enough to hold his remains. Since the discovery, pilgrims from across the Christian world have taken the pilgrimage because of its miraculous powers, and to receive forgiveness for their sins. Also, with the fall of Jerusalem, and Rome in the state it is in now, the Camino has become the most popular pilgrimage in the world.

"St. James has been known to appear on the Camino either as a pilgrim, as you described, or as a warrior. You have been blessed, my son." Ronan shook his head in amazement.

Etienne still felt jubilant. The adrenaline was still pumping through his veins. He wondered what purpose he had been called to here on the Camino. After his encounter with Santiago, he felt it had something to do with Isabella. He needed to talk to her.

CHAPTER 6

SAHAGUN

There was great excitement as the caravan entered Sahagun. Children rushed out to see the wagons and pilgrims, knowing that a caravan meant food, toys, and stories of faraway lands. The merry band of pilgrims made their way to the monastery in the main square. Everyone was in good spirits, except Gerhart, who had a gnawing feeling in the pit of his stomach.

"Are you sure you want to stay here with Katsuji and the caravan?" Gerhart asked Mariano.

"They are paying a good price."

"I feel like they will need us," Gerhart said reluctantly, looking at Clair.

"When did you develop feelings? What happened to Gerhart the Destroyer, mercenary for hire?"

"I just feel… I feel," Gerhart stuttered.

"There's that word again. Don't let feelings get in the way of work. We need this job," Mariano said sharply.

As day turned into night, the company joined together for one last meal, and a sort of melancholy fell over the camp. Gerhart couldn't shake the feeling that they were making the wrong decision by staying. He had never felt like this before. It was easy for him to go from job to job. It didn't matter to him who he had to hurt, as long as they were paid. The only person he had an attachment to was Mariano. They had been brothers in arms more times than he could count. Mariano was always there for him, always getting them work, always looking after him. This was the first time he had ever questioned his judgment. *Is it because of her?* he thought, looking at Clair, who was avoiding his gaze. He shook it off and took a large bite of a drumstick. He ate like a caveman, tearing the flesh from the bone, lost deep in thought.

Gerhart walked to Andy, Ronan, Etienne, and Tristan who were going over the plans for the next day's travel. He figured he should know the route just in case he wanted to join them.

"Since we can't walk openly on the Camino, due to the Moors, I think it will take us about a two days' march to reach Leon. I can't know for sure though, it has been many years since the last time I ventured there." Ronan said.

"Hold on fur just-a moment," Andy said, disappearing briefly into their albergue and returning with a large, musty, leather-bound book. "I 'ave just the thing!" he exclaimed.

"What is that?" asked Tristan.

"'Tis the Codex Calixtinus,[17] the guide to the Camino de Santiago. 'Twas the only thing I was able to save from the fire." Andy's eyes moistened. He quickly opened the book and thumbed through the pages. "See 'tis complete with maps," he said, stopping on a page that had a beautifully drawn map. It was labeled, "The Kingdom of Leon," in bold, gold leafed, Celtic letters. Gerhart leaned over the others to get a good look.

"You are full of surprises," Etienne said, smiling at Andy. The five of them sat and poured over the pages to get the lay of the land. Having no interest in books, Gerhart turned his attention back to Clair.

Isabella watched as Clair stood abruptly and walked away from the group of men. Isabella quickly left her conversation with Katsuji and chased after her.

"May I join you?" asked Isabella, running to catch up to her.

"As ye like lassie. Ah canno' stand that big oaf starin' a' me," said Clair.

"I think he is in love with you," Isabella said with a kind smile.

"Whooda luv an ol' bat like meh?"

Isabella dropped her gaze to the ground, feeling the weight of her guilt. She could see how Clair might feel unwanted, and she felt ashamed that she'd tried to leave without saying goodbye. She was sure that was why Clair had been avoiding her all day.

"Clair, I think I owe you an apology," Isabella began. "I didn't mean to hurt you this morning by trying to leave without saying goodbye. I was trying to keep everyone else safe, because I was afraid that my presence was putting you all in danger. I thought that if I didn't say anything, it would be easier to walk away. But I see now that it was wrong of me. Can you forgive me?"

Claire's expression softened as she looked at Isabella. "Aye, chil', ah forgi' ye," she said, and wrapped Isabella in a warm hug.

They walked arm in arm down the cobblestone street to the stone bridge and rushing river. The sound of water splashing, mixed with the frogs and crickets, created a symphony that filled the night air. They sat under a willow tree; its long wispy branches blew in the night breeze, bringing the stars in and out of view.

"Thank you," Isabella said sincerely.

"Fer wha', chil'?"

"For holding me and comforting me, back at the convent. I can't remember the last time I was held like that. My mother seldom came to see me. When we did meet, it was a queen meeting a princess, not a mother meeting a daughter. I think I reminded her of my father, and she couldn't stand him. He can be an incredibly cruel man at times, and my mother resented him greatly. She only saw him in me." Isabella stared blankly at the flowing water contemplating how much she had not experienced in life.

"How cud a mother act li' tha'? I woulda giv'n my life for my 'Eather." Clair's expression froze and hardened. Isabella touched Clair's shoulder, and Clair took her hand. "'Tis alri', she's up there with tha angels."

"I have never met a woman—or man, for that matter—who is as strong as you. I will miss you when we part ways."

Isabella and her companions had departed in the morning, leaving Gerhart and Mariano with Katsuji. Mariano was glad to be rid of them. Had they never entered the boathouse, he would still have Alba. Gerhart, on the other hand, was upset. Mariano had never seen him act like this before. Gerhart had never second guessed Mariano's decisions. Mariano was happy they had work. It was something to take his mind off of Alba's death.

The day wore on and sales were good. The wagons had been transformed into three large stalls, housing the exotic clothes Katsuji was selling. The fabrics made a rainbow of color and texture. Mariano watched the people

from town all come to see what Katsuji was selling, and sell he did. His charisma shot through the crowd. The townsfolk were excited by the adventures
Katsuji and his caravan had gone through to bring these fabrics from the Far
East. He talked about the magical properties each fabric held and encouraged
the wealthy townspeople to touch the silk just once.

As Mariano and Gerhart stood guard at either end of the stalls, keeping a
vigilant eye on the goods, a Spanish woman with almond-shaped eyes smiled
at Mariano. Mariano's shoulders slumped and he stared at the ground. *She has
Alba's eyes. Mi amor.*

The bells for evening mass chimed, and the crowd dispersed. "Let's pack up.
That is good for today." Katsuji motioned for Mariano and Gerhart to come
closer. "You two come with me: we must deposit the gold with the Templars."

Until three days ago, Mariano had dreaded the word Templar; now it made
him think of Ronan and Etienne. They were the first Templars he had known.
Being a conman and mercenary, he'd tried to avoid Templars, instead of traveling in their company.

Once they'd accompanied Katsuji to deposit the gold he'd earned, Mariano
said, "I think I will retire early." A wave of grief had overcome him and he
didn't want to be in the company of others. He needed time to mourn Alba. He
needed time to think and process his emotions.

"Are you sure?" Gerhart asked. Mariano nodded and his old friend walked off
with Katsuji to the tavern.

Rest will do me good, he thought as he continued down the lonely street.

At the inn, Mariano hadn't been able to sleep, Alba's death played in his head
again and again. He shivered as a cold breeze blew through the room. His grog-
gy mind began to wake; he hadn't left a window open.

"Mariano, why couldn't you save me? You killed me."

His eyes shot open. *Mi amore!*

Thoughts of Alba's death had plagued him all through the night, but this was
different: those words came from inside his room.

There was another whisper in the darkness Mariano lay still for a moment,
listening for movement. All was silent, but the hairs on his arm told him not to
trust it. As he reached slowly for his knives, careful not to make a sound, he
heard the hiss of metal cutting through the air. Heart racing, he rolled off the
bed just as the blade descended. It barely missed him, slicing open the pillow
that still had the heat of his head clinging to it.

The Shadow let out a hideous noise as it withdrew its sword. Mariano saw
nothing but blackness and the glint of moonlight on the silver blade. He
kicked the wooden frame of the bed with all of his might, sending it crashing

into the creature's shins. *If only I could reach my throwing knives.* He looked desperately at the night table next to the Shadow, calculating whether he was fast enough to make it.

Deciding to take a chance, he dove, but the Shadow screeched again, knocking into him before he reached the table.

He kicked at it, but his legs didn't connect. Light spilled into the room from the now open door, and he saw two large hands pull the Shadow into the hallway. He heard the creature hiss as its body hit the torch. Mariano rushed into the hall. Gerhart's large arms held the Shadow fast from behind. He let out a loud roar and rolled onto his back. Using his legs and the momentum of the fall, Gerhart kicked hard and sent the Shadow out the window. Mariano rushed to the window; below, there was nothing but the ground, and all was silent.

Gerhart pulled Mariano to his feet. "We have brought a terrible thing upon this house, Mariano. Two people are dead. Those things must have been looking for Isabella. We must leave immediately; we may be able to reach our companions before the Shadows do."

As the two fled the town, Mariano kept thinking of the voice he heard. *It couldn't have been her.* A chill ran up and down his spine. *I will avenge you, mi amore, so you can rest in peace. Forgive me for failing tonight.*

CHAPTER 7

PARIS

King Philip IV of France sat on his red velvet throne and gripped the golden armrest tightly, feeling the metal heat up under the pressure. He focused on his knuckles that were whitening from his tight grip. Releasing the tension, he watched the blood slowly returning to his hands. He paid no attention to the man pleading before him. This was just a formality, an illusion to make the populous believe he was just and fair. But Philip had no space in his calculating mind for justice, only for control. Philip had decided this man's fate long before he had entered the throne room.

This man is an utter fool. Did he really think he could compromise my power by rousing a rebellion? Did he not know that I would destroy him and his companions? At the thought of destroying his enemies, Philip gripped the throne again tightly, then released.

"Hmm, hmm, Your Grace," said his closest advisor.

"What is it, Pierre?" Philip asked, still distracted by his grip on the throne.

"The man has finished stating his case," Pierre said cautiously.

"So he has." After a pregnant pause, Philip continued, "Have him and his followers hung, drawn, and quartered. Then have their remains placed at the towers surrounding the city to be a reminder for those who may have similar ideas."

"As you wish, Your Majesty." Pierre clapped his hands, and the guards seized the man who struggled and pleaded.

"What's next?" Philip barked.

"We have news of your daughter, Your Majesty."

"Ah, excellent. Send in the messenger." Philip smiled and placed his clasped hands under his chin. The doors to the great chamber opened and a road-weary messenger entered the throne room. The red dust from the Camino de Santiago still clung to his clothing. The man approached the throne, took off his hat, and knelt on one knee. "Rise," commanded Philip, "and tell me of my daughter."

Avoiding eye contact, the messenger rose. "The Baron of Castrojeriz sends words that your daughter's caravan was attacked by the Moors just outside of Castrojeriz. All were killed, except Her Highness and the captain of her guard, Tristan. They managed to make it to the safety of the city. This news comes from the Baron of that small town. Knowing it wouldn't be safe for them under the siege of the Moors, he ordered them taken to the Kingdom of Leon. The Templars accepted the task and snuck them out of the city. They haven't been seen or heard of since."

"The Templars! The Templars!" Philip roared. "They are a plague to the land and threaten this kingdom. Their power and wealth have become too great. Now they possess my daughter?!" Philip gripped the throne tightly. "I must speak with the Pope immediately."

Though he was raging on the outside, inside he was smiling. This gave him the perfect excuse to execute his scheme. He couldn't have planned it better himself.

CHAPTER 8

BENEATH THE STARS

Isabella watched the small fire spark and crackle as the wind blew; it was the one thing that brought her peace in the exposed, dark woods. At dusk, they had left the Camino and set up camp a little way off the road. Isabella had never slept under the open night sky before, but the next town was still miles away; this was their only option. She didn't want to show how terrified she was as the sky grew dark—how every noise made her heart race, how she constantly felt like insects were crawling on her skin, or how she felt like she was being watched from beyond the firelight. She wanted to stay composed and not reveal her discomfort.

The others all seemed at ease with being in the woods. Andy slowly spit-roasted the rabbit Etienne had caught. Clair was preparing some mushrooms they had found before sunset. Tristan was on watch, and Ronan lay looking at the stars above. Etienne sat staring at the fire. Isabella watched the flames gently dance in his dark eyes. She had missed those eyes, especially when they were smiling. He used to give her a half-smile that made her feel giddy inside. But since they had been reunited, Etienne had barely even looked at her.

"I will go get more firewood," Etienne said, breaking his trance. This was the perfect opportunity to talk to Etienne alone. It had been hard to find a moment to speak to him, especially when Tristan was always so close to her side.

"I will join you," Isabella said, standing.

Etienne hesitated for a second. "As you like." He shot her his half-smile, and her stomach fluttered in response. In anticipation of this moment, she had rehearsed many times what she was going to tell Etienne. She would tell him what happened the day he was sentenced to death, and she'd tell him her feelings.

They walked away from the tiny fire, gathering some sticks in the moonlight. Etienne was silent. She was going to have to speak first.

Isabella took a deep breath to calm her nerves. "I can't believe this is our first moment alone." Isabella put her hand to her forehead. She was embarrassed that she'd just blurted that out. Of all the things she'd rehearsed, that was not one of them.

Etienne stopped gathering sticks and walked closer to her with purpose. The thought of him embracing her crossed her mind. She dropped the sticks in her hands ready to receive his embrace.

Etienne bent down to pick up the sticks she had dropped. "I have to talk to you about something." He rose and looked deep into her eyes. "Yesterday on the Meseta I was visited by Santiago…" This wasn't what she was expecting at all. Her shoulders slumped and she took a step back. "He told me that I had been called on the Camino because I was needed here. When he was speaking to me, I realized the purpose for me being here is you. I was called here for you."

Isabella's heart lifted as she smiled inside. Was this him telling her his feelings? No, he had just told her a realization, not his feelings about her. Isabella was unsure of how to interpret what he said. She was putting her own emotions into his words, overanalyzing the situation. She closed her eyes for a second. *I must not let my emotion fog my thinking.* She reminded herself of her mission.

"Etienne, I do need you." She looked lovingly into his eyes. *Stay focused Isabella.* She shifted her mind to think of her father and Edward. *I need you, Etienne, just not in the way you think.* She needed Etienne to help her find the treasure. Etienne and Ronan had already led her to one of the doors. She needed to stay with them to discover more. She did have feelings for Etienne, and thoughts of him found their way into her mind more often than she'd like to admit—but she had to stay focused on her goal. If she found the treasure, then she would be free. She could even be with Etienne if she chose to be. But until she found the treasure, she was trapped.

"Isabella, you're biting your lip. You always did that if there was a secret you were trying to hide."

Isabella smiled. "You still know me so well." He had always seen her for who she was; he'd understood all her small quirks better than anyone. "I have something to talk to you about as well." She paused for a moment. "I need to tell you what happened the last day I saw you." His body became rigid. It seemed that he had put back on all of his armor. "Etienne, my heart broke in that throne room. Your sentence killed a piece of me, as well. I loved you." Isabella couldn't believe she had just said that as well. What was happening to her?

"Some love," he said coldly. He crossed his arms and looked like an impenetrable fortress. "When you love someone, you save them when you have the opportunity. You just stood there and watched me be sentenced to death."

Isabella clenched her jaw. "That isn't true!"

"Yes it is, Isabella, and you know it!" His words hit her like daggers, every single one piercing her heart.

"Leave me alone." Isabella said coldly, whipping around to turn away from him.

"With pleasure," Etienne said, walking back toward the fire.

Rage ran through her body. She had just made herself vulnerable, and he had twisted the knife that had been stuck in her side for two years. She picked up a stick and swung it at a tree to let out some of her frustration, breaking it in half.

Isabella heard a twig snap behind her and turned, "Etienne, I don't—" A dark figure slammed Isabella against a tree. She felt pain bloom in the back of her head as she lost consciousness.

Etienne had taken a few moments to himself before heading back to the fire. He'd been wanting to talk with Isabella, but hadn't imagined it happening like that. He was ashamed that he let his anger lash out at her. He had often wondered why Isabella had been willing to let him die, and just now, when he could have gotten that answer, he'd pushed her away.

"Ach, where have ya been? The fire almost went out," Andy said, turning the spit. "Where's Isabella? Dinner is almost cooked."

Etienne's face was flushed and his body tense. "She needed a minute alone."

Ronan sat up. "You left her alone out there?"

"Donna worry, I'll go'n find her fer dinner," Clair said, getting up from her log and walking into the woods.

As Clair was calling out to Isabella, Etienne was starting to get unnerved that she hadn't responded yet. *No, she probably just doesn't want others to see her upset.* Clair shouted back to camp. Etienne couldn't understand what she was saying, but he leapt to his feet and ran to where he had last seen Isabella. Clair was standing in shock, and pointed to blood on the trunk of a tree. Etienne glanced around; there was a clear path of broken sticks and disheveled leaves leading to the east. "Isabella!" His heart sank deep in his chest.

Ronan threw Etienne his sword. "You will need this." In his haste, Etienne had left everything behind. "It looks like there were five or six of them. Quickly, we might be able to overtake them."

Etienne led the charge. He had failed Isabella. *She had told me she loved me.* He couldn't stand the thought of letting her die. He would save her. They followed the trail for a half hour, and stopped when several campfires and tents came into view.

Etienne looked back at his companions. "Where's Tristan?" he whispered. It would take all of them to get Isabella out of this situation. There had to be at least fifty soldiers at the camp.

"He hadn't come back from watch before we left," said Ronan. "Look." Ronan pointed at a group of five Moors, one of them carrying Isabella's limp body into a tent. Etienne moved forward, but was restrained by Andy and Ronan.

"'Tis too many of them," Andy said.

"He's right we need to be smart about this." Ronan let go of Etienne's arms. Etienne looked at the soldiers around the fire, and then at his dark hands, and a plan began to formulate.

Isabella awoke with blurred eyes. Her head throbbed in pain and her mouth was dry. She scanned her surroundings: *a large tent, animal furs, men talking...* Isabella struggled to keep her eyes from closing, as she fought to regain consciousness. Her vision came into focus, and a few feet away she saw a group of men sitting around a table smoking a strange glass water pipe. All of them were bearded and wore turbans. Isabella tried to move her hands and feet, but both were bound.

"Release me at once," Isabella demanded.

Her captors spoke in a language she had never heard before, and laughed. Well, she thought she had never heard it before, but her head felt so fuzzy it was hard to tell. A man stood and brought Isabella a glass of water. "Come, you must be thirsty. I'm Nazir," he said in the common tongue, holding the glass to Isabella's lips. He tipped the water into her mouth, and she spat it back at her captor. The others all laughed again.

"Come, that is no way to treat your host, Your Highness." Isabella froze. Her eyes widened and her mouth gaped. They knew who she was. Nazir read the shock on her face. "Of course we know who you are, and about your mission. That is why we are here." Isabella felt exposed, unclothed from her disguise as a pilgrim.

"How do you know..."

"Does this surprise you? We know everything, and are everywhere. We are from the Order of the Assassins.[18] We cannot let you succeed in your mission. Had we caught you at the Arc, we could have avoided so much bloodshed, and you would have been seen safely back to Paris. But now, you may know too much. We were just deciding your fate when you woke. Perhaps you need that drink now." Nazir held the water to Isabella's lips and she accepted the liquid. Her captors all laughed again and Nazir joined them at the table.

Isabella felt absolutely helpless. Assassins don't take prisoners, nor send ransom notes, they just kill their victims. What was she still doing alive? She needed to escape. She wished she wouldn't have made Etienne leave. She wished their last words weren't in anger. Isabella looked more closely at the men; their complexions and features were similar to Etienne's.

"What are you looking at?" Nazir said.

"I thought you were Moors when you first attacked us. But you're different. You remind me of someone."

"Usually, your people think we all look the same," her captor grunted. "We hired the Moors to fight with the six of us. We had to make it look like it was their doing. Assassins are invisible." Her captors all laughed again. Him telling her all this, confirmed the fact that they were going to kill her.

Is Etienne an assassin? The question came up unconsciously. Had Etienne been spying at her father's palace, and now on the Templars? Maybe that's why my father wanted him executed. Etienne had almost seemed as interested in the door in Castrojeriz as she was.

Yelling came from outside, and a soldier rushed into the tent. He exchanged hurried words with the assassins. Nazir directed one of the men to stay with Isabella, as he and the others rushed out. Adrenalin kicked into Isabella's body. She struggled with her bonds until her wrists bled. They were too tight; she had to find another way. Isabella scanned the tent quickly and saw her opportunity as the guard looked out the front flap of the tent. Isabella rolled herself across the furs on the ground, knocking into the table and causing the glass water pipe to shatter on the floor. Isabella took a piece of glass in her hands and tried to cut her bonds. With each movement the glass edge penetrated deeper into her skin. The guard turned and kicked the glass out of her hands. Isabella's body stiffened as the guard raised his arm to strike. But the blow was intercepted by a soldier who grabbed him by the arm and flipped the guard backwards.

As the two men fought, Isabella grabbed another piece of glass and began on the knots again. Her heart raced, yet she stayed calm and focused. This was her chance. Even though the fighting was happening right in front of her, her whole attention was on cutting her feet free. She gasped pushing through the pain of the glass. The soldier swung, but her guard caught his arm and twisted it behind his back. In response, the soldier rammed his head into her guard's face.

Isabella coughed—where the water pipe had landed, the hot coals had lit the furs on fire. Black smoke filled the tent and Isabella's lungs. She didn't have time to cut her ropes any longer, she rolled herself toward the door, clutching the glass in her bloodied hand. It was her means of freedom, but also one last defense should anyone try to attack.

The two men rolled away from each other and regained their feet inches from where Isabella lay. She froze. "I don't have time for this," the soldier yelled, pulling his sword. The guard pulled his sword as well, but the soldier spun in and slit the guards throat. The guard dropped to his knees, then fell forward, his body bleeding out next to her.

The soldier rushed to Isabella and untied her bonds. As soon as her feet were free, she kicked him in the groin and ran to the tent flap.

"Isabella, it's me," said the soldier from the ground. Isabella stopped. "Etienne!" She rushed back to help him up, and together they escaped into the cool, dark protection of the forest.

CHAPTER 9

LEON

"We're here!" Andy shouted.

Isabella crested the hill and felt a weight removed from her shoulders. Below lay the magnificent walled city of Leon. *We made it.*

Andy danced around and started hugging everyone. Isabella felt like doing the same, but she was too exhaustaed. Last night she'd thought she was going to die. Isabella unconsciously clutched her bandaged hand. After they'd all escaped the camp, they'd found Tristan and headed west. They'd kept to the woods, and had been careful to cover their tracks.

Isabella looked below again, she saw safety, but she also saw uncertainty. *Is this the end of our companionship?*

Ronan and Etienne had only agreed to escort her to Leon, and she hadn't learned Andy and Clair's plans. *Will they stay here with me as I await my father's directions, or continue on?* Isabella wondered if she should enlist their help in her quest. Andy was very intelligent, and she loved Clair's company.

"Would ya look at that! The most powerful kingdom in Spain!" Andy exclaimed as they hurried down the hill. "Ya know, over the years, the kingdoms of Castile and Leon 'ave been joined an' separated many-a time..." As he continued, Isabella noticed Clair feigning interest. She often did this when Andy went on a historical purge. He continued, not even noticing, "However, six years ago in the year 1300, John reconciled with Ferdinand and entered his service, unitin' the two kingdoms." Clair clapped slowly.

Isabella smiled slightly. "It is amazing how much you know."

Puffing his chest proudly, Andy said, "Well, I'm a scholar, after all."

The walls of Leon towered above the pilgrims, and two large doors stood between them and the bustling metropolis. Ronan knocked on the wooden door with his staff.

"Who goes there?" shouted a guard from the wall above.

"Pilgrims on the way to Santiago in search of refuge," Ronan replied.

"You may pass."

The two giant doors opened, revealing one of the greatest pearls in Spain: Leon. Isabella took a moment to let her eyes inhale the splendor of the city. The cobblestone streets stretched off in all directions, each holding its mystery. Amongst the stones, scallop shells marked the path of the Camino. Her eyes followed them to the majestic cathedral in the distance; it stood as a testament to the strength of both God and the city.

The travelers were greeted on either side by merchants selling their goods, each stall more colorful than the last. The smell of cooking food and candy made Isabella stomach rumble. She restrained herself, but Andy couldn't. He walked to one of the candy stalls and indulged in a sample of the wares.

"Come, we have no time to waste," Ronan called to Andy. "We must reach the cathedral before the doors are shut." Andy ashamedly put back his second helping of sweets and rejoined the group.

Isabella and her companions' gray cloaks and dusty shoes were a stark contrast to the vibrant colors all around them. Once again, they were out of place; they were of this world, but no longer belonged to it. There was something that separated them.

"Buen Camino," Isabella heard, again and again, as they traversed the streets. The salutation given to pilgrims was a blessing for a good road, a safe adventure, and the fulfillment of their pilgrimage. Every time Isabella heard it, her body was rejuvenated. The kindness of those who lived along the Camino was legendary. Time and time again, she had experienced it. So many people willing to help. So many people wanting the pilgrims to succeed in completing their pilgrimage to Santiago de Compostela.

Andy pointed to a scallop shell on the side of a building. "Ya know, the scallop shell is a metaphor for the Camino de Santiago. Its lines represent all the different routes pilgrims travel from around the world, to meet at one destination: the tomb of St. James." Isabella had followed these shells like north stars along the Camino. She knew very well what they meant, but she liked the look of joy on Andy's face whenever he got to explain something.

The main street opened into the square, revealing the first full view of the immaculate cathedral. It towered above the rest of the city, glowing orange as the sun set behind them. The phthalo blue sky heightened the contrast between the cathedral and the heavens above.

"The Cathedral of Leon," Ronan said. All stood for a moment, taking in its sheer majesty before they made haste to the front doors. There were three large pointed archways that served as the entrance to the cathedral. Above them was an intricate rose stained glass window that shone like a rainbow in the mist. It reminded her of Notre Dame.

People were exiting the middle door from the evening prayer. Isabella admired the archway; not a single inch of space was wasted. Small figures were carved into the arch, their forms curving with the structure as it ascended. Below the archway stood two inlaid doors. In the center between them was a statue of the Blessed Virgin Mary holding our Lord Jesus.

"That is The Virgin Blanco; the most famed statue of the cathedral," Ronan said, noticing her admiration.

"The mass has ended and the cathedral is closing," a clergyman said as they entered.

"We have pressing business and must speak to the bishop immediately," Ronan said in a commanding voice.

"All peregrino business can wait until the morning. Let me show you to the albergue," insisted the clergyman.

"We are not mere pilgrims," Ronan said. He shifted his outer garments to reveal his white mantle and the blazing red cross of the Knights Templar. "I am Ronan, Seneschal to Grand Master Jacques de Molay.[19] We accompany Princess Isabella of France, whose life has been in great peril," he said, motioning to Isabella.

"My apologies. I didn't recognize you in peregrino clothing. I will notify the Bishop at once. Enjoy the cathedral while you wait."

Isabella nearly gasped out loud. Ronan was second in command to the Grand Master of the Templars. No wonder he knew about the tunnel in Castrojeriz. *He probably knows where all the secret doors are located. I must figure out a way to get more information from him.*

"You are the seneschal to the Grand Master?" Etienne said, his mouth gaping. He thought of all the moments he'd treated Ronan as an equal, when the reality couldn't be farther from the truth. Etienne's shoulders slumped. He was only a sergeant, the lowest ranking of Templar. He wasn't a knight before he joined the Templars, so he would never ascend the ranks of the order. The things Ronan had shown him in Castrojeriz, and what they had spoken about were way above his station. He felt the unworthiness he had felt from childhood creep in.

"It is so, my son," Ronan said as they walked apart from the others down the south side of the cathedral.

"You are his right hand! The second highest ranked Templar there is." Etienne shook his head. "I'm unworthy to even breathe the same air as you."

Ronan stopped. "We are all brothers. You are worthier than most I have met. A title doesn't make a person; their morals, values, and actions do."

Etienne didn't know how to take the compliment, so he asked the first thing that came to his mind. "Why are you in Spain? Shouldn't you be in Cyprus—"

Ronan placed his hand on Etienne's shoulder. "If we are through with this, there are more important things to discuss. What do you notice about this church?"

"It is a true work of art," replied Etienne, admiring the stained glass windows. Etienne thought it was the most interesting church he had ever been in. So much of it was covered in strange carvings of what looked like scenes out of mythology and lore.

"No, what do you notice that the others may not?" Ronan asked sternly.

Etienne looked around the giant space. Behind him, the last rays of sun shone in from the stained glass window above the entrance. "The cathedral is positioned facing east."

"Search deeper. What else?"

Etienne looked up and scanned the perimeter of the cathedral. "The stained glass windows to the south are incredibly beautiful and colorful, while the ones to the north are dark." As he said this, Etienne knew what Ronan was trying to convey. "It's built to resemble Solomon's Temple."

"Very good, my son. All the cathedrals along the Way of St. James were built in this manner, and serve as signposts that point to the secret the Camino holds. As you may know, our order found a great treasure in the Holy Land under Solomon's Temple. What the original nine discovered gave them unimaginable power and wealth. If this treasure ever fell into the wrong hands, it could destroy everything we hold dear. Etienne, there is something about the Shadows that I can tell only you. Swear to me, on your oath as a Templar, that you will guard this secret with your life."

"I swear it," Etienne said solemnly. He didn't feel worthy to receive this information, but if Ronan thought he was, Etienne would defend it with his last breath.

"The fate of the Shadows is tied to that of the treasure. The Shadows first appeared after the battle of Montgisard when Grand Master Odo de St. Armand used the treasure to decimate Saladin's army. He killed 26,000 of Saladin's soldiers with only 80 Templars, 200 knights, and a few thousand infantry men. All the Grand Masters had been warned not to use the treasure, but Odo didn't listen. When he used it, he unleashed the Shadows, and much worse things, on the world."

Ronan looked around anxiously. "Knowing the Holy Land would fall, Odo's successor Grand Master Arnold of Torroja took the treasure and hid it on the Camino. As a precaution, should anything happen to the Grand Master and his Seneschal, the whereabouts of the treasure was encoded in the cathedrals along the Camino. Like a giant puzzle, each cathedral holds part of the secret that leads to the treasure's location. The day the Shadows attacked Arnold, he was putting the final clue into the Cathedral of Santiago de Compostela," Ronan finished with a somber look on his face.

"I heard rumors of a treasure, but didn't know it actually existed." Etienne felt excitement coursing through his veins. Then the weight of Ronan's words sunk in. The only reason he would be telling him this information is if Ronan thought misfortune was upon himself or the Grand Master.

"Shhh, very few do. Now that the Shadows have returned, I fear our fates are tied to this treasure once more."

"Why is that?" Etienne didn't know if he should ask questions or not, but he needed to know if he was the cause of the Shadows—if they were the souls of those he had killed.

"Besides leaving a map to the treasure's location in the cathedrals, the Grand Master bound the treasure, and the evil it brought into the world, behind seven doors. When unlocked, each door presents both a trial and a treasure. The Shadows are one of those trials. Whether it was by accident or on purpose, someone has unlocked one of these doors. Only when these treasures are united and the trials overcome, will a person be worthy to stand in the presence of the one true treasure."

"What does that have to do with us?" Etienne's body tingled, and the hairs on his neck stood up.

"Many of the complexities of the Shadows are still unknown, but I do know this: one of our companions at the boathouse is the person who has opened this door. There were nine Shadows at the boathouse and nine of us companions. Our worthiness is being tested, and we are the only ones who can destroy the Shadows."

"There are only eight of us, though."

"The ninth was Alba." Ronan took a moment of silence. "I am afraid that others in our company will meet the same fate. Follow me"

Etienne tried to grasp what he had heard as Ronan led him further down the southern side of the cathedral. The echo of Andy's laugh bounced off the walls. For a moment, Etienne had forgotten the others were still in the cathedral. *My companions.* Etienne couldn't bear thinking about any of them facing the Shadows again, but now, it looked like their fates were intertwined. Etienne was overwhelmed by a wave of questions and uncertainty, but he tried to push those aside to stay focused.

Ronan and Etienne rounded the nave behind the altar and passed three small alcove chapels, the fourth of which Ronan entered. "I have something to show you." Etienne didn't know how much more information he could take. His whole world paradigm had shifted. Etienne was relieved the Shadows hadn't appeared because of him. He didn't remember opening any secret doors. *Who could have opened it?* To protect the Templar treasure, Etienne would have to kill this person.

"Why are you telling me all of this?"

"Because of Santiago's message, that there is great need for you on the Camino." He took a large breath. "And because of the reappearance of the Shadows. With the treasure coming back to life, I would feel better knowing you have this information. I am old, my son—I don't have many battles left in me, and there are some in the Templars that I do not trust."

"No, you can't say that." Ronan was a mentor and friend. He had filled a void in Etienne that he had felt since his father's death. "I accept the responsibility of this secret, but your time is not over."

"We shall see," Ronan looked over his shoulder again. "Very well, let's continue." He held a torch to the right side of the alcove, revealing a sarcophagus with a well-carved effigy. Etienne's eyes studied the figure for a few moments, then moved upward. Above the tomb he saw something strange: on the wall was carved the face of a man with wild hair and antlers.

He turned to Ronan and asked. "What is this face? I remember something like this from my childhood. It was carved into the wall that surrounds the Palais de la Cité. It used to scare me as a child."

"Ahh, so you have seen Cernunnos[20] before. What you saw was the Pilier des Nautes,[21] or Pillar of the Boatmen, in the common tongue."

"Yes, Cernunnos. I remember that name carved above it. Who is he?"

"He is a pagan god of fertility, life, animals, wealth, and the underworld."

"Why is it carved on this church?"

"You shall soon see." Ronan moved the torch to the opposite wall. Once again, Etienne saw a sarcophagus, this time of a woman. Her effigy was beautiful. She looked so peaceful, so calm. Above it, was a carving of a goat's head.

"Why is there a goat's head above this tomb?" Etienne asked raising an eyebrow.

"What shape does the goat head make with its two horns?"

Unsure of the importance of the question, Etienne replied, "A triangle with the point facing down."

"The triangle has always been a sign of divinity. With the point facing down, it represents the female aspects of divinity; with the point up, the male. It is a symbol of unity, and that which results from that unity. The tip of the triangle is the meeting of all worlds."

Etienne furrowed his brow. "I don't understand."

"Soon all will be clear." Ronan raised the torch to the back wall of the alcove. Here, on the same level as the other images, was a carving of a severed head.

"Baphomet?"[22] Etienne took a step back.

"Yes, it is an image of Baphomet. What do you know of its origin and legend?"

"Some say the severed head is regarded by us Templars as our savior, bringing great wealth and power. It is also said that it will make the land germinate and the trees grow no matter the season. Is this legend true? Is Baphomet the secret treasure? Etienne asked with raised eyebrows.

"Do you know the Atbash Cipher?" Ronan asked with a half smile. Etienne wasn't surprised Ronan couldn't tell him who or what Baphomet was directly, but perhaps Ronan was trying to give him a hint.

Etienne thought back to every code he had learned in his few short years as a Templar. "Yes... Yes, it's Coptic. It is a substitution cipher. You replace the first letter of the alphabet for the last, and the second for the second to last, and so on."

"Good. Then you have the tools to learn what the Templars truly worship, and what makes the trees bloom and the fields germinate. This will be the first test of your worthiness."

Etienne's heart raced. He wasn't going to let his feelings of unworthiness stop him. This was too important. He took Ronan's hint and scratched out the word Baphomet and the cipher*[1] on a stone with his dagger.

A B C D E F G H I K L M N O P Q R S T U V W X Y Z

Z Y X W V U T S R Q P O N M L K I H G F E D C B A

Etienne put the word Baphomet into the cipher, but came up with, 'Yzlsmovg.' The letters didn't spell anything. Etienne stroked his chin.

---

1. The letter "J" didn't exist until the 16th century. Therefore, all ciphers and alphabets are based on 25 letters as opposed to 26.

"Wait a minute. It's Coptic, which means it's in Hebrew." Etienne wrote out the Hebrew alphabet forward and backward. He then spelled the word in both directions.

אבגדההוזחטיכלמנסעפצקרשת
תשרקצפעסנמלכייטחזוההדגבא

בפומת
(Baphomet)

שופיא
(Sophia)

"Sophia... wisdom... The Templars worship wisdom—this is what makes the trees bloom and the fields germinate."

"That is so," Ronan said with a proud look in his eye. "You have proven yourself worthy to receive more wisdom. I feel you will need this information on the Camino, and it will render great service to mankind." Ronan took the dagger from Etienne and scratched out the carved letters. "All I have told you, you must keep to yourself. I am one of the protectors of these secrets, and now you are as well. Guard this knowledge with your life."

Etienne dropped to his knees and said, "I swear it by God, I will guard this secret with my life."

"Rise, my boy, and receive more wisdom while there is still time. I will now share with you how to read the symbols that lead to the clue of this cathedral." Etienne stood and waited patiently. "As in all cathedrals, the location of the code is revealed by a symbol of Baphomet. Actually, in this case, all three symbols are representations of Baphomet. What shape do they make?"

Etienne looked right, left, then straight ahead. "They make the shape of a triangle."

"That is correct, it is the perfect trinity." He motioned to the severed head. "This is the symbol for wisdom." He then pointed to the goat head. "The triangle is the symbol of the divine on earth." He pointed straight across at the man with antlers. "And he represents nature. The clue in this cathedral can be found where there is wisdom of the divine in nature—" Ronan stopped abruptly as the sound of footsteps approached.

"The bishop will see you now," the clergyman said as he and the others came into view.

"Where is Tristan?" Etienne asked, looking around. He thought it was strange that he wasn't with the group.

"He is sending a message to my father. We need to let him know of our arrival, and learn his wishes for our next steps." Isabella said.

"His most Reverend Excellency, Bishop Gonzalo Osorio,"[23] announced the clergyman as the band of travelers entered the ornate chamber. Isabella marveled as her gaze swept the entire room—it was completely gilded in gold.

"Would ya look at that," Andy said, "They weren't joking when they said the streets were paved with gold." Clair nudged him in the gut. Andy rubbed his stomach and gave her a look that said, *What?* This made Isabella smile. She and her brothers never had interacted like these two. Even with all the bickering, Isabella knew they loved each other.

The bishop looked like he had dozed off while waiting for them. By the time they reached him, he had put on his state face—the face of authority men like him always wore when Isabella met them. He was a representative of the church—the most powerful authority on earth—and his face showed his belief in that fact.

The Bishop extended his hand, which had a large gold ring with a black onyx stone in it. Isabella took his hand and kissed the ring. The stone felt cool on her lips, and the bishop's hands smelled slightly of roses.

She lifted her head and said, "Your Excellency."

After the formalities were finished, Isabella continued, "Thank you for seeing us this evening. I know the hour is late, but our plight is desperate."

"You are welcome, my child. God's house is always a place of refuge for those in need. I take it you are Princess Isabella? I knew your father when he was a young man," the bishop said, with the polish of a politician. "Please, tell me, how may I be of service to you?"

"Your Excellency," Isabella said, "my caravan was attacked by the Moors outside of Castrojeriz." Isabella didn't have to tell the bishop that the Moors were hired by the assassins. "None survived except for myself and the captain of my guard. We were saved by the bravery of the Knights Templar, who brought us to the Baron of Castrojeriz. He advised us to continue on to the safety of Leon to seek protection and council. Along the road, tragedy befell our small band once more, as we were attacked by Shadows, by the Immortals—" The bishop raised his hand stopping Isabella mid-sentence.

"Shadows..." The bishop muttered, sitting back in the large throne of a chair. He placed his fingers together and pressed hard, appearing to be deep in thought. After a moment, he said, "You will be safe here tonight, my child. We have actually been expecting you. Your father wrote with the instructions that you should return to France..."

Isabella's heart dropped. Her quest was over. She had failed. She would have to return and marry Edward. If her father only knew what she'd discovered, he wouldn't be summoning her.

"I fear you cannot go back the way you came," the bishop continued, "but I think I have a solution. As we speak, Jacques de Molay is at the Templar castle in Ponferrada, which is a four-day walk west on the Camino."

"Really? He's here on the Camino?" Etienne asked. Both Ronan and the bishop nodded.

"That is why I am on the pilgrimage," Ronan said. "I was summoned to meet him there."

"Am I suppose' ta know who this Jacques de Molay is?" Andy asked. Clair elbowed him and smiled politely at the bishop.

Etienne turned to Andy. "He's the Grand Master of the Templars. He is said to be the best leader the Templars have ever had."

"Yes, yes..." interrupted the bishop. "So he has... anyway, I am told he will stay another week before returning to Cyprus. I also heard they have a convoy returning to France from Finisterre by ship at the end of the month. If you hurry, you will catch him before he departs and obtain his permission to travel on this transport. I will send a message ahead of you by rider to Ponferrada to delay him. I feel it will be best for you to carry on by foot, so as not to be detected by the Moors or Shadows. Outside the walls of the city, the road is still dangerous." The bishop clasped his hands loudly, giving Isabella a start. "With this, I bid you a good evening and wish you a buen Camino." Turning to the clergyman he said, "Brother, will you escort our guests to their chambers." Isabella looked at Etienne. She still needed to resolve their past. They hadn't had a moment alone together. Isabella bit her lip and resolved to speak to him again tomorrow.

After the morning Vigils, the pilgrims congregated for mass. Isabella and Clair seated themselves at the pew across from Etienne, who was deep in meditation. Isabella gazed at him as he knelt with his eyes closed. She examined every detail of his face, her eyes absorbing each line and contour. She missed their evenings together walking through the palace courtyards, where they'd talked about running away together to far off lands, and laughed until their cheeks hurt. She'd always felt safe when he was around, even when she'd let her own guard down.

She wondered what it would be like to touch his cheek. She could almost feel the warmth of it, and the roughness of his stubble. Her eyes then moved to his lips, but before she had time to indulge herself in their contemplation, the prayer bell rang, and Etienne's eyes shot open. Isabella quickly composed herself and leaned back into her seat.

The monks chanted in the common tongue, and all who knew Psalm 148 joined. It was a volley of words back and forth between those sitting on either side of the altar.

"Praise the Lord. Praise the Lord from the heavens; praise him in the heights above," came from those on the right.

"Praise him, all his angels; praise him, all his heavenly hosts," was returned by those on the left.

"Praise him sun and moon; praise him all you shining stars."

"Praise him, you highest heavens and you waters above the skies."

"Let them praise the name of the Lord, for at his command, they were created,"

Isabella found it hard to concentrate; thoughts of Etienne were still rushing through her head. She had never had these feelings for another man, especially not Edward. She had tried to push her feelings to the back of her mind since the first moment she saw Etienne. But now, here they still were. She needed to talk to him again.

"Amen," the congregation repeated.

The Lord's Prayer began, and, as was custom, everyone joined hands. Etienne stepped to the middle of the aisle and took her hand. It was the first time their hands had touched since they were young. He cradled her hand gently, like a child holding a butterfly; it was a sharp contrast to the strength and coarseness of his rough skin. Isabella lost herself in this sensation, masking the pain she still felt in her hand. Her mouth automatically said the prayer, but her full focus was on his touch. Her thumb caressed him.

His eyes snapped to hers in surprise, and she blushed, unsure about what was happening, drunk on the emotions and feelings arising in her.

"Amen." She squeezed his hand gently, not wanting to let go. She wanted to hold his hand forever. Isabella noticed that his hand lingered as well. It was almost as if some force was binding them together.

She sat through the rest of the mass pretending that nothing had happened, but in her heart, she knew something had awoken that couldn't be denied.

"Everyone is gone, my son. Quickly, the cathedral is revealing the wisdom of the divine in nature," Ronan said.

Etienne looked up from his prayer to Ronan pointing at a green ray of light. Its path led directly to an archway close to where they had stood the evening before. The light settled on a carved face of a man with leaves and vines coming out of his mouth.

"Quickly, we don't have much time before the sun shifts," said Ronan. "We must find every Green Man[24] that is illuminated and take an impression with this." Ronan held some parchment and charcoal.

Though he was confused as to what the faces with leaves and vines had to do with the clue, Etienne took half of the paper and they began the task. Etienne discovered nine illuminated green faces and copied them in charcoal. As he finished the last etching, the sun changed and the green was gone.

Etienne rejoined Ronan at a pew and wiped the charcoal off his hands. "What was that?"

"That was the secret of the Cathedral of Leon. It is held by the Green Men who do not speak. They are the divine wisdom in nature." Ronan placed the first etching down on the pew and drew an "A" in the bottom left corner. He took Etienne's drawings and laid them out in order next to his and numbered each 1–18.

"These Green Men hold the secret of this cathedral. Their mouths have been bound with vines. However, Green Men are tricksters, and reveal the secret in another way. What do you notice about all of these?"

Etienne observed the etchings deep in thought. After a moment, he said, "Every Green Man has vegetation coming out of his mouth, yet some have a larger amount coming out of the right side, and others have a larger amount coming out of the left."

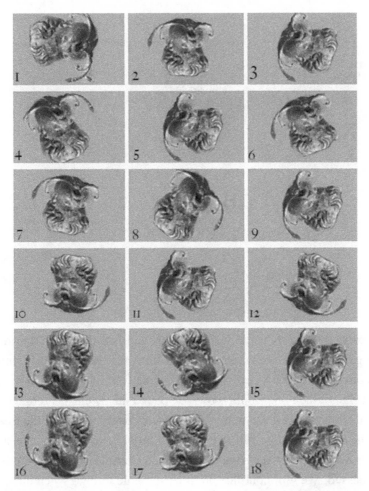

Ronan smiled. "Very good," he said, clasping his hand over Etienne's shoulder. "But that isn't enough to give you the secret. You'll need to look further."

Etienne's brain churned as he examined the pictures. "Six of them appear to be facing the same direction, but I cannot make out what it all means."

"Ach, there ya are," shattered the silence. Andy approached and Ronan quickly gathered the papers. "Breakfast is-a almost finished. If ya donna hurry, you'll starve on the road." Noticing the papers in Ronan's hands, he asked, "What do ya 'ave there?"

"Nothing for you, my friend," Ronan said kindly, with a smile.

Andy looked inquisitively at the papers, shrugged, and said, "Let's eat." Etienne watched Andy suspiciously and remembered Ronan's words from the night before. Could Andy have opened the door that released the Shadows? Was he after the Treasure?

CHAPTER 10

THE LAKE

The day carried on in its usual fashion. Clair and Isabella walked arm in arm, laughing gaily, and Tristan walked ahead with Andy. Ronan and Etienne were deep in conversation. They kept a little distance from the group so none could hear. Isabella wished she could slow her pace and listen to them. She knew Ronan had shown Etienne something in the cathedral to do with the treasure.

When the sun reached its full strength, the small band found a lake surrounded by a grove of trees. "We should get off the Camino and rest here until the heat has passed. We will continue on to Hospital de Orbigo when dusk sets in," Ronan said. "I will take the first watch."

Etienne had wandered off soon after Ronan announced his watch. Isabella had wanted to follow, but she was detained by Tristan who wanted to talk about the letter he sent to her father. Even though the conversation was important, she found herself longingly watching Etienne as he walked away instead. Etienne had disappeared into the woods, and Isabella wished she had a reason to go after him. Their conversation was still unresolved.

Tristan walked to his sack. "I was saving this for a special occasion," he said, pulling out a large bottle of wine. "I want to celebrate that we will be going back to France. I feel like we should drink it today."

"Ach, would you look at tha'. 'Tis straight from France," Andy said examining the bottle and licking his lips.

"You are full of surprises." Isabella straightened, realizing this was the perfect opportunity. "I will go get Etienne to join in the celebration."

"You go do that, lassie," Andy said, not taking his eyes off the bottle.

Clair hit Andy. "Are ya shure?" Clair asked Isabella, with a motherly look in her eye.

"The lake is just over there. I will be fine," Isabella said with a smile. She rose and made her way to the water. The woods were beautiful with golden rays of sun bursting through the trees. After the trauma of being kidnapped, Isabella needed the peacefulness of these woods. She felt as if all was right in the world again—as if the previous days had just been a dream.

Isabella arrived at the stony shore of the lake, but didn't see Etienne.

She gazed out over the placid water, a perfect reflection of the sky above, searching for Etienne. The reflection was shattered as an arm shot out from the water. It looked as if it was reaching out from a different world, breaking into her reality. Soon, the arm was accompanied by a head and an incredibly strong back, the muscles rippling as it stretched out of the water toward the sky. Her face flushed and she quickly looked away, her gaze settling on a pile of clothes behind a stone. *Those are Etienne's.* Not wanting him to see her, she turned and ran away from the lake into the woods.

"Isabella! I'm here!" Etienne yelled as he caught up to her. She froze at the sound of his voice, her body petrified to the spot. Unsure what to say or do, she just stood there.

"What are you running from? Where are they?" he said.

"I, I was running... I saw..." Isabella said without turning around.

"You saw what?"

"I saw you in the water," she said, finally facing him. Seeing Etienne shirtless, she tried to look away but couldn't. Her eyes soaked in his body as he stood before her. His well-formed chest rose and fell with every deep breath. The water clinging to his body gave his skin a certain quality that made it shine.

Hoping to distract him, and herself, from her inability to look away, she crossed her arms. "Do you not have any shame standing there before me half naked?"

"My apologies, Your Highness. I would endure any shame if I thought it would save you. I couldn't let you be taken again."

Isabella could have kicked herself. Once again that was not the way she wanted to start this conversation. She looked at the ground then back at Etienne. "Thank you for coming for me when they took me."

"I should have never left you alone. I didn't mean to say all of those things in the woods. When I'm around you, somehow the wrong things come out of my mouth."

Isabella smiled. "The same thing happens to me, especially when you're shirtless." Etienne flashed her his half smile.

"I should have listened to everything you said before cutting you off. I just have been angry for so many years. Angry at Tristan, your father, and you. Being with you was the only place I ever felt I belonged. You were the only one who accepted me and loved me for who I was. You were the only person I ever trusted, and I felt so betrayed by you. Why didn't you tell your father the truth about us?"

Isabella fought off the urge to start running again. She had run from this for too long, she had to take responsibilities for her actions. "Etienne, you made me feel so seen, so loved. I felt like I could be myself with you, as well."

Isabella placed a hand on Etienne's arm. She wanted to touch him but also brace herself for her next words. "I'm sorry. I have wanted to say that to you every day since you were taken from me. I'm sorry for not saying anything. I'm sorry for letting you get so close to me when I knew it wasn't allowed. I'm sorry for any pain that I have caused in your life. I tried to speak in the throne room, but fear robbed my voice from me. After they took you, I went to my father and begged for your life. On my hands and knees, I begged him to spare you. However, this only seemed to strengthen his resolve to have you executed." It felt as if a thousand-ton weight was lifted from Isabella's shoulders.

Etienne looked at Isabella with his deep soulful eyes. "I'm sorry I never came back for you. We could have run away together."

"Isn't that what we are doing right now." They both laughed. Isabella felt so light, as if the only thing keeping her tethered to the ground was her hand on Etienne's arm.

"It's good to see your smile again. I have seen hundreds of sunrises on the Camino and none of them can compare to your smile."

Isabella took a step forward and stroked his strong face. "Etienne," she whispered. "My heart broke the day I thought you died."

Etienne placed his hand on hers and slowly moved it down to his lips. He gently kissed the wound on her palm, sending chills through her body. He watched her, his eyes deep and disarming, as he then moved her hand down to his chest. Isabella felt the muscle underneath his skin and his heart beating steadily, calling to her.

"This has always been yours, and always will be, my lady." Isabella felt like this was a dream she never wanted to wake from. His words made her feel whole and loved in a way she felt she didn't deserve.

Isabella raised up on her toes, and time stopped as their lips met. Her senses left her, and the only thing that existed was their kiss, frozen for an eternity.

"Ahhh!!!" A piercing scream shot through the air, shattering the Garden of Eden that surrounded them. Isabella startled away from the heaven she'd momentarily found.

Eyes wide, she looked at Etienne. "That sounded like Clair." Without thinking, she grabbed his hand and rushed through the woods.

When she and Etienne got to the camp, Andy and Clair were each sitting with a half-drunk bottle of wine in their hands. "Ahhh!!!" Clair let out again, followed by uncontrollable laughter. Andy couldn't contain himself and he laughed as well.

"Ach, you're the best siser a man could ask fur," Andy slurred, putting his arm around Clair. "I'm 'appy to be he'ar with ya." Isabella and Etienne exchanged a look and smiled at each other. She noticed he was still holding her hand. He hadn't let go.

"Ach, me tooooo. You're the only family I've lef'," stammered Clair.

"Well, we still 'ave this member of the family," Andy said, lifting his bottle of wine. Clair lifted hers as well and they toasted. "Ta the ones we've lost," he said, and they both drank their fill.

Isabella loved their relationship. She wished her and her brothers were as close as the two of them.

When Andy finally noticed them, he said, "Ach, there you are! Ya almost missed the party." holding up his bottle. "Actually, looks like I missed the party. Why are you shirtless?" Noticing them holding hands, he winked.

Etienne reddened and let go of Isabella's hand. "I was swimming and...never mind. Where did you get this wine?" Etienne asked.

"Well..." Andy said pointing to the bottle in Clair's hand. "Tha' bottle came from Tristan. And this one..." he held up his bottle, "...this one is from my private reserve. Although I do 'ave ta admit, I had some of the good stuff before I opened 'er." Andy winked. "Bu' we wanted ta save a little for ya."

Clair handed Etienne her bottle of wine.

"I wanna make a toast..." Andy said, once again holding up his bottle. "I would like ta make a toast ta lying, stealing, cheating, and drinking. If you're goin' ta lie, lie for a friend. If you're gonna steal, steal a heart..." He winked at Etienne, and Isabella looked away. "If you're gonna cheat, cheat death. And if you're goin' ta drink, drink with me!" He held up his bottle in a toast, and Etienne followed suit.

When the bottle reached Etienne's lips, he paused and asked, "Where are Ronan and Tristan? Something doesn't feel right."

"Ach, they 'ave been gone for ages. Almost as long as you two," Andy said, winking again.

"I should have never left you unprotected." He picked up his sheathed sword and fastened it around his waist.

Isabella looked around, trying to figure out what Etienne was worried about. "What is it?"

"The first watch is well over. Ronan would have returned immediately back to camp to protect you. Did Tristan drink before he left?" Etienne asked.

"Settle down, laddie…" Andy hiccupped, as he said this, "… I'm sure they're fine, and no, he didna drink."

"I have seen you drink four bottles of wine by yourself and not be this drunk." Etienne traced his finger around the rim of the bottle and put it to his lips. "This wine has been compromised."

Isabella's eyes shot to him. There was no way someone could have gotten close enough to their supplies to poison them. She opened her mouth to say so, when Clair swayed and fell over with a dull thud.

Andy rushed over to her shouting, "Clair! Clair!" He bent down and cradled her now limp head. He looked up at Etienne with pleading eyes. "She drank more from tha' bottle than I did."

"Andy, quickly boil some water and find some stinging nettle. It will help to flush the poison out. It is only a matter of time before she is dead, we must get her to the next town. I'll find Ronan and Tristan; which direction did they go?" Etienne demanded.

Andy raised a shaky finger and pointed to the trees.

"Isabella, do you have your dagger?" Etienne asked.

Isabella nodded her head. "Yes, why?"

"You may need it. If I am not back soon, carry on west to Hospital de Orbigo; it is only one and a half miles away. You will find help there." With predatory stealth, Etienne disappeared into the woods.

Isabella felt her chest heave. She knew in her heart Tristan had done this, but she didn't know why.

Etienne rushed through the woods. He thought of Isabella and Andy back at camp, and wondered if he'd made the right decision leaving them. He bent to the ground and saw two sets of tracks heading east. If Tristan did poison that wine, it meant Ronan was in great danger. Ronan had become more than a mentor to Etienne, he was the first person in years to believe in him. With all the negativity Etienne had received over the years, he found it hard to have self-belief. Being told you aren't good enough—or even wanted—had burrowed its way into his identity. Etienne pushed himself to be the best, but no matter how good he was, it was never enough to drown out the voices telling him he was worthless.

A twig snapped, and Etienne turned into the shoulder of a Moorish soldier tackling him. The two of them hit the ground and rolled. Etienne pulled his dagger and maneuvered himself on top. With one swift movement he brought the dagger down on the soldier's throat, then jumped up. He was surrounded by five Moors and a man wearing a hood and face covering. The Moors moved in, but the man raised his hand and they all stopped. The hooded figure said something to Etienne in a language he didn't understand.

Seeing that Etienne didn't comprehend him, the man removed his hood and mask. Etienne stepped back and his eyes widened. "Ah, so you are as surprised as I am,"

Etienne nodded his head. "I have never seen anyone like me before." In Katsuji's caravan there were others with the same skin tone, but this man could have been Etienne's older brother.

"It is a shame you don't speak our language, brother, I am Nazir."

"If you are chasing after those I care for, then I am not your brother." Etienne thought of Isabella and Andy. He wanted to give them as much time as possible to escape, even if it meant his death.

"But we are of the same people, possibly the same blood. Have these infidels ever truly accepted you?" Etienne's body went cold. It was as if the stranger knew his greatest pain, and had disarmed him with a few words. "I see by your expression they have not."

Etienne shook his head. "One has, and I will protect her until my dying breath."

"Very well. It has been said that you don't know someone until you have fought them; come, let's find out who you truly are. I will give you the privilege of drawing your sword. I won't attack until after you are properly armed." Nazir raised his mask, covering his face once more.

Etienne drew his sword, but Nazir remained unarmed. This concerned Etienne; he had fought many people, but had never experienced anything like this. He moved into striking range and stabbed quickly. Nazir slapped the sword away with one hand, spun in, and backhanded Etienne with the other hand. Etienne staggered backwards. He felt a tooth had dislodged and spat blood. Nazir laughed, as did the Moors around him.

Etienne's mind calculated all of the actions that had taken place in the attack. He ascertained the speed of his foe. He wouldn't make the same mistakes twice. He was going to have to fight differently—smarter. Etienne slashed at his opponent slower than he normally would. Nazir dodged the first two swings easily. On the third swing, Etienne swung fast and hard. Nazir had either underestimated Etienne's speed, or overestimated his own—either way, Etienne's blade grazed Nazir's cheek. Nazir corrected and punched Etienne in the solar plexus, sending him back once again.

Nazir touched his cheek. "It has been many years since anyone has cut me in battle. I'm going to enjoy this." Nazir's eyes smiled behind his mask.

Etienne motioned to the Moors. "That is because you let other men do the fighting for you." Etienne needed to draw him in. He needed to provoke him. Etienne knew he wouldn't win if he fought any other way.

"You insolent boy." Nazir ran at him with full force. He easily dodged Etienne's thrust and flipped him to the ground. Etienne wheezed; the wind had been knocked out of him. Nazir brought his foot down hard above Etienne's head. Etienne dodged, missing the full force, but Nazir redirected and kicked him in the ear. Immense pain shot through his body. He was disorientated and couldn't breathe. Nazir had defeated him in three moves.

"I will send your regards to Isabella," Nazir said. It was hard for Etienne to tell where his voice was coming from, but Isabella's name brought him a new focus. He had to win. He had to save her and the others.

Nazir drew his sword and thrust it down hard. Time slowed, and Etienne turned his body, narrowly avoiding the sword. Nazir tried to retract his weapon, but it was stuck fast to the ground. Etienne rolled into the flat edge of the blade and knocked it from Nazir's hands. At the same time, he kicked up hard into his attackers stomach. Nazir caught his foot, twisting until Etienne spun. Before he put him into a leg lock, Etienne pulled his dagger and stabbed Nazir in the foot, then kicked his knee. There was an awful popping noise and Nazir dropped to the ground. He hoped this blow would buy his companions more time to escape. Nazir would need a horse now.

Etienne tried to punch, but Nazir grabbed his hand and locked it behind his back. Pushing Etienne's face in the dirt he asked, "Who trained you?"

"I was trained in the palace of King Philip."

"No, who trained you before? You were the best there before you arrived, weren't you? Think back."

A vision of Etienne's mother teaching him a punching sequence flashed in front of his eyes. "M-my mother," he stammered, shaking his head. "How is it possible that she trained me? What is this?" He didn't have many memories of his mother—they seemed to have been erased from his memory. He'd assumed it was too painful to remember her, so his mind had blocked her out.

Nazir nodded pensively. "I cannot fight you. You are blood of my blood."

Confused, Etienne watched as Nazir sheathed his sword. "What do you mean?"

"You have the blood of an assassin in you. There is no other explanation. Your mother must have been my sister. She was sent to France on a mission and never returned. Three years we searched for her in vain. She must be your mother; that is the only explanation."

Etienne shook his head.

"My fight isn't with you." He released Etienne and was lifted by two Moors.

Nazir made to leave, but Etienne stood and grabbed his sword. "I can't let you hurt Isabella."

"We are at an impasse, then." Nazir nodded to a Moor who threw a dagger into Etienne's arm. Etienne pulled out the dagger, becoming lightheaded. He dropped his sword and fell to the ground, fading in and out of consciousness, as poison rushed through his body.

"I am sorry, nephew..." was the last thing his senses told him before the world went black. In the darkness, all of his senses were dead, but his mind still worked. Then he heard it. It was faint at first, just a slight melody. Gentle and flowing like a stream, it coursed into his ears and gave his body strength. It was the most beautiful thing he had heard in his whole life. Was this the voice of God calling to him?

The darkness was replaced with a golden light. Etienne felt his eyelids still closed, but it was as if he could see with the song that was now flowing through him. His body was light, as the song surrounded him in a golden glow. The song seemed so familiar to him, but he couldn't place it. He felt that he'd known it for his whole life, knew it before he was born. As it came to the chorus, a lifetime of memories passed in front of his eyes, and he recognized it. It was the song his father had sung to him in his infancy.

"Father," he cried, daring to raise his head and open his eyes. At first, all he could see was a golden glow. As his eyes focused, he saw his father standing there, singing, surrounded by the same golden light that Etienne felt around his body. He smiled gently down at Etienne and extended his hand. Etienne grasped it. His hand felt rough, like it had in his childhood, so large and strong. It was warm, but the warmth didn't stop at the skin, it continued deep into him, into his muscle, sinking into his bones.

They walked hand in hand. If love could be felt by the senses, this is what it would feel like. The whole time, his song surrounded them, sustaining him for those few moments he needed to reach the ones he loved so deeply.

They reached the clearing where the camp was, and his father squeezed Etienne's hand. Then he was gone. Etienne dropped to the ground, feeling all the warmth that surrounded him turn back to cold and darkness. Footsteps approached and Etienne looked to see Gerhart where his father had stood.

Gerhart and Mariano bent down over Etienne. "Is he alive?" Gerhart asked.

"He is breathing," Mariano said. "Quickly, pick him up. We have no time to spare." Gerhart placed Etienne on his shoulder and they made their way to the remains of the camp. All that was left were empty bottles of wine and nothing else.

"What happened here?" Mariano asked.

"The Moors…" Etienne managed.

The sound of horses approaching became louder. "Quickly, we must go," urged Mariano. Gerhart repositioned Etienne, and they ran westward down the Camino.

When Isabella had heard the sounds of fighting from camp, she knew it was time to flee. Now she and Andy struggled to carry Clair down the dusty road.

"Ach, for such a small woman ya sure are heavy," Andy said to Clair's limp body. His face was red with the strain of carrying her.

Holding up her hand, Isabella whispered, "What was that?"

Andy stopped. "'Tis footsteps."

"We must hide." Isabella desperately looked around, but there was no cover, except a tree that blocked the bend in the road.

Andy shook his head with a grim look. "No, lassie, this is it. This is our final stand." He gently put Clair down and drew his sword.

Isabella followed suit and unsheathed her dagger. There they stood ready to meet their fate. Isabella wasn't ready to die, but she also wasn't ready to kill. The life she took outside of Castrojeriz had been eating at her. She wanted to be tough and help Etienne, but she hadn't fathomed the emotional toll taking a life would have on her.

The footsteps grew louder as they approached the bend in the road. Thankful for the element of surprise, Isabella clutched her dagger tightly. As the figures rounded the bend, Isabella and Andy attacked. Leaping from behind the tree, Andy tripped over Isabella's foot and went flying, sending him to the ground before the battle had begun. Isabella took a swing with her dagger but found herself bound tight in the grip of a giant hand before she knew what had happened.

Isabella heard a loud laugh, followed by the words, "Oh, there you are." She followed her captive's arm up to see Gerhart smiling at her. "Where is Clair?" he asked, letting go of Isabella. She smiled and wrapped her arms around his massive body.

"I am so happy to see you," Isabella said, her emotions of gratitude, relief, and fear had all mixed to form tears that streamed down her face.

"We don't have time for this," Mariano said. "The Moors are coming."

"Clair is there." Andy motioned to her body as he stood up and brushed the dirt from his clothes.

Gerhart followed the direction that Andy had motioned. Clair's small body was lying on the side of the road. "No!" he roared. "Is she? Is she dead?"

"Not yet," Isabella said gently, hoping to ease Gerhart's distress. "We have counteracted the poison, but I fear she doesn't have much time." Isabella patted him on the arm. That's when she noticed Gerhart was carrying someone on his shoulder. "Who is that?" she asked, afraid that she already knew the answer.

"It's Etienne," Mariano said. Seeing the fear in her eyes, he quickly added, "He is alive, but none of us will be if the Moors reach us. Let us make haste to Hospital de Orbigo." Gerhart bent down, and with gentle care he lifted Clair, placing her on his free shoulder. As soon as she was secure, they ran.

They rounded the next bend in the road, revealing the expansive bridge of Hospital de Orbigo with the river raging below. There was still hope. A wave of relief crossed Isabella's face, just as the sound of horses thundered on the road behind.

"Run! Don't turn back!" Mariano yelled. "Run with everything you have." The slope of the hill gave them greater speed than they would have had on the flat ground, and the dark of night made them a hard target for the incoming rain of arrows. Isabella wasn't as scared as she had been at the Arc of San Anton. Was it because of her companions, or that she had grown so much as a person since then? She'd braved things she never thought possible before, and had survived. She would survive this as well.

The horses were approaching quickly, but so was the bridge and safety. Isabella could tell Gerhart felt the strain of carrying two bodies, as he fell to the back of the group. She knew he would make it. He would save Clair at any cost.

They were steps away from the bridge when Isabella heard bells cutting through the night air. The town was being called to arms. Isabella saw horses approaching fast from the far side of the bridge. In the torchlight, she saw a white eight-pointed cross on a black banner and knew the night wasn't lost. The Knights Hospitaller,[25] were riding to their rescue.

The Knights overtook the band of travelers, parting like the Red Sea as they passed. The lead rider lay the first Moorish pursuer to waste. As the rider turned to urge on the others, Etienne groggily said, "Santiago. It's Santiago..." Then he fell silent. Isabella wondered if he was having another vision of the saint. Silently she prayed that Santiago would protect them, heal Etienne, and save Tristan and Ronan from whatever misfortune had found them.

CHAPTER 11

HOSPITAL DE ORBIGO

After ensuring the others were being cared for, Gerhart and Mariano rushed through the halls of the hospital, passing wounded soldiers as they left to join the battle against the Moors. They followed the blood-stained floors like birds following breadcrumbs. As they exited the building, the sounds of war filled the air and the glow of fire made the night almost as bright as day. Mariano was ready for a fight—he still had so much pain to release.

Gerhart and Mariano reached the bridge as the archers let a volley of arrows fly. In the air, the steel tips reflected the fires below and made a glistening arch hitting their marks on the other side of the river.

With rage in his heart Mariano ran halfway across the bridge to the center of the battle. The Hospitallers were holding the line fast despite the bloodstained ground below them. It was a mass of bodies pressed against shields with the occasional sword passing through the line.

"Hold fast!" a grizzly-looking Hospitaller commanded. The Hospitallers grounded their feet and pressed their shoulders hard into their shields. The second line used their large broadswords to reach over the top of the shields, making contact on the other side. There was a white flash and a deafening sound; the blast broke through the line, sending Hospitallers flying backward.

Mariano caught one man and saw the life drain from his body. All he heard was ringing as he cleared his eyes. Moors pushed through the hole in the line and were coming toward him and Gerhart at full speed. Gerhart raised his mighty ax and swung it wildly. With one swoop, he knocked four men off the bridge, on the reverse swing another two. The Moors stopped dead in their tracks, looking at the giant that stood a good two head lengths above them.

When the Moors regained their courage, they charged him. Mariano threw his knives at the lead attackers, his blades striking with pinpoint accuracy and sending his prey to the ground. He sprang forward, pulled his knives out of the dead bodies, and attacked again, thinking of Alba with every thrust. Next to him, Gerhart let out a loud battle cry and charged the oncoming Moors with the abandon of a man who had nothing to lose. They pushed the Moors back, and the knights rallied around them, regaining the line.

Mariano was drenched in sweat, and the smell of dead bodies was everywhere. Cries of agony came from a distance, and he dared to look above the shields. Narrowly avoiding a sword coming straight for his head, he saw the Hospitaller cavalry had returned and were plowing through the Moors at the other end of the bridge. The Moors were now trapped, and their line broke as the Hospitallers pushed harder.

In the distance, a horn blew, sounding the retreat. The day was theirs; the Moors were defeated.

Mariano was elated. He and Gerhart exchanged a nod and smiled. The horn blew again, and where the sound was coming from, there was a lone figure on a horse with six Shadows flanking him. The figures vanished in an instant, and were replaced by the first rays of morning sunlight. The joy Mariano had felt moments before disappeared along with the Shadows, and was replaced by a burning desire for revenge.

The room the Hospitallers had provided was a large wooden chamber with six beds and a fire burning brightly at the far end. Andy set their meager belongings down. They had next to nothing now. All had been abandoned at the camp, save a few small things. He took Etienne's satchel off his shoulder and threw it on the closest bed. As it hit, rolls of paper spilled out. He sat down next to the papers, put his head in his hands, and wept.

He was too proud to cry in front of the others. Etienne, Gerhart, and Mariano were all such strong warriors, and he was just a simple scholar. He couldn't take all of this fighting and death. Ronan and Tristan were gone, and now his Clair, his most precious Clair, lay in a hospital bed below.

'Tis all because I am a drunken fool.

Tears streamed down Andy's face even harder. He took a piece of paper from the bed and brought it to his nose. He was about to blow when he realized what this paper was: it was what Ronan and Etienne had been keeping secret from him in the cathedral. He used his sleeve to blow his nose and wipe his eyes, then unrolled the scroll. A strange face stared back at him.

How peculiar.

He studied the face for a long time before unrolling the other pieces of parchment. Each had a face on it. Some were larger, some smaller, but all had vines and leaves coming out of their mouths. On the bottom left corner of every drawing was a number. Andy laid all nineteen images on the bed in sequential order. There was one image without a number in the corner; instead, there was the letter "A." The vines coming from its mouth also differed to the other drawings. They were equal on both sides and spiraled inwards, like a mustache, instead of being shorter on one side and longer on the other. Six of the eighteen numbered images were facing the same direction, all the others were tilted to varying degrees.

The black charcoal images on the tan parchment burned themselves into his mind. He racked his brain for any information he knew about these strange pictures, but nothing came to mind.

The agonizing screams of war had subsided. Andy's curiosity pushed him to the window. He had to know who had won. At the bridge, the Hospitallers banners were flying triumphantly. The fighting had stopped, and the Moors had retreated. He caught sight of Gerhart, who raised his mighty ax. He brought it down hard on the head of a Moorish soldier. The man let out one last terrified scream before the ax found its mark. Andy turned away. He fought from time to time, but in his heart, he deplored violence. It made him sick to his stomach.

Andy tapped his fingers on the windowsill incessantly. *I need a drink.*

He had passed the kitchen on his way to their room and was backtracking his way there when he stopped suddenly.

Ach no, 'tis the drink that got us into this mess.

Andy redirected himself to a large red door and opened it. Sunlight and bird song shot into the stone corridor. When Andy's eyes adjusted to the light, he stepped into the covered walkway and looked through the stone arches to a cloistered garden. The garden was beautiful; roses climbed up the pillars supporting the arches, and there were flowering plants of many varieties. He recognized some of them as healing plants. "'Tis the medicinal garden," he mused. It had the feeling of sanctuary and healing; it was a relief to the carnage that had passed in the night.

Andy walked to an opening in the arches and stepped into the garden. He was met with the scent of rosemary. He picked some and brought the sprig to his nose. The scent made him smile; it was a smell of comfort and normalcy. He reached the center of the garden, which was adorned by a large stone sundial. "Would ya look at that," he mumbled, examining the magnificent centerpiece. The masonry on the stone base was outstanding, and the face had golden Roman numerals for each hour of the day.

A loud *clank* sound reverberated off the wall behind him, startling Andy from his perusal. He clutched his chest and took a few deep breaths, preparing to be told off.

"She's awake! I have been searching all over for you," Isabella said.

Still clutching his chest, Andy turned to see a weary Isabella standing in the doorway. "She... she's awake... my Clair's awake!" Tears rolled down his cheeks at the news. Andy's spirits soared. He had been so worried about Clair.

"Yes, Gerhart is with her now. He just arrived from the battle."

"Ach, he's a good man." Andy looked down and ground a small rock under his foot. After a moment, he looked up at Isabella. "And Etienne?"

Isabella turned away from him, but not before he saw the tears welling in her eyes. With a small stutter in her voice, she whispered, "There is no change, he is still unconscious. He is barely holding on to life."

"I'm-a sorry, lass."

"What are we doing just standing here talking? Clair is waiting to see you." Andy took one last look at the sundial and rushed after Isabella.

The closer Andy got to the infirmary, the more blood appeared. The signs of war hung heavy in the air. They turned the corner to a hall filled with the wounded from the battle. There were makeshift beds lining the walls all filled with soldiers who had fought valiantly to protect them. Andy clutched his stomach; the sight was too much for him.

In the infirmary the nuns were attending the wounded. It was a frenzied place with so many souls hanging in the balance between life and death.

"Where are Etienne and Clair? They were just right here." Isabella motioned to beds with wounded soldiers. She grabbed the nearest nun. "Where are they?"

The nun brushed off her hand. "The big man moved them up to your chambers. We needed those beds to take care of our own."

Isabella straightened, narrowing her gaze. "He was too sick to be moved. How could you do that?"

The nun looked her squarely in the eye. "You see that boy laying there with his leg barely attached to his body? He is my sister's son and his life is much more valuable to me than that of any Templar."

A look of rage came over Isabella, and Andy's hands shot out to stop her as she lunged toward the nurse. "Coom on, Isabella," he said calmly. "Let's see them in our chamber. Etienne will be a-needing ya now more than ever."

"I won't forget this," Isabella said.

On exiting, Andy asked in a hushed voice, "I thought being a Templar, Etienne would be considered one of their own?"

Isabella, still upset, replied, "There is no love between the Templars and the Hospitallers. They fight against a common foe, but they are not friends. The moment they found out Etienne was a Templar, they all but abandoned him to my care."

"What 'appened between them?"

"My father told me after the fall of Jerusalem the Templars and Hospitallers lived in Acre. It was there that a rivalry and mutual distrust formed between them. They often had violent encounters. When both orders moved to Cyprus, the Hospitallers complained that the Templars had ceased to be a religious order and were just bankers making a fortune off of others. They also said the Templars weren't even Christian anymore. My father holds these same beliefs."

"Ach, but Etienne and Ronan are some of the most devout men I've met."

"I know. The story doesn't add up."

Andy opened the door to the bed chamber. At the far end, closest to the fire, Gerhart sat holding Clair's hand. Both turned their heads and smiled.

"Thank ya for taking care o' my sister once again," Andy said to Gerhart, avoiding eye contact. "Without ya she'd be... we'd all be..."

"Ach, quit yer blubbering," Clair said with a weak smile.

Andy smiled back and replied, "I always knew the drink would kill ya, but I never expected it would be like that." Everyone laughed.

Gerhart's laugh rumbled loudly rolling off the walls and Etienne stirred slightly from his comatose state. Isabella moved to his bed and caressed his forehead.

Andy looked around the room once more, his forehead creasing. "Where is Mariano? Did he na make it?"

Gerhart let out another loud rolling laugh. "Of course, he did. He left with a party to hunt down the remaining Moors to get his revenge."

Andy nodded. They each had their vices to deal with pain; Andy's was eating and drinking, while Mariano's was fighting.

Isabella put a hand on Etienne. "He's burning up. Andy, quickly hand me that cloth and dip it in water." Andy followed directions and soon the cool rag was on Etienne's forehead; at this, his body relaxed. Isabella smiled tenderly at Etienne and kissed his head. "He needs more medicine or he won't make it; the poison is too strong."

"Can't ya get it from the infirmary?" Andy asked.

Gerhart shook his head. "These Hospitallers have no hospitality. Hospitallers, my 'arse,'" he spat, borrowing a word from Clair and Andy's vocabulary.

Andy loved how raw and blunt Gerhart was. He had become quite fond of him, but he would have to correct him. "Ach, they werena' named Hospitallers because of their hospitality. The order began at the Hospital of St. John of Jerusalem, which originally cared for pilgrims—"

"Seems they forgot their origins," interrupted Isabella.

"'Tis true," Andy said. "At first the hospital took on mercenaries ta defend it against bandits. But by 1160, they 'ad become a full-blown military order and defended the frontier from the Muslims."

"Well, now those who used to care for others, appear to only care for their own," Isabella said, gritting her teeth. "They've informed me they have no more medicine to spare."

Andy grinned, the image of the cloistered garden, and all its herbs, flashing in his mind. "I think I know where ta get some."

CHAPTER 12

NOTRE DAME

Pope Clement V [26] sat in the front pew of Notre Dame admiring the rose stained glass window. *What marvels men have created to the glory of God.*

He placed his hands on the pew and pushed himself up to his feet. The wood was coarse under his fingers and his frail body was sore from the ride. He had grown tired of sitting, and, for that matter, tired of waiting.

I hold the most powerful office in the world and here I am at the beck and call of a king, like a servant. He shook his head. *Not only that, he has left me waiting for over an hour in the empty shell of Notre Dame.*

He raised his head to the cross behind the altar and prayed, "God, grant me strength and guidance for this meeting."

The Pope looked at the stained glass window once again, pacing up the aisle. His footsteps echoed in the empty building. The whole cathedral had been vacated under the pretense that King Philip would give his *confession.* But Clement knew he was to hear no confession today. No, today he would only hear how he fit into King Philip's plans to rid them both of a common threat. *It is time to pay the piper.*

Clement reached a stand filled with small candles—each candle a prayer for some poor soul who thought God was listening. Clement extended his hand over the candles and prayed that their prayers would be answered. However, in the back of his mind, he knew he was just warming his old, tired, cold hands. "It is freezing in here," he muttered.

The door at the far end of the cathedral creaked open and footsteps approached. Clement kept his eyes closed and his hands over the candles, still pretending to pray. The footsteps stopped behind Clement, but he remained steadfast in his stance.

He made me wait an hour. I will make him wait a few minutes.

After sufficient time had passed, Clement turned to see King Philip dressed in ostentatious regal garb.

"King Philip," Clement said in his most authoritative voice.

"Your Holiness," Philip replied dryly. Clement extended his hand for Philip to kiss the Papal Ring. Philip looked down at the large ring on his frail finger and smiled. "I will kiss yours if you kiss mine," Philip said sarcastically. "We are equals, my friend, unless you would like to think of me as your better. It is only because of me that you are in the position you now hold."

"It was God's will that I am Pope. How dare you speak such blasphemy in His house," Clement said, but in his heart, he knew that Philip spoke the truth.

"His house." Philip chuckled. "I could have it destroyed tomorrow if I so willed it. Just as I could have you destroyed tomorrow. Do not forget your place and who put you there, or in which country you stand." Philip's steely gaze cut through Clement and sent a chill through his body.

"Have I made a deal with a man or the devil?" Clement shook his head. "God help me." The year prior, Philip had helped Clement secure the papacy. There was a deadlock between the Italian and French Cardinals for nearly a year. Seeing an opportunity, Philip manipulated the situation and arranged for Clement to win. Clement had asked what Philip wanted in return, and Philip had just said, '*Favors.*' Clement hadn't realized these *favors* meant he would be at Philip's beck and call. He had already done so much for him.

"God won't be able to help you out of this deal," Philip said with a slight smile. "The only thing that will release you is to fulfill your obligation, or forfeit your life. Once the task is done, we will see if it is God's will or the devil's. Until then, it is only my will you should be worried about." With this statement, Clement knew Philip had won, and he pulled back his hand.

"And what is it you will?" asked Clement, cautiously.

Philip clasped his arm around Clements' shoulder with a victorious smile. "First, we must rid ourselves of Unam Sanctam. The Bull of Boniface VIII, which gives the pope supremacy over all other rulers. This law is absurd. I have just proven we are equals," Philip said, keeping a tight grip. Clement cringed at Philip's touch. They most centrally were not equals in Clement's eyes. The church was the supreme power on the earth, and he was its representative.

Philip continued, "Second, and more importantly, we must destroy the Templars. They are a standing army without a war, and I fear they have their eyes fixed on setting up a kingdom within mine. They pay no taxes, they can travel through any border, and they do not have to answer to any monarchy. They only have to answer to one person, the Pope, and as we established before, we are more than equals. They are too powerful, and a danger to all of us."

Clement chuckled, saying, "You only want to be rid of them because you are deeply indebted to the Templars and have no way of repaying them. You are afraid that they will collect the money you owe them."

"Silence!" Philip bellowed, temporarily losing his cool disposition. "These men, should they be called that, are heretics. They are responsible for usury, credit inflation, fraud, heresy, sodomy, immorality, and abuse. I don't need to tell you what happens in their initiation ceremony. The church has tolerated them long enough and has given them too much power." Philip snatched Clement's hand and held it over the open flames of the candles. Clement felt his flesh burn, then the smell reached his nostrils. He struggled, but Philip was too strong. "And if the church isn't with us, we will move on our own... and perhaps a new pope will need to be installed."

"AGHHH!!!" Clement let out a scream that echoed through the church. "I... I am with you. The church is with you." Philip released Clement, who cradled his hand.

"The good thing about giving cowards power is that they are easy to manipulate. Isn't that so?" Clement sat there, fuming at Philip's smug tone but fearing what would happen should he disagree. "I said, isn't that so?" demanded Philip. Clement nodded his head slowly.

"Excellent. Now that we see eye-to-eye," Philip squeezed Clement's burnt hand for emphasis, "you will order the Templar leadership to France under the guise of meeting with the Hospitallers to make amends. Make it appear that there will be another crusade. Once they are assembled, we will make our move and show the world just how corrupt these men are." Philip shot a cruel smile at Clement, whose eyes were now filled with tears of pain.

CHAPTER 13

THE SECRET OF THE GREEN MEN

Long after most were asleep, Andy would make his nightly journey down the stairs, through the large door, and into the open courtyard that contained the medicinal garden. This had become his nightly ritual for the last few days. He took great care to pluck only what he needed to treat Etienne. Just enough to help him, but not too much to get caught.

The night air was brisk and a canopy of stars met Andy as he stepped through the archway. The small sliver of moon had disappeared an hour earlier, leaving the stars to shine in all of their glory. At this point, Andy didn't need any light, he knew his path well. First, he made his way to the calabar beans, a plant he didn't even know existed until five days ago. The Moors had brought this plant from Africa. It was the only thing that could combat the poison running in Etienne's body.

After he collected a few of the oddly shaped bean pods, Andy made his way behind the sundial to collect the Tanacetum parthenium and the Mentha piperita. The pretty white flowers with the yellow center of the Tanacetum parthenium, also known as feverfew, were easy to spot even on a night as dark as this. For the Mentha piperita, Andy used his nose. He would recognize the smell of peppermint anywhere. Both herbs had been used to reduce Etienne's fever, which was all but gone now. Still, though, he gathered some as a precaution.

When he was done harvesting, Andy stopped to admire the sundial. He didn't know why, but this had become his nightly ritual. He admired the beauty of its shape and ran his hands across the face. He loved that this device could tell you exactly which hour of the day it was. The golden Roman numerals were cold and slightly raised from the stone face. He traced his fingers around the circumference I, II, III... until he reached XII. *A full twelve hours... I wish I could see this again in the daylight.*

Andy returned to the room and heard the monstrous roar of Gerhart's snore coming through the door. He had no idea how Clair and Isabella could sleep through it. Although, they said he snored just as bad, and sometimes it sounded like two animals fighting when he and Gerhart were sleeping at the same time. Andy slowly opened the door, trying not to make any noise.

Not that it matters with him snoring away.

The room was warm and cheery when he entered, the fire still glowing at the far end. Clair was fast asleep, with Gerhart in the bed next to hers. Isabella sat by Etienne's side, holding his hand. Andy could tell Etienne needed the herbs and set about preparing them. Andy moved to the fire and took the kettle off. He poured the boiling water into a glass with the peppermint and the feverfew. As the decoction steeped, he looked at Isabella. Her face was tired and sad. Andy walked up to her and put his hand on her shoulder. "'Tis alright, lass. Why dunna ya get some rest."

Isabella looked up at him with her large eyes and they said everything. They spoke of her sorrow, of her hope, her thanks, and her love for Etienne.

"Thank you. I could use some rest."

Andy helped her to the bed next to Etienne's. Within moments, Isabella was fast asleep. For the first time in days, Andy saw the stress leave her face, and he saw the girl he had first met at Castrojeriz.

What great sorrow and stress this has brought to all of us.

Etienne groaned. Andy reached for the decoction and brought it gently to Etienne's lips. He poured the warm liquid into his mouth. "This will do you well, laddie. You saved my life once; I hope these herbs can repay the favor."

Andy moved to his bed and took out the small bag that contained the drawings of the strange faces. *We're gonna figure this out,* he thought, looking back at Etienne.

He shuffled through the papers, studying each image. After a few minutes of getting nowhere, he sighed. "Ach, 'tis useless."

Andy looked at the numbers on the bottom corner of each page and placed them on the ground in sequential order. He raised the image with the letter "A" on it. "And where do ye go?"

As he continued to study the faces, his mind wandered back to the garden with the sundial at the center. "Focus," he said, pursing his lips. "I have ta figure this out." Andy stared hard at the images and they stared back, almost mocking him, smiling with the vines coming out of their mouths. "That's it. Ha, ha, 'tis it. The large vine is like the shadow of a sundial. Why didna' I see this sooner?"

Andy drew a circle like the sundial that was separated into twelve parts, one for each hour of the day. He then wrote letters at the numerical divisions. He went around twice and realized that his theory was off. Twelve times two is twenty-four and there are twenty-five letters in the alphabet. He was so close he knew it.

Andy looked down at the papers again and then at the face with an "A" in the corner. "'Tis it... 'Tis it," he said, smiling. "The alpha is the missing letter. If I use it for the letter 'A', it works." Andy bounced up and down where he sat, the excitement ready to burst out of him.

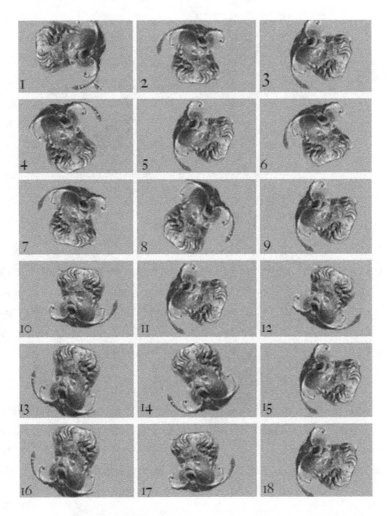

Andy rubbed his hands together. "And now, ta figure out which letter goes where." He paused deep in thought again. He looked at the image that appeared six times. "Tha' face 'as ta be the key." From his many years of study, Andy knew the most frequently used letters in the common tongue are "A" and "E." "Well-a, since 'A' is taken, that leaves 'E.'" Andy mused. "Let's see if this works." He placed the image inside the sundial he had drawn, and the long vine coming out of the mouth on the right side pointed directly at four o'clock.

Andy realized that if the vine is longer on the right side of the face it represented the first part of the alphabet and, if it was longer on the left, it represented the second half. Using this theory, he drew letters around the circle creating a cipher.

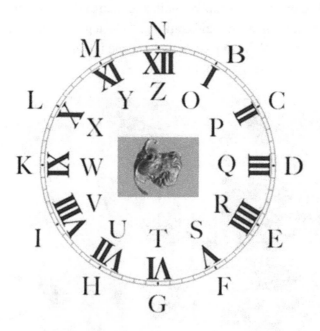

After the cipher was complete, he placed each face over the sundial in sequential order and the vines pointed perfectly to the letters. Quickly, he drew another grid below the cipher and placed each number and corresponding letter into the boxes.

W H E R E F I V E B E C O M E O N E
1 2 3 4 5 6 7 8 9 10 11 12 13 14 15 16 17 18

"Where five become one.' What the 'ell does that mean?" Andy blurted out. He excitedly rushed over to Etienne's side and whispered, "I have it, laddie. I've-a figured it out."

Etienne's eyes shot open, and he replied, "Figured what out?" Andy flew back and tripped over the chair. The noise woke up the others.

Isabella jumped out of bed. "You're awake!!! You're awake!!!" she said as she bent down and held him.

"The Moors are here. We have to be careful," Etienne said.

All laughed at this. Andy picked himself up and replied, "I donna think we will have to worry about them again. We are safe now, laddie." Etienne closed his eyes and Isabella stroked his head. Andy felt a warmth in his body. It wasn't the warmth from the fire, nor the excitement of his discovery, it was the warmth of friendship and love.

CHAPTER 14

THE ALCHEMIST

The heat from Mariano's horse warmed his body. The beast had borne him diligently all night. Now, it was twilight and Venus was rising with the sun. His horse was uneasy and took a few steps from side to side. *We are close*. Mariano felt tension in the air and knew that in the dark woods ahead, he and the Hospitilars would find their quarry.

They had already dispatched several Moorish deserters, riding them down as they fled. He showed no mercy, but this was not the revenge Mariano wanted. He only cared about destroying the Shadows who had taken Alba. The thought of the Shadows made the hairs on his neck stand up. Somehow, they stripped him of his courage. Facing them was like facing every fear he'd ever had. The last time he fought the Shadow, it had somehow used Alba's voice. His worst fear was that he was the cause of her death; he should have been behind her to block the knives.

A branch snapped as his horse shifted her hooves. Mariano took a deep breath, focusing on the woods ahead. All thoughts left his mind, and he felt very still. He took another deep breath, feeling his lungs expand. As he exhaled, a flash of silver streaked across the dark woods. By the time the air left Mariano's lungs, all the knights around him had fallen to the ground, blood pouring from their bodies. Mariano's horse also gave way, trapping his leg under her weight. The pain was excruciating. It radiated up his leg, but he stifled his scream. *Have we been ambushed?* Mariano scanned his surroundings, he didn't see or hear anything. His senses were heightened, ready for an attack.

Mariano caught the glint of a silver blade reflecting the glow in the east. The curved sword was dripping with blood. *The sword of a Shadow*. A chill ran through his body. His fear outweighed his pain and he struggled to free his leg.

The Shadow turned its attention on Mariano. "You cannot save yourself, just like you couldn't save me." Alba's voice came out of the Shadow again, as it approached slowly.

Mariano slipped out of his boot, freeing his leg. He tried to stand, but his foot was broken. Mariano grabbed his knives, and in a blink, the Shadow was now overhead.

A woman's melodic laugh filled the air.

The creature let out a terrible screech and fled into the blackness of the woods.

From the ground, he peered over the dead horse and saw a woman smiling at him. She was dressed as a woman of the desert with a head covering and long robes. She had high cheekbones and had facial tattoos on her dark skin. Her eyes were the most captivating Mariano had ever seen; they held the vastness of the desert and the skies above them. Her whole being was a single-minded focus, and she emanated a blissful joy.

Mariano turned away. He couldn't withstand the pure presence she had.

"Stand up," she said.

"I cannot, my foot is broken," Mariano said sheepishly.

"Stand up," she said, once more lovingly. Mariano looked at her eyes and couldn't help but fall in love. It was like looking at pure light. He repositioned himself and pushed up from the ground, his foot no longer in pain.

"I don't understand...my foot, it was just broken. How is it that I am standing?"

She held his gaze and he felt more present, more alive, and more joyful than he had his entire life. "Are you an angel?"

"I am not an angel," she responded. "I have many names, but the one you will be most familiar with is, 'The Alchemist.'"[27] Mariano had heard that name before. It was in the story Ronan had told about the Shadows. Was she the one he needed to find to defeat the Shadows?

"How is it that I am alive and my comrades are dead? The Shadow was frightened of you. Why?"

The Alchemist reached a hand forward and stroked his face. Her touch was soft, and Mariano felt her warmth flow through him. He hadn't been stroked like that since he was a child. "You were in the present moment and they were not," she said, motioning to the dead men. "That is why you were unharmed. And the Shadow, as you call it, was forced to flee when exposed to someone who lives only in the here and now. In the present moment.

"The Shadows only exist outside the present moment. They can do no harm to those in the here and now. All of these men were thinking of the past or the future. None of them were here, in the now. Tell me, what were you thinking of before this thing attacked?"

Mariano took a second to recall and answered, "I was not thinking of anything. I took a few deep breaths and was focusing on the woods. I was fully present."

The Alchemist walked over to a Hospitaller with a blood-stained beard. "This one was thinking of what he would feast on when he returned to town. Gluttony." She walked over to another attractive looking corpse and stroked his face. "This one was thinking about how marvelously he had fought and what a hero he was. He was thinking of the hero's welcome he would get on his return. Pride."

"How do you know what they were thinking?"

She smiled. "I can tell you what you are thinking."

Mariano tried to clear his thoughts, but the image of the beach he used to play on when he was a child came to mind. The more he tried to ignore the image, the stronger it became.

"You are thinking of the beach you used to play on. The sun is shining; the sand is hot; the water is gently hitting your little toes, as your mother is calling your name."

Mariano took a step back. "How?"

She looked at him sharply, her eyes piercing him. "My love, we are all made of the same thought. That is all we are. We come from the same place. One thought split into every person you have ever met. Everything you have ever seen, smelt, or touched." She stroked his cheek gently. "Why, my love, you don't even exist."

Mariano stared at her blankly. He understood her words, but not their meaning. Was he dead? To him she did look like an angel. "What do you mean I don't exist? I am here speaking to you. I felt your hand on my cheek."

"Are you sure that the words you 'spoke' are yours? Is it true that I even have a hand to stroke your face?" she said gently.

Mariano opened his mouth. "But…"

She looked at him again and all of his words were lost. He struggled as hard as he could to say something, but not a sound came out. He drew a knife and held it to her neck. She smiled gently, touched the blade with her pinky, and pushed it away with the force of ten soldiers.

Mariano stumbled backward and found that he had regained his ability to speak. "How did you… What just happened?" Mariano could see now why the Shadow fled from her. Mariano wanted to flee too, but he had to figure out her cryptic speaking. He needed to know how to defeat the Shadows.

She smiled tenderly. "I didn't do anything to you. It was done to you. Did anything just happen to you?" She smiled again and laughed. "Once you understand the nature of reality, you realize nothing has ever happened nor will it happen. You realize that you never existed, and that you are nothing more than a thought getting to know itself. Created in every present moment, then ceasing to exist until the next present moment when you appear.

"There is a saying that the Camino will provide everything you need. It isn't always what you think you want, but it is what you need. I am here to tell you this."

Mariano thought of Alba dying in his arms. "How could I have needed her death?" Mariano murmured to himself.

"You only suffer if you fight against what has passed... *'She shouldn't have died.'* This thought has caused you nothing but torment and stress. Can you know that she shouldn't have died?"

"Yes," Mariano said with pain in his eyes.

"Are you sure beyond a doubt?"

Mariano thought for a moment. "I guess there is no way I could know if it absolutely is true. But still…"

"Perhaps she died for no other reason than to create a better story of life… What happens to you when you think the thought, 'S*he shouldn't have died?*'"

"I feel rage and anger. I feel guilty that I couldn't protect her. I feel a pain in the pit of my stomach, and I want nothing more than revenge."

"It must be very painful for you to believe that thought." Mariano looked away trying to hide his sadness. She continued, "What if it was impossible for you to think the thought, '*She shouldn't have died...*'"

Mariano tried to recall the thought that she was mentioning, but nothing came to mind. "Which thought are you speaking of?"

"The thought that was giving you so much pain," replied the Alchemist.

Mariano racked his brain, trying to remember this thought, but nothing came. "I'm not in pain. I'm just here with you. There is no thought."

The Alchemist snapped her fingers and the thought, *"She shouldn't have died,"* pierced Mariano like a blade, and he wept.

"What happened when the thought, '*She shouldn't have died,*' disappeared?"

Mariano responded with a confused look on his face, "I just experienced a world where I couldn't think that thought, and then another when I believed it. When I believed she shouldn't have died, I found suffering. When I couldn't think that thought, I was at peace. There was no suffering. I was just here with you. Enjoying the beauty of the world around us."

"Do you see how believing these thoughts is the origin of suffering, nothing more? It takes you out of the present moment and makes you live in the past. You are so unkind to Alba and yourself. She is murdered again and again in your head, not just once. There is nothing in this present moment causing you or her to suffer, only the thought of a past, that may or may not have existed." Mariano just sat there, trying to comprehend.

"Only when we see these thoughts for what they truly are can we let go of our Shadows and find peace. If we don't, they will pursue us for our whole lives. As if life exists anywhere else besides this present moment." She laughed merrily.

She continued, "The Shadows of the past and fears of the future are destroyed in the present moment. They have no power to stand up against the 'here' and the 'now.' Question the thoughts that give you pain and be in the present moment. It is only here, and only now, that you will ever find peace."

The Alchemist took Mariano's head in both hands and kissed his forehead. Her lips were soft and supple. When their warmth left, Mariano opened his eyes and found she was gone.

He watched the sunrise and felt as if he were experiencing it for the first time: as if the world was coming to life for the first time; as if he was feeling the sun's heat on his face for the first time—even the song of the birds was new. The beauty of the world filled him with joy and he stood in peace.

CHAPTER 15

BEAUTIFUL LIFE

Etienne awoke to a bright room with wooden cross-beams high above. He felt clammy and pushed the covers down. Clair and Gerhart were asleep in the beds across from him, and to his left was Isabella. The rays of light landed gently on her angelic face, her hair falling softly over her brow.

The last days since he was poisoned were such a haze. The only things he remembered were her touch and gentle voice. She was the one thing that had kept him bound to this world. His love and duty to her were stronger than the pull of death.

Isabella opened her eyes and met his. Their gaze locked and a large smile spread across her face. It was a smile of relief, contentment, and love. Etienne had never been looked at like that before. He felt a sense of belonging in her eyes. Joy welled up in him and spread through his body.

"Welcome back," Isabella said touching his cheek.

Etienne clasped her hand, pressing it hard against his skin. "Thank you... I felt you here with me the whole time," he said hoarsely.

Isabella smiled gently. "There is no place that I would rather have been." Etienne felt the stubble of his beard brush her delicate skin as she pulled away her hand. "Do you need some water?" she asked, filling up a cup.

"How many days have I slept?" Etienne sat up and the world spun. He placed his hand firmly on the bed.

"Careful," Isabella said, steadying him. "I have lost count of the days myself. It has been about two since you regained consciousness for the first time."

Etienne broke her gaze. "I don't know how to thank you... No one..."

Isabella pressed her finger to his lips. "You are a part of me. You have always been a part of me." Etienne took hold of her hand and Isabella blushed. "It wasn't just me that cared for you. Andy snuck into the garden every night to get the herbs we needed to heal you. He cares deeply for you as well."

Etienne looked around the room. "Did Ronan and Tristan ever show up? I wasn't able to find either of them. I was ambushed in the woods by a group of Moors and a man who resembled me." Etienne wasn't ready to tell Isabella that the man might have been his uncle.

Isabella straightened up. "That man was one of my kidnappers. I hope to never see him again. As for Ronan and Tristan," a look of sorrow crossed Isabella's face, "they never returned." Etienne's insides churned. He felt responsible for Ronan. Had he not gone swimming, this could have been avoided.

"Hey! Welcome back," boomed Gerhart, as he and Clair waved from across the room.

Etienne waved back and asked, "Where's Andy?"

The door swung open revealing Andy with his hands raised. Behind him stood a Hospitaller Master, a nun, and several guards.

The nun pointed to the table with the herbs. "See, Master Francisco, I told you they were stealing from us! We need that medicine for our men. I saw this fat one sneaking around our gardens and knew he was up to no good."

Isabella glared at the nun, and she shot back an arrogant look.

Gerhart rose from the bed and took his battle ax. "You let that little man go. If you touch one hair on his head, this ax will find a new home in your heart."

"All a'right everyone, settle down," Andy said calmly. "We are 'appy to pay for the herbs."

"These herbs are priceless in a time of war. I should have known better than to take in Templar scum," the Hospitaller Master, Francisco, said with disdain. He looked around the room and sized up Gerhart, who took a step forward. "You are no longer welcome in this house. You must leave immediately."

"I am the only Templar," Etienne said weakly. "There is no need for blood." He noticed Francisco's gaze sweep across the room, lingering on Andy's bed. To his horror, Etienne saw the pictures of the green men carelessly strewn across it. His eyes shot to the Hospitaller, hoping the Grand Master didn't know what the images meant. The look on Francisco's face as he sheathed his dagger destroyed any hope inside him.

With a smug smile, Francisco said, "You are right, young man. There is no need to draw any more blood, but you all must leave immediately. Pack your things and my guards will await you in the hall." Francisco once again glanced at the papers before turning away.

Etienne watched Francisco leave, a sinking feeling taking over his entire being. Just one more problem he would have to deal with.

Once they'd left the Hospitallers, Gerhart and Andy wrapped their arms around Etienne, helping him every step of the way. They followed the scallop shells out of the town back onto the Camino. Etienne had very little strength, and was glad they could take the most direct route to the next town without the threat of the Moors. "I hate being so weak and vulnerable. I am supposed to be strong for Isabella. Strong for all of you."

"'Tis alright to be helped by others. Ya don't always have ta be the strong one."

"That job is already taken," Gerhart said, laughing.

"Hush up, I'm being serious. Ya shoulda listen, too. Being weak and being vulnerable are'na the same thing. True connection can only happen with vulnerability. If ya are always walking around being the *tough one* with your walls up, no one ever has the opportunity ta get ta know ya. They can have an image of ya, just like looking at a suit of armor, but they donna get ta *know* ya. 'Tis only when we let our walls down and let people in that we can truly connect and love others. If ya ask me, being vulnerable is one of the bravest things a person can do."

Etienne took Andy's words to heart and let them sink in.

He looked around to the group, belatedly realizing they were short one person. "What happened to Mariano?"

"He went to hunt down the Moors and the Shadows with the Hospitallers after the battle. No one from the expedition returned. Not a single one. I should have gone with him," Gerhart said, slumping his large shoulders.

"I'm sure 'e is still alive," Andy said.

"He has to be. He is all I have. Without him, I wouldn't... I wouldn't know what to do."

"Well, ya have us now," Andy said, "And we won't let anything 'appen to ya."

Gerhart nodded, his eyes straying to Clair up ahead.

"I can-a take it from 'ere," Andy said, noticing as well.

Gerhart smiled softly. "He's all yours." Gerhart placed a walking staff into Etienne's left hand and quickened his pace like a large puppy to catch up with Clair.

"Now don't ya be angry with me. I saw the look ya gave me about them pictures. I was'na snooping. Those pictures just fell on ta the bed and I... Well, I couldna help myself." Andy looked apologetically at Etienne.

"Those pictures are sacred and a secret. Only three Templars know of their existence." Etienne looked pained. "Well, I guess now just two." Ronan had entrusted him with this secret and he had failed already. This just reinforced Etienne's feelings of unworthiness to be responsible for this secret.

Andy placed his freehand over his heart. "Aye, 'tis a shame we lost Ronan. A better man ya couldna find. But, he may still be alive. We donna know." After a moment of silence, he continued, "See, they fell on ta the bed the night of the battle. I needed something ta take my mind off Clair, and… Well, and it worked. It took me a few days, but I figured it oot."

Etienne looked at him sharply. "What do you mean you figured it out?"

"'Twas a code. I woudna 'ave gotten it without that sundial. See, each hour represented a different letter, and once I matched the letters with the hours of the day, 'twas quite easy… You Templars need to come up with more complicated codes." Andy reached into Etienne's bag he was carrying for him and pulled out the grid. He showed it to Etienne.

W H E R E F I V E B E C O M E O N E
1 2 3 4 5 6 7 8 9 10 11 12 13 14 15 16 17 18

"Where five become one… What do ya think it means?" asked Andy.

Etienne shot daggers out of his eyes. It was all he could do. He couldn't even make a fist. "Destroy this at once. If this fell into the wrong hands… If you were anyone else and I had the strength, I would kill you where you stand." But, Andy wasn't anyone else. What would he do now that Andy knew the code?

Andy stopped and looked at him with large hurt eyes. "Well, ya Templars shoulda come up with something more difficult…"

They walked in silence. Etienne's stomach churned. He had taken an oath to protect the secrets of the Templars. Would he have to kill this man who was so dear to him? Andy felt more like a brother to him than any Templar ever had.

"Beautiful life." These words interrupted Etienne's train of thought. "Beautiful life." He heard again. Past Andy to the right was a small oasis in the distance. There sat a solitary man cross legged under the shade of a handmade shelter. "Come, peregrinos," the man said, beckoning them.

The company looked at each other. "Well, some shade would be nice from this heat," said Isabella.

The man was thin but strong, with long curly hair pulled back. Once again, the man said, "Beautiful life," with a giant smile on his face. Etienne felt like punching him. It didn't feel like a beautiful life at the moment.

"What do you mean, 'Beautiful life?'" asked Isabella.

The man replied, "It is a beautiful life." The words didn't relieve Etienne's anger, but he was happy to have a distraction. He didn't like thinking that he may have to kill Andy. Etienne was also relieved to have a break from walking. His body was extremely fatigued, and the conversation with Andy had drained him even more.

"What are you doing living out here all by yourself?" asked Isabella.

"I am here to offer shelter to the peregrinos on their way to Santiago. There is no other occupation that I would rather have. Here I sit and the whole world comes to me, nation after nation. There are so many good people all searching for something, and I have found my beautiful life right here," the man said, beaming at them. "Come have a seat, eat and drink with me. Tell me of your adventures until the heat has passed. We shall enjoy the time as old friends. For the miles you have walked, I would like to walk with you now."

The man brought food and water and they recounted their tales. The man was in rapture. He loved every minute of it. The hours passed and the sun's heat waned. Telling this man of all their adventures made Etienne realize how much they had endured together. He had grown so fond of each of his companions. For the first time in a long time, Etienne felt like he belonged. Like he had a family.

"We must go," Isabella said.

"Not yet." The man walked into the shelter and came out again holding a sack of fruits, vegetables, and a bit of bread.

"What is this?" asked Isabella. "We have no money to pay you," she said sheepishly. Etienne bet she had never had to say that her whole life.

"I do not seek payment." The man handed Isabella the sack of goods.

"Thank you," she said, with tears of gratitude in her eyes.

"We are all pilgrims in this life traveling to one destination. Buen Camino."

CHAPTER 16

ASTORGA

Some time later, the small band of pilgrims arrived at a large hill. From the top, Isabella could see the whole countryside opened before them. There, in the valley below, lay the walled city of Astorga, its cathedral's towers mimicking the grandeur of the snow-capped mountains that lay beyond. It was still a three-day hike west on the Camino to meet Jacques de Molay in Ponferrada, but Isabella knew they had to stop here. She looked at the Camino snaking into the majestic mountains. There was no way Etienne's exhausted body could make the trek over the high peaks.

Isabella led the group through the village that lay outside Astorga's city walls. She admired the multi-colored rocks in the wall; each boasted of the beautiful mountains that lay just beyond. The grays, reds, and whites, all reflected the sun differently. The wall stood thirty feet high and surrounded the entire city. Every fifty feet the wall was rounded, which created aesthetic beauty and practical defense. Something about this wall reminded her of the wall that surrounded Paris.

"This would be a hard city to conquer," Gerhart said, sizing it up.

They turned down the last street of the village to see a large flight of stairs leading to the wall's entrance. Worried, Isabella looked back at Etienne, the exhaustion clear on his face. Andy shook his head. "'Tis the cruel joke of the Camino. Ya walk all day and finally make it to your destination, then you 'ave ta climb something like this."

"Ach, quit yer belly-achin'," Clair said.

"At least you can walk by yourself," Etienne said, half-jokingly.

"Aye, true, laddie," said Andy, slipping Etienne's free arm over his shoulder. "Let's do this together." Andy looked at Gerhart, who was supporting Etienne on the other side, and together they climbed the stairs.

When they reached the last step, even Gerhart was out of breath. They sat for a moment on a bench just outside the wall. Two young and well-dressed guards approached. "Welcome, peregrinos. What news of the Camino?" the taller guard asked.

"Much turmoil on the road these past few days. Our company has sustained great injury and loss at the hands of the Moors," Isabella said, standing to greet them.

"We heard of such reports," the taller guard said.

"You will find safety and rest within these walls," the other said. "Welcome to Astorga."

"Thank you, kind sir," Isabella replied. "Where can we find a Templar Commandery, and an albergue?"

"After you enter the gate, go straight and you will find the Church of San Francisco. Across from it is a good albergue. To find the Templar Commandery, go right at the church and follow the main street to the town square. You will find it there."

They followed the guard's directions to a beautiful red stone church with several bells adorning the roof. Across from the church, was a friendly-looking albergue with smoke gently rising from the chimney.

"This must be it," Andy said, still out of breath from the stairs. "I'll stay here and get us a room."

"And how do you intend to get us a room without any money?" Isabella asked.

"You leave that to me." Andy winked. He turned from the company and headed toward the albergue.

Isabella and the others continued up the main road to the town square, which was teaming with people. To her left, was a large church with two spires and a bell tower in the middle. The beautiful gray and white stones complimented the surrounding buildings. Merchants were selling their wares, and Isabella spotted several pilgrims. They were easy to spot amongst the townspeople.

Isabella looked at her garments. No one would ever expect that she was the princess of France. Even she didn't feel that she was anymore. In Carrion de los Condes she had been embarrassed at her poor appearance; now she embraced it. She was just like all the other pilgrims. All equal, all the same. Shedding her former identity had been liberating, but painful; all growth is.

In the far-left corner of the square was the Templar Commandery. The red cross on the white background was a welcoming sign.

"So how do you propose we get the gold we need from the Templars? Tristan always took care of the expenses before. I lost my credentials back in Castrojeriz," Isabella said, the thought of that night still heavy on her heart. She hadn't thought about Jessica and the others she had lost in a few days. She had been too concerned with saving herself and those around her to properly mourn. There hadn't been enough time.

"Ach, mine too," Clair said.

"I can let the Templars know of our plight and my brothers should be able to supply us with what we need," Etienne said.

"Any time someone finds out who we are, we get attacked. We don't know who we can trust," Isabella whispered.

"It's alright," said Gerhart, pulling a piece of parchment from his sporran. "Katsuji paid us well, and I made a large deposit. Will you three be alright here by yourselves?"

When Isabella nodded, Gerhart sat Etienne on a bench in the middle of the square and disappeared into the crowd.

As they waited, Isabella, Etienne, and Clair watched the townsfolk. Children went running through the square, chasing one another. Young lovers stood in the archways courting each other, and the elderly yelled at both. There was so much color and laughter.

"Ach, 'tis 'ard ta believe this is what life was like," Clair said.

"It was never like this for me," Isabella remembered her many days indoors by herself studying. She would look out the window and wonder what lay beyond the walls of the Palais de Cite. Her only interactions were with her brothers, servants, and Etienne when she could sneak away.

"I always longed for a life as simple and free as this," Etienne said. "I was a slave to hunger before I entered the palace." Isabella took hold of his hand and gently squeezed. His eyes seemed mournful. It looked as if there was more pain beyond the hunger. After her days on the Camino, Isabella could empathize with those who were poor and hungry for the first time in her life. She vowed to herself that when she made it back to her palace, she'd have more compassion for her country's poor. Together they sat hand-in-hand and continued to watch the simplicity of everyday life.

"You know, you're the reason I took this pilgrimage, Etienne," Isabella said.

"What do you mean? There is no way you could have known I was stationed in Castrojeriz."

Isabella looked down. "I was never able to forgive myself for your death, no matter the confession I gave, nor the indulgences I received. I thought walking the Camino would help me forgive myself."

Etienne squeezed her hand firmly. "Isabella, I—"

"They are criminals," Gerhart said as he reached the group.

"They didn't give you your money?" Etienne asked.

"They did, but not all of it. They charged me a storage fee. I should take my ax and go back there to get what's mine."

Etienne laughed slightly. "Aw, you think this is funny, do you?" Gerhart asked.

"My brothers charge everyone a fee for storing their gold."

Gerhart glared at him. "Well, a man should keep all of what he has earned."

"We-a better be checking in on Andy," said Clair, to change the subject. "Let's see if 'e got us tha' room."

The smell of soup cooking on a fire greeted them as they entered the albergue. "Ach, there you are," Andy said, perched at the bar, surrounded by a group of pilgrims. They all had drinks in their hands and Andy's face was red. "Well, I wasna able to get us a room, but I did manage to get a free drink." He raised his glass in a toast with the other pilgrims. "Com' on an join us."

"I thought ya quit the drink after what 'appened," Clair said, narrowing her eyes.

"We need to get a room, Andy," Isabella said sharply. She couldn't believe he had just been sitting idly by. Etienne needed to rest.

"Suit yer self." Andy turned to his new friends. They all laughed.

"Drink will be the death of that man," Isabella said under her breath as they turned to find the owner of the albergue.

The owner was a thin older Spanish man with a curled mustache. It looked as if, in his youth, he could have been a great traveler. His old eyes still had adventure in them and Isabella could see the sharpness in his gaze.

"Ah hello. Your Scottish friend said you would be arriving soon. We already have your room prepared."

"What?" Isabella's eyes grew wide. Andy smiled at them from the bar and raised his glass. If she wasn't so concerned about Etienne's wellbeing, she'd be amused at Andy's deception.

"Ach, 'e always has been a troublemaker," Clair said.

The old man continued, "We never turn away pilgrims whether they can pay or not. It is the way of the Camino."

"We can pay," Gerhart said. He still sounded upset about the storage fee. "How much?"

"It is donativo. Pay as you like."

"Hmm," Gerhart grunted, handing him a small amount of money.

The old man smiled back at him. "Thank you. Now if you will follow me." The old man led them down the corridor and up a flight of stairs to the first bedroom on the left.

"There are only four beds in here," Isabella said. "There are five of us."

"Your Scottish friend will stay with the Italian pilgrims in another room. This was the best I could do, and he didn't mind." Turning to leave, he said, "Should you need anything else, don't hesitate to ask, my name is José. Also, we will have dinner soon with all the other pilgrims. You are welcome to join as our guest."

Etienne looked longingly at the bed closest to him, but Isabella knew he should eat before he rested. They followed the others back out to the main room. Andy was sitting with the same pilgrims he had been drinking with earlier. He raised his hand and beckoned them to come over. "Every'un I'd like ya ta meet my sister and um her... her... her Gerhart." All laughed at the poor introduction. When the laughter died down, he finished introducing Etienne and Isabella. Isabella was glad Andy remembered not to say she was a princess in his inebriated state.

A handsome man, with olive skin and wavy black hair, put a hand on his chest, bowing his head slightly. "My name is Vincenzo Fellini. My brothers and I are making the pilgrimage from Torino, Italy. Have you ever been to Italy?" When Isabella shook her head, he said, "You must come; it is the greatest country on earth. We have the most beautiful mountains and, more importantly, the best food." The whole table erupted in laughter.

"Clair, wud ya like a drink?" Andy asked, passing her his glass.

"Ach no... Do ya na remember ya daft fool. That almost killed me..." A look of shame crossed Andy's face, and he stared at the glass.

"It has almost killed me once or twice as well," Vincenzo said in his thick Italian accent as he filled Andy's glass. Isabella didn't like that Andy was drinking so much again. Mistakes happen when people drink too much. She was enjoying safety and anonymity too much.

Vincenzo started making eyes at Isabella, and she avoided his gaze. Etienne noticed and said, "Friends, please excuse me. I think I must rest after our long journey."

Isabella wrapped her arm around Etienne firmly to show both Etienne and Vincenzo that she was with Etienne. "I'll go with you." Turning to Clair, she said, "If you would be good enough to bring us some soup on your return..."

At Clair's confirmation, he and Isabella walked slowly back to their room. Isabella was happy to have more time alone with Etienne. Vincenzo was handsome, but Isabella knew that Etienne could give her more than any other man in the world. He made her feel whole.

CHAPTER 17

SWEET CHARITY

The next morning, the energy had returned to Etienne's body. Isabella was fast asleep on the bed next to his; her arm hanging over the edge. Etienne slowly made his way down the stairs. Andy was still sitting at a table looking like he hadn't slept all night.

"Good morning," Etienne said.

"Achhhhhh, 'tis morning already," Andy said groggily. "I couldna sleep, those Italians snored worse than Gerhart. You're lookin' better though."

"Some strength has come back to me."

"Good, laddie, good. Now that you have your strength back, where you be off ta?" Andy asked with a raised eyebrow.

"I am going to the cathedral for my morning prayer."

"Do ya mind if I join ya? I've just been sitting 'ere for a long while and could use a change of scenery."

"I would love the company for the walk, but in the church I must focus."

"'Tis fine, laddie. Maybe I can find some rest there."

The sun was just rising and the first pilgrims were leaving their albergues to continue on the Camino. Etienne heard the echo of their staffs hitting the cobblestone road as they went. Andy and Etienne continued to walk in silence as they passed the main square. On the ground, scallop shells mixed in with the cobblestones led to the cathedral.

The red rocks reflecting the morning sun gave the cathedral an ethereal glow. Etienne removed the hood of his cloak and stared up at the magnificent building, its spires reaching to the heavens. It seemed that almost every inch of the edifice was covered in detailed sculptures. They walked toward the three arched entryways. The center one was ornately decorated and had a large wooden door.

"Sure is something, isn' it," said Andy. "'Tis as if the story of the whole world is told right 'ere in this one archway." Etienne gently smiled and tried to open the door. It didn't move an inch.

"Ach, figures. Just 'ere for decoration." They walked to the door on the right and entered.

The church smelled of incense and every sound echoed. Etienne gazed at the ceiling. It looked like a meadow of giant white flowers, opening to greet the morning. Etienne walked the distance of the great hall to the second pew in front of the altar. He knelt in prayer and was lost to the world.

When again he opened his eyes, Andy was sitting a few seats away, patiently waiting. It took a few seconds before Etienne was fully present.

Andy had a giant grin on his face. "Ach, back to the land of the living," he said. "I 'ave something to show ya. I coudna' help myself. It was right there."

Etienne furrowed his brow. "What?"

Andy pointed his plump index finger to the crucifix. "There, above the altar."

Following Andy's finger with his gaze, Etienne shrugged. "It is our Lord Jesus."

"No, behind him."

Etienne strained his eyes and saw what Andy was pointing at. Behind the crucifix was the strangest picture Etienne had ever seen. It was a ring of twelve skulls, surrounding a golden disk, with a triangle in the middle that contained a thirteenth skull. Below it was a red sun in the sky over the city of Astorga. Just above the city flew some strange large black birds.

"It has ta be it. The next clue," Andy said excitedly. "I've never seen anything like that. The triangle is the perfect symbol for you know what."

"No, I don't know what," Etienne said cautiously. His body tensed. Did Andy know more about the treasure?

"'Tis like what Ronan said. The triangle is the symbol for—"

Before Andy finished, Etienne pinned him against the pew by his throat. His body reacted without him thinking. He made a vow to protect this treasure and he would keep it. "How do you know about that?" Andy croaked and pointed to his throat. Etienne lessened the pressure so he could speak.

"Settle down, laddie. I know it from ya." Andy continued, "When ya were unconscious ya talked in your sleep, and I coulna' 'elp over 'earing."

"Do the others know about the drawings and what I said?" Etienne asked, still pinning Andy. Etienne was worried that all of his companions would have to die for the information he'd let slip out. He had been right: he wasn't worthy of protecting the secret. He wished Ronan had never told him about the treasure.

"They dunna know about the drawins'. I kept those ta myself. And they thought you were talkin' nonsense. You are as much ta blame for talk'n as I am for listenin'." Etienne loosened his hold, and Andy took a deep breath. Etienne was relieved Andy was the only one who knew.

"I should kill you for what you know…" Etienne shook his head. "I took a vow…"

"Ya didna break any of your vows consciously. Ya still 'ave your honor," Andy said, with all seriousness. "Everything 'appens for a reason. Ronan wanted you to solve that puzzle, and I donna know if ya could 'ave done it on your own." Andy massaged his throat. Andy was right. Etienne had puzzled over the green men and hadn't come up with anything. He wouldn't have been able to solve it on his own.

"I need you to swear to me here and now with a blood oath, in front of God, that you will protect these secrets with your life. When we see Jacques de Molay in Ponferrada, he will decide both our fates: mine for revealing the secret, and yours for knowing,"

"Aye, let it be done." Andy held out his hand. Etienne drew his dagger and made an incision on Andy's palm. He then did the same on his own. They put their hands together and Etienne said, "Do you, Andy Sinclair, vow to keep secret that which you have discovered regarding the Templars, on the penalty of death?"

Andy looked at him solemnly. "Aye, I will keep these secrets, and if I shall ever break my oath, my life I forfeit."

Etienne continued, "As God is our witness, let it be so." They parted hands and each bandaged their wounds.

"So, shall we try to solve it?" Andy asked, his eyes bright with anticipation.

With a small chuckle, Etienne shook his head. "Your curiosity will kill you one of these days."

"I already took the blood oath not to tell anyone, and if the Templars decide to kill me, so be it. I may as well figure out the puzzle and make it worthwhile." Andy crossed his arms.

Etienne smiled. "Well, you do have a good point. But I'm not going to help you."

"So, what do ya think it means?" Andy raised an eyebrow.

"It just looks like a painting of the apocalypse to me," Etienne said, hoping to quiet Andy's curiosity.

"That's it, ha-ha! Why didna' I see it earlier? You're brilliant. I've been sitting here nearly twenty minutes trying ta figure out the darn thing, and ye get it the first time."

Looking back at the painting, Etienne's forehead creased. "I don't understand."

"Don't ya try to hide it. Revelation, the book of Revelation. It has ta be. There are twelve skulls and one in the middle, so that would be Revelation chapter twelve verse one. That is where we will find the secret of this cathedral. We need to find a bible." Andy rushed off toward the altar, leaving Etienne still confused in his seat. He wasn't trying to help him. He wanted Andy to just quit searching. When Andy reached the altar, he thumbed through the bible. He stopped and read with an excited look on his face.

"'Tis it, 'tis it. Come 'ere." Andy beckoned Etienne to join him.

Etienne slowly made his way to Andy and knelt as he passed the altar. Andy pointed to the passage.

Revelations 12:1, A great sign appeared in heaven: a woman clothed with the sun, with the moon under her feet and a crown of twelve stars on her head.

"And what does this have to do with anything?" asked Etienne, putting his hands on his hips.

"Twelve skulls, Twelve stars. I bet if we find this woman, we'll-a find the clue we are looking for. We need ta find a statue or painting of a woman, with the moon under her feet and crowned with twelve stars." Andy rushed away from the altar and frantically searched the church for the image.

Other pilgrims and townsfolk had entered the cathedral to admire its beauty and say their morning prayers. Etienne was ready to head back to the albergue. He was sure the others were awake by now, and even if Andy was on to something, he didn't want him to find it. In his eyes, the less they knew the better. He had already divulged one secret; he didn't want to be responsible for another. Although, he couldn't help feeling curious about the next clue.

After he had searched the whole cathedral, Andy sat next to Etienne dejectedly. "I could have sworn tha' was it."

Relieved, Etienne placed a hand on his shoulder. "I'm sure it is for the best that we found nothing here. As you said before, everything happens for a reason."

Andy smiled at him and the two of them left the church. They walked down the main street back the way they came. Andy stopped for a second and looked at the cathedral longingly.

"Wait a minute. Wait a minute," Andy ran back to the cathedral. Instead of heading for the front doors, he made for the side entrance. Above it was a sculpture of a woman glowing orange with the rising sun. Two angels were crowning her, and she was sitting upon what appeared to be the moon.

When Andy reached the entrance, he climbed a pillar next to the door. For a man of his size, he moved incredibly quickly. Etienne thought he looked like a bear climbing a tree and had to laugh. "Maybe there is something to the saying 'mad as a Scotsman."

"I found it!" Andy climbed down the pillar. "The sign of the triangle and skull were bookending a passage written on top of the entrance facing the sky."

"What did it say?" Etienne asked, not sure if he should feel excited or concerned.

"I donna know, it is written in code," Andy said as he drew it in the dirt on the ground. When he finished, both of them looked at the markings in silence.

∇▷>▷◊◁◊▷△✕>▷>∨◁◊▷◊>∨◁∇◁∨>∇

"How did you remember all of that?"

"I donna ken. Since I was a wee one, I had the ability ta remember anything I saw."

"Excuse me, what are you drawing? I like to draw too," said a small voice behind them.

Etienne erased the markings with his foot and turned around. The voice belonged to a young girl, she couldn't have been older than eight, with blonde hair parted into two braids.

"Where are your parents," Etienne asked.

"I don't have any," the girl responded.

Her words struck Etienne to his core, and he was taken to his own childhood after his parents died and all the many nights he spent on the cold streets. He wanted to help this child. "Do you have a name? Can we help you in any way?"

The girl smiled sweetly. "My name is Charity."

"'Tis a beautiful name."

"Do you have anything you can share with me?" Charity asked with large eyes.

"We don't have much, just the clothes on our backs and our weapons. Sometimes even adults are impoverished." Etienne wished he had money or food to give to Charity. His heart welled up inside him and felt like it was caught in his throat.

Andy put his hand on Etienne's shoulder. "Ach, I think I 'ave somethin' for ya." He winked at Charity and asked Etienne, "May I have your sword sir? I feel like dancing." Etienne smiled. He knew what was coming.

Andy crossed the swords in an x on the ground. He clapped his hands, both Etienne and Charity joined. Andy danced to and fro singing a silly song that made Charity smile. Etienne loved that even when they had nothing, Andy still found a way to give. Andy finished the dance and took a bow.

"That was wonderful," Charity said, vigorously clapping her hands.

"If you come back to the inn with us, I'm sure we can get you something to eat," Etienne said, extending his hand.

"No, thank you. But I do have something for you." Charity took them both by the hands and led them back to the door below the statue of the virgin. She let go and walked to the left side of the door. Hidden in plain sight was a carving of the tree of life. Charity pushed on the circles in a zigzag pattern leading down to the bottom. As she pressed the last one, the circular images on the door turned and five points of light emanated from the center. Etienne could hardly breath. *Who is this girl?*

Etienne shielded his eyes from the bright light. When the light decreased, he saw an open door and a set of steps leading down. He remembered Ronan's words, *behind each door there is a trial and a treasure.*

"Follow me," Charity said sweetly as she skipped down the stairs.

Andy stood with his mouth gaping and hands on his hips. "How'ed she—?"

Etienne stopped Andy from moving forward. "We must be prepared for anything down there. Be on guard."

Etienne went first; as he reached the fourth step, there was a bright light and the door closed behind them. The corridor now glowed with a green light coming from the foot of the steps. Etienne wished Ronan was with them. He would know what to do. Etienne steadied his breath and focused on taking one step at a time.

"Come on. You're so slow," Charity shouted from out of sight.

"I'm scared, Etienne," Andy said.

"Keep your hand on my shoulder. I will be right here with you." Etienne could feel Andy's hand shaking as it reached him.

At the foot of the steps was another door that was wide open. Etienne froze and Andy ran right into him. "Andy, look." Just beyond the door lay a vast treasure. Gold coins were mounded high. There were treasure chests filled with rubies and pearls. Etienne had never seen so much wealth in all of his life.

"Welcome to my home," Charity said from the middle of the room spreading her arms wide.

"Well, I'll be." Andy reached for a large sapphire by the door.

Etienne stopped his hand. "Don't touch anything." Etienne didn't know what the test was. He didn't want Andy to get hurt. He had already lost one friend. He couldn't take losing another.

Etienne cautiously walked closer to Charity. "You have a beautiful home." Charity grinned from ear to ear. "You said you had something to give us."

Charity brought both hands to her face and ran in place. "I'm so excited! Since you both gave to me out of your poverty, I get to give each of you something special." Andy looked like a statue, the only thing moving was his eyes. Etienne's mind was apprehensive, but his body was relaxed, it gave him no indication of danger.

Andy broke his trance. "Well, donna keep us waitin'."

"Perfect, first Etienne. Charity took Etienne by the hand and led him toward the back of the room. They passed mounds of gold, until they came to one that reached at least twenty feet high.

"Your gift is behind there."

Etienne let go of the girl's hand and slowly turned the corner, ready for whatever beast may lay behind.

"Ronan!" Etienne ran and embraced the old Templar, who was badly wounded. "I can't believe you're alive. I thought you were dead."

"I'm so happy you like your gift!" Charity exclaimed, jumping up and down.

"Thank you," Etienne managed still clutching his long-lost friend.

"You're welcome, thank you for your kindness. Andy, I have so much to show you. Let's go play."

"'Tis good ta see ya again," Andy said as Charity pulled him away.

"How did you get here? What happened?"

Ronan leaned back in the throne he was seated in. "When I was on watch, Tristan drugged me. As I was passing out, the Moors appeared and I learned it was Tristan who had betrayed Isabella from the beginning. He received a sum of money from the Moors and pointed them to our camp. There was nothing I could do. I was paralyzed."

Etienne punched the wall hard. He felt his knuckles crack open and bleed. Tristan was the person who had caused Etienne the most pain in his life, and now he had hurt him even more. "Tristan sold his own princess to the Moors. If I ever see him again, I will kill him."

"I am not sure if you will get that chance. I will explain more later. I must finish my story first, though. When I awoke, Tristan interrogated me for several days about the treasure. I knew I couldn't escape. When I learned all that Tristan knew about the treasure, I decided he needed to be stopped. I devised a plan and led Tristan to this door. As I said to you in Leon, there is both a trial and a treasure behind each door. I put Tristan to the test and unleashed Charity. As you can see, he failed."

"Charity? What trial could she present to defeat Tristan?"

"A trial so terrible I never want to see it again. Each door is bound with a duality; this treasure is bound with greed or charity. She reflects whatever is in your heart. When Tristan saw all of this gold, he stuffed his bags full. As we were leaving, the girl you know as Charity approached and asked if we had anything to share with her. Tristan pushed her aside. In that moment, Charity's opposite side appeared, Greed. She's a coin that has two sides. Greed stole everything from Tristan, including me. She will plague him until he has nothing left, and then will take his life."

Etienne shook his head and finally found his words. "Why are you still here?"

"I sacrificed myself by not giving Charity anything. I couldn't have Tristan discover the secret. Since I didn't give her anything, she is taking the only thing

I have left, my life. This is only a last chance to say goodbye." Etienne's heart felt like it was about to burst.

"No...no it can't be." Etienne shook his head vigorously.

"It is so, my son. I have one thing left to tell you. To find the other doors, you must unlock the tree of life as I did in Castrojeriz. This is the pattern." Ronan drew the same pattern he had seen Charity push moments earlier. "The doors that bind the treasure must be unbound by making this sign on them. Ronan drew a backwards z. Once the task is completed, or the person who opened it dies, then the door will be sealed once more."

Ronan told him all of this with urgency, as if Etienne was his last hope. "Should anything happen to Jacques de Molay, you must find these treasures and unite them at the location the code of the cathedrals depicts. Remember, the codes to the treasure's location are revealed through Baphomet. Then you have to move the one true treasure to safety."

"Why must I do that?"

"Because there is a traitor in the Templars who seeks to control the treasure for himself, and Molay is too stubborn to see it. I must go now, my son." Ronan gripped his hand tightly. "Do not grieve for me. I'm going home." With these words, Ronan gave up his spirit. Etienne couldn't follow Ronan's last request, tears formed in his eyes as he held the corpse of his mentor.

A few moments passed and Charity came skipping around the corner. Etienne managed the words, "Thank you." Charity ran to him and gave him a hug that only an eight-year old could.

Andy ran up out of breath. Sorrow crossed his face. "I'm sorry for your loss, laddie."

"Time is up," Charity said. She clapped her hands and Ronan disappeared along with everything else in the room.

Etienne dropped to his knees, nauseated by grief and a strange energy that sped through his body. He closed his eyes to stop the spinning of colors circling him. A moistness hit his skin and his eyes opened. They were now in a dark cave illuminated by the same green glow as before. Andy was laying on the ground next to him. "Are you alright?" asked Etienne, shaking him.

"I feel like I 'ave a hangover," Andy said sitting up. "Where are we?"

"Jerusalem," answered Charity, who sat patiently in front of them with her legs crossed. "Andy, I need to give you your gift." Charity took them by the hands and led them through the cave accompanied by the glow. She ran forward and dropped to the ground in front of something wooden at the edge of the cave. Etienne thought it was a bit strange, but then again, everything about this was strange.

"What is this?" Etienne asked as he reached her.

She looked at him with tearful eyes. "This is the one True Cross."

Etienne looked at Andy and both of them dropped to their knees placing their heads to the ground.

"I'm not worthy to be here," Etienne said, pressing his head even harder into the ground. He wanted to make himself as small as possible.

Charity pet his head. "Yes, you are. You both are. You both gave from your poverty the only thing you had. You are worthy of receiving this gift. Andrew Sinclair, rise." Andy hesitantly stood but kept his head down. Charity walked to the cross and took a sliver of wood from it. "I give you this piece of the One True Cross. This gift is yours for your kind, generous, loving soul. It is one of the keys to unlock the greatest treasure of all." She placed the small shard of wood in Andy's hand.

Andy closed it in his fist. "I will protect this and keep ya in my heart."

Charity clapped her hands together again and they were back outside the cathedral looking down at the code. Etienne patted his body all over, ensuring he was really there. He felt Andy as well for good measure. They were definitely there, but Charity was gone.

Andy still had his fist outstretched and looked just as confused as Etienne felt. "Do you have it?" Etienne asked. Andy slowly opened his hand to reveal the splinter of wood sitting in his palm. "You better put that in my bag with the drawings for safe keeping."

Andy reached for the bag, then looked at Etienne blankly "'Tis na here." Andy smacked himself in the forehead with his free hand. "Ach, 'tis ok, it's in my room." Andy said, staring hard at the shard in his hand.

"You left one of the best-kept secrets to mankind unattended, in a room with people you don't know!" Etienne wished he would have taken his bag away from Andy last night. Once again, he was just as much to blame as Andy was.

Etienne burst into the albergue and all eyes in the bar turned to him. Clair, Isabella, and Gerhart rushed to him. Before they could reach him, José, the owner of the albergue, asked, "Whatever is the matter, peregrino?" As he spoke, his curled mustache quivered.

Out of breath and still holding on to the door handle for support, Etienne asked, "Andy, what room was Andy in? I must go there immediately."

"Follow me," José said.

Isabella touched Etienne on the arm gently. "Is everything alright?"

"I don't know yet." Etienne hoped beyond hope that the bag was still there, but in the pit of his stomach he felt it would be gone.

José led them to the last door at the end of the hall. It was empty; there were no Italians, no Andy, and no bag.

"Where's my broder?" Clair asked, the concern in her voice was palpable. "Did 'em Shadows get 'im?"

"Nah, Clair, I'm-a right 'ear." All turned to see Andy at the entrance to the hall, his head hanging low in shame. "Now I wish them Shadows woulda taken me."

"José, have you seen the Italians this morning?" asked Etienne.

José shook his head. "I have been up since just after the sun rose and haven't seen them. Whatever is the matter?"

"They took something of great importance," Etienne said. He wasn't going to let José know more than that. "We must find them." Etienne felt his legs buckle underneath him. He swayed and braced himself against the wall.

Isabella rushed to his aid. "You shouldn't be going anywhere in your state."

"There are some things that are more important than my health," Etienne said sharply. "More important than my life. This is one of them, and you are the other." By Isabella's look, he could tell she didn't know how to take his statement. He also wanted to tell her that Tristan had betrayed her, but this was not the right moment.

"What are we waiting here for?" asked Gerhart, taking his ax. "Let's go hunt some Italians." Etienne shot him a smile, and he winked back.

"Since we are on this side of town, let's ask the guards at the gate if they saw anything," Etienne said.

As they approached the gate, the tall guard from the day before stepped forward and said, "Hello again."

"Hello," Isabella said smiling.

Before she could continue, he asked, "What's happening on the Camino?"

"What do you mean?" Isabella asked.

"It isn't every day you see two groups of pilgrims backtracking on the Camino before breakfast. Have you heard of some trouble on the road ahead?"

Etienne's gaze zeroed in on the guard. "What did this other group of pilgrims look like?" Even the effort of speaking was a strain on his body now.

"They were a group of three men. I think I heard them speaking Italian. They arrived yesterday shortly after you did," the second guard said, walking forward.

Etienne looked directly at him. "How long ago did they leave?"

"Just before the sun rose," responded the taller guard. "So, is there trouble on the road?"

"No, we think those men stole—" Etienne was interrupted by a cheerful song being whistled at the bottom of the steps. Relief flooded his body when he saw it was Mariano whistling, as he spun Etienne's leather bag around his finger in a great circle.

"Gaaahhh!!!" Gerhart let out a roar of joy and went bounding down the stairs. He lifted Mariano in a giant bear-hug, spinning him around in a circle high off the ground.

Everyone smiled at the spectacle. Etienne turned to the guards. "Thank you for your kindness. I think we found what we were looking for."

Gerhart and Mariano rejoined the group at the top of the stairs and they walked back to the albergue. Mariano handed the bag to Etienne. "I believe this is yours. Happy to see you are alive," he said with a smile.

"I could say the same for you." Etienne returned the smile. Something was different about Mariano. Whatever had happened to him, Etienne was glad for it. He seemed more like the Mariano they had met at the boathouse—lighter, somehow. Etienne clapped his hand on Mariano's shoulder before looking in the brown leather bag at the pictures. "How did you find this?"

"Let's just say it's only gambling if you have a chance of losing." Mariano winked. "On my return to Hospital, I found out you had left for Astorga. So, I pressed on through the night and camped a few miles outside the city. When I broke camp this morning, I crossed paths with a band of three pilgrims. I recognized one of them. A very handsome man. Not as handsome as me, but still handsome, all the same. You don't forget a face like that—"

"That must have been Vincenzo," interrupted Andy.

"Yes, that is his name," Mariano said. "He recognized me as well, but neither of us could remember where we had met. I asked them to join me for breakfast. Soon, I realized I had seen him on the battle of the bridge. We had fought side-by-side against the Moors. He was one of the Hospitallers that had held the line so valiantly."

"He was a Hospitaller?" Etienne straightened. An image of the Hospitaller Master's eyes lingering on the drawings across Andy's bed immediately rose in his mind. "They know..." He cut himself off before he revealed anything to his companions.

The Hospitallers must know about the code. That is the only reason they would go to such lengths to get my bag.

"Are you alright?" Isabella asked.

Etienne shook off his thoughts. "We must make it to the Templar castle in Ponferrada with great haste."

"Yes, for more reasons than what is in that little bag," Mariano said, "When I asked Vincenzo why he was dressed as a pilgrim and not as a Hospitaller, he said he had some business he needed to attend to that required a guise. As he said this, I noticed him clutch the bag around his neck."

"After traveling with you for so many miles, I knew that bag was yours, but when I asked him of the bag, he claimed it was his. This meant that he had either killed you or stolen from you. Either way, I didn't like Vincenzo much anymore.

"I challenged him and his companions to a game of Thimble-rig for the bag. Needless to say, they lost. They didn't want to give me the bag, but my knives were much more effective than their swords at close range. One of them got away, so the Hospitallers will come for more than what's in that bag. It is good we have a days' start on them." Mariano didn't seem troubled by any of this. He was relaxed and calm.

At the albergue, José greeted them with a smile. "That was quick."

"We found what we were looking for. If anyone comes asking about us, or this bag, tell them you saw this." Etienne reached into the bag and pulled out all the drawings. He took them to the hearth and placed them in the raging fire. Within moments, the paper had disintegrated into ash.

José looked at him gravely. "I will tell them what I witnessed. One question though. Why destroy something that you would forfeit your life for?"

Etienne looked at his companions. "I destroyed it because I am not willing to forfeit their lives for it. Thank you for all of your hospitality."

CHAPTER 18

THE PAPAL COURT

Cardinal Leonardo Patrasso[28] awaited the Pope's return to Poitiers. The Papal Court had been assembled there since Clement's coronation. Late in the evening, the ornately decorated papal coach appeared, pulled by two beautiful white horses. Leonardo hastened from the doors of the palace to meet the coach, wanting to be the first to see the Pope on his arrival. There was much unattended business that needed to be dealt with, and no time to waste.

When the coach came to a stop, Leonardo opened the golden door. The red velvet interior was even more lavish than the exterior. *Does God's servant really need all of this? How many mouths of the poor could we feed with this one coach?*

Leonardo shook off these thoughts as the Pope emerged. Clement extended his hand and Leonardo kissed the papal ring. "Your Holiness," he said, bowing. When his lips met the top of the Pope's hand, he noticed the texture of cloth. He opened his eyes to see that the Pope's entire hand was bandaged. Leonardo let go immediately. "Are you well, Your Holiness?"

Clement looked at him with road-wearied eyes. "Nothing that ever passes is excluded from God's plan." Leonardo helped Clement out of the coach, and they walked to the palace.

"Your Holiness, there is much work to do and no time to spare. I met you out here to inform you that the Italian delegation of cardinals arrived yesterday, and they have grown impatient for your arrival."

"Very well. Have their congregations been paying their tithe to the church?" asked Clement.

"Of course, Your Holiness."

"Good, then I don't think we will have much to discuss."

"Much to discuss? Much to discuss?! Why, indeed, we do have much to discuss," a booming voice came from down the long corridor in front of them. "Let's begin, shall we? First of all, why has the Papal Court been moved to Poitiers and not kept in the Holy City of Rome? It isn't even in Italy!"

"Ahh, Cardinal Giovanni Boccamazza.[29] I am sure the Pope will answer all of your questions tomorrow. He has only just arrived and is weary from the long travel," Leonardo said.

Pope Clement raised his hand to silence Leonardo. "Cardinal Boccamazza, whom has God deemed infallible on this earth?"

Reluctantly, Cardinal Boccamazza responded, "The Pope, Your Holiness."

Clement continued. "Do you not think that there is a reason why we are here and not in Rome at this moment? Perhaps it is for the very same reason you are here to see me now. Or am I mistaken?"

Cardinal Boccamazza stood in silence.

"Rome has become a dangerous place. That is why I am proposing to move the whole Papal Court to Avignon, which is not a part of France, but a fiefdom held by the King of Sicily. The Papacy will always remain on Italian soil," Clement said reassuringly. "If that is all, I will retire for the evening." Cardinal Boccamazza bowed and kissed the Pope's hand.

Leonardo and Clement turned and left Boccamazza still bowing. They went through a large door into the Pope's private chambers. "Your Holiness, there is one more thing. This came for you yesterday." Leonardo held up a letter. "It is urgent news from the Hospitallers."

Clement took the letter from his hand, broke the seal, and opened it. A smile spread across his face. "Do you believe in divine providence?"

"Of course, Your Holiness."

"God has just given us something that will wipe away all of these problems," Clement said, crumpling the letter in his bandaged hand.

CHAPTER 19

RABANAL DEL CAMINO

Three miles west of Astorga the road sloped upward into the foothills. Mariano enjoyed the beautiful trees and wild mountain flowers dotting the hills with their royal purple splendor. He saw the world completely differently now, as if a veil had been lifted from his eyes.

The pilgrims passed several farms with old stone walls, marking the territory of one farmer to the next. They also passed small towns made up of only one or two stone houses. Each had smoke merrily piping out of the chimney. Along with the scenery, the air became brisk as they climbed. Mariano savored all the places the wind had traveled to meet him at this very spot.

"Are you sure it is safe for us to be on the Camino in the open?" asked Isabella. "So many people have seen us." Mariano smiled at the days when they had to walk in the woods to avoid being seen.

They had met several pilgrims along the way from many countries, each traveling to Santiago for the forgiveness of their sins. Some had entered their company for a short while, others just passed by in silent contemplation. It was the most interaction they had had with others on the Camino besides Katsuji's caravan.

"I assure you we are fine," Mariano said, grinning. "The Moors were completely disbanded."

"And wha' about...the Shadows?" Andy asked with a hushed voice.

"The sun is shining. We are jolly. There is no place for fear to hide here." Mariano placed his arm around Andy's shoulder and squeezed him tightly.

Gerhart looked at Mariano dumbfounded. "Okay, what happened to you out there?" he asked, pulling Mariano off Andy's shoulder.

"All right, all right," Mariano said, beckoning the others to come closer. "I met her."

Gerhart started laughing. "Only you would go on a hunt to kill Moors and come back in love with a woman."

"I didn't fall in love, I met love itself," Mariano said. He was as giddy as a schoolchild. Mariano knew there were seven names for love in Greek. The closest one that described her was agape, that universal love God has for all of mankind.

"What are you talking about? Did you go mad out there?" Etienne asked.

"Maybe mad, or maybe sane for the first time in my life. Either way, it was because of her."

Isabella raised her eyebrows. "Who is *her*?"

"The Alchemist. I met the Alchemist. We were in the woods, waiting to kill the last of the Moors, when one of the Shadows attacked. It killed all twenty soldiers I was with, but then she appeared and laughed. Her simple laugh made that Shadow flee in terror."

"Ach, I 'ave heard of the Alchemist before but didna know he was a she," Andy said, crossing his arms.

Both Clair and Isabella shot him a look. "And why shudn-a she be a woman?" Clair poked him hard in the chest.

"I mean... I mean yeah, of course, she-a could be a woman," Andy said, backtracking.

"What did she say to you?" Etienne asked.

"It is hard to put into words. She has me questioning my whole reality. I am still trying to understand what happened," Mariano said with a contented grin on his face. "After she kissed me, everything in the world seemed right, and I saw reality for what it is. I no longer fought against it. I realized: it was my own thinking that has caused me to suffer all of these years."

Andy doubled over with laughter. He regained his breath and got the words out, "You kissed a nine-hundred-year-old woman." He began another fit of laughter.

"Well, to be fair, she kissed me, and it was only on the forehead. But it was the best kiss I have ever had. I guess nine-hundred years of practice makes perfect." As the others laughed until their eyes teared up, Mariano remembered the sense of pure light traveling through his body as she kissed him. It felt as if the light had purged something in him.

After they had regained their composure, Etienne asked, "So what did she say about the Shadows?"

"She said they can only be fought in the present moment. That is the only place they are powerless. Actually, that is the only place any of us exist. If your consciousness is in the past or future, they will kill you. But then she said, *Can you fight against reality? Can you fight against your Shadow?* After this, she added, *We have to let go of the thoughts that cause us to suffer, so we can live in the moment."*

"Wha' the 'ell does all o' tha' mean?" Andy asked.

"I guess we will get a chance to find out, sooner or later," Mariano said with a smile on his face.

"How can you say that smiling? We will die if we donna figure this out," Andy said, shaking Mariano.

"Die?" Mariano asked, unaffected by Andy's shaking. "Do we even exist, my friend?" Everyone stared at Mariano blankly.

"Yep, something definitely happened to you out there," Gerhart said.

That evening they stopped at Rabanal del Camino, a small mountain community located just before the highest point of the Camino, and found lodging at a local monastery.

Since Andy, Etienne, and Gerhart each decided to use the time before supper in their own ways, Isabella and Clair went outside for some fresh air.

Isabella closed her eyes, enjoying the sun on her skin. The mountain air was fresh and the wind gently pushed through her hair making the small strands tickle her face.

"It's beautiful here. So quiet and peaceful."

Clair nodded, "Aye."

They walked on for a bit and came to a point where the view opened to reveal rolling hills and snow-capped mountains in the distance. The sun was sinking in the west, giving the landscape a golden glow.

Isabella turned to Clair. "I am so happy you are alright. I am so sorry for all that has happened to you and Andy because of the Moors...and Tristan." Isabella had to remind herself that Tristan had given Clair the compromised wine. She still didn't know why. She wondered if he was still alive and if she would ever see him again.

"'Twasna your fault. 'E was no good." Clair put a reassuring hand on Isabella's. "Plus, I got a guard'n angel oottuv it."

"You mean Gerhart?"

"Aye. He is a good man. I ain't never met the likes-a 'im afore. It seems that ye 'ave adopted a puppy as well." Clair winked at her and Isabella felt her face redden.

"I have always… He has always…" Words seemed to evade Isabella, no matter how hard she tried to find them. Since the first time she met Etienne she'd had feelings for him. She couldn't put her feelings for him into words. He moved something inside of her. When they were young, they always talked about running away to a far-off land together, and now they were here. But they still couldn't be together. The smile left Isabella's face.

Clair patted her hand. "I-a know, lassie."

Isabella shook her head. "He is bound to his duty, and I'm bound to be married."

"I've learnt we're all jus' pilgrims on this road." Clair winked again at Isabella, "And all will be forgiven when you reach Santiago." They both laughed.

They sat together and watched the day fade in fiery reds and oranges. The bells of the monastery rang in the distance, calling them for dinner. Isabella and Clair rose from their grassy hill and made their way back.

Andy met them at the door dressed in an apron, having helped the monks prepare the evening meal. He was in true form. He offered them each an arm and said, "My ladies." He escorted them into the refectory, where everyone was seated. He placed Clair next to Gerhart and Isabella next to Etienne. When their eyes met, she and Etienne exchanged a smile.

Andy disappeared into the kitchen and reappeared with the first course. It was a simple salad with lettuce, tomatoes, and olives, served in deep wooden bowls. Before they ate, a kindly monk with a long white beard stood.

"I'm Brother Xavier, and I would like to welcome you dear pilgrims. If you would please bow your heads in prayer." Isabella closed her eyes. "Dear Lord, thank you for this food which we are about to receive, may it come into our bodies and give us strength for the road ahead. May you bless each and every one of the pilgrims on their Camino, especially those sitting at this table. We pray that you will walk with them every step of the way. Amen."

"Amen," all said in chorus, and ate.

Andy was beaming with pride. "What do ya think of tha' salad dressin'. I made it myself."

"It's lovely," Isabella said, putting a hand to Andy's ear and whispered, "It would rival any salad in a palace."

Andy was ecstatic. "Wait until ya try the main!"

Andy dashed off into the kitchen. After a few moments and the sound of many clanging pots, he reemerged carrying a wild boar with an apple in its mouth. Isabella salivated at the smell.

"God has been good to us today," said Brother Xavier. "Peregrino Jacob has brought us this boar as his donation for the evening."

All applauded, and Jacob stood to take a bow.

Andy placed the boar in the middle of the table and carved it. He turned to Etienne. "This one has my special honey glaze." Andy was in his element.

Isabella leaned over to Clair. "I didn't know your brother was such a cook."

"Aye. 'E loves food and drink. That's why 'e's so fat."

"We all have our vices," Mariano said, overhearing the conversation.

Andy took the best piece of the boar and put it on Isabella's plate. She brought a bite-sized morsel to her lips and blew lightly. The smell was intoxicating. She took a bite and the morsel melted in her mouth. All the different flavors overwhelmed her taste buds. It sent warmth and joy rushing through her body, and her rapture came out in an audible, "Mmm."

It had been a long time since she'd enjoyed such a meal. They often would feast like that at the palace. Isabella loved trying different exotic foods. It was one of her passions in life. She did miss that about her old life—and the baths. A wave of nostalgia came over her. She missed her father. He was depending on her to save their kingdom. *What if that isn't what I want to do anymore? What if I want to run away with Etienne? I was never given a choice, and we were never given a chance.* She took another bite of food, hoping the pleasant rush from the taste would take away these thoughts—and it did.

Etienne watched Isabella. The pleasure on her face reminded him of the moment they had shared in the woods. He felt the blood rush through his body. She looked so beautiful, her lips pursed, blowing on the food. Distracting himself, Etienne took a deep breath and turned to Xavier. "Thank you for the wonderful meal and hospitality tonight."

"It is God's hospitality, my son." He put down his fork and knife. "Look at the birds of the air: they do not sow nor do they reap, nor do they gather into barns, and your Heavenly Father feeds them. Are you not much more valuable than they?"

"Mathew 6:26," Etienne said, recognizing the passage.

"It is one of my favorites. It always reminds me that God will provide whatever we need. It is so easy to forget this, especially with the perceived difficulties of life." Xavier took a drink, then continued, "If we are hungry, he provides food. If we are lonely, he provides love." Xavier motioned to Isabella with his head. "I couldn't help but notice the way you two look at each other. I thought you were married when you arrived."

Etienne straightened up at this remark. "There is great love between us, but I am afraid it can never be. We both have our oaths and obligations to uphold." Etienne felt his face harden and his cheeks fall from the smile he had moments before. "Just as yourself, I have taken the oath of poverty, chastity, and obedience."

"My son, it sounds like there is something you want to confess. I don't think here is the time or place." Xavier looked at Isabella, who was laughing at one of Andy's jokes. "I will take your confession, if you feel so compelled."

"I would like that very much."

"Meet me in the chapel following our meal."

After dinner, Etienne took a deep breath and pulled back the red cloth that veiled the entrance of the confessional. Etienne had committed many sins since the Arc of San Anton, all of which hung heavy on his heart. He knelt inside and Brother Xavier opened the small wooden panel between them. Through the grill, Etienne said, "Forgive me, Father, for I have sinned. It has been about a month since my last confession. I accuse myself of the following sins: I took three lives in the defense of a pilgrim at the Arc of San Anton. I have had lustful thoughts about Isabella and kissed her, breaking my oath of chastity. This sin resulted in the death of a dear friend, the mortal wounding of an enemy, and great sickness for myself and another in our company. I should have been more vigilant in the observance of my oath. Beyond that, Isabella is bound to marry another. I also let a great secret escape that now puts our company in peril."

Xavier sat patiently and listened to him. When Etienne had finished, he said, "Which order did you take an oath with?"

"I took the oath of the Knights Templar," Etienne said, straightening his posture.

"Ah, I see," said Xavier, "It seems that you have kept your oath in protecting pilgrims, which is one of the sworn duties of a Templar. There are times when God needs soldiers on earth to protect his flock from the wolves in life. Tell me, how did you come to be a Templar?"

Etienne told his story, and the whole history with Isabella, to Xavier. When he had finished, Xavier said, "Did you take the oath of your own free will?"

Shock coursed through him at the question. He had never thought of the circumstances of his oath. After a moment's pause, Etienne shook his head. "No. The Templars saved my life, and took me to the Arc. I didn't think I had a choice. I just went with them, not knowing what to do. I had to leave France and was used to taking orders. I never once considered that there was another option."

"My son, it sounds like you need to examine this. Does an oath count if it was not made of your own free will? When I entered the Benedictine order, my heart was ready and desired nothing beyond the life of service to God. I made that oath with every fiber of my being, through my own free will. God wants us to come to him willingly. He doesn't want us to be forced into his service. Perhaps you need to find where your heart truly lies."

Etienne sat in silence, allowing the weight of his words to sink in. "You're right, I didn't exactly make my oath willingly. I thought it was my only option," he said.

"Your friend did not die because of you, my son," Xavier said compassionately. "As for your sin of lust, is it lust or love that compels you? It is true she is betrothed, but is it of her own free will? At that table I saw a young man and woman in love—not a princess being unfaithful, and a Templar breaking his vows. Love is the language of God, not guilt and shame."

Etienne sat, unsure of what to say. He was reevaluating his oath to the Templars, something he thought he would never do.

"Is there anything else, my son?"

Regaining his composure, Etienne shook his head. "For these and all the sins of my past life, I ask pardon of God, penance, and absolution from you, Father."

Xavier answered, "For this and all your sins, say five 'Our Fathers' for your penance and sin no more. Remember to move the way your heart makes you move, not the way fear and shame make you move." Xavier closed the small door that covered the grate, finishing the confession.

Etienne left the confessional and knelt at a pew. "Our Father who art in heaven..."

After Etienne finished his prayers, he looked at the crucifix and felt a great weight had lifted from his shoulders. He bowed low to the altar and exited. The cold mountain air on his exposed skin sent a chill through his spine, but he still held the inner warmth of the chapel at his core. He gazed up at the stars above. The Milky Way looked like a giant river of white dots streaking through a cobalt sky. He thought of the saying, *For every pilgrim who walks the Camino de Santiago, there is a star in the Milky Way* and wondered which stars were theirs.

Etienne entered the sleeping chamber and closed the door quietly. He walked to his bed, next to Isabella's. She was sleeping peacefully with a smile on her face. As he sat on his bed, Isabella opened one eye and smiled at him. Instead of being conflicted about his feelings for her, all he felt was love. Etienne leaned forward and kissed her forehead. "Isabella, I love you."

She looked at him tenderly. Her hand reached out to his face and brought his lips to hers. The heat and passion from their kiss tore into the cold of night, destroying it utterly. "Etienne, I have always loved you."

Isabella moved her hand from his face down his strong arms. Etienne's muscles flexed as her hand passed over them. Isabella pulled him in tight for an embrace and whispered, "My love." The words melted Etienne. He felt whole, and like the only place he ever belonged was in her arms. He pulled her even closer.

"Do you remember when we were young and we would dream about running away to foreign lands together." Etienne smiled. Of course, he remembered, it was one of his favorite memories from childhood. "Let's do it. Let's leave all of this behind and just be Isabella and Etienne, not a princess and a Templar. Let's finally be ourselves for once in our lives. Come with me. I have an idea," Isabella whispered, taking his hand and leading him to the door.

Etienne wasn't sure if he was dreaming or not. She had just said everything that was in his heart.

CHAPTER 20

CRUZ DE FERRO

Watching the clouds change, Isabella felt like she was a whole new person. She and Etienne kept exchanging glances. They had a secret none of the others knew. Xavior had been the only one present at their vows. For the first time in her life she had done something for herself—something she truly wanted. The way Etienne had looked in the moonlight the previous night would forever be in her mind. She loved him even more than she had before. She didn't think such a thing was possible.

Isabella thought of how furious her father would be, but she didn't care. She would probably never see him again. She and Etienne would walk on the Camino with the others to Santiago, and then disappear together, forever. Her father would have to send someone else to find the treasure, and she most certainly would never marry Edward. Etienne shot her his half smile, and Isabella felt her knees become weak.

"I couldna help bu' notice that you're walkin' a little pained," Clair said to Isabella.

Isabella looked at her, trying to hold back a smile. "It's nothing."

Clair pointed at her. "Donna try an' lie ta me."

Heat blossomed across her cheeks as she again thought about her night with Etienne.

Clair put her hand to her mouth and took a deep breath in. "Auhhh, ya did?"

Isabella nodded her head, unable to contain the huge smile from spreading across her face. "We became man and wife last night. We said our vows before God, then we—"

Clair gasped and put her hands on her hips. Before she could speak Andy shouted from ahead, "This must be Cruz de Ferro!"

"Xavier said that pilgrims often leave a small token or stone from their homelands here in place of a troubling thought they want to leave behind on the Camino," Etienne said once she and Clair had caught up to them.

"That's a bit like what the Alchemist told Mariano," Isabella said.

"What did I say?" Mariano asked, he seemed a little off. It looked as if he had just woken up with a large hangover, even though he hadn't had a drink last night.

"You said, the Alchemist told you we had to let go of our stressful thoughts and live in the present moment," Etienne said.

Mariano looked really confused. "I did? I feel as if I have been dreaming the past few days. It is all hazy now." Mariano placed his hand on his head.

Gerhart laughed and put a large hand on Mariano's back. "The spell of the witch's kiss is wearing off. Welcome back, my friend."

They turned the corner, and there was a large cross in the middle of the road raised on a hill of small rocks. Andy pointed to the pile. "I suppose each of these wee rocks is a thought some pilgrim wanted to leave behind."

They climbed the little hill of stones and stopped at the foot of the cross. "I donna have anything from home ta leave behind," Andy said.

"I don't think any of us do. But I do have this." Isabella reached into her sporran and pulled out her small stone the nun had given to her. "I feel like it has been a lifetime since we were at Carrion de los Condes."

"Ach, good idea, lassie." Andy and the others pulled out their stones.

"Sister Fransie said these stones would be a light in dark times. Let's leave them here to be a light for other pilgrims who struggle to leave something behind."

Isabella turned to the cross, thinking on which burden she would have Jesus bear for her. She squeezed her stone tightly, squeezing into it all the guilt she felt for the lives lost at her expense, especially Jessica and those who had accompanied her from France; and what about Tristan? Isabella didn't know if he was dead or alive. She thought of those wounded or dead at Hospital. She squeezed all of that pain, all of that suffering, all of that guilt, into the rock. It was too much for her to take. Tears streaming down her face, she threw the rock into the pile. It was as if a dam had been released. She couldn't stop the flood of tears. Clair put an arm around her, and together, they left the heaviness of their burdens behind them. They made their way back to the Camino, gradually feeling lighter with every step.

CHAPTER 21

MOLINASECA

Etienne waited a few moments after the others left and watched the rising sun.

My Lord, thank you for forgiving my sins. I pray that I will leave behind the guilt for the lives I have taken and the guilt of breaking my sworn oath for the love of Isabella. I leave these here at your feet, your humble servant who cannot bear this burden on his own.

He tossed his stone on the pile and a ray of sunshine broke through the tops of the pine trees hitting his face. The sensation was too much for him, and for the first time that he could remember, tears streamed down his cheeks. He sat there and watched the sunrise, weeping with gratitude.

It wasn't long before Etienne caught up with the others. Everyone was walking in silence, each meditating on the thoughts they had left behind. The top of the mountain range was hilly. Just as they reached the peak of one hilltop, another would rise in the distance. Andy had dropped to the back of the group and was walking alongside Etienne. "Ach, these hills are killin' me! I donna know how much more my knees can take with all of this up and down. I preferred the Meseta."

Etienne smiled kindly at him. "It is more difficult, but much more beautiful."

"I donna mind the ups so much, but 'tis the downs that kill me." Andy rubbed his knees.

"Have you tried walking in zig-zags on the way down? It will lessen the pressure on your knees greatly," Etienne said.

On their next descent, Etienne and Andy snaked down the hill, going back and forth diagonally. When they reached the bottom, Andy had a big smile on his face. "Ach, 'tis much better. Thank you, laddie. So, what do ya think it means?"

"What?"

"The code." Andy over exaggeratedly waved his hands in the air.

"It is not for us to know. We should forget about all we have seen and heard." When we reach Ponferrada, we will inform the Grand Master of what we have discovered. He will deal with us accordingly. He is a fair man. If it is death for us, at least it will be quick and just." Etienne dragged a finger across his neck like a knife. Etienne, was planning on forgetting everything about the Templars. He hadn't told the others yet, that they wouldn't be stopping at Ponferrada. Isabella and he wanted to surprise them when the time was right. Plus, it was fun to play a joke on Andy for once.

Andy stopped dead in his tracks. "Ya donna think…" Etienne couldn't contain himself any longer and laughed.

"Ha, Ha, very funny! On another note, I coudna help but notice that you and Isabella 'ave been actin different today. Ya keep holding hands and lookin' at each other. Did somthin' 'appen last night?"

Etienne stopped suddenly. "Did you hear that?" he said in a hushed voice. Andy was about to speak, but Etienne put his hand over his mouth. He knew Andy heard it when his eyes widened. The sound of hooves coming down upon them. Quickly they ran to the others and ushered them off the road into a large grove of trees, where they waited patiently with bated breath, covering up as best they could. The thundering hooves got closer and closer until finally they were upon them. Etienne peered out from behind the trees to see twenty Hospitaller knights dressed for war, riding at full speed. It took only a few seconds for the cavalry to pass, but the dust they kicked up lasted long after their departure.

After five minutes, Etienne was the first to come out of hiding, and Andy was soon to follow. "Ach, what do ya think those miserable bastards were in such a hurry to catch?"

"Us," Mariano said, emerging from the trees. "To them, it would have looked like I killed a host of their soldiers in the woods, then two more just outside of Astorga."

"Ach, but that one was a thief, and the Shadows killed the others." Andy crossed his arms.

"I know, but to them I'm a murderer, and I'm sure they will also be after the secret that was in that bag. I saw the look on Vincenzo's face when he held the bag. He had the same look all men get when they have just received treasure or great power—both of which, men won't give up easily."

"But, everyone in the albergue saw me burn the contents," Etienne said, scanning the Camino ahead and behind, wondering how many more the Hospitaller

Master, Francisco, might have sent for them. "I think we should stay off the road until we get to Ponferrada."

Later that afternoon, Etienne sat as he reached the summit of another hill. One by one, as the others joined him, they took a seat. Andy was the last to join. As he reached them, he was gasping and holding his chest.

"This is one of the most beautiful things I have seen," Isabella said, lost in the sweeping landscape in front of them. Below lay a city nestled in a valley, on a river, with high mountain walls coming up on all sides. It looked like something out of a fairy tale. Something so beautiful that it could only exist in an imaginary world. Etienne took in the scenery with a critical eye.

"Aye, 'tis Molinaseca," Andy said.

"It is beautiful, but the descent will be treacherous, and we won't have much cover. We will have to do it as quickly as possible, so as not to be noticed," Etienne said, bringing everyone back to the reality of the situation.

As he led the group down the sharp mountain face, they found some cover behind boulders and shrubs. Etienne wanted them to be invisible, he wanted to protect his wife. He looked at Isabella lovingly. He felt like the luckiest man in the world. All they had to do was pass Ponferrada undetected and they would be free. They were so close to their goal.

They skirted two small villages on their way down, staying hidden from the inhabitants. They trekked through the woods, as much as they could, until they reached the outskirts of Molinaseca. There were small houses and a church that lay outside the city on the opposite side of the river.

The band of pilgrims came out of the woods and hid behind a big boulder above the Camino. "So how do ya suppose we cross tha' river without being seen?" Andy asked pointing to the bridge which had several Hospitallers blocking it.

"Katsuji!" Isabella exclaimed. All of them looked at her in surprise. "It's Katsuji's caravan." She pointed at four covered wagons coming to the last bend in the road before the bridge.

Etienne watched in horror as Isabella broke their cover and ran down to the road. He shouted her name, but it did no good. Etienne knew that when Isabella set her mind to do something, she would follow through. The only thing he could do was chase after her.

The first wagon stopped and then all the others. A second later, Katsuji jumped off the coach and greeted Isabella.

Etienne was the first to reach them. Katsuji extended his hand and the two of them shook.

"Isabella told me of your troubles. We had our own run-in with some bandits. We sustained some losses but were able to fend them off," Katsuji said, looking at Gerhart and Mariano. "We could have used you in that battle, but now knowing what I do know, I can understand why you had to leave so quickly. She is a much greater treasure than anything we carry." Katsuji bowed once more to Isabella. "If the Hospitallers are searching for you, we need to get you off the road as quickly as possible." With that, Isabella, Etienne, Gerhart, Mariano, Andy, and Clair all got into the first coach, and Katsuji covered them with his many fabrics.

Etienne was happy the Camino had provided for them once again. However, he was now questioning their decision to pass the safety of the Templar Castle in Ponferrada. Etienne knew going there meant he wouldn't be free to make his own choices. But to protect his wife and friends, he was willing to make that decision if it came down to it.

Isabella was hot and uncomfortable underneath the fabrics, but it was a small price to pay for safe passage. The coach carried on down the dusty road to the only bridge crossing the river. There, blocking the passage, were four Hospitallers clad for war on horseback. The coach came to a stop and Katsuji jumped down.

Isabella covered her head under some garments and listened to the muffled voices. "Allo, allo," Katsuji said, his voice dripping with charm. "Can I interest you gentlemen in any garments? We have the most unique fabrics from the far east." After a small pause, he said, "Perhaps something for the missus."

"We are sworn to chastity, poverty, and obedience. There is nothing you can offer us," one of the Hospitallers said with displeasure.

"Well, if I can't offer you anything, how may I be of service?" Katsuji asked, in high spirits.

"We are searching for a band of six pilgrims. Two women and four men. There is a Scottish brother and sister. A beautiful young woman. A young Templar." The guard spat at this. "A giant of a man, and possibly a Spaniard. The Scottish man is a thief and has stolen from us. The Spanish man is an assassin and has taken the lives of several of our order. He is friends with the giant."

There was another pause before Katsuji said, "I have seen them."

His words made Isabella's heart race with worry. *Is he about to betray us?* She took a deep breath and reached for her dagger.

"I hired the Spaniard and the giant over two weeks ago to protect our caravan. They were paid and then left us in the middle of the night." He paused, and continued, "I haven't seen them since. If you find them, I would like my gold returned for the services they didn't render."

"Those sound like the same ones," the Hospitaller said. "Do you mind if we search your wagons?"

"By all means," said Katsuji.

Isabella felt a bead of sweat run down her face as she heard the Hospitallers ride to the back of the wagon. The fabrics covering Isabella began to shift.

At that moment, Katsuji yelled, "Snake!" and hit the horse on the butt, causing the wagon to take off like a shot.

"Where?" A Hospitaller asked over the sound of the rumbling wagon.

"The horses must have trampled it. There are its remains in the water. Now, having taken the vow of poverty, how do you intend to pay for any goods that are damaged?" Isabella heard Katsuji say in the distance.

CHAPTER 22

PONFERRADA

Etienne was jostled around in the coach along with the others as it bucked wildly. He hurriedly climbed out to the front of the coach, but the reins had fallen down between the horses. Without thought, he made a dive for them, belatedly realizing his mistake. He'd stretched too far and lost his balance. He grasped for the reins, as he was about to go under the coach.

Instead of fear, Etienne felt his own stupidity. He'd survived a royal execution, Immortal Shadows, a poisoned dagger, the Moors, but a wagon was about to kill him. He could've laughed at the irony. He felt himself slipping and closed his eyes, saying a silent prayer, when two massive hands grabbed his ankles, keeping him from going under. Etienne strained his back and lifted himself up. He reached with all the length he could muster and took hold of the reins. Gerhart hoisted him up, and Etienne steadied the coach, calming the beasts.

The wild ride had taken them through the city and back onto the Camino. They were now approaching Ponferrada and the Templar castle quickly. Etienne knew he had to make a decision fast as the castle came into view. They would either have to take their chances with the Hospitallers or seek safety with the Templars. He looked at Isabella and the others. *She's not going to like this.* He would have to change their secret plan. They had to stop at the Templar castle for help and protection, it was too risky to travel forward with the Hospitallers on the hunt. He and Isabella could make their disappearance when the Camino was safe once more.

The Templar castle was unlike anything Etienne had seen on the Camino. He felt as if a dragon could climb out from behind the majestic gray stone fortress at any time. Mariano slowed the coach as they climbed the ramp leading to the drawbridge. At the top of the old wooden bridge was a large door symmetrically framed by turrets.

"State your business," a loud booming voice called out.

Etienne placed his hands to his mouth to amplify the sound. "Sanctuary! And we seek an audience with Jacques de Molay."

After what felt like an eternity, the doors on the other end of the bridge opened to a small courtyard. The wagon entered and a delegation of Templars stepped forward. Etienne had never been so happy to see members of his order. He had always been on the other side, always the one granting sanctuary and safety. Now he knew the gratitude the pilgrims felt toward him and his brothers every time they came to their rescue.

"Hold," ordered a Templar with a strong jaw. The wagon came to a stop and all the pilgrims dismounted.

"The Grand Master is detained with other business and will be here momentarily."

A Templar in his sixties entered the courtyard, and all the knights in the yard stood at attention. He had the air of authority and looked as if he possessed great wisdom—the kind of wisdom that can only be earned through experience. Etienne sensed the loyalty and respect these men had for him. They would die for him and follow him into any battle. Etienne felt the same loyalty, even though he had never met the man. His mere presence evoked trust and fidelity. With all his grandeur, there was no doubt in Etienne's mind: this *must* be the legendary Jacques de Molay.

"Ha! These are the very ones we are searching for!" a broad shouldered Hospitaller exclaimed from behind the Grand Master. "Looks like we won't be needing your services." The Hospitaller signaled for his companions to follow, and they quickly made a move to restrain Etienne and the others. Etienne drew his sword, Gerhart raised his large axe, Isabella drew her dagger, Clair grabbed her staff, and Mariano readied his knives. They would not be taken. The Templars in the courtyard also drew arms.

"Hold!" Molay said in a commanding voice, raising his hand. All followed his order without hesitation. The Hospitallers stopped, the Templars sheathed their swords, Etienne and his companions lowered their weapons.

"These men and women are murderers and thieves," said the commanding Hospitaller.

"Diego, steady yourself," Molay said. Turning back to their wagon, Molay asked, "What do you have to say for yourselves?"

Etienne was about to speak, but Isabella put a hand on his arm and stepped forward. Etienne noticed Molay's eyes rest on her hand. "I am Princess Isabella of France, daughter of King Philip the IV. These people are my guardians and companions. We are not thieves, nor murderers." She motioned to Etienne. "This is Etienne LaRue, a Templar and guardian to all pilgrims. These siblings are Andy and Clair. They are our guides and companions, fellow pilgrims on the road to Santiago. And this is Mariano and Gerhart. They are two of the finest warriors in the land, whom I have engaged to help protect our party. I can vouch for all of them." Etienne had hoped Isabella would understand why he had brought them here.

"Ha, Princess. I saw you in our halls tending to the sick, especially this one." The Hospitaller that Molay had called Diego pointed to Etienne. He then pointed to Andy. "The fat one was stealing much-needed herbs." He then motioned to Mariano. "And the Spaniard helped to kill an entire company of our men, and later murdered our Brother Vincenzo."

"We can vouch for that," said another Hospitaller. Etienne recognized him as one of Vincenzo's companions.

"Ach, he was the thief," Andy said, unable to control his temper. "Vincenzo stole our belongings. They stole something of great value, both to us and to you." He looked directly at Molay. "Mariano caught that thief." Etienne wanted to put his hand over Andy's mouth. He wanted to speak to Molay alone before he found out what both of them knew about the treasure.

"I did kill Vincenzo," Mariano said.

"What more do you need than that?" Diego spat.

Mariano shook his head. "I noticed that he had Etienne's bag. I asked him to return it and he drew the sword. I was forced to defend myself."

"This man can't be trusted. He led a company of our men to their deaths. Straight into a trap set by the Moors," Diego all but yelled.

"It was not I who killed them. It was a Shadow," Mariano said sternly. "It is by the grace of God that I am alive." Etienne couldn't believe all what his companions were giving away. At this rate they would all be killed by the Templars, not the Hospitallers.

"It is true that we had to use some herbs from the herb garden," Isabella said. "Once the Hospitallers found out that Etienne was a Templar, they refused to treat him. I had to take full responsibility for his care. They said they needed the bed space and medicine for their own. We were forced to do what we had to."

Molay regarded them silently for a moment, his gaze going from one to the other. Etienne had the feeling he was weighing their words in his mind. "Etienne, advance and give me the grip and password of a Templar," Molay commanded. Etienne sheathed his sword and walked up the ramp from the courtyard to Molay. Their hands met and they exchanged the ancient grip, as Etienne whispered the password in his ear. Etienne didn't feel worthy to be doing this. The night before he had forsaken his oath as a Templar. He was going to abandon them and all that he had been entrusted with. But, he must play the part to get Isabella to safety.

The Grand Master nodded. "There is truth in their story," Molay said in a manner that immediately ended the discussion. "Bishop Gonzalo Osorio of Leon said they would be coming. I have been waiting several days for you. This is why I have delayed my trip to Cyprus. I was expecting to see Brother Ronan with you."

Etienne's being filled with sorrow. He bowed his head, unable to keep the sadness from his face. "Ronan fell in his duty as a Templar. He died protecting myself and the good people you see before you."

"A finer Templar there has never been," Molay said. His tone of voice reflected the pain Etienne was feeling inside. "We had fought side by side many times when we were younger men." Etienne thought of Ronan dying in front of him. He wished he could have saved him.

Molay turned to Diego. "I offer these pilgrims sanctuary and see no fault in them. You are to leave these lands immediately and pursue them no more. Before you go, take whatever herbs you need from our stores to repay the debt owed to you, and let us part as brothers, not foes."

Diego straightened, outrage plain on his face. "The order of the Hospitallers will not be satisfied until the Spaniard and the fat pilgrim are handed over."

"Then you will have to leave unsatisfied and leave knowing these travelers are under the protection of the Templars. No harm shall befall them."

Diego began to speak, but Molay cut him off. "I will hear no more. The matter is settled."

The Hospitaller turned to Mariano and Andy with a glare. "Your protection can only reach so far and for so long. Perhaps you have less time than you think." He motioned for his companions to follow and they rode out of the courtyard.

Molay motioned to a few of the Templars nearby. "Follow them and make sure they leave the borders of our lands doing no harm to our inhabitants." The knights nodded, and in a manner of minutes, they were on the road.

"Thank you," Isabella said.

Before Molay could respond, Etienne heard the sound of coaches approaching. All turned and looked out past the drawbridge to see Katsuji and his caravan. The remaining wagons had been badly damaged.

"Oh no!" Isabella exclaimed as she and the others quickly rushed out to aid their friends. Katsuji was wounded, and many of the fabrics were torn to shreds.

Katsuji managed a smile as they approached. "I guess they didn't want to pay."

"I am so sorry," Isabella said. "This is all our fault. Thank you so much for helping us out there."

Katsuji looked at her sternly. "You would have done the same for me."

"'Tis true." Andy put a hand on Katsuji's shoulder. "'Tis true."

"Get these pilgrims to the infirmary immediately," ordered Molay. "And take their wagons into the safety of our walls." With these words, it was done. "Take Princess Isabella and her companions to our guest chambers," Molay said to the Templar on his right. "Etienne, walk with me, we have much to discuss."

Etienne obeyed. He felt the freedom he had experienced the day before disappearing quickly. He also felt a nervous energy in his body. He didn't know what he was going to say to the man he had idolized for the past two years.

He and Molay turned and walked up the ramp. It led under the fortified wall and into the main courtyard of the Templar castle. The open courtyard showed the expanse of the property. There was a fortified wall with turrets surrounding the whole perimeter. At the far end was a giant stone castle and immediately to their right was a two-story palace that served as the living quarters for the knights.

Molay ascended the stone stairs that led to the wall and walked toward the old castle. Over the edge of the wall was a hundred-foot drop to the river below. Upstream beyond the castle lay two bridges, and behind, mountains towered in the distance. On the opposite side of the grounds, the towers of the cathedral were barely visible above the outer walls of the compound.

"I like to come up here to think," Molay said, stroking his long silver beard. Etienne needed to think as well. Would he tell Molay everything Ronan had entrusted him with? If he did, he probably would be forced to remain a Templar. Also, what about Andy? Etienne felt closer to Andy than any Templar, except Ronan. He couldn't let Molay kill him.

Molay placed his hands on the wall and surveyed the land that stretched in front of them. "We took a vow to protect these people, to protect these lands, and all of those who travel upon them. We are the shepherds of God that tend to his flock, making sure the wolves do not devour them. I saw many things in the Holy Land. But there... there you always knew who your enemy was.

"Here in these lands, it is much harder to tell who your enemies are. They are your friends. They pray to the same God as you. However, they are often wolves in sheep's clothing, or even worse, wolves in shepherd's clothing." Molay turned his sage eyes to Etienne. "Tell me, why were these wolves in shepherd's clothing hunting you?"

Knowing he had betrayed his vow to Ronan and to the order, Etienne took a deep breath. "The secret of the green men." Molay's eyes widened slightly in surprise.

Etienne wanted to honor Ronan's last wish—he had to protect the treasure. Molay needed to know all that had passed. "Ronan taught me how to locate the codes hidden in the cathedrals, but not how to decode them. At the Cathedral of Leon, we had made charcoal drawings of the green men, and I had placed them in my bag. As we were traveling, we were betrayed, and attacked by the Moors. Ronan was taken by a traitor and I was poisoned. I would have died if it weren't for my companions. When I was ill, my Scottish friend discovered the papers and… well, he figured out the secret of the green men. Upon leaving the Hospitaller stronghold, they discovered the papers as well. That is what they tried to steal from us in Astorga. I immediately destroyed the papers in the fire once they were returned to us."

Molay had been quiet as Etienne spoke. He nodded slowly, regarding Etienne thoughtfully. "Ronan must have trusted you immensely to share this secret with you. Why did he have such great faith in you?" Etienne felt like Ronan's trust was misplaced. Just this morning, he had almost completely abandoned the Templars for a life with Isabella.

Etienne took another deep breath. "Because Santiago appeared to me and said there was great need for me on the Camino. Also, because of the reappearance of the Shadows. He said our fate was intertwined with them and that one of our companions had unbound a door."

Molay slammed his fist onto the stone wall. "He should have never told you about the existence of the doors."

"I also think he chose me because I am a nobody, just a sergeant. Ronan thought there was a traitor in the Templars."

"He has believed that for years, but I have found nothing wrong with the line of succession. My knights are all worthy men. That was not his decision to make." Molay stroked his beard again. After a long pause he continued, "Although, there is no way the Hospitallers would have known what those drawings were unless they knew about the code in the Cathedral of Leon. Perhaps he was right."

Feeling like he must confess everything, Etienne broke the silence. "We also found the secret in the cathedral of Astorga…" Etienne stopped before telling him about receiving the treasure from Charity. Ronan said there was a traitor. *Could it be Molay?*

Molay stopped stroking his beard and looked at Etienne sternly. "No Templar, except the Grand Master and his Seneschal, is to know more than one secret that leads to… How may I know you to be speaking the truth?"

Etienne cleared his throat. "It was written in code, below the Virgin. We didn't copy the code, nor try to solve it."

"Forget what you have seen and never speak of this again," Molay ordered.

"I swear it by my life. I will never utter the secret again," Etienne said. "I think the Hospitallers know that Andy possesses the secret too. He has taken a blood oath with me on the penalty of death not to give the secret to anyone... Yet he is not a Templar. I couldn't bring myself to kill him. He has been a true brother and comrade to me. I told him we would let you decide our fate."

"This is grave news. If what you say is true, it is a small thing to sacrifice your whole flock to keep the world safe. If the secret that this road holds should fall into the wrong hands... God help us all." Molay stroked his beard again.

After a moment of contemplation, he continued, "As for your friend. Perhaps it is God's will that you both know. The Camino provides what you need. Perhaps there will be a need for both of you to have this information. You will take Ronan's place as protector of the secret of Leon. As for Andy, he will have a choice. He can either become a Templar by binding himself to this order and protecting its secrets, or die. His fate is in his hands."

CHAPTER 23

TEMPLAR CASTLE

Etienne had barely seen Isabella and the others since they arrived at the castle. It felt strange for him to be back amongst the Templars. He felt out of place here—like he didn't belong. In the small cell he had in the Templars' quarters, his only company was the crucifix that hung over the bed. Etienne had always chosen solitude in life, but now it was different. He longed to be with his comrades. He longed to be with Isabella.

Knock, knock, knock. Etienne rose from his bed and opened the door.

"Hello, brother, it is time for the evening meal," said a short, slender Templar that had a spark in his eyes and a more youthful energy than men half his age. "If you would follow me to the refectory," the Templar said, motioning for him to follow. "My name is Brother Andre. I am the Guest Master; welcome to Ponferrada. I hope your Camino has been a good one," he said with a slight smile and a hop to his step.

"Thank you, brother," Etienne said as they walked down the long hallway leading to the refectory. "Will the pilgrims I traveled with be joining us for dinner?"

"Yes, yes. They will be there," Brother Andre shook his head vigorously and clasped his hands behind his back. "You have traveled many miles together and have become very fond of them, haven't you? The Camino has a way of doing that. People become dear to you, almost like family."

"Yes, it is so."

"Don't become too attached; all things pass. Life is like a running river. People come and go, like a leaf on the current, yet you stay the same, unchanged always the river."

Etienne thought about this for a moment. "True brother, but there are some people that shape the course of the river of your life. They are like the rocks that plant themselves, diverting the flow of the water."

"Hmm," said Andre, closing the door behind them. "But with time, these stones will become pebbles and will float downstream. So it is with life."

They passed through another large door and Etienne sensed the sounds and smells coming from the refectory. He didn't know why, but he didn't have an appetite. He was more excited to see his traveling companions than to eat.

Etienne smiled broadly when he saw Isabella and the others sitting at the outermost table. The room was set up with one large table stretching the length of the long space and the others meeting it perpendicularly, like the letter "E." Etienne broke away from Brother Andre and moved toward his friends.

"Hmm, hmm." Etienne stopped and turned to face Andre. "That table is for visiting pilgrims only." Etienne's smile disappeared. "This way." Brother Andre motioned to the head table. Etienne followed him obediently and was seated next to Molay.

"I hope you found your accommodations comfortable," Molay said.

"They were more than adequate," Etienne responded, his gaze returning to his friends.

"You will have time to speak with the pilgrims after the meal. I want you to deliver a message to Andy. But, in the meantime, join me, brother." Etienne leaned back in his chair, but he couldn't relax. "That will be all, Brother Andre. You may continue with your duties." Brother Andre left them and moved to a pulpit at the edge of the head table.

Etienne glanced over at the pilgrims table and Isabella smiled at him. He returned the smile discreetly. She was his wife. He still couldn't get over that. But how would they deal with this situation? Everything that seemed so clear that morning was now murky.

A loud bang quieted the room, and all eyes turned to Brother Andre. He stood at the podium with an open book in front of him. He cleared his throat. "Proverbs 21:21. He who pursues righteousness and loyalty finds life, righteousness, and honor. One who is wise can go up against the city of the mighty and pull down the stronghold in which they trust. Those who guard their mouths and their tongues keep themselves from calamity…"

The words seemed almost like a warning. Etienne looked at Isabella and his faithful companions, wondering how best he could serve them now. Should they all run away in the night, or should he fulfill his obligation and have them continue on?

When the meal had finished, Brother Andre stopped reading and all the Knights Templar rose. Etienne stood and Molay grabbed his arm. "Remember where your loyalties lie. One thing I have come to know in this life is that people are not always what they seem." Molay directed his gaze at Isabella. "There are things at play in this world much larger than you or I. Now, shall we find out if Andy truly wants to become your brother." Molay released his grip, and Etienne walked to his friends. Ronan had told Etienne that one of his companions had unbound the door releasing the Shadows. He assumed it was Tristan, but what if it wasn't.

Everyone smiled as he approached. Andy was the first to speak. "Why were ya sitting with that lot?" he asked with a huff.

Etienne placed a reassuring hand on Andy's shoulder. "Here, I am not a pilgrim, but a Templar, and I must obey the commands of my order."

"Ach, sounds like you have a stick up your arse," Andy said and they all laughed. It was nice to cut through the tension and awkwardness of the situation. He felt the distance from those he had been so close to.

Isabella reached for him. "It is nice to have you back." Her face reddened as her hand made contact. Etienne let her hand linger awhile, soaking in the warmth of her touch and the tenderness behind it.

Regaining his senses, he pulled away. "I can't, not here," he said in a lowered voice.

"What has gotten into you? Etienne, why did you bring us here? Why didn't we just continue?" Isabella's eyes betrayed her hurt. He felt her pain like it was his own. All he wanted to do was take her into his arms and kiss her—to let her know that he was still with her and still loved her—but his duty restrained him.

He raised all of the emotional walls that he had used for so many years to shield himself from the torments of the world, cutting off his own feelings in order to do what had to be done. With a blank face, he stood up straight. "I need to speak to Andy alone."

Isabella slammed her cup on the table and turned. Clair put her arm around her and gave Etienne a look that said it all, but he forced himself to keep his emotional facade in place as they walked out of the refractory. Gerhart and Mariano were soon to follow.

"I have informed the Grand Master of the knowledge you have," Etienne said reservedly once he and Andy were alone.

"Ach, quit with the formalities. 'Tis just you and me here now."

Etienne softened a bit. "He has given you a choice. Either join the Knights Templar and become a keeper of these secrets, or face death."

He looked at his friend gravely. If Andy chose death, Etienne wasn't sure what he would do. He couldn't let his friend die.

Andy burst out laughing, surprising Etienne out of his thoughts. When he composed himself, he said, "Ya mean, all I had ta do ta become a Templar was ta figur' oot one of yer secrets." He laughed more. "I 'ave always wanted to become a Templar, but didnna think I could, due to my constitution and dislike for fighting." he said, patting his large belly. "'Tis great news, laddie. Great news indeed."

Etienne exhaled. "Now I can truly call you my brother." Etienne wrapped his arm around Andy. "I will inform the Grand Master, and we will perform the ceremony tonight."

"What shudd-ah wear?" Andy winked.

Isabella went straight to the sleeping quarters after dinner. She couldn't hold in her emotions. Try as hard as she could to restrain them, the tears just kept coming. *How could have I been so stupid?*

She slammed the door and lay in her bed face down. She took her pillow and screamed hard into it. Her body went limp and she lay there.

A warm hand touched her back. "Do ya mind if I sit?"

Isabella didn't move; Clair sat next to Isabella and stroked her hair. "'Tis allrigh', child."

Isabella faced Clair. "No, it's not alright. I should have never married Etienne. I have abandoned the future of my kingdom for…I thought it was love. I have only ever loved him." Isabella sniffed loudly and her tears slowed. "I thought Etienne was different, not like all the other suitors."

"I've seen love before and 'e looks at ya like a man desperate in love. 'Ere, though, 'e is bound ta his duty. 'E canno' be 'imself." Clair patted Isabella on the back. "But, sometimes love is na enough. Ye both 'ave yer duties. 'E is a Templar, an you—you are due ta be wed ta another man. Neither of ya can get outta yer duty." Clair looked at Isabella kindly. "Wha' did ya expect to 'appen when the Camino ended?" Isabella knew exactly what she wanted to happen. She wanted to run away with Etienne. She wanted to have a life with him and raise a family. This thought burned the coals of anger even hotter.

"I don't know." Isabella hit the bed with both hands. "I just thought we could disappear on the Camino and have a normal life. We would be free, and not be bound to duty. Although, I would have regretted every single day had we not been wed."

"Well, now ya can live withou' regret for tha'. Wha' a gift ta be able to live so free."

"I guess when you put it like that it was a gift. I just expected our marriage to last longer. I can't even imagine kissing Prince Edward, let alone…" Isabella buried her face in the pillow. After a moment, she raised again and said, "I do have a duty to my father and my country. I need to put that above my selfish wants and desires."

Isabella thought of her quest again of how she had failed her father. With the distraction of Etienne gone Isabella resolved to make her father proud. She would bring him back as much information as possible about the treasure. She thought back to the Cathedral of Astorga; she knew Etienne and Andy had found something there. Andy was clenching something in his hand that whole day. Perhaps Isabella could bring her father more than just information.

Clair stroked Isabella's hair again. "I think ya can be selfish until the end o' the road. Etienne will-a be back to 'imself when we leave this place."

Isabella gave Clair a warm embrace. "Thank you. Thank you so much," she said. "I don't know how I would have been able to survive this road without you."

Night fell across the land, and Andy had a knot of excitement, fear, and anticipation in his stomach. He sat on the edge of his bed looking at the door expectantly. He had been in this position for a few hours. Any other night his body would have already been fast asleep, but he didn't notice a hint of tiredness. He heard the echo of footsteps coming down the hall, then the light of a torch filled all the cracks in the old door. The handle turned and opened to show a dark figure holding a torch.

Andy's eyes adjusted to the light. "Etienne, ach, thank God 'Tis you, laddie. I was near-abou' ta piss mysel'," Andy said, jumping down from the bed.

Etienne handed him a blindfold. "You will need to put this on and come with me." Andy put on the blindfold and the entire world became darkness.

"How am I suppose ta know where ta go?"

Etienne hooked his arm. "Take hold and have no fear."

They walked for about fifteen minutes traveling up and down, turning left and right. Descending a large set of stairs, the air became moist and smelled of earth. He wanted to ask, *Where are we?* but thought it best to keep his mouth closed for once and follow blindly. He had full faith in Etienne.

After a few paces, Andy heard the noises of many bodies in a large chamber shifting and coughing. He and Etienne came to a stop.

"Brother Etienne LaRue brings before you Andrew Sinclair, a hopeful candidate for initiation into our holy order. Are there any objections?" boomed the authoritative voice of Molay. The room fell silent for what seemed like an eternity. Andy breathed in and out. He tried to keep his breath steady to hide his fear.

"There being no objections, lead the candidate to the adjoining room, to await further testing." Etienne moved again and Andy followed suit.

They entered another room through a small doorway. They had to turn sideways to fit through it together. Etienne led Andy to a bench and said, "Sit and await further instruction." The bench was cool and a little moist. Etienne exited the room, and Andy heard the door shut behind him.

Testing. What are these tests? What if they find me unworthy? Ach.

The door swung open and footsteps approached.

"Do you wish to be made a Templar?" Andy recognized the voice of Brother Andre.

"Aye," responded Andy. The footsteps walked away, and the door closed once more.

After a few more moments, the door opened again. Andy heard a deep gruff voice ask, "Do you wish to be made a Templar?"

"Aye, I do." Andy was unsure why they were asking him a second time.

The footsteps walked away, and the door shut.

Another few moments passed and he heard the door open again. "Do you wish to be made a Templar?" Etienne asked.

"Aye, that I do."

"Rise and follow me." Andy rose and took Etienne's arm. Together they walked into the large space once more, which was warmer from the heat of all the bodies. They came to what Andy assumed was the center and stopped.

"Remove his blindfold," Molay said. It took Andy's eyes a few moments to adjust to the torchlight. They were in a place the likes of which he had never seen before. It resembled a cathedral, but it was underground. There were no windows, and the walls were made of stone. The only light came from torches that surrounded the room. Plus, the light from the two small candles on either side of the altar.

Molay sat on the far side of the altar, flanked by two men. He rose and began, "The rules of our order are strict, and you are beginning a life of endurance and not one of ease." At this, Andy tried to look as tough as he could.

Molay continued, "It is a life of self-denial and danger. You will have to watch when perhaps you will be sighing for sleep; to endure fatigue when you greatly desire rest; to be hungry and thirsty when you are longing to eat and to drink." Andy winced a little at this last remark. "And to leave one country for another without a moment's hesitation, if your vow requires it. Do you really wish to be a Templar?"

Andy took a moment to consider all the trials listed. He cleared his throat and said, "Aye, I do."

Molay then asked, "Are you in good health?"

"Fit as a fiddle," Andy replied with a smile. Noticing the silence, he said, "Yes."

"Are you betrothed or married?"

"Ha." Andy grabbed his gut with both hands. "I tried that before but it dinna' work out. No, I am neither."

Smiling a little at the last remark, Molay asked, "Are you in debt and cannot pay?"

"No."

"Do you belong to any other order?"

"No." Andy shook his head as he answered.

"Finding no fault with your answers, and you being in good standing and willing by your own free will to become a Templar, I implore you to take the vow of a Templar. It is a vow of poverty, chastity, and obedience. If you still wish to become a Templar and take this vow, move to the altar, kneel, and place your right hand on the Holy Bible, raising your left in the air."

Andy took a few steps forward to the altar, knelt, and placed his hand on the holiest of holy books. He then raised his other hand high in the air. Finding his position satisfactory, Molay said, "Repeat after me: I swear to defend with my life, my strength, and my speech, the holy doctrines of the Trinity and the Catholic faith."

"I, Andrew Sinclair, swear ta defend with my life, my strength, and my speech, the holy doctrines of the Trinity and the Catholic faith."

Molay continued, "I promise to be obedient and submissive to the Grand Master," Molay shot Etienne a look, then focused back on Andy, "and to travel by sea or by land if need be, to defend my brother Christians against the infidels."

Andy repeated back, the words perfectly.

Molay nodded and continued, "My right hand and sword shall be dedicated to the service of the church against the infidels, and I swear never to shun a combat with any miscreants, if only three in number. I will fight them in single combat and never fly from an enemy."

Andy took a deep breath, knowing he wasn't much of a fighter and repeated the vow.

When Andy finished, Molay continued once more, "Having taken the oath of a Templar, and satisfying all the requirements, I now ask you to rise, not as a common man, but as a brother Templar." As Andy rose, he felt a sense of pride and worthiness that he had never felt before. Reaching his feet, the other knights gave three resounding claps. Andy smiled widely and looked at Etienne, who returned the smile.

Molay moved from behind the altar to Andy with a bundle in his arms. "This is the Tabard and woven belt of the Knights Templar, which are never to be removed." Andy took the garments and put them on. Then Molay placed both hands on Andy's shoulders and kissed his lips. It shocked Andy. He didn't know what to do. Molay's beard tickled his face. Molay then moved to Andy's belly and posterior, kissing both.

Andy was so uncomfortable and nervous, he let out a little giggle.

Molay rose and took Andy's hand, entrusting him with the grip of the Templar. He then whispered in Andy's ear the secret word of the Templars. Andy returned the word with a solemn look on his face. Molay took him by both shoulders. "Welcome, brother, to the Knights Templar." These words finished the ceremony.

Andy stood frozen to the spot. "I canna believe tha' just happened."

"Welcome, brother," Etienne said with a big smile. One by one the other knights congratulated Andy on his initiation. After all the knights had done so, Etienne clasped Andy on the shoulder. "Come." Following his lead once more, they entered an adjoining room where there was food and libations.

Andy smiled at the sight of the feast and said, "I think I'm gonna enjoy being a Templar." With this, they entered and spent the remainder of the evening feasting and strengthening the bonds of brotherhood.

CHAPTER 24

FIRSTS AND LASTS

Andy awoke feeling like a whole new man. One of his life's dreams had now been fulfilled. He couldn't help but smile. *I'm a Templar.* The evening before seemed like such a blur, he worried it was a dream.

Raising his head, he saw the solitary chair in the cell. On it was his very own mantle. He saw the red cross on the black background standing proudly. Since he wasn't a knight before becoming a Templar, he was now a Sergeant, just like Etienne, "Ach, definitely not a dream," he said, as a surge of excitement coursed through his veins again.

He jumped out of bed like a child at Christmas. *What other secrets will I learn?*

He took the mantle and danced around the room. After a few spins, he put it on and looked at his reflection in the window. "Andrew Sinclair, you're a Templar Knight." He seemed like a different man standing in the reflection. He almost didn't recognize himself: he looked proud and noble.

The door creaked open, revealing Etienne. Andy ran to him and wrapped his arms around his torso. "Thank ya, laddie." His eyes moistened.

Etienne smiled at him. "Don't thank me yet. You don't know what you got yourself into. There is a lot to learn."

"It donna matter what I got myself inta. For the first time in my life, I feel like I 'ave a meaning. That I 'ave a purpose. As for learnin', 'tis my specialty." Andy winked.

"Okay, you can let go now," Etienne said, tapping Andy on the shoulder. "We will be late for the morning prayer."

"Right, right." Andy loosened his grip and took a step back, straightening his mantle. "How do I look?"

Etienne smiled and said, "Like a Templar."

The two of them set off down the long hall toward the chapel. Andy had never been so excited to go to a prayer. It would be his first as a Templar. He wanted to remember all of his Templar firsts.

As they entered the chapel, the rays of sun shone through the stained glass windows. All the pews were filled with Templars of different shapes, sizes, and colors. But despite their differences, the bonds of brotherhood united them all. Etienne and Andy took a seat next to Brother Andre.

"Good mornin', Brother," Andy said with such enthusiasm and excitement that it made the old man chuckle. Brother Andre held a finger to his lips, silencing Andy. He realized a hush had fallen over the chapel. It created a silence so thick, it was palpable. The first note of the chant cut through the air. Andy struggled with the ritual, but Etienne helped him. Andy fidgeted in the pew, too excited to sit still.

After the prayer, they made their way to the refectory with the other Templars. "Wait until Clair sees me like this," Andy said beaming. "She's gonna be so proud."

Andy entered the refractory and tried his hardest to look stoic in front of the pilgrims. But he couldn't help himself, he waved at Clair like a madman and pointed at the mantel. Clair gave Andy a proud smile. Isabella, on the other hand, was clearly doing anything she could to avoid Etienne's gaze. She turned to Katsuji and engaged him in conversation. Andy could tell that she was faking laughter—he'd never seen her so sad.

Etienne and Andy sat at one of the long tables and ate their breakfast in silence. *Ach, my first breakfast as a Templar.* Andy shook his head in disbelief.

When breakfast finished, Molay stood and broke the silence. "Brother Sinclair, Brother LaRue, and your traveling companions, meet me in the library. All others are relieved to their usual duties."

"I canna' wait to talk ta Clair. It felt so strange not being with them," Andy said to Etienne as they cleared their plates.

"I understand the feeling." Etienne looked longingly at Isabella, who was just about to exit.

"I can see that." Andy nudged him in the side to break his gaze. "Come on, we canna' keep the Grand Master waiting."

When they reached the door to the room, Andy heard Clair, Isabella, Mariano, and Gerhart. They stepped inside, and the library smelled of old books and beeswax candles. *Ahh the smell of knowledge.* The walls were covered with leather-bound books bursting with wisdom, and in the middle of it all were his friends. Andy ran past the others, straight to Clair. He gave her a massive hug and picked her up in the air, spinning around.

"Ach, pu' me doon."

After one more spin, Andy set her down on the ground. "Can ya believe it? I'm a Templar."

"Aye, tha' ya are," Clair said, smiling. "Mother would-a be proud, and I am-a proud too." She kissed him on the cheek.

"Ah, nice of you to join us. I thought you had become too good for us," Gerhart said as Etienne entered the room. He chuckled, then put his massive arm around Etienne's shoulder.

Etienne looked past Gerhart's arm straight at Isabella. "Here, I am bound by my oath and must be obedient to what my order demands."

"Not just here, Etienne," Molay said from the doorway. He gave Etienne a stern look. "In every step of life, you have taken the vow of obedience." He entered the room, and all eyes were on him. Gerhart removed his arm from Etienne's shoulder. Etienne took a step back and stood at attention. Andy thought Molay's entrance was a bit rude, but he now understood why Etienne was acting the way he was.

Molay turned to Isabella. "I hope your stay has been pleasant." His words were kind, but his tone wasn't. Andy wondered what he had against Isabella.

Isabella shot him an icy look. "It has been more than adequate." Andy had seen a lot of passive aggression before, but this was next-level. It made the room feel very uncomfortable. *What was going on between these two?*

"Happy to hear," Molay said, bringing his hands together. "One of our ships will leave from Finisterre at the end of the month for France. You will find passage to your home country onboard, Your Highness. I will send word to them, as well as to your father, so they can make the preparations for your return. I will give you a company of knights to ensure safe passage to your destination."

"Thank you," Isabella said with a bow of her head.

"Oh yes, there is one other thing." Molay took a piece of parchment from under his mantle. "Here are new credentials for you. Whatever gold you desire will be given and the balance will be added to your father's *debt*." Molay put an emphasis on the word debt as he handed her the paper.

Isabella gave him a cold look as she took the parchment from him. Andy had never seen her behave like this.

"Ha, would ya look a' that." Andy bent down to pet a cat at his feet.

"It seems Puna likes you," the Grand Master said. "That is a good thing, as you will be spending a lot of time together."

"Ach, she is sweet…" Andy looked up, Molay's statement sinking in. "What do ya mean by a lot of time?"

"The pilgrims will depart in the morning." He looked directly at Andy. "You will stay here to serve as an apprentice to the master of the library."

"Bu' I canna stay." Andy looked at Clair. "I canna leave, Clair." Andy heard Molay's words but he couldn't believe them. Clair and he had never been apart for long. Andy didn't know how to be in the world without her. He obviously hadn't thought this whole thing through.

"You have taken a vow of obedience, and you will best serve the order by staying here." Molay's tone brooked no argument. For the first time, Andy realized exactly what he had given up by choosing to be a Templar.

Clair took Andy's hand. "'Tis alri', Gerhart is a goo' man and we will look after each other."

Andy shook his head. "Bu' I thought I would just continue on with ya, like Etienne."

"Etienne will also not be joining the pilgrims," Molay said. As the words left his lips, both Isabella and Etienne looked at each other like desperate animals. "He will join my personal guard." Etienne's face turned to stone and showed no emotion again, but Andy noticed his hands trembling.

"I suggest that the pilgrims explore the town today and take advantage of this beautiful weather," said Molay.

"Thank you once again for all of your *kindness.*" Isabella spat the word. Andy was sure that if it were possible, her gaze would strike the Grand Master dead on the spot. "I hope that the knights you provide will be as brave and loyal as the two you are taking away from me." She walked confidently out of the room, leaving everyone else in her wake.

Andy and Etienne stood by and watched as their friends and companions left them one by one. Molay called for the master of the library. When he arrived, Molay said, "Brother Bernard, take Brother Andy and show him the details of your work."

"This way, Brother Andy," he said, motioning to a door at the back of the library. Andy lingered a moment, then followed. He looked pleadingly back at Etienne, who stood there, as firm as a stone. But his friend couldn't save him this time. He couldn't even save himself. Andy cursed his curiosity for getting him into this mess. It would cost him his Clair.

Etienne felt an inferno raging inside his body. His jaw was clenched and his fist held tight. Molay had just taken his wife from him. Etienne felt a pain that was unimaginable. He wished they hadn't stopped here. Why hadn't he just given the Hospitallers what they wanted and just continued on? They would be free now if he had. Etienne wanted to punch Molay, but that wouldn't do anyone any good.

"You may hate me right now," Molay said, breaking into his thoughts. "I know the love you hold for Isabella. I saw the way she touched you in the courtyard, and the glances you exchange." Etienne's back stiffened. How could Molay possibly know the fathomless love he had for Isabella?

Molay continued, "You must listen to me. Isabella can't be trusted with the secret you carry. It is too dangerous. You know who her father is, and that he is a cruel man engaged in many wars. If he ever got his hands on the treasure we possess, God help us all."

He began shaking his head before Molay had finished speaking. "Isabella is trustworthy," Etienne said. He hadn't noticed how tightly he was clenching his jaw until he spoke.

"Answer me this, Etienne. Before the Camino, when was the last time you saw her?"

"Over two years ago."

"I visited Philip's court recently to discuss his debt to us, and Isabella was present. Philip insisted on having her at all of his meetings so she could learn from him. I watched her. She admired her father with absolute devotion. She would do anything for him. Her responses were as cruel and calculated as his. I also saw the way she manipulated the men around her. In minutes, she had them in the palm of her hand, expressing undying love and a willingness to sacrifice their lives for hers. Her father reveled in her coolness and boasted about her skills in manipulation. Perhaps Isabella isn't who she presents herself to be. Think about it: where were you when Ronan was abducted?"

"I was with Isabella in the forest. She was running from something. When I caught up to her, I found there was no threat. Andy's cry called us back to camp," Etienne said.

"And when you were in the forest, what happened? Tristan took Ronan and poisoned Clair. Don't you think it odd that she kept you away from the camp? This distraction gave Tristan an opportunity to strike. It is my understanding that this attack also happened directly after you had the first clue from the cathedral in Leon. I do not think this is a coincidence."

"But Isabella didn't know about the Green Men," Etienne said, his head trying to make sense of the person Molay was describing, versus who he knew Isabella to be.

"If Andy knew, so did Isabella and Tristan," Molay said sternly. "Isabella is smart, she would keep you and Andy around as long as possible if she were after the treasure."

Etienne thought back on all that had happened. What Molay was saying made sense. Etienne's mind wandered back to the door in the tunnels of Castrojeriz... Was it a binding door? Ronan had said it led to either heaven or hell. Etienne remembered Isabella pricking her finger. He tried hard to recall the shape her bloodstain made. *Oh my God.* The shape was the same Ronan had shown him to unbind the doors, but backwards. Isabella had opened the door in Castrojeriz. She was after the treasure.

Etienne had to be sure, though. He had to take a chance. "Grand Master, you ordered me to never speak of the doors again but, I need to know: is the door in Castrojeriz related to the Shadows?"

A look of disbelief crossed Molay's face. "What was Ronan thinking? Did he show you everything!"

"No, we used the tunnels to escape. I just realized now that one of our companions unbound that door."

"Yes, they are the trial of that door. Which one of your companions opened it?" Etienne's heart stopped. He would either have to betray Isabella and tell Molay the truth, or blame it on Tristan.

Etienne weighed his decision carefully. He thought back to Santiago. Etienne had felt that his purpose had to do with Isabella, not the treasure. "It was Tristan, the one who took Ronan."

Molay smiled. "That is a relief. Someone who is after the treasure for greedy reasons will never succeed. The Shadows or one of the other trials will get him. I would have been more worried if it was Isabella. She wouldn't be looking for the treasure for her own self-interest. It would be for her father."

Etienne hoped he had made the right decision. His heart wouldn't tell him if he had or not. He loved Isabella. She was his wife; he could never betray her. But what if she had just been using him the whole time? Etienne wished Isabella had never come to Castrojeriz.

"I know it is a lot to take in, and I know you love her, but you must understand that this threat is real. Take the afternoon off from your duties, go to the chapel for reflection and prayer. I hope that Andy's oath last night was a reminder of the oath you took when you became a Templar. That will be all." Molay walked slowly out of the room, leaving Etienne utterly alone with his thoughts.

After the meal that evening, Isabella returned to the guesthouse with the others. The cheery room was the exact opposite of how she was feeling. A dark cold room would have better fit her mood. Etienne had not looked at her once during the meal, a fact Molay seemed smug about. Sighing, Isabella sat at the large table where they had passed the last several evenings.

"Well, at least Molay said we would get to say goodbye tonight," Gerhart said, putting a comforting arm around Clair. "Andy and Etienne will both come."

"Ach, it wonna be, 'Goodbye,' just, 'Until next time.'" Clair looked up at him, feigning a smile.

"I just don't see why Andy and Etienne can't come with us." Isabella crossed her arms. "He said at the library that he would provide an escort. Why not give us back our... our... our trusted companions?" Her fists trembled.

"I donna know chil', I donna know." Clair shook her head.

Katsuji took a seat by the fire. "Every Camino is like a lifetime: some people walk with you for a day, others a few cities, still others come in and out at the perfect moment. But there are a rare few who will walk with you until the end of the world."

"Does this mean you will join us to Finisterre?" Isabella uncrossed her arms and looked at him hopefully.

"No, I am not well enough to travel, and I still need to sell my wares to make up for my losses. I am more like someone who comes in and out, at just the right time."

"I will be your first customer. Will you sell me that silk you said only a queen or princess could afford?" Before Katsuji could answer, Isabella tossed him a small bag of gold. "This should be enough."

Katsuji opened the bag. "Isabella, I can't. This is too much."

"You saved us out there. It is the least I can do. Plus, I really liked that silk. It will remind me of you and all you have done for us."

The door opened and Isabella could barely make out the red Templar cross in the dark hallway. Her heart skipped its rhythm. "Etienne, is that you?"

"Ach, no, 'tis just I," Andy said, stepping into the light.

Isabella dropped her head in disappointment, but Clair smiled broadly and said, "I dinna recognize ya. Ya look good in uniform... Ahve always been so proud of ya." The two of them embraced. Soon, Gerhart's large arms wrapped around Andy as well, then Mariano, Katsuji, and lastly Isabella joined.

"'Tis the most love I've ever received," Andy said, sniffing and drying his eyes.

They released the embrace and stepped back. Andy looked at all of them and said, "I will do ya all proud."

"I ken ya will." Clair placed her hand on his cheek.

"Where is Etienne?" Isabella asked.

"I donna know." Andy raised his shoulders and hands. "Sittin' next ta him at dinner was like sittin' next te a wall. I donna know what Molay said ta him, but it surely affected him. He still migh' come, but it may be too hard for 'im to say goodbye. He doesna do well with emotion. He just shoves it down inside."

"When you see him, tell him he is a coward for not coming," Isabella said, crossing her arms again.

"I'm-a sure he has his reasons," Andy responded.

"Come, let's have a drink," Katsuji pulled out a bottle of wine.

"None for me, thank ya," Andy said.

Isabella sat with the others, and they recounted the stories from the road and memories from back home. They felt like a family now. The bonds of suffering and endurance had tied them closer together than blood. Isabella smiled on the outside, trying to conceal her emotions, but she missed Etienne. He was a part of every story they told. He had been with her since the beginning.

After some time, the bell rang signaling the evening prayer for all the Templars. Andy said his final goodbyes to everyone and was heading for the door when Clair stopped him. "I wish ya were comin' with us. You're-a fine knight, Andy Sinclair, and the best broder a sister could 'ave." They both teared up and embraced a final time before Andy exited the room. Isabella wished she could hug Etienne one last time. This wasn't fair.

The morning came way too quickly. Isabella awoke and the first thought in her head was, *I can't believe he didn't come.* She had slept terribly. Every small noise she heard in the night held in it the hope that Etienne would appear and embrace her. She wanted one last kiss. She still remembered the warmth of his lips and the way his body had felt with hers. She shook her head violently. *No, no, no. I shouldn't allow myself such thoughts.* She rose from the bed and dressed.

When Isabella entered the common room of the guest house, Mariano, Clair, and Gerhart were already waiting for her, packed and ready to go. Looking at them, she said, "Our company seems so small now. I am happy you'll still accompany me."

"Ach, we are with ya 'til the end of the world," said Clair, hugging her. "Ya canna get rid of us that easily."

Both Molay and Etienne had been absent from the morning meal. Isabella wondered what Molay had said to Etienne to make him abandon her. Or did something worse happen? Did Molay find out about their marriage and kill Etienne for it? Isabella scrunched her face at the thought.

Isabella walked outside with the others. She was thankful Andy was allowed to escort them to the gate. She had to find out what had happened to Etienne. She could feel her face turning to stone at the prospect of not seeing him again.

Andy hooked Clair's arm as they walked across the grand courtyard. "Clair if I woulda known—"

Clair patted his hand gently. "It doesna matter now. It doesna matter."

Unable to contain herself any longer, Isabella turned to Andy. "I didn't see Etienne or Molay at breakfast, and there seem to be fewer knights. Where are they?"

Andy looked at her gravely. "I'm na' supposed ta tell ya." After a long pause, he laughed. "Na, I'm-a joking. They left early this morning ta go ta Crete. Molay took Etienne with him." Isabella's heart moved to her throat and she swallowed hard. Etienne was already gone. She felt the last ray of hope to see him leave her.

"Maybe that is why he didn't come last night," Isabella said.

"Maybe, lassie," replied Andy. They reached the main gate and were met by a company of ten Templars and four extra horses at the ready.

Andy stopped. "Ach, I wish I was coming with ya."

"Us too, Andy." Isabella kissed his cheek, causing Andy to turn bright red. "At least we got to see you again this morning. I will miss you." Isabella wished he was coming too. Not only for Clair's sake but for her own. If she could convince Andy to help her find the treasure with her, she wouldn't be alone in her quest. She knew he wanted to find it as badly as she did.

"Until we meet again," Mariano said.

"Goodbye, little man." Gerhart embraced him.

"G'bye, big fella. Watch out for my sister and Isabella." Andy's eyes teared up.

"I will." Gerhart patted Andy's head with his large hand.

"Clair... I," started Andy as he embraced her.

"You donna' have ta say anything. I love ya." Once again Isabella admired their relationship. Isabella's brothers had barely said goodbye to her. She wasn't looking forward to seeing them when she returned to France. They were jealous of their father's love for her. She was his favorite and often reminded them of it.

"I love ya too." They released the embrace and Clair followed the others through the gate, leaving Andy alone in the courtyard. He watched as they mounted their horses and rode off into the west, leaving a trail of dust behind them. Isabella took one last look back at Andy. They exchanged a smile, and then she was gone.

CHAPTER 25

O CEBREIRO

The difference between riding a horse and walking had never been so apparent to Isabella. She felt it throughout her body: new muscles were being used, and a completely different kind of soreness was present. But they were certainly covering far more ground. The powerful muscles of the horse shifted as they sped past the countryside. Before noon, they reached Villafranca, a beautiful town that lay in a deep valley, nestled in the mountains. Isabella wished Etienne was with her to enjoy the view. They had just left Ponferrada that morning yet it felt like she had been apart from him forever. Seeing Clair and Gerhart's infatuation didn't help her melancholy. It made her miss Etienne, her husband, even more.

The scenery and the look of the people shifted the higher they climbed. The strangers they met were fair-skinned and some of them had red hair.

Clair rode up next to Isabella. "Ach, I feel like I'm in the highlands."

"Is this what your country looks like?"

"Aye, and the people are similar. Just as mean," replied Clair, and both laughed. "Why da the people look like they belong in the highlands?"

"They are Celts as well," Mariano said riding up to join them

"No, ya donna' say! I didna' know they were 'ere too." Clair turned to Gerhart. "Let's get a summer home 'ere."

"Um…a." Gerhart rubbed his head.

Isabella felt a pain in her chest: she knew she would never have that with Etienne again.

Night approached and fires gleamed on the hill that rose above them. A Templar rode up to Isabella. "We are entering the Kingdom of Galicia and that is the town of O Cebreiro. We will rest there for the evening. Oh, and don't stray off tonight alone, this town is rumored to have witches."

Isabella wasn't too concerned about witches, but throughout the night she kept close by the others just in case.

In the morning Isabella arose before her companions. She dressed quickly to keep the cold off, moving as quietly as the sun tracing its way across the sky. She exited the circular stone albergue and admired its architecture. The design was unique and quaint. It had rounded slate stone walls and a slanted thatch roof to match. It reminded her of a building wearing a pointed hat. This brought a small smile to her face.

The smell of baking bread and pastries filled the small streets as Isabella walked to the entrance of the city. She admired the valleys and rolling hills which lay far below; it was a palate of green, gold, and blue, dotted with purple, stretching out for as far as Isabella could see.

In the east the sky shone, and the clouds emitted a silvery glow as the sun reached over the farthest ridge. Just to the right of the rising sun was the morning star; something about it reminded her of Etienne.

"Beautiful sunrise, isn't it?" a raspy voice came from Isabella's right. She knew that voice from somewhere but she couldn't place it.

Isabella turned and stumbled backwards when she saw the crone who had told her about the doors. "I met you in Burgos."

The crone took Isabella's hand. Her body wanted to recoil at the crone's clammy skin. "Yes, yes, you did, and you have done well with the information I gave you. There has been so much death since." The old crone cackled.

"What do you mean?"

The crone patted Isabella's hand. "My payment was blood, and you have spilled so much. When you unlocked the door in Castrojeriz, you unbound the Shadows. Everyone who has died at their hands is a result of you unleashing them. I forgot to tell you that behind every door there is a treasure but also a trial. I only showed you how to unlock the trial. I got it backwards, oops." The crone released Isabella and cackled.

"You witch!" Isabella's fists shook. She felt so used and taken advantage of.

"Yes, I am a witch. If only you would have known that sooner." She cackled again. "And, there will be another six deaths ending with you, my dear. Each of your companions will die at the hands of the Shadows because of you. So much glorious death." Isabella felt her insides turn. She was going to vomit. "They will only stop after you are dead." Isabella felt queasy, and retched despite her attempts to swallow down her nausea. She wanted to die. All of those deaths were because of her. "You can always kill yourself to stop the Shadows." The crone cackled and walked away.

The guilt overwhelmed Isabella and she ran to the edge of the cliff to throw herself off. As she reached the edge she stopped and crumpled in a little ball. She didn't know how long she sobbed there, thinking of the lives her quest had already cost her. She couldn't take her own life; she was too afraid. Isabella hated herself even more for being a coward. She lifted herself up and slowly walked back to the albergue with a heavy heart.

Isabella joined her companions in the bar and Clair dished her up a heaping slice of the meat pie. "'Tis good ta have-a 'arty breakfast," Clair said smiling. "Aye 'ave a feeling 't'will be a long day."

Isabella looked at her grimly and said, "It already has been."

"What 'appened ta you this mornin'?" Isabella shook her head. She couldn't tell Clair that the Shadows had appeared because of her. She looked at Mariano—Alba was dead because she had unbound that door.

Isabella took her first bite of food. The flaky crust crumbled in her mouth and all the flavors inside the pie mixed into a perfect harmony, but it didn't help her mood. She felt dead inside.

"It is a specialty in this region," Mariano said, trying to lighten her mood.

"How do you know so much about Galicia?" Isabella asked. She tried to act normal, but she couldn't look at Mariano. The love of his life was dead because of her.

"Gerhart and I have worked many times in these mountains, either protecting people or robbing them." Mariano shook his head. "That seems like a lifetime ago now. I cannot imagine…" He looked down.

Isabella touched his hand. "This road will change you, and all of your sins are forgiven when you reach Santiago." She hoped that was true; she had so many sins now—so much blood on her hands. She looked at each of her friends knowing that if she didn't kill herself, they would all die.

After breakfast they left O Cebreiro, and the morning fog hung thick as a blanket on the west side of the mountain. They slowed their speed as they plunged into the fog line. The moisture of the fog clung to Isabella's hair making it thick and heavy. Isabella couldn't see five feet in front of her, but she knew there was a sheer cliff drop to her right. She almost wished her horse would take a miss-step.

A blood-curdling howl cut through the fog like a knife.

Isabella stopped and her horse neighed uneasily as it took a few paces forward then back again. "Steady, girl," she whispered, stroking her horse's mane. Isabella's self loathing was replaced with a primal fear.

Howls came from all around her. *Wolves.* She sensed she had been singled out from the others and was surrounded on all sides. She looked desperately to her left and right, but the fog was too thick to see anything.

"Isabella!" She heard Mariano through the blanket of fog, but she couldn't see anyone. She was alone. A new desire to live shot through Isabella—she didn't want to die! The old crone had probably tricked her again. Isabella drew her dagger. She would fight to the end, with the wolves *and* the Shadows.

A low growl came from Isabella's left. Her horse reared up high in the air, kicking wildly to ward off the attackers. Isabella leaned forward, squeezing tightly with her thighs to stay seated. When they came back down, three massive wolves, large teeth bared, surrounded her and her horse. Their eyes glowed yellow and fierce. They looked like demons staring up at her. Isabella was ready. If she died, the others would be saved, and if she lived, she would do everything in her power to stop the Shadows from taking those she loved. One of the wolves attacked her from the side, pushing her mount toward the precipitous drop. Isabella felt her horse's hooves give way and slip. *Lord, don't let me die like this.* Her beast scrambled, trying to regain its footing, but all was lost. She screamed for Etienne as she and her horse went toppling over the cliff's edge.

CHAPTER 26

THE TEMPLAR COMPANY

Etienne and the large company of Templars pressed southward. They had left Ponferrada yesterday, long before the sun had risen. The journey was uneventful. Etienne had kept to himself, still thinking about the words Molay had spoken to him. *Did Isabella open the door? The symbol was backwards... Was she just using me? Maybe this is why Templars take the vow of chastity. Did my love for her cloud my intuition?* He felt no peace in his body, only sorrow, anger, and confusion.

After the morning meal, Etienne heard Isabella's voice in his head. It was almost as if she was next to him. *Help.* It was a gentle whisper on the wind. Try as he could, Etienne couldn't shake the feeling that Isabella needed him. The more miles they rode, the more it pressed on him. He wondered if he had made the right choice, or if he had abandoned the only family and the only love he'd ever had.

Etienne skipped the evening meal and made his bed slightly away from the others. He needed to be by himself; he needed to think.

Etienne was startled awake by a loud crashing thunder. His eyes shot open, but there wasn't a cloud in the sky. Everyone at the camp seemed undisturbed. The only movement came from the two Templars keeping watch, and the horses as they grazed. Another loud crash of thunder jolted through Etienne's body. He turned his head away from camp toward the sound and saw Santiago towering above him, with lightning in his eyes.

"You are needed on the Camino." Santiago's words reverberated through Etienne's body.

Santiago lifted his staff and placed it on Etienne's forehead between his eyes. A silver prayer streaked through the sky and hit his staff. As the prayer made contact, Etienne was shot through a tunnel of light. On the other end, he saw Isabella covered in blood. A giant wolf, his mouth about her neck, dragged her across the ground. Etienne tried to scream out her name but found he had no power of speech. He was helpless to watch as the beast salivated down her spine. Tears filled Etienne's eyes. There was another flash, and Etienne saw a lone church on top of a hill. On the inside he saw strange markings on the wall, the likes of which he had never seen before.

With another flash, Etienne was back in camp, Santiago still towering high above him. "Go now! There is still time!"

Santiago disappeared, and behind where he had stood were thundering clouds in the distance. Etienne hurriedly gathered his things, mounted his steed, and galloped back in the direction they had come. He heard the cries of the guards behind him, but he sped on. He had made his decision. He knew it meant death, and that Molay would send the Templars to capture him. But that didn't matter. To him, all that mattered was saving Isabella.

CHAPTER 27

THE TEMPLAR LIBRARY

Andy sat patiently transcribing the book that lay in front of him. *Ach, I've never felt so alone in my life.*

Even though he was surrounded by people, he felt a certain emptiness inside. "I miss my family," he muttered as he continued to write.

"At least I have you, Puna." He stretched out his hand to stroke the gray cat with black stripes. Just as his hand was about to touch her, she moved out of reach. This annoyed Andy. *Figures,* he thought, as he stretched further.

Having nothing to do with it, Puna jumped off the table narrowly avoiding his hand. This caused Andy to slip and knock a book to the floor. As it hit, the book opened to reveal the same coded language he had seen below the statue in Astorga. Andy's annoyance immediately turned to excitement. He looked down at the cat and said, "'Tis the same as... We found it, Puna."

"What is all of that noise?" Brother Bernard said.

"Ehh... 'Tis nothin'; just dropped a book."

Brother Bernard looked over and saw Andy staring at the coded book on the floor. Brother Bernard shut the book on his desk firmly. "I hope you didn't damage anything." He raised his book from the desk and ordered, "Now, take this to the back room."

Andy took the book from Brother Bernard and left the room. When he returned, he noticed that the code book that had fallen was nowhere to be found. He looked at Brother Bernard who gave him a sneaky smile.

"I have some things to attend to. I trust I can leave the library in your care." Brother Bernard raised his eyebrows in question.

"Of course," said Andy, standing taller.

Looking at him skeptically, Brother Bernard walked to the door. As he was about to exit, he turned to the cat. "Puna, you watch after him." The cat meowed.

Andy began his work again. "Ach, who would have thought working in a secret library would be so boring. Guess I got used to life on the road." He looked over his left shoulder, then his right, to make sure no one was around. He took out a fresh piece of parchment and wrote the code he had memorized at the foot of the Virgin.

He was about halfway through when he heard a low growl. He looked up from his work, directly into Puna's yellow eyes staring right at him. Andy stopped writing. "Wha'? Ya canna be serious."

Andy wrote again. He made three strokes and Puna's paw pushed his hand. She meowed. "I know, I'm not supposed to write this out, or try to solve it, bu' I canna help myself." Andy picked up the parchment and turned his back to Puna. He wrote out the last few symbols as quickly as he could. Just as he was about to finish, he felt claws on his shoulder. Puna had jumped from the table and was now on his back. "Ha, you're too late. I'm done," Andy said. Puna sunk her claws into his shoulders one last time and jumped off.

$$\nabla \triangleright > \triangleright \Diamond \triangleleft \Diamond \triangleright \triangle \times > \triangleright > \vee \triangleleft \Diamond \triangleright \triangleleft > \vee \triangleleft \nabla \triangleleft \vee > \nabla$$

"Now where is that book?" Andy stood up and searched the library for the book he had knocked off the table. He scoured the shelves, wasting no time. But to his dismay, it was nowhere to be found. After searching in vain, Andy turned to Brother Bernard's desk, and there sat Puna on the book with the coded language. They stared at each other in a battle of wills.

"Ach, so you've been a hidin' it." He approached the desk, and Puna didn't move. She growled as he neared. Andy reached out his hand and Puna arched her back, ready to pounce.

"Now Puna, that's no way to treat a guest." He extended his hand again and Puna took a swipe at it with her paw. Andy withdrew his hand immediately.

"Now we can do this the hard way, or the easy way," Andy said, looking squarely at Puna. "I choose the easy way."

Andy walked over to Puna's food bowl. He opened a bottle of milk and poured it into her bowl. Immediately, Puna was off the desk and purring at his feet. He placed the bowl on the ground and stroked Puna on the head. "Ya put up a good fight," he said and walked back over to Brother Bernard's desk. The leather of the book was smooth and inviting to the touch. He made his way back to his desk and sat.

Andy took a deep breath and opened the book. He turned from page to page; each was written in the secret code—the same code that he had just etched on the scroll. There was only one picture in the book. It was a picture of a lonely church on top of a hill. The church was very simple, made of stone, with one stained glass window. Below the church was written the caption:

Andy decided the picture and caption were the best chance he had at decoding the cipher. He quickly copied the caption and tried to draw the church as best he could. He focused hard and worked diligently. The light from the beeswax candles flickered, sending a sweet honey aroma into the air. Andy wasn't much of an artist, but when he finished, he took a step back and looked at the two drawings side-by-side. "Not too bad," Andy said. As soon as the ink dried, he rolled up the parchment and placed it under his garments. He placed the codebook back on Brother Bernard's desk, in the exact position he had found it.

"What do you think you are doing?" Brother Bernard asked from the door. Andy froze, his body obscuring Brother Bernard's view of the desk. His heart pumped wildly as he tried to figure a way out of this situation. Out of nowhere, Puna appeared on the desk. Andy reached forward and picked her up, sending her a silent thank you. Turning, he said, "Just getting Puna. I felt like a little company." Puna purred peacefully in his arms.

"Ahh," said Brother Bernard. "It is good that you two are becoming friends." Looking over at Andy's desk, he continued, "Looks like you haven't gotten much done since I left. It is best that you leave Puna alone now and get back to work." Andy dropped Puna and made his way back to his chair. He dipped his quill into the ink and continued his work.

The evening carried on as all the other evenings had: dinner, then evening prayer. Andy couldn't wait to get back to his cell. He wanted to decode what he had discovered in the library. As soon as the last words of the evening prayer were spoken, Andy rushed back to his little room. The distraction of figuring out the code took his mind off the loneliness that had consumed him since his friends had left.

He spread the parchment out on his tiny bed and looked up at the crucifix. "Forgive me, Lord, if this is a sin."

At first glance, the caption below the picture just looked like a random collection of symbols: triangles, triangles with dots in them, V's, X's, and diamond shapes.

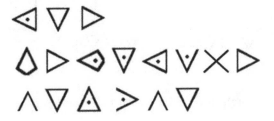

Andy focused on the first set of shapes. He thought of all the three-letter-words he could. Placing each into the shapes before him: and, the, can, two, for…

Looking at all the possibles the only word that seemed to work was "The," because the word "The" often starts a sentence. He assumed he had the first word of the code figured out. He then placed the corresponding letters in place of the coded symbols.

◁▽▷ ◊▷◈▽◁∨✕▷ ∧▽△≽∧▽
T H E   E   T   E   H   H

Andy racked his brain, "What word has "H" as the second and last letter; and what words have "E" as the second and last letter?" He paced the room, going through his internal thesaurus. After a few minutes deep in thought, he walked back to the bed and looked at the code. He then saw the drawing of the church he had made. "That's it!" he said, "Church. How could I be so daft? Of course, 'tis church." This realization confirmed that the first word was "The."

◁▽▷ ◊▷◈▽◁∨✕▷ ∧▽△≽∧▽
T H E   E   T   E C H U R C H

This didn't help him much with the second word of the caption. He only had the "E" and "T." He still didn't know what the code was. He couldn't see the pattern.

Are they just random symbols to replace letters? No, there has to be a pattern.
He turned his attention to the parchment with the inscription they had found
below the statue in Astorga. He filled in the letters below the symbols he knew.

▽▷⟩▷♡◁♡▷△✕⟩▷⟩
H E R E   E U   E R

∨◁♡▷◇⟩∨◁▽◁∨⟩▽
    E   T   R

"Well, that didn't help too much, but it is a good start. What if I separate
some words?"

▽▷⟩▷
H E R E

"And I think this one is under."

△✕⟩▷⟩
U N D E R

"Now let's see where that puts us."

▽▷⟩▷♡◁♡▷△✕⟩▷⟩
H E R E   E U N D E R

∨◁♡▷◇⟩∨◁▽◁∨⟩▽
    E   D   T   R

"Hmm, now we are getting closer. Let's put these into the caption."

◁▽▷ ◊▷◇▽◁∨✕▷ ∧▽△⟩∧▽
T H E   E   T N E C H U R C H

Andy paced the room again, his head swimming with the symbols. They were
like floating puzzle pieces connecting and disconnecting in his mind. He tried
several constructions. "How do these shapes fit? What is the pattern?"

He paced the room for another fifteen minutes and finally gave up.

Well, 'tis a good start. Best get some sleep now.

He wasn't used to getting up at four A.M. every morning. He folded up the papers and put them under his mattress. He blew out the candle, and the sweet smell of beeswax mixed with smoke filled the air.

Andy lay there with his eyes closed, but his brain kept spinning, the shapes still shifting and morphing in his head. Soon, images of Clair and the others occupied space in his mind.

Ach, I hope you're alright. Lord, please watch over them, he prayed.

Thinking of them made Andy feel alone once again. He missed them so much. He had never been apart from Clair for long. They had been best of friends since they were children—always looking after one another, always getting into trouble together. Now, she was the only family he had left. His eyes filled with tears as he thought about never seeing her again. "I dina' think it would be like this, Clair," he said softly. "I miss ya."

Before the sorrow overwhelmed him; he focused on the puzzle. He needed to take his mind off them. His logical mind switched on, blocking emotion. He saw the shapes melting together before his eyes. Then he noticed his mantle, which he had lazily thrown on the chair; the red cross was illuminated by the moonlight. "That's it! That's it! I knew I had seen those shapes before!"

Andy jumped out of bed and reached for the papers under his mattress. He lit the candle again and scribbled all the different versions of the Templar cross. When he had finished, he said, "This is every possible shape that is in the code and it equals all the letters of the alphabet."

Andy quickly went to work and filled in the empty spaces with the letters he had discovered.

Andy tried to fill in the rest of the alphabet, where he thought the letters would go logically, but it just produced gibberish. Now, he had to use a process of elimination. He didn't mind though, working on the puzzle kept his mind off of Clair. After many trials and failures Andy finally stumbled on the correct combination. "It works!" He jumped up in excitement.

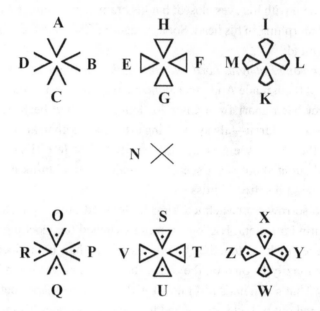

"It works!" he said again. Even though he was alone, he turned his head from left to right to make sure no one heard. He was a little unsure if he should proceed or not. He started with the code from the caption. "Now, on to the middle word."

◁▽▷ ◊▷◇▽◁∨✕▷ ∧▽△▷∧▽
T H E   K E Y S T O N E   C H U R C H

"Wow!" said Andy. "This must be 'The Keystone Church,' whatever that is. Now to decode the inscription from Astorga."

▽▷≫▷♡◁♡▷△✕▷▷≫
H E R E I L I E U N D E R

∨◁♡▷◁▷∨◁▽◁∨▷▽
A F I E L D O F S T A R S

"Here I lie under a field of stars." Andy sat for a minute, then said, "All of that work, for this. *Here I lie under a field of stars.*" He had been expecting some big revelation. "Maybe it will make more sense if I put it together with the clue from Leon. *Where five become one. Here I lie under a field of stars.* He looked over at the picture of the church on the bed. "I wonder what this Keystone Church has to do with anything?"

Andy shook his head and gathered the papers. Not wanting to make the same mistake as before, he held the papers to the flame of the candle and watched the parchment slowly burn. As soon as the last of the parchment turned to ash, he opened his bag to look at the shard of the True Cross Charity had given him. The bag was empty. Andy shook it upside down, but nothing came out. He slapped himself on the forehead.

Etienne is going to kill me.

CHAPTER 28

THE GALICIAN FOREST

"Isabella! Isabella!" Mariano cried as they descended the steep ravine. Their progress had been slow due to the fog and the sharp gradient of the cliff. Mariano, Gerhart, Clair, and two of the Templars zigzagged across the rock face, finding footing wherever they could. The other Templars had stayed above to watch the horses and supplies.

"Aye lassie, don't ya worry, we are a-comin'," Clair shouted as she raced down faster than the others. Gerhart took up the rear. His body was made for fighting, not scrambling down steep cliffs. It had taken them much longer to make their way down than Mariano had expected. The fog obscured just how far the fall was.

"There is no way she could have survived the fall," said one of the Templars.

Clair shot him a death look. "Don't ya doubt."

By late afternoon, the fog cleared and Mariano could see the valley floor below. It looked like something from a murder scene. Blood and entrails were strewn everywhere. The birds of prey and scavengers had already moved in on the carcass of the horse.

Seeing the carnage, the Templar said, "See, there is no way she survived this. We should go back before the night sets in."

Clair grabbed him by the shirt and pulled him down to her height. "We are na' goin' back." The Templar stumbled at this and almost lost his footing.

Mariano was the first to arrive at the valley floor. "Isabella!" he shouted at the top of his lungs, "Isabella!" He ran to where the horse was scattered across the ground and lifted his shirt to shield his nose from the smell.

Clair quickly ran up behind him. "Is she?"

"No, she isn't here. I don't see her anywhere," Mariano said. "This is just the corpse of the horse." He took a few steps back and something to his right caught his eye. About ten feet away, on the ground, was another blood stain with something white in the middle.

He ran over to the spot, stooped down, and picked up the pieces of a shattered scallop shell. "Over here!" he yelled. All rushed past the corpse of the horse to his side. "This must be where she fell," he said, showing the others the shattered shell.

"Tha' was 'ers. 'Twas always on her bag." Tears filled Clair's eyes.

"Where is the corpse?" asked one of the Templars.

Mariano stood and looked at him furiously. "How could her body disappear? She must still be alive."

"Or dragged into the woods by the beasts." The other Templar pointed to the trail of blood leading into the forest.

All looked in the direction he was pointing. "Noo," Clair gasped.

"That doesn't mean she is dead. She could have dragged herself to the cover of the woods," Mariano said. He couldn't save Alba, but there was a chance he could still save Isabella. "I won't believe she is dead until I see her body." He moved to the blood-stained trail. Just as he reached the tree-line, a blood-curdling howl cut through the air. This stopped him dead in his tracks for a second, then he continued.

"If death is what you seek go ahead. You will be devoured by these devilish beasts. I am heading back to camp before nightfall," said the first Templar.

"Cowards!" cried Clair.

"Men I can face, but these things were sent by the devil," the other Templar said as he headed back to ascend the cliff. Maybe that was true, but Mariano had already faced the devil and returned. He would do it again.

"Ha, run back to the safety of your castle." Bellowed Gerhart, as Mariano and his companions took their first steps into the Galician forest.

CHAPTER 29

OLD ACQUAINTANCES

The bells for vigils cut through the air and Andy's eyes shot open. "Ach, no, I overslept." He rolled out of bed and dressed quickly, wiping the sleep out of his eyes. *I donna' think I will ever get used ta this.*

When he arrived, the giant wooden doors of the church were closed, and the knights were already deep into the chant. Andy turned the knob slowly and pushed. It made a hideous creaking noise, and Andy cringed. He stopped when the door was just wide enough for him to slip through. The knights were still chanting their ancient chant, undisturbed.

For a moment, Andy thought he had gotten by without being heard, but when he closed the door, it made the same awful noise again. Brother Andre looked at him and shook his head. Andy waved and took a seat at the back pew. When he sat, the bench moaned under his weight. Andy placed his hand on his head and turned red.

After the vigils were over, Andy remained seated as the other knights filed out. He figured he would put in some extra time with God to make up for being late. Soon, the sound of footsteps leaving the chapel stopped. Andy raised his head and peeked out of one eye. Standing next to him was Brother Andre. Andy jumped back, making a loud commotion as he hit the bench.

"Are you about finished making noise," Brother Andre said.

Andy opened his mouth to speak but quickly shut it again and nodded.

Brother Andre shook his head slowly in disappointment. "For your tardiness and disruption, you will have to pay some penance. Instead of helping Brother Bernard in the library today, you will assist in cleaning out the latrines."

Andy sunk into the pew and his shoulders slumped. Brother Andre shook his head and made his way out of the church. He opened the large wooden door, and it was silent. Andy shook his head in disbelief. Brother Andre closed the door, and once again there was no noise.

How did he do that?

After breakfast, a broad-shouldered, burly Templar came up to Andy. "So, what did you do to get on latrine duty?" he asked in a robust voice, his grizzly black beard moving with each word.

"Ach, aye was late for vigils this mornin'," Andy said, "Suppose you are 'ere to take me ta the latrines?"

The corners of the grizzly knight's mouth raised. "How did you guess?" He motioned for Andy to follow. "Come on then." Andy rose reluctantly and followed the man into the kitchen.

"What are we doing here?" asked Andy.

"We are collecting ash from the fireplaces to put over the waste in the latrine."

"Since we will be working together, don't ya think 'tis good to know each other's names. I'm Andy." He extended his hand.

"Baron." The grizzly knight took Andy's hand and squeezed tightly.

"Quite a grip you 'ave there," Andy said, rubbing his hand. "So, Baron, what did you do to get on latrine duty?"

"I volunteered today."

"Why would ya do a thing like tha'?"

"To better serve my brothers," Baron said. "Come, we have much do."

They took two shovels and scooped out the ash from the massive fireplaces in the kitchen. Once their wheelbarrows were full, they carted them past the grand courtyard to the front gate. The portcullis opened and the guards let them pass. On exiting, they turned right and followed the massive wall of the castle to the riverside.

Andy could smell the waste long before he saw it. The smell was disgusting. "'Tis a terrible smell." He pulled his tunic over his nose.

"Here, try this." Baron handed him a piece of cloth. The cloth felt wet in Andy's hands, but he thought nothing of it. As he placed it over his mouth and nose, he felt the large arms and strong hands of Baron wrap around him. He held Andy tightly and pressed the cloth hard against his face. Andy struggled to free himself and took in a deep breath to yell for help. As he did so, the vapors from the cloth filled Andy's lungs and the world went black.

Andy opened his eyes. His consciousness was slow to come back to him. *What happened?*

He felt like he had been run over by a carriage. He blinked, and above him, a wooden roof came into focus. He tried to move and found his arms and legs tightly bound to a bed. He struggled some, and the ropes rubbed and burnt his skin.

Andy tried to speak, but found he was gagged. Slowly his senses came back to him and the feeling returned to his body. To his right, Baron sat in a chair holding a sword. There were two other men in the room that looked vaguely familiar. He squinted his eyes to get a better look. Then it all came rushing back to him. He remembered the cloth and Baron's tight grip around him.

"Ahh, you are awake," Baron said loudly.

"Welcome back," said one of the other men, and all three laughed. Andy recognized one of the men. He had accompanied Vincenzo. *They must be Hospitallers.* Andy struggled to free himself and tried to speak.

"What is that? You have something to say?" Vincenzo's companion asked mockingly. "Shall we hear what he has to say? I remember he does like to talk."

Baron loosened Andy's gag.

"Ach, how could ya. We're brothers," Andy said accusingly.

Baron laughed heartily. He motioned to the two other men. "These are my brothers. I'm a Hospitaller. I had been assigned to Ponferrada to spy on the Templars. But it was worth exposing my cover to retrieve you. We know you have some very valuable information.

"'Elp!!! 'Ehhhhlp!!!" Andy yelled at the top of his lungs. The damp rag covered his face again and the world went dark.

Andy didn't know how much time had passed. He opened his eyes once more and found himself still tied to the bed. All light had escaped the room, save the embers of the fire still glowing in the hearth. Two of his captors were sleeping in the surrounding chairs; one was still awake, looking out the window, keeping guard. Andy turned and twisted his wrist as quietly as he could; he felt the rope cutting into his skin. *'Tis nothing compared ta the torture they will inflict on me ta get me to talk.* He struggled harder to free himself.

Andy turned his head to the door. *If only I could get free of these ropes and get out that door. Someone will be there to 'elp me.*

The door slid open slightly, not making a sound. The Hospitaller keeping guard didn't notice, he continued looking out the window. Andy stilled, watching the door. To his horror, a Shadow appeared and quietly swept into the room.

Terror froze Andy as he watched the darkness attack Baron, as he was the closest. Baron made a slight gurgling noise as the Shadow slit his throat. Then the Shadow quickly moved to the other man sleeping in the chair. He soon met the same fate as Baron. Hearing the noise, the guard at the window drew his sword. The Shadow turned on him with lightning speed, and Andy saw the man drop.

A cold shiver ran up and down Andy's spine, and his perspiration soaked the bed. He tried to recount what Mariano said about the Shadows, *something about being present*. Andy couldn't remember with the Shadow now slowly moving to him. It raised its massive sword. He closed his eyes and cringed.

So, this is how I die.

Instead of a deathblow, Andy found his bonds were severed. He scrambled out of the bed to the floor, hands out pleadingly. The Shadow moved closer to him.

"Andy, calm yourself." The Shadow pulled back the hood of his cloak to reveal Etienne. Relief broke through him, and Andy burst into tears, throwing his arms around Etienne's waist. "Howdya' know I was 'ere'," Andy said through thick sobs.

"I was refilling my water at the spring just below the window when I heard you scream out this afternoon. I would recognize your voice anywhere. I recognized one of your captors from Astorga and knew the Hospitallers had you." Etienne helped Andy to his feet. "Come, we must go quickly." The two of them disappeared into the night like shadows.

Using the cover of darkness, Etienne and Andy passed through Ponferrada undetected. Though they resembled the seal of the Knights Templar—two knights riding on one horse—people looked at them strangely as they passed. It was a rarity to see two Templars on one horse. They were both wanted men now for deserting and disobeying direct orders from the Grand Master. Etienne had given Andy the choice to stay and return to the castle, but Andy had refused.

"Something 'bout this reminds me of my home," Andy said as they passed through the stone entrance of O Cebreiro. "Not quite sure what it is, but it almost feels like the highlands."

Etienne hadn't spoken much to Andy through the night. He wanted to give him time to recover from the kidnapping, and it gave him time to sort through all that had happened. Etienne wasn't sure how he would confront Isabella about the treasure. Everything Molay had told him still lingered in the back of his mind. Those things wouldn't even be an issue if they couldn't save her in time. Santiago gave him hope that there was still a chance, and the Saint couldn't have made it any clearer where he was needed. And truthfully, that's where Etienne wanted to be.

"We should stop here for breakfast and ask if anyone has seen Isabella and the others," Etienne said, slowing the horse. The vision of Isabella being dragged through the forest by the neck kept replaying in his mind. Etienne felt a tightness in his throat. He was afraid that he may never see her again. He regretted acting as he had at the Templar castle.

Both dismounted and Etienne fastened the mare tightly to a post. There were several people milling through the small town: pilgrims getting ready for the day's journey, shopkeepers opening their small stores, and of course, the kitchens that had a hot breakfast waiting for any who desired.

They walked to the closest bar and descended the stone steps. Inside there was a counter with a grim-looking barkeep, as well as several pilgrims and some town folk well into their meat pies. All eyes turned to them as they entered. The stares weren't threatening, nor inquisitive. They were more like the stares that said: *We don't know you, and we don't care to know you.*

Andy sat at a wooden table by the door, and Etienne walked to the bar. "Two meat pies," Etienne said to the grim-looking man.

"Lots of your type here in the past few days." The barkeep motioned to Etienne's tunic. He continued through gnarly teeth, "Have ya finally come to take care of the Hounds of Hell?"

"Hounds of Hell?" Etienne asked, recalling his vision of the wolves. His heart raced.

"Yeah, the other day, ten of your lot came through here with four pilgrims, one of which was larger than any man I had seen before. Rumor has it, the hounds attacked them on the road." An image of a beast's jaws clamped around Isabella's delicate neck appeared again. Sweat broke out on his forehead knowing that the vision was true. "We've been trying to get you Templars to help us rid ourselves of them for years. They're evil beasts. There is one that is twice the size of the others. Him and a white one steal children and take them for their own. He is the evilest of them all, able to take down a cow by himself and drag it by the neck for a quarter mile. Some people say they are just wolves, but us Galicians, we know they are the Hounds of Hell collecting the souls of pilgrims." A little spittle fell from the grim man's mouth as he finished speaking.

"That is exactly why we are here. To kill those beasts and reclaim the pilgrims." Etienne gripped the bar tightly. "Did any of the party return?"

"Not a one," said the man. "Some folk say the Templars turned tail and rode back through here by night, without the pilgrims. But you would have known about that if they had." The barkeep eyed Etienne up and down.

"So how do we find these hounds?"

The man laughed heartily and wheezed, "Yea can't find the devil. He comes to find you." He handed Etienne two meat pies. "It don't look like your friend would be much help if ya do find them," the barkeep said, nodding to Andy.

Etienne paid and took the pies abruptly. "He is one of the smartest people I have ever met. I think he could even outsmart the devil."

"What took ya so long?"Andy asked as Etienne approached the table.

"The barkeeper told me he saw them the other day."

"Tha's good."

Etienne looked at him grimly. "He also said that they were attacked by the Hounds of Hell, and that the Templars may have passed in the night without the pilgrims."

"That's not good," Andy turned very solemn. "What are these hounds?"

"He says they are the devil himself, especially the largest one. He described them just as I had seen them in my vision. I hope we aren't too late."

"Ach, me too." Andy took his first bite. With a mouth full of food, he continued, "You never told me much about this vision. What exactly did you see?"

"First, I saw Santiago with lightning in his eyes. He said I was needed on the Camino. Then I saw a flash of a giant wolf, dragging Isabella by the neck."

"The Hounds of Hell," Andy interrupted. "Sorry, sorry, continue."

"Then Santiago said there was still time, and he showed me a flash of a church on a hill, one that I have never seen before. Then it was done."

When Etienne finished, Andy leaned closer. "Did you say church on top of a hill?"

"Yes, why?"

Andy dug around under his tunic and pulled out a piece of parchment. He unrolled it and laid it on the table. Etienne's eyes widened. It was exactly what Santiago had shown. "Did you have the same vision?"

"No. I copied this from a codebook in the library. I also figured out how to decode the second clue from Astorga." Etienne shot Andy a disarming look. He thought Andy had stopped. He couldn't believe he was still searching. "Don't ya worry. I burnt all the evidence except this drawing. In the book, they called it the Keystone Church, whatever that means. I think it has something ta do with decoding the next part of the riddle. Do ya want me to tell ya what the decoded message said?" Andy asked, his eyes bright.

Etienne crossed his arms. "You were supposed to stop trying to figure it out."

He waved a hand in the air. "I thought since I was a Templar now, it didn't matter. Well, do you want to know?"

Etienne leaned in and whispered, "Here I lie under a field of stars."

Andy jumped back. "How d'ya know that?"

"It is a very common code for Templars to know. When we need to send messages, we often use this coded language."

"Why did ya na' tell me?" Andy asked, a hurt look on his face.

"It was for your own safety. The less you know the safer you are."

"I would hardly call m'self safe. Ya found me strapped down ta a bed, about ta be tortured." Andy crossed his arms in a huff.

"That is true," Etienne said with a smile. After a moment he continued, "Santiago said there was still time for our friends. We must find this Keystone Church, before anything happened to his wife. Etienne felt like he was the worst husband who had ever existed. He would make it up to Isabella: he would save her.

CHAPTER 30

THE GUARDIANS OF GALICIA

Mariano was an expert tracker, but he had never experienced anything like this. He examined the nearest patch of blood, accompanied by paw prints, unsure what to make of what he was seeing. The prints were definitely canine, but larger than any he had seen. On either side of the prints there were drag marks and blood. He had no idea how they were traveling so quickly. If Isabella were dead, why would the animals carry her this far?

The woods became dense overhead and the evening sun was having trouble pushing through. "We cannot go any further," Mariano said looking at the others. "If we continue in this light, we will lose the trail and all hope of finding Isabella." Gerhart plopped down on a large log.

"We 'ave to keep goin'," Clair said, putting her hands on her hips defiantly.

"We almost lost the trail last night. We cannot take another chance." This was their second day of tracking, and Mariano knew if they didn't find Isabella soon, their search would be futile.

"Mariano is right. If we lose the tracks in the darkness, we may never find them again. I'll start a fire," Gerhart said. He gathered some sticks and twigs around a felled log and quickly built a fire.

"I just canna' give up the feelin' that she's close." Reluctantly, Clair sat next to Gerhart. "Isabella!" she shouted one last time.

A howl called back through the dark night. Mariano looked into the forest wondering if that was the wolf who had Isabella. Another howl came, this time a little closer, then a chorus erupted around them. His hopes were dashed. This was something different: this was a whole pack.

Mariano grabbed his knives. "Quickly, take your weapons and stand back-to-back. They will try to attack from behind. Do not give them that opportunity."

The night became silent. They waited, back-to-back, with the small fire glowing at their side. Mariano felt neither fear nor anticipation, he was simply present. He had both Gerhart and Clair at his side. The three of them wouldn't go down without putting up a fight.

A large black wolf, with eyes so blue they looked white, stepped into the radius of light. The wolf bared his teeth and saliva dripped from his fangs. Another wolf appeared at his right, another at his left, and two more approached flanking the small band. Mariano and his companions breathed as one person. He focused on keeping that breath calm and purposeful, unsure if it would be his last.

The black wolf took a step closer, growling.

"Get ready," Mariano said, holding his knives loosely at his side.

Gerhart let out a loud battle cry, but this only made the black beast growl more. It lowered its body, preparing to attack, and the other wolves followed suit. Before Mariano could register what happened, the black wolf leapt at Clair. He felt her body jolt, preparing for the inevitable blow, and she raised her arms in defense.

Just before the black wolf made contact, he was intercepted and knocked to the ground by a huge gray wolf with blood-matted fur. The larger wolf sunk its teeth deep into the black wolf's neck and pinned him to the ground. The pack moved to attack the larger wolf, and he released his death grip to snarl at the other wolves.

This distraction gave the black wolf a moment to recover. He lunged up at the large wolf, sending it back. The black wolf pounced on the larger wolf's back, sinking its teeth into the already bloodstained fur. The large wolf threw its body to-and-fro. It smashed the black wolf against a tree, sending both to the ground. They fought viciously—they fought savagely. Blood painted all that surrounded them. Mariano knew this was a battle to the death.

The larger wolf was dominating the fight now. Another wolf lowered its body to attack. Before it left the ground, Mariano threw one of his knives. It found a home deep in the beast's neck, sending it to the ground whimpering until all life left its body. The other wolves backed up warily.

The larger wolf pinned the black wolf on its back. He lowered his head and his teeth sunk deep into the black wolf's neck. When he pulled back, he tore the black wolf's throat open, sending blood spilling out over the ground. The large wolf faced the pack, blood dripping from its jowls, and all the other wolves disappeared into the forest.

The large wolf took one step toward the band of travelers, then collapsed. Concerned for their savior, Mariano filled a gourd with water and rushed to the wolf. When he was a foot away, the wolf raised its head and snarled. Mariano stopped dead in his tracks and placed the water on the ground, then backed up slowly, saying, "Thank you." The wolf inched its body toward the gourd and drank. Mariano wished he could do more for the victor. That had been one of the most spectacular fights Mariano had ever witnessed.

The bushes behind them rustled, and a boy jumped out from the foliage. He ran at them with a knife clenched between his teeth. Mariano thought he was human, but he moved like an animal. The boy surveyed the scene, then growled at Mariano, who backed up to give him space. The boy rushed to the large wolf and cradled him in his arms, licking his wounds. Mariano felt like he was watching something out of a legend. He looked at his companions for confirmation that this was actually happening. Both Clair and Gerhart nodded.

The boy howled, and out of the same woods appeared a white wolf, who had something on its back.

"Isabella!" Clair cried. Mariano looked closer at the wolf and saw a bloodied Isabella draped over its back. Isabella raised her head then lowered it again, obviously too weak to keep it lifted.

Sensing the boy's distrust, Mariano said, "Put down your weapons." Once their weapons were on the ground, the boy seemed to relax. He communicated something to the white wolf, and it walked to Gerhart, lying down as gently as possible to roll Isabella softly to the ground at his feet. Immediately, the white wolf joined the boy and the large wolf.

The boy turned to the others and growled, "Benedictus... Help... Follow."

"Can I help carry him?" Gerhart pointed to the wolf. Even though Gerhart was a force to be reckoned with, Mariano knew he had a soft spot for animals.

The boy looked at Gerhart, then looked at the large wolf. He nodded and Gerhart lifted the large beast onto his shoulders. Mariano and Clair lifted Isabella. The white wolf approached and stood between them, looking at Isabella expectantly.

"Moira help... quicker," the boy said. The wolf whined, as if telling them to place Isabella on her back. Mariano and Clair lowered Isabella gently onto white wolf. "Come," the boy said, rushing into the forest.

Mariano and the others followed their strange guide until they came to the edge of the forest. In the distance was a small village with a stream running through it. Mariano headed toward the village.

The boy ran in front of him. "No!" He pointed at Moira and the other wolf. "Kill... Benedictus help."

They continued on the edge of the forest to the massive hill behind the village. Up and up they climbed. As they reached the top of the hill, the trees opened, revealing a simple church. "Benedictus," the boy said, rushing forward.

The boy let out a piercing howl, and a few moments later a light appeared in the chapel. The door swung open, filling the ground with light. Adjusting his eyes, Mariano saw a benevolent-looking monk dressed in a brown robe with a cord about his waist. He had a short silver beard and resembled someone from antiquity.

The boy looked up at the monk pleadingly. "Benedictus, help."

"Oh, my child," said the monk, with a compassionate voice. He stepped aside from the door and ushered the travelers in, leaving the cold of night and the wilderness behind them. As they entered, the monk asked, "Do you speak the common tongue?"

"Yes," Mariano replied.

"What on God's earth happened?" he asked, looking at the large injured wolf and Isabella laid out on Moira's back. Mariano looked at him blankly; he didn't quite know how to explain what had just happened.

The Monk shut the door. "We need to act quickly. Come." He led them to the front of the church. They went to the left at the altar, into a humble room with a bed and a solitary chair.

"Place her on the bed," the monk said. Mariano swiftly followed orders. The monk laid out the extra linen on the floor and made a nest for the large wolf. Mariano had so many questions for this old monk. He never expected this would be the outcome of their expedition.

"Place Bennie in here," the monk said as he completed the nest.

"Bennie?" Gerhart asked, placing the large wolf amongst the blankets.

"Yes, yes. This is Benedictus, Moira, and Raphael. We will do formal introductions later. Right now, we need to work quickly." He hastily bandaged Bennie to stop the bleeding, then moved to Isabella. He removed her bandage, exposing a broken leg and a wound that had festered. Mariano had seen many wounds in battle, but it was hard to see Isabella like this.

"In that cupboard—hand me the alcohol," said the monk. Gerhart rushed off in the direction he was pointing. While he did this, the monk patted Isabella on the shoulder. "This will hurt, my child." He took both hands to her leg and reset the bone. It made a terrible sound as it found its proper home. Mariano cringed at the noise.

Isabella screamed and Moira howled with her. Gerhart reappeared with a bottle containing a clear liquid.

"My apologies once again." The old monk poured the alcohol over Isabella's wound and she whimpered.

The monk turned to Clair. "Can you sew?"

Clair shook her head.

"I can," Gerhart said.

The monk fished through a drawer and produced a needle and thread. He put the needle over the open flame to sterilize it, then handed it to Gerhart. "This wound needs to be threaded." He turned his attention to the giant wolf that lay stoically in the nest of sheets. "Benedictus, what have you done?" He petted the wolf gently.

"'E saved us," said Clair, looking fondly at the animal.

"I would expect nothing less," the old monk said as he tended to the wounds of the unflinching wolf.

When the work was done, the sun had already peeked above the horizon. Gerhart opened his large mouth and yawned widely. Mariano felt weary as well, but he wanted answers for all that was going on.

"I think that is all we can do here," the monk said. "I would offer you a bed, but mine is already taken. All I can offer are the pews in the chapel."

"That will work just fine. Thank you, Benedict, for all of your help," Mariano said.

"My name's not Benedict. I'm Brother Philip."

"Why did the boy say, 'Benedictus, help,' and then lead us to you?" asked Mariano.

"I am a Benedictine monk," Philip said kindly.

"Ahh... and how did you come to know these... this pack?" Mariano motioned to the boy and two wolves curled up together.

The old monk smiled, his beard lifting as his cheeks raised. "I found Moira and Benedict when they were pups and raised them here. When they became large enough, they left for the wild. I didn't see them for many years. When they returned, they had this young one with them. I named the boy Raphael and taught him what speech I could. The three of them didn't stay long. A wild animal at heart can't be kept within walls. I haven't seen them in many years and I assumed that they had joined a pack. Every now and then, as the rare pilgrim would pass through, I would hear stories of the boy with two wolves. They got the nickname 'The Guardians of Galicia.' Pilgrims have told me he and the two wolves had protected them along the road to Santiago." Mariano was even more amazed at the pack after Philip had told the story.

The old monk smiled at Raphael, Moira, and Benedict. "I am very proud and happy to see them. I didn't think I would see them again on this earth."

"Come on, let's go to bed." Gerhart placed a large hand on Mariano's shoulder. "Are you coming, Clair?"

Clair remained on the bed next to Isabella. "Ach, No I'm gonna stay with Isabella tonight. See ya in the morn." Gerhart smiled.

In the chapel, Mariano and Gerhart each picked a large wooden pew to call a bed for the night. Mariano stared at the ceiling and thought of all that had happened that day. During the fight, Mariano hadn't felt fear, just curiosity. He had been in many dangerous situations, and before, he'd always felt the slightest bit of fear. But now it was gone. Mariano wondered what the Alchemist had done to him.

CHAPTER 31

THE EMPTY

Isabella awoke in Clair's warm embrace. She was curled up in her arms, her head resting on Clair's bosom. She tried to move, but felt pain in her leg. Her wound was now sewn shut and her leg in a splint.

"Ach, good mornin'," Clair said groggily, having woken from Isabella's movement. "'appy to see you are feelin' better."

"Thank you. Did you—?" Isabella motioned to her leg.

Clair shook her head. "'Twas Gerhart an' Philip. I didna know he could sew."

"Who is Philip?"

"That would be me." Brother Philip entered the room with a large tray of food.

Smelling the food, the wolves and the boy stirred from their slumber and poked their heads up from the nest of blankets on the floor. The larger wolf yawned widely and whined a little as he exhaled. The second wolf stood and shook out her body, she then stretched her front paws forward and lowered her head. Even though they had huge fangs, Isabella didn't feel frightened by them.

Both Mariano and Gerhart entered at the same time. "Is that breakfast I smell?" Gerhart asked.

"Ach, you big lug, is tha' all ya think about?" Clair smiled at him and nodded her head toward Isabella.

Gerhart looked bashful. "Oh... uhh... Good morning, Isabella. It is great to see you feeling better."

Isabella smiled. "Thank you, Gerhart."

"I wasn't planning on all of us eating in this small bedroom, but since we are here, I will fetch the rest of the food." Philip set down the large tray on the end of the bed, and Clair helped him distribute the plates of eggs.

Brother Philip turned to leave, but Isabella grabbed his arm. "Thank you for everything."

Brother Philip looked at her with a fatherly smile. "It is all in the service of God, my dear. No need to thank me."

During breakfast, the others had told her of the ordeal she'd gone through, and that she had the boy, Raphael, and the wolves, Benedictus and Moira, to thank for her survival. Isabella was astounded at the story. She thought she had dreamt being carried by the wolves.

When all the others had gone off to help with chores. Moira rose from the floor and walked up to Isabella. She rested her white head on the mattress and looked up at her like a puppy. Isabella stroked Moira's neck. "Thank you for saving me." Moira nuzzled into Isabella's arm and licked her hand.

Gerhart appeared in the doorway. "Would you like to come out to the garden to get some fresh air? It's a beautiful day."

"I would love that." Gerhart picked her up and Isabella asked, "How is the work going?"

"I would rather carry you than clean the chicken coop," said Gerhart. "That's why I am here." He winked and both laughed.

Gerhart was right, the day was spectacular. The sun was shining brightly and there wasn't a cloud in the sky. The temperature was just right with a slight breeze. Gerhart carried Isabella to the back of the church, where she saw a beautiful garden. There were many colored plants, some bearing fruit, and just beyond the garden lay the woods. There was a great sense of peace about the whole place. It had the feeling of growth and healing, with a simple natural beauty.

Gerhart put Isabella down on a log and placed a large stump under her leg. She cringed as he lifted her leg, but knew it was for the best.

"Gerhart, Gerhart, where are you? I have another job for you." The kindly voice of Philip filled the air. "There is something I have been trying to reach for years but haven't been able to… Gerhart!" Isabella and Gerhart exchanged a smile.

"You better go. It sounds really important."

Gerhart sighed loudly and said, "Coming." He rose and walked toward Philip's voice.

Isabella sat admiring the garden. She was so grateful to be alive, to feel the sun on her face once more, to hear the birds singing. Her body was in pain, but her spirit was high. After facing death, the things that had troubled her before didn't seem to matter. Her worries seemed like the worries of another person. A different life. All she felt was gratitude for this moment.

A loud crash came from the grape vines. A second later, Raphael appeared with a dead rabbit between his jowls. Isabella smiled at him and the boy walked over to her on all fours. Her smile was more from curiosity than amusement. Raphael hunted like an animal. How did he have those instincts?

"How did you know there was a rabbit there?"

The boy dropped the rabbit, and without missing a beat, he pointed to his left. "Mouse." Then across the garden, "Butterfly." Then to the edge of the forest, "Hawk." Isabella followed his finger and saw all the creatures after straining her eyes to find them.

"How do you see them?"

"No see... Feel... Nothing connects. Empty connects." Raphael closed his eyes and pointed to a rock three feet away. "Lizard."

Isabella saw a small lizard sunning himself on the rock. He pointed next to Isabella's feet. "Ants." Isabella looked down and saw a few small ants. He stuck out his finger. "Butterfly." As he finished saying the word, a beautiful yellow butterfly landed on his extended finger.

"You... Feel nothing... All around... Close eyes."

Isabella closed her eyes at these strange instructions and tried to feel nothing. She shook her head. *How do you feel nothing?*

"And what are you two doing?" Brother Philip's question startled Isabella's eyes open.

The boy smiled. "Feel nothing."

"Ahh, I see," Brother Philip said. "May I join you?"

"Of course, you can, but I'm not really sure what we're doing," Isabella said, making space on the log next to her.

Brother Philip sat down. "Would you like me to explain?" Isabella nodded. Philip picked up a stick and cleared the dirt in front of them.

When he was finished, Brother Philip asked, "What is this?"

She looked down at the ground. "Just some dirt."

"No, it's the ocean," Philip said with a smile.

Isabella raised an eyebrow. "I don't see it."

Brother Philip drew with his stick. When he was finished, he pointed to his rudimentary drawings of fish. "Does this help?"

"Yes, now I see fish, but I still don't see the ocean."

Philip bent down again and drew a box around the fish and some squiggly waves between the fish and the top of the box. "What about now?"

"Yes, now I see the ocean," Isabella said, still unsure of the point he was trying to make.

"Good," Brother Philip said. "God is like the blank canvas, formless. It can only know itself by adding form. Just like when I added the fish and waves, you knew it to be the ocean. So, by creating the heavens and the earth, separating day and night, God began to know itself. But if you look down at the picture, you will notice all the forms on the ground are connected by empty space. Without the empty space between them, the forms wouldn't exist. God is the empty space between forms that connects us all together. Man has forgotten this and sees himself as separate, but we can never be separate. It is this formlessness that gives us form. If you can feel this formlessness all around you and in you, you will know God. That is what Raphael means by saying, 'the empty connects us.'" Isabella let this soak in. It was one of the most profound things she had ever heard.

"So, you are saying that God is the empty space between me and that tree?" asked Isabella doubtfully, pointing to the closest tree.

"Without that empty space between you and the tree, there would be no you, and there would be no tree. There would be no form, there would be no existence." Philip erased the picture creating a blank canvas.

Isabella thought about his words deeply as Brother Philip drew. "It isn't just the physical space between you and the tree. It is the space between each thought. It is the space inside you. This is why, when you let go of your past, you are open to becoming what you are to be filled with next."

A flower appeared where the ocean had been. "This flower could have never come into existence unless the space had become empty once again. This is what is meant by, 'Doing God's will.' The emptier you become, the more ways God can draw you."

Brother Philip erased the flower and drew a box with the shape of a vase in it. "What do you see now?"

"I see a vase."

"I see two faces."

Her eyes narrowed at the image, trying to see what he saw. Finally, she shook her head. "What do you mean? It is a vase."

"Focus on the empty, not on the form." Isabella squinted her eyes. After a few moments, she saw it. The empty space around the form of the vase made two faces about to kiss.

"How is this possible?"

Brother Philip smiled. "Life is like this—you will see what you focus on. Whether you focus on the form, or the space creating the form, will determine if you will live in heaven, or in hell. It will determine whether you will live separate from everything, or connected. It is all perspective. The tree loses its leaves when it is done with them. The snake sheds its skin when it no longer fits.

They grow out of the form they were, without question, without hesitation, and the formless is always there, to perfectly surround its new form. The snake is now taking up more space; the tree less."

Brother Philip continued, "You can't have something without nothing. It is impossible. This creates a duality, but the trick is to know that we are all connected to the formless, and nothing is everything. Every form you have ever seen is made of the nothing surrounding it. Now close your eyes and feel this space."

Isabella closed her eyes, trying to feel the empty space around her. Then she felt it: an insect flying a few feet away from her, its wings sending ripples through the nothing, creating a new form with each stroke. She smiled.

Noticing, Brother Philip said, "When one thing affects the formless, all forms are affected."

Isabella felt a leaf fall from a tree in the woods. It was as if her body was connected to everything. She felt every movement of the leaf as it fell through the air. It sent ripples out into the formless forever, just like a drop of water on the ocean sends out ripples in all directions.

Isabella opened her eyes. "That is amazing!"

"It is the miracle of God," Philip said smiling. "Bringing form to the formless." He placed his hand on her wound, and in an instant, her leg was healed. Isabella looked at her leg, then at Philip, then back to her leg again. Isabella had no explanation for what just happened. She had experienced a miracle.

Isabella managed the words. "Thank you," with tears in her eyes.

"I am just an empty vessel. Thank God," said Philip kindly.

Isabella closed her eyes. She longed for the connectedness she had felt moments earlier. She wanted to feel the nothing again—to feel herself as everything, and everything as her.

CHAPTER 32

PORTOMARIN

Etienne was sore from riding all day. They only took a short break to ask travelers if they had seen the church in the picture. To Etienne's dismay, no one they encountered had seen it. They passed the towns of Triacastela and Sarria, which had several small gray stone houses. As the sun was setting, they reached the town of Portomarin. They stopped and watered their horse at the river in front of the city.

To Etienne's right, there was an old fisherman, sitting lazily holding his pole. He wore a large hat that covered his eyes. After filling his gourd with water, Etienne walked to the old man and cleared his throat.

The old man lifted the brim of his hat. "How may I be of service to you, young man?"

Etienne pulled out the parchment from his tunic and brought the paper close to the old man. "Have you ever seen this church before?"

"And what do two Templars have need of a church for? Is there something you need to confess?" The old man laughed until he started coughing.

"That is our business." Etienne's blood began to race. He wished the old man would just answer his question.

"Well, it is my business then if I have ever seen it." The old man lowered his hat and ignored Etienne. Just at that moment, he got a bite on his pole. He struggled with the fish for a few minutes then pulled it out of the water. "She is a beauty," said the old-timer, holding up the fish. "I haven't gotten a bite all day. Maybe this is a sign. All right, I will tell you. The church you are looking for is just up there, on that hill, behind the city. Rumor has it that a saint lives there, but the Hounds of Hell keep him prisoner. Most who have ventured there have never returned." Etienne was elated. He could have kissed the old man.

Etienne smiled and said, "That's the place we're looking for. Thank you." He was ready to face the Hounds of Hell to save his wife.

"The garden healed you?" Gerhart asked Isabella.

"Yes, we were sitting there talking and then my leg was healed," Isabella moved her leg forward and backward. She felt no pain; her leg was completely restored. She didn't like lying to the others, but Philip asked her not to tell him that he had healed her.

"This truly is a magical place," said Mariano. "Maybe we should just stay here."

"You are more than welcome to stay as long as you'd like," said Philip, "It is nice to have company after so many years of being alone." Isabella felt a tug on her heart. She thought this would have been an excellent place for her and Etienne to run away for a while. No one would think to find them here.

"Pass the potatoes," said Gerhart, with a mouth full of food.

Clair nudged him in the side with her elbow. "Swalla first." Gerhart finished chewing and swallowed the large mouthful. Isabella smiled and passed him the potatoes.

"Thank you so much for your kind invitation, but I must take a ship back to France. I have responsibilities." Isabella took the bowl back from Gerhart, who had served himself a large portion.

"I understand," Philip said. Isabella did have responsibilities. After facing death, she realized her responsibility was to her friends. If she left them, perhaps the Shadows would only pursue her. Also, maybe her father would give up his quest if she married Edward. There would be peace with England and he wouldn't need the treasure. After her experience with the crone, Isabella realized her search for the treasure had only brought death, and she wanted nothing to do with it. Thinking of France made Isabella think of Tristan; she still didn't know if he was dead or alive, nor why he had tried to poison them.

After dinner, Isabella returned to the small bedroom off to the side of the chapel. Philip refused to take back the room, even after Isabella's miraculous healing. Benedict laid nestled in the blankets on the floor. His wounds seemed to be healed as well. Moira and Raphael were nowhere to be seen. Isabella supposed they were off in the forest doing whatever it is wolves do at night.

There was a gentle rapping on the door, and Benedict's head shot up, his ears at attention.

"Come in," said Isabella.

Philip opened the door with a kind smile on his face. "I was just coming to check on my patients." He walked to Benedict and patted him on the head. He looked him over, then he turned to Isabella. "All looks to be in order here. And how are you feeling?"

"I am fine," she replied. "A little tired, but fine. Why didn't you want me to tell the others you healed me?"

"Because it wasn't me that healed you." Philip stood, brushed off his robes, and walked to the door.

As he was about to exit, Isabella said, "You know, Philip is my father's name."

"He must be a great man, to raise such a daughter as yourself," Philip said, turning to look at her.

"He is great, and terrible. The sad part is, I admired him unconditionally and would have done anything to get his approval—even betray my friends." Isabella lowered her head.

Philip walked back to the bed and sat next to her. "That doesn't seem to be who you truly are. I see a loyal, loving, and grateful person in front of me."

Isabella looked up at him. "This road has changed me. Love has changed me. But, I am afraid of what I have done, and who I will become when I return home. I don't want to become that person again. I don't want to betray my friends. I have come to love them so much, as well as those who gave up their lives to protect me."

Philip looked at her with kind eyes. "It sounds like you need to let go of your past, to create space for God to fill you. He will guide you to become what you are meant to be next. Just like the snake or the tree—"

A howl filled the air, interrupting their conversation. They looked at each other and said, "Moira!"

"She only howls when there is danger," Philip said rising.

Gerhart and Mariano were already at the main entrance with weapons ready. Mariano counted to three and they all burst through the front door, ready to fight. Isabella saw Moira growling at two riders on a horse. The lead rider dismounted and pulled his large sword. Before he took two steps, Benedict leapt past Isabella. The two wolves attacked the man, pinning him to the ground.

"Ach, no!!!" the second rider said.

Isabella's eyes widened, and she looked back at Gerhart and Mariano briefly. "Andy, is that you?"

"Course 'tis, and we came to save ya from these savage beasts."

The other rider continued to wrestle with the two wolves, but they were too strong. Benedict pinned him and lowered his jowls to bite.

"Benedict, Moira, that is enough," Philip said. Reluctantly the two wolves turned and came back to the door.

"Who is with you?" Isabella asked. She hoped beyond hope she knew the answer, but didn't want to get too excited.

"It's Etienne. He—"

Isabella gasped, thanking the Lord for bringing him back to her. Before Andy could finish his sentence, she rushed to Etienne and cradled his head in her arms.

"I should have let them eat you," she said half-jokingly.

Etienne looked up at her, and she saw the love she so missed in his eyes. "I couldn't leave you in danger. You're more important than... than..."

"It's alright, we can talk later." Together they rose and walked back to the church with the others. Seeing Etienne again felt more surreal than having her leg instantly healed. *This truly is a place of miracles.*

Andy dismounted the horse and joined them. "Clair... where is Clair?"

The sound of wood dropping made him jump. "I am right 'ere," Clair said lovingly, running up to him and wrapping her arms around his stomach.

"I missed ya so much." Andy hooked Clair's arm and together they walked into the church.

"Etienne, Look, 'tis the same code—" Etienne quickly covered Andy's mouth.

Isabella pulled them both in tightly for another hug. "I am so happy to have you both back." She brushed aside her anger over how he'd acted when she last saw him, happy that he was here now. There'd be time to clear the air later. She just wanted to hold them now and forget about everything else in the world.

Andy awoke to a wet slobbery feeling on his face. He opened his eyes to the white wolf's tongue coming in for another round. He tried to move, but it was too late. Moira's tongue licked his cheek, and he sat up quickly to avoid her getting another taste. "Ach, so you're the Hounds of Hell." He patted her on the head. "Ya aren't so scary in the daylight." Moira stared up at him with her purple eyes and set her head in his lap.

Andy placed his hand on the small of his back. *My bod is killin' me from sleeping on this pew.* He had spent the whole night in fear of falling off and hitting the stone ground. The pew just wasn't wide enough for someone of his size.

Everyone was still asleep and Gerhart's loud snore filled the chapel, but by this point, it was like music to Andy's ears. It was the familiar sound of home. The church was small and simple; the only decoration was the ornate wooden altar framing pictures within its construct. All in all, the chapel wasn't special in any way, except for the code carved into the large gray stone blocks that the church was constructed of.

Moira whined. "I didna forget about you, girl." He continued to pet her. "Well, no time like the present." He reached into his bag and pulled out the picture of the church. Turning it over, he copied down what was on the walls. He recognized all of the symbols form the Templar code on one wall, but he had never seen the symbols on the opposite wall. Both codes were twenty-six stones high by twenty-six stones wide.

Wall 1

```
  ∨ < ∧ > ▷ ◁ △ ▽ ⊽ ◊ ◇ ○ × ∨ < ∧ >
∨ < ∧ > ▷ ◁ △ ▽ ⊽ ◊ ◇ ○ × ∨ < ∧ > ▽
< ∧ > ▷ ◁ △ ▽ ⊽ ◊ ◇ ○ × ∨ < ∧ > ▽ ◁
∧ > ▷ ◁ △ ▽ ⊽ ◊ ◇ ○ × ∨ < ∧ > ▽ ◁ △
> ▷ ◁ △ ▽ ⊽ ◊ ◇ ○ × ∨ < ∧ > ▽ ◁ △ ▷
▷ ◁ △ ▽ ⊽ ◊ ◇ ○ × ∨ < ∧ > ▽ ◁ △ ▷ ◊
◁ △ ▽ ⊽ ◊ ◇ ○ × ∨ < ∧ > ▽ ◁ △ ▷ ◊ ⊽
△ ▽ ⊽ ◊ ◇ ○ × ∨ < ∧ > ▽ ◁ △ ▷ ◊ ⊽ ◇
▽ ⊽ ◊ ◇ ○ × ∨ < ∧ > ▽ ◁ △ ▷ ◊ ⊽ ◇ ◌
⊽ ◊ ◇ ○ × ∨ < ∧ > ▽ ◁ △ ▷ ◊ ⊽ ◇ ◌ ∨
◊ ◇ ○ × ∨ < ∧ > ▽ ◁ △ ▷ ◊ ⊽ ◇ ◌ ∨ <
◇ ○ × ∨ < ∧ > ▽ ◁ △ ▷ ◊ ⊽ ◇ ◌ ∨ < ∧
○ × ∨ < ∧ > ▽ ◁ △ ▷ ◊ ⊽ ◇ ◌ ∨ < ∧ >
× ∨ < ∧ > ▽ ◁ △ ▷ ◊ ⊽ ◇ ◌ ∨ < ∧ > ▷
∨ < ∧ > ▽ ◁ △ ▷ ◊ ⊽ ◇ ◌ ∨ < ∧ > ▷ ◁
< ∧ > ▽ ◁ △ ▷ ◊ ⊽ ◇ ◌ ∨ < ∧ > ▷ ◁ △
∧ > ▽ ◁ △ ▷ ◊ ⊽ ◇ ◌ ∨ < ∧ > ▷ ◁ △ ▽
> ▽ ◁ △ ▷ ◊ ⊽ ◇ ◌ ∨ < ∧ > ▷ ◁ △ ▽ ⊽
▽ ◁ △ ▷ ◊ ⊽ ◇ ◌ ∨ < ∧ > ▷ ◁ △ ▽ ⊽ ◊
◁ △ ▷ ◊ ⊽ ◇ ◌ ∨ < ∧ > ▷ ◁ △ ▽ ⊽ ◊ ◇
△ ▷ ◊ ⊽ ◇ ◌ ∨ < ∧ > ▷ ◁ △ ▽ ⊽ ◊ ◇ ○
▷ ◊ ⊽ ◇ ◌ ∨ < ∧ > ▷ ◁ △ ▽ ⊽ ◊ ◇ ○ ×
◊ ⊽ ◇ ◌ ∨ < ∧ > ▷ ◁ △ ▽ ⊽ ◊ ◇ ○ × ∨
⊽ ◇ ◌ ∨ < ∧ > ▷ ◁ △ ▽ ⊽ ◊ ◇ ○ × ∨ <
◇ ◌ ∨ < ∧ > ▷ ◁ △ ▽ ⊽ ◊ ◇ ○ × ∨ < ∧
◌ ∨ < ∧ > ▷ ◁ △ ▽ ⊽ ◊ ◇ ○ × ∨ < ∧ >
```

Wall 2

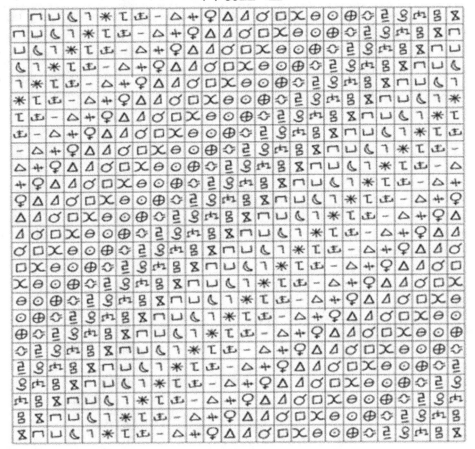

Moira quickly got bored with Andy ignoring her and went over to Gerhart, whose massive feet were hanging over the edge of his pew. She sniffed them a few times, then licked vigorously. Gerhart squirmed and let out a loud laugh that awoke everyone else from their slumber. Satisfied with the job she had done, Moira turned and left the chapel for the small room with Isabella and Benedict.

Noticing Andy writing furiously, Etienne left his pew and sat next to him. "You don't waste any time, do you?"

"Well, Moira woke me up. The beast almost ate me," Andy said with a smile. "I didna' want to wake you lot, so I figured I would make good use of the time."

"Nothing I can say will make you stop looking, will it?"

"Once my mind is set into action, I just canna help it. It works on its own. Why, I almost have this-a one figured out. It seems ta be another coded grid. It 'as the alphabet going across and up and down." Andy pointed to his right "I knew the symbols on that wall from the Templar code and assumed that these new symbols were the mirror opposite." Andy pointed to the other wall. He then held up the paper to show the code and below it, written out in letters, was this strange grid.

```
    A B C D E F G H I K L M N O P Q R S T U V W X Y Z
A   B C D E F G H I K L M N O P Q R S T U V W X Y Z A
B   C D E F G H I K L M N O P Q R S T U V W X Y Z A S
C   D E F G H I K L M N O P Q R S T U V W X Y Z A B C
D   E F G H I K L M N O P Q R S T U V W X Y Z A B C D
E   F G H I K L M N O P Q R S T U V W X Y Z A B C D E
F   G H I K L M N O P Q R S T U V W X Y Z A B C D E F
G   H I K L M N O P Q R S T U V W X Y Z A B C D E F G
H   I K L M N O P Q R S T U V W X Y Z A B C D E F G H
I   K L M N O P Q R S T U V W X Y Z A B C D E F G H I
K   L M N O P Q R S T U V W X Y Z A B C D E F G H I K
L   M N O P Q R S T U V W X Y Z A B C D E F G H I K L
M   N O P Q R S T U V W X Y Z A B C D E F G H I K L M
N   O P Q R S T U V W X Y Z A B C D E F G H I K L M N
O   P Q R S T U V W X Y Z A B C D E F G H I K L M N O
P   Q R S T U V W X Y Z A B C D E F G H I K L M N O P
Q   R S T U V W X Y Z A B C D E F G H I K L M N O P Q
R   S T U V W X Y Z A B C D E F G H I K L M N O P Q R
S   T U V W X Y Z A B C D E F G H I K L M N O P Q R S
T   U V W X Y Z A B C D E F G H I K L M N O P Q R S T
U   V W X Y Z A B C D E F G H I K L M N O P Q R S T U
V   W X Y Z A B C D E F G H I K L M N O P Q R S T U V
W   X Y Z A B C D E F G H I K L M N O P Q R S T U V W
X   Y Z A B C D E F G H I K L M N O P Q R S T U V W X
Y   Z A B C D E F G H I K L M N O P Q R S T U V W X Y
Z   A B C D E F G H I K L M N O P Q R S T U V W X Y Z
```

"What do ya make of this?" Andy asked.

"I don't know," replied Etienne, looking at the grid.

The door to Isabella's bedroom creaked on its hinges and she appeared. Isabella looked radiant, silhouetted by a soft white light.

"Excuse me." Etienne rose and walked to Isabella. As he approached, Isabella crossed her arms and her gaze narrowed. Etienne knew he would have to answer for the way he had treated her at the castle. He needed to take responsibility for his actions. "May I talk with you?" he asked. "There is something I need to explain."

Isabella looked past Etienne's shoulder at the others and said, "Let's go to the garden." She walked across the chapel to the small door and exited.

The morning air was brisk, and the birds were merrily singing their songs. As they reached the garden, Isabella stopped abruptly and asked, "Why did you leave without saying goodbye? Why were you so distant in Ponferrada? It was as if the moment we stepped into that castle, I was nothing to you and after we... after we made a vow to God and..." Etienne put a hand on her shoulder and she shrugged it away.

"I... I have failed you as a husband. There's a conflict between the oath I took and my love for you," Isabella turned to face him and he continued, "I chose wrong in Ponferrada. I realized after I left that my love for you is more important than my oath; more important than my life. I can't imagine a world without you in it. It has always been that way. You were the only light in my life. My one reason for everything I did at your father's castle when we were young. I never dared to think I would see you again; and now that I have, I never want to let you go." Isabella took his hand. Her skin was warm and soft. They exchanged a smile. Etienne took a breath, knowing he had to tell her the reason he'd abandoned her. "Also, Molay said something that made me leave."

"What did he say?" Isabella asked, her eyes becoming guarded.

"He said that maybe you weren't the person I thought you were. He said maybe you and Tristan had been working together and that you kept me away from camp so you could steal the secret we were carrying. Isabella, I know you opened the door in Castrojeriz and that you are after the treasure." Isabella's eyes got cold and distant. This look confirmed everything to Etienne. He took a breath and continued, "Molay said that he had seen you in your father's court and you were ruthless. This made me question everything I knew about you. I believed him and didn't listen to my heart."

Isabella withdrew her hand from his and held her head down for a long pause. As she raised her head, her features seemed somewhat harder and her eyes colder. It seemed that Isabella had discarded her guise of innocence. "We all have our duties and responsibilities in this life: you to your order, and me to my people and the future of my kingdom."

It was almost as if Etienne didn't recognize the person in front of him. The Isabella who had been so sweet and loving was now a thousand miles away, with a glacier of ice separating them.

"My father's kingdom... My kingdom is destitute and indebted to your order. Do you really think I was taking this pilgrimage to purify myself before my dreaded marriage to that English prince? My father had heard that the Templars greatest treasure lay on the Camino. He said if I found this treasure, I wouldn't have to marry Edward. He said we would be the most powerful kingdom in the world. We would be free, Etienne. Help me find the treasure and together we can rule as man and wife."

Etienne took two steps back and put his hand on his sword. Molay had been right, Isabella had only been using him to get closer to the treasure. Etienne felt like a fool for falling into her trap. She had used him.

"Now you will kill the one to whom you just professed your love? Saying that her life was worth more than your own?" She laughed at this. "Maybe I was wrong about you. Maybe you are just like all the other men."

"What about Clair, Andy, and the others?" asked Etienne. He wanted to buy time to decide what to do.

Isabella laughed again. "They are pawns, just like you; the means to my end. You all are nothing to me. I only care about the treasure and my kingdom. I will make my father proud. Tristan would have taken my offer to rule alongside me."

A white heat flashed through Etienne, he drew his sword and ran it through Isabella. "Tristan betrayed you. He was going to sell you to the Moors." Isabella's eyes widened, and she fell to the ground.

CHAPTER 33

PALAIS DE LA CITÉ

King Philip sat in his throne room; his long fingers pressed hard together just below his chin. He was lost deep in thought, his cunning eyes out of focus, staring into the void.

I didn't think our new Pope would be so much trouble. My, how people change when they are given power. That is why having power is reserved for people like me: people who actually know how to wield it.

Philip smiled cruelly as he re-lived burning the Pope's hand. He'd loved the way Clement had whimpered. Philip's mind went in six different directions, each one leading to a strategy for an endgame with the Pope. The one he favored most was watching the Pope burn alive after being caught in the act of devil worship. But alas, the one that was most likely was the Pope following orders like the little sheep he was.

The large doors at the end of the throne room opened, interrupting Philip's daydream. Pierre, his closest advisor, rushed to him; his heavy footsteps echoed in the hall as he approached the throne.

Philip dropped his hands from his chin. "Why are you disturbing me, Pierre?"

Pierre's footsteps quickened at this, and he was soon kneeling in front of the throne, his head bowed low. "Your most Excellent Exalted Majesty. There is a delegation from England here."

"What do they want?" Philip barked. "Were we expecting them?"

"No, Your Majesty, we most certainly were not expecting them. They are here about... about Isabella," said Pierre.

"Very well, make yourself useful and let them in," Philip clutched his throne in annoyance. As Pierre got up to go, Philip added, "And Pierre, make sure not to be too polite to them. You must remember that we are their betters."

"Yes, Your Majesty, of course we are." Pierre flashed a proud grin and bowed low. He rose, then sped off to the large doors at the end of the hall, his footsteps echoing the whole way.

I really need to put down carpet, or get that man new shoes, Philip mused.

Within minutes, Pierre reappeared with two large brawny men, neither of whom portrayed a single ounce of elegance or refinement. They looked so dull compared to the beauty of the room. The men plodded down the length of the throne room. When they were about twenty paces away from the throne, Philip raised his hand. "That is far enough." All the men stopped immediately.

"Your Majesty, may I present Sir David Smith, and Sir Richard Williams, representatives of, King Edward I Longshanks," said Pierre.

Sir David stepped forward. "Your Majesty—"

"Do they not teach you any manners in your country? Here, lessers wait to speak, until they are spoken to," Philip said, raising his hand.

Sir David, obviously angered by the statement, looked up at the king and waited. After an obscenely long pause, King Philip nodded for him to continue. Sir David opened his mouth and continued, "Votre Majesté, nous sommes ici–"

"Oh my, Pierre, was that supposed to be French?" Philip asked mockingly.

"Why yes, Your Majesty, I believe it was," Pierre replied in the same mocking manner.

"I would rather hear a cat screaming as it is being butchered than hear you butcher our beautiful language. Let us proceed in the common tongue," Philip commanded.

Sir Richard's face turned a blustery red, and he took two steps forward. "Why you—" As he did so, the guards around Philip drew their swords.

"I don't think that is a good idea, Sir Richard. Remember, we have a peace treaty," said King Philip. Sir Richard hesitated, then grudgingly stepped back.

"That is precisely why we are here. In the peace treaty of 1303, between our great nation and yours, your daughter Isabella was promised to our crown Prince Edward II. His Majesty heard news that your daughter has gone missing on the Camino de Santiago. If this be true, the treaty will be void... Unless equal compensation can be presented," Sir David said.

A flash of anger streaked across Philip's face. "There is no compensation that will ever be equal to that of my daughter." He pounded his fists on the throne. Then took a breath and composed himself. "There is nothing to be concerned about. I have just received word that Isabella is in the safekeeping of the Knights

Templar, at the castle in Ponferrada. Also, the Moorish forces were defeated by the Hospitallers. As we speak, she is being escorted to a ship in Finisterre, which will ferry her directly back here."

"We are happy to hear of her safety. King Edward would greatly like to hear news of the princess upon her arrival," Sir Richard said.

"I am sure the whole world would like to hear of her safe arrival, and so they shall," said Philip. "Tell Edward congratulations on catching that William Wallace.[30] It never ceases to amaze me that you let those savages in the north beat you so many times."

Sir David and Sir Richard bowed rather than rise to the bait. *What a disappointment.*

"Your Majesty," they said, then left the king's presence.

CHAPTER 34

THE DARK NIGHT OF THE SOUL

"Nooo!!!" Etienne yelled, opening his eyes. Looking around, he found himself back in the dark chapel, his body damp with sweat. *It was just a dream.* He saw Andy working diligently, just as he had before. The others were waking up and Moira disappeared into Isabella's room.

This was all happening like it did in his dream. His next step had been talking to Andy. If Andy was working on the code like he had been, then Etienne knew his dream had been a warning.

Etienne left his pew and took a seat next to Andy. Seeing Andy working on the code, Etienne repeated the words from his dream. "You don't waste any time, do you?"

"Well, Moira woke me up. The beast almost ate me," Andy said, smiling. "I didna want to wake you lot, so I figured I would make good use of the time."

"Nothing I can say will make you stop looking, will it?" It was as if he had memorized a script. He knew every word Andy would say before it happened.

"Once my mind is set into action, I just canna help it. It works on its own. Why, I almost have this one figured out. It seems ta be—"

"Another coded grid with the alphabet going across and up and down," Etienne interrupted. Andy looked dumbstruck.

"How did ya know?"

Isabella appeared. "I will explain later. There is something I have to do," Etienne walked to Isabella. It was all happening like his dream. Was it inevitable to have this fate? Was there any way he could avoid it. He was afraid real life would end exactly as the dream had. Feeling more like an actor than his true self, he walked to her and took up his sword as he passed. Etienne didn't know why he had received so many visions. Were they all leading him to this moment?

"May I talk to you?" he asked Isabella. "There is something I need to explain."

"Let's go to the garden," Isabella said, walking across the chapel to the small door.

The garden looked exactly as it had in Etienne's dream, even though he had never stepped foot in it.

Isabella halted and asked, "Why did you leave without saying goodbye? Why were you so distant in Ponferrada? It was as if the moment we stepped into that castle, I was nothing to you and after we... after we made a vow to God and..." Etienne put a hand on her shoulder and she shrugged it away.

"I... I have failed you as a husband. There was a conflict between the oath I took and my love for you," Isabella turned to face him and he continued, "I chose wrong in Ponferrada. I realized after I left, that my love for you is more important than my oath; more important than my life. I can't imagine a world without you in it. It has always been that way. You were the only light in my life. My one reason for everything I did at your father's castle when we were young. I never dared to think I would see you again; and now that I have, I never want to let you go." Isabella took his hand. Her skin was warm and soft. They exchanged a smile. Etienne's smile quickly vanished. He knew he should continue but he didn't want to. He didn't like where this path ended.

"What is it," Isabella asked with a concerned look.

Etienne took a breath; he knew he needed to continue. "Also, Molay said something that made me leave."

"What did he say?" Isabella asked, her eyes becoming guarded.

"He said that maybe you weren't the person I thought you were. He said maybe you and Tristan had been working together and that you kept me away from camp so you could steal the secret we were carrying. Isabella, I know you opened the door in Castrojeriz and that you are after the treasure." Isabella's eyes got cold and distant. This look confirmed everything. He hated himself, but he took a breath and continued, "Molay said that he had seen you in your father's court and you were ruthless. This made me question everything I knew about you. I believed him and didn't listen to my heart."

Isabella held her head down. "I have something to tell you," she said quietly, "There is some truth to what Molay said."

Etienne took a few steps back, composing himself. His thoughts flew to what she'd told him in his vision, but he forced himself to reserve judgment until the real Isabella spoke. "What do you mean?"

Isabella raised her eyes to meet his. "I would have done anything to get my father's love and approval. It was the only thing that mattered in this world to me. He loved it when I was cruel and ruthless. He often told me he wished I would have been born a boy, so I could rule his kingdom. I was better at strategy than any of my brothers. It was a fun game. However, I didn't realize the true horrors of war until my pilgrimage, when I saw it first-hand. Until then, it had just been an intellectual game, with the sole purpose of winning at all costs. The Camino has changed me."

Isabella continued, "I did not begin this Camino just as a pilgrim seeking to purify myself before marriage. I came for another reason as well. I came in search of the treasure your order possesses." Etienne grabbed the hilt of his sword. It felt as if an uncontrollable force was guiding his movements and words. Isabella placed her hands on his chest.

Etienne thought of his vision. This was different, Isabella was different. Could he avoid the fate of killing her? He prayed that this situation would work out for the best for all of them.

"Etienne, if my father controlled it, the war with England would end and both of our nations would be at peace, without me marrying Edward. We could be together. I would be free."

Etienne didn't know what to say. Anger entered his body and he became rigid. "You told me you were taking the Camino because you thought you killed me when we were young. Was that a lie as well?"

Isabella dropped her head. "No, that was true. I have never forgiven myself for what happened to you." Isabella tried to stroke Etienne's face but he pulled back.

"Etienne, the Camino has changed me, you have changed me. That is why I am telling you this. I have brought so much death on this land in my quest. I understand now that if I ever possessed the treasure, it would only bring more of the same. My soul cannot take it any longer. I'm not asking you to forgive me, but pleading with you not to discuss the treasure or code in my presence. I don't want to be tempted."

Etienne clenched his teeth and asked, "What about Tristan? Did you distract me so he could steal the secret?"

Isabella looked at Etienne with all sincerity. "Tristan acted on his own that day. My love for you... I wasn't expecting..." She shook her head, as if to clear her thoughts. "Everything between you and me has been true. My heart has loved you since we were young. That is why I have made a decision to go back to France to marry Edward instead of searching for the treasure. I hope this sacrifice will end my father's quest and save my country."

Etienne felt betrayed by Isabella, once again she was abandoning him. He was so upset he let out the one thing he knew would hurt her most. "Tristan was the one who betrayed you. He was going to sell you to the Moors." Isabella stepped back and put her hands to her mouth. "Ronan told me as he was dying from the wounds Tristan had given him. There is another one to add to the list of people your quest has killed." Tears formed in her eyes. Etienne had to fight every urge he had to comfort her and hold her in his arms. "I cannot trust you now," he whispered. "But I will still protect you. We must leave immediately" He turned and walked back toward the chapel.

"Etienne, I—" Isabella called after him.

Etienne stopped for a moment then continued to the door. "You are no longer my wife." Etienne was seething, not only from Isabella's betrayal, but from the way he had treated her.

The night was dark, darker than any other Isabella had experienced in Galicia. The clouds were obscuring any light from the stars above, and the moon was barely visible. The landscape matched what was in Isabella's heart. It was filled with sorrow and darkness. Etienne hadn't spoken to her since they left the church and set out on the Camino again that morning. None of the others knew what had happened between them, but they sensed all was not well.

"Ach, I am a soakin' wet," Andy said, peeling his drenched garments away from his body.

"Well, come an' join me by the fire." Clair motioned to Andy to sit next to her.

Andy moved in closer to the little fire Mariano had started and warmed himself by extending his hands and rubbing them together.

"I think we have enough wood to last us through the night if we keep the fire small," Etienne said, as he and Gerhart placed the last of the branches onto the woodpile.

"Good thing the rain has stopped. Otherwise, it would have been an unpleasant night," Mariano said.

"I don't know how Raphael does it," Isabella said.

"He is part animal," Etienne snapped. His tone was like a blade to her heart, and she looked away, unable to face him.

"Ach, do he and his beasts ever sleep?" Andy asked. "They guided us all day, an' now, they are keepin' guard. Wish I 'ad that stamina."

Moira's howl came tearing through the night air. Isabella knew Moira only howled when there was danger. Everyone grabbed their weapons and rushed off through the dark night toward the noise. The last days at the church, there had been no threats or attacks, it had given Isabella a false sense of security. Within minutes, they came upon Moira; she was whimpering and curled up on the ground. Etienne was the first to reach her. She snarled and bared her teeth at him as he tried to touch her. A pool of blood had gathered around her.

"Easy, girl," Isabella said soothingly, extending her hand slowly. She placed it on Moira's side and stroked her, calming the wolf. Isabella stroked her again and felt the shaft of a broken arrow protruding from her side, closest to the ground. "She's been shot. We have to take this arrow out immediately."

Mariano and Gerhart peered into the darkness, pulling out their weapons.

"It could have been a hunter," Etienne said, pulling his weapon as well. "But if it wasn't, we all need to find cover." Etienne looked around, the concern on his face clear. "We have to move her to the protection of the trees. Whoever shot her must still be close."

Before Isabella knew what had happened, Benedict came flying toward her, knocking her backward, the breath whooshing out of her. Snarling, Benedict stood between her and the others. He was ferocious, his fangs like white daggers gnashing toward them. His low growl rumbled through Isabella, bringing up a primal fear. He positioned himself ready to attack. Etienne raised his sword. Isabella placed her hand on his and caused him to lower it.

Within seconds, Raphael was next to Benedict, also on all fours. He looked wilder in the forest than he had in the garden. "What happened," he growled in a low menacing voice.

"She has been shot by an arrow. It is still inside of her, she is laying on the broken shaft," Isabella said. Raphael's wiry muscles twitched and he let out a howl. Benedict did the same, then started growling at them, coming even closer.

"We need to turn her over," Isabella said. Raphael put his hand on Benedict's large paws, stilling him.

"You help," Raphael growled.

"If we hurry, we might save her," Isabella said.

Raphael and Benedict stepped out of her way but blocked the others. Moira sniffed Isabella's hand and bowed her head, allowing Isabella to pet her. "We have to turn you over, girl."

Isabella tried to shift the wolf's massive weight and Moira let out a whimper of pain. Benedict turned and growled at Isabella, baring his teeth. Raphael reached out his hand and steadied him. Isabella had shifted Moira enough to expose the wound. She reached around and pulled out the arrow lodged in her side.

Moira let out a whimpering howl again that caused a shiver to run up and down Isabella's spine. The wound gushed blood and Isabella looked frantically around for something to bandage it. Not finding anything, she placed her hand over the wound. "We need to turn her more," Isabella said in desperation.

Raphael jumped over Moira and assisted Isabella in this task. Another arrow went flying. It narrowly missed Benedict and hit Moira again. The wolf looked at Raphael one last time before her spirit left her body, and she went limp.

"Noo!" Raphael yelled. His scream was halfway between a man's and an animal's howl. Benedict also let out a howl and bounded off at full speed, in the direction the arrow had come from. Raphael dipped his fingers in Moira's blood and placed it under his eyes. He took off like a shot after Benedict.

"Take cover!" Etienne yelled, as he picked up Isabella from the ground.

More arrows flew and everyone scrambled for the cover of the grove of trees. Tears streamed down Isabella's face. She punched the tree and wished the pain in her hand would take away the pain in her heart. She had loved Moira.

The sound of a man being torn apart came from the woods where Benedict had run. Another cry came, this time in a slightly different direction. The arrows stopped flying and Isabella could hear men fleeing on the other side of the clearing. Then all was quiet. A little too quiet. All sounds of night had stopped. There were no more insects chirping. There was no more wind in the trees. Nothing but silence, darkness, and a bitter cold.

"Do you feel that?" Isabella asked.

"Aye, it just got colder, and wha' 'appened to all the sounds? There is nothin' now," said Andy.

"I don't like this," Gerhart tightened his grip on his ax and looked over to Clair.

"Something moved." Etienne pointed across the clearing. "It's too dark—as if night has swallowed the world. Quickly, let's get to the camp where there is light."

Running back to camp, Isabella could almost feel the darkness pushing against her. It filled her with a sense of dread and fear. When they arrived at camp, the embers from their little fire were still glowing. Etienne placed more wood on it and the fire burned brightly once again. It lit only a small circle, and the surrounding woods devoured all else. To her horror, the darkness broke off into six pieces. They were surrounded.

Etienne drew his sword, his eyes on the Shadows around them. He could hear the others arm themselves as well. All but Mariano, who had sat down by the fire, with his eyes closed and a peaceful look on his face.

"What are you doing?" Gerhart yelled. "Draw your weapon. The Shadows are about to attack."

"There is no need to draw my weapon, just a need to be in the present moment," Mariano said calmly. "I suggest you do the same."

Etienne shook his head, uncertain what was going on with Mariano. He brought his attention back to the impending fight. A Shadow lunged forward toward Etienne, their swords clashing. He felt the strength of his foe. Never had he battled with something so strong before. The Shadow struck him on the face and sent him flying across the campsite. As he landed, Etienne felt as if every joy had been sucked out of his body, and all that remained was pain, fear, and anger. But most of all fear. Once again, Etienne was petrified to the spot unable to move.

Isabella moaned as she was hit hard. His love for her snapped him out of his trance back to the present moment. He had to help her. Etienne ran and tackled the Shadow that was now on top of her. The Shadow escaped his hold and Etienne sprung back to his feet.

Gerhart, Clair, and Andy stood back-to-back as three Shadows approached them. Gerhart let out a loud battle cry and swung his ax wildly through the air. The Shadows easily dodged each swing. Not once did Gerhart make contact. "Mariano, what are you doing. Help us, we need you!"

Mariano sat and smiled at them. "They don't exist. Not here, not now," he said. "These Shadows have no power in the present moment. Stop fighting against what has passed. The Shadows can only hurt us when we relive these painful memories, and fight against them. We only suffer when we believe these Shadows of the past are real. But here, in the moment, they don't exist, unless we give them life."

Mariano laughed so hard that Etienne was distracted from the Shadow attacking him and Isabella. They all stopped fighting and turned to him, including the Shadows.

"Look at them, just look at them and see them for what they truly are, accept these things and be at peace," Mariano said, still laughing.

Etienne's forehead creased, wondering what Mariano was talking about, but he looked at the Shadow that loomed over him. Under its hood he saw every painful memory he had ever had. He saw the death of his parents. He saw the loneliness and abandonment he had felt his whole life. He saw the persecution because of the color of his skin. He saw his many years of isolation and solitude. He saw his fights with Isabella. As he observed it, the Shadow shrunk.

The last face to appear was Tristian's. Tristan killed his friend in childhood, Tristan got Etienne thrown out of the palace, Tristan betrayed Isabella, and he killed Ronan. Etienne felt rage run rampant in his body.

Tears filled Etienne's eyes and he attacked the Shadow of Tristan with all of his might. Their swords crossed as the Shadow kept growing in size, until it towered over Etienne. Adrenaline coursed through Etienne as he attacked. It was time to take the life of the person who had taken so much from him.

Their swords hit, again and again. Etienne had always been the better swordsman, but the Shadow of Tristan was stronger. Etienne knew it was only a matter of time until it would devour him. The Shadow's fist shot out, and Etienne felt his bones crunch and blood gush from his nose. He staggered back and fell hard to the ground.

The Shadow of Tristan stood over Etienne and taunted him. "You always were weaker than me," he said, raising his sword for the death blow. Etienne rolled to his left as the blade came down and, with one swift movement, pulled his dagger. Etienne thrust it into the Shadows thigh, but there was no reaction. He looked in desperation at his friends who were all staring blankly at their Shadows. Mariano was the only one who seemed to be unaffected, but he wasn't helping.

The Shadow of Tristan lifted Etienne into the air by the throat. Etienne felt the life being squeezed out of him when he heard Mariano say. "Anger, sadness, and pain feed them. Just look at them and observe them for what they are. The Shadow you're fighting is your pain, but you are not defined by your pain. By reliving these bad memories, we are making them happen over and over again. We are giving these Shadows their power. In the present moment, pain and thoughts of the past have no power to make you suffer. It is insanity to give them that power over you."

Etienne tried to wrap his head around what Mariano was saying, as he struggled to free himself.

"Etienne, let go. You know what it is to be in the present. I have seen you there when you meditate and pray. Bring your mind to that quiet space where there are no thoughts, just the here and now." Mariano said.

Etienne stopped fighting, and started being. He took a deep breath and let his mind go to a place of quiet. He observed the Shadow and the thoughts of Tristan that constructed it. The more he observed the thoughts, the less effect they had on him. The pain associated with each memory disappeared. As he let go of each thought, the Shadow let go of his throat.

Mariano continued, "It is only when we don't accept what has happened, or is happening, and fight against it, that we lose. 'This shouldn't have happened.' 'She should still be here.' 'They shouldn't have died for me.' 'I am an outcast.' 'We will never survive.' 'What if they abandon me?' There is nothing in this present moment causing us to suffer, except these thoughts from the past and fears of the future attacking us. These things have no power here in the present moment. Nothing can cause us suffering in this present moment, unless we believe and feed these painful thoughts."

Mariano turned to his Shadow, that had shrunk to the size of a small child, and said, "Thank you. You have been an invaluable teacher." There was a great flash of light and his Shadow disappeared.

Etienne watched every negative feeling he had ever had play under the hood of the Shadow. Now though, when he looked at them, they had no power over him. He just sat and observed them. Etienne closed his eyes. When he opened them again, his Shadow was gone.

Everything went dark and a blinding white glow appeared in the middle of the camp. Mariano averted his eyes. When he looked back, in place of the white glow stood the Alchemist. He could tell her presence mesmerized everyone. Her brown eyes seemed to look right through each of them, tearing their flesh away from their bones.

"You've learned much since last we spoke," she said.

Mariano smiled happily. "I would still be living in a place of rage and anger if you had not intervened."

The Alchemist gave Mariano a mysterious smile. "It was your sadness and anger that was attracting them. They feed off these emotions. Had I not intervened when we first met, your Shadows would have consumed you and prevented each of you from fulfilling your destiny."

"If they don't exist, what are they? And what would have happened to us if they had won?" asked Isabella.

The Alchemist looked at her gravely. "The Shadows are made of the realites you fight against and the future you fear. It is a battle that always leads to suffering. When you unbound the door, a physical Shadow was generated for each of your companions who had a possibility of finding the treasure. This was a test of worthiness for all of you. Only one who has overcome their Shadow can stand in the presence of the true treasure. If the Shadows had won, you would have turned into the shadow-self permanently and lived in eternal suffering, feeding off the pain of others."

"So, in a way, I did kill those men in the forest, and Alba," Mariano said. He was at peace with this thought. He didn't argue about how it shouldn't have happened. He simply accepted it.

"Yes," replied the Alchemist.

"Did you destroy these Shadows?" Etienne asked.

"They were not mine to destroy. Only you can face your own Shadow. The Shadows can't be fought against—fighting them will only feed them and make them grow. As soon as they are observed for what they truly are, it brings them into the present moment, where it is impossible for them to exist. Once your consciousness is in the present moment, you realize there are no problems: you cannot change the past and you cannot control the future, you can only act in the present. And therefore, the Shadows of the past and future cannot exist in the present moment."

"Ach, if we passed the test where is the treasure?" Andy asked

"The door was opened backwards so only a trial was presented. The door must be opened correctly to claim the prize. However, what you have experienced from this trial is more valuable than your weight in gold."

"Aye that 'tis."

The Alchemist moved to Mariano and kissed him on the forehead. "You all have proven yourselves worthy and have passed the trial of this door. If it is God's will, we shall meet again." With these words, she vanished just as quickly as she had come.

After the Alchemist left, a strange peace set in on the camp. Isabella felt intoxicated. All of the others had a childish grin on their faces. She felt more peaceful than at any other time in her life. There were no problems in this present moment. She tried to remember the past that had given her trouble before, but it seemed like an echo of a life that was no longer hers. The memories of her father's cruelty, those that had died, and the guilt she had felt were gone. They didn't exist in the present moment unless she brought them there.

Benedict's all too familiar howl pierced the night air.

Andy turned his head and looked at the others. "Well, I suppose tha' is the signal for us to go." Isabella couldn't help smiling at this. Life was showing them the way, and she would offer no resistance.

"Shall we then," Etienne said, and they were off into the dark woods. Within minutes, they were back at the spot where Moira had fallen.

Isabella looked at her corpse and no longer felt sorrow. She just observed it and thought, *Moira is as beautiful as ever, laying there peaceful-*

ly. Isabella fully accepted the reality of the moment. There was no longer war inside her.

Benedict appeared on the other side of the clearing with a corpse in his mouth, followed by Raphael. The two of them crossed and stopped in front of the group. Benedict opened his massive jaws, releasing the neck of the corpse. Hitting the ground, the corpse rolled over to reveal Tristan. His lifeless eyes staring up at the stars above.

"Tristan? Ronan was right, greed did eventually take him." Etienne said. "For the first time in my life, seeing him no longer makes me feel angry." Etienne looked at the corpse. "It is as if I knew Tristan, but had never truly seen him before."

Raphael walked to Moira, "Moira now part of everything. She is nothing." Isabella smiled at this, knowing the depth of what he was saying. He let out an ear-piercing howl and Benedict joined him.

Isabella walked a little way into the field and picked the white flowers that covered the ground. She returned with a handful of flowers and placed them over Moira. She took Raphael into her arms and as she held him, the others picked more flowers and laid them on Moira, covering her completely. Where Moira lay, now looked like a mound of the purest snow, impervious to the changing seasons of this world.

CHAPTER 35

SANTIAGO DE COMPOSTELA

A single bird chirped its morning song. Isabella opened her eyes to see shafts of light darting through the canopy of leaves. She blinked a few times and focused on the small bird singing merrily. Joy, the likes of which she'd never known, welled inside the depths of her. Everything seemed so clear and the colors so vibrant. It was like a waking dream, a beauty so pure it didn't belong in this world.

Isabella noticed the feeling in her body. She ran her right hand across the ground. She could feel every piece of grass and every piece of dirt that crumbled under the weight of her fingertips. These sensations made her feel like a child, experiencing life for the first time.

She focused her attention on her left hand. The sensation she felt was very different from the right. Instead of the cool damp grass, she felt her hand cradled in the nest of a warm and coarse human hand. Her fingers traced the lines and calluses that lay just below the fingers. She had a vague memory of what skin felt like, but it didn't do justice to the feeling of every contour she was exploring.

Her fingers rested again and pressed gently. Her perception moved past the rough skin to the blood pulsing below the surface. She could feel each pulse of the heart that belonged to the hand holding hers. The hand squeezed hers—life, from the dormant perfection that she was observing.

She turned her head to see Etienne smiling. He blinked his eyes, as if they couldn't absorb everything he was seeing. He looked up at the leaves and the light coming through them. He smiled, then focused back on Isabella.

He looked deeply into her eyes. Isabella felt him see past her flesh, past what lies underneath, past the concept of Isabella, until he reached her soul, the only thing that was true and real.

Etienne parted his lips. "I have never seen anything so beautiful."

"Ach, thank ya. You're not so bad yourself." Isabella heard coming from her right side. She turned to see Andy resting on his elbow, staring at them. And Andy did look beautiful! It seemed almost as if he was glowing. She perceived every small detail of him, her eyes drinking up the smallest movement.

"I must be drunk. I 'ave never been so 'appy before, and the lot of ya look like angels."

"It wasn't a dream," Mariano said, sitting across from them. "She came to visit us. This is what I felt after the first time I met her. This is being in the present moment. Paradise is here! Now!"

"So, we destroyed the Shadows?" Andy asked.

Mariano smiled and handed them some food. "You cannot destroy that which does not exist."

As Isabella put the first bite of food into her mouth, it was as if she was tasting for the first time. She chewed slowly, noticing the bread crumble and become moist. She could feel each sensation as the bread touched the different parts of her mouth. She noticed the flavor constantly changing as she chewed slowly. Swallowing, she knew that this bread would become a part of her body. It would *become* her body. She felt gratitude for each bite, knowing that the bread was her, and that she was every crumb.

After breakfast, they started the day's journey. Raphael was the only one unaffected by the night before. All the other pilgrims seemed as if they were experiencing the world for the first time: all so inquisitive about each stone, or the bark of every tree. Raphael waited patiently as they explored the world and their senses. If one of them would stray from the pack, Benedict would kindly find them and escort them back. Each was in silent contemplation as they walked. They were all too enthralled with the world around them to put the experience into words. There were no words, there were no concepts, only experience after experience in the present moment. Each one replaced by the next present moment.

They crested a large hill, and there below them lay a beautiful town, like a precious jewel set into the crown of the earth. Its red roofs, adorning the tops of each of the houses, appeared as rubies glinting in the sun. The large spires from the cathedral stretched up, always reaching toward God.

Raphael pointed and said, "Santiago."

"We made it," Isabella whispered as tears formed in her eyes.

Isabella felt Clair's strong wiry arms wrap around her. "Aye, lassie, tha' we did."

Thinking of the future beyond Santiago, Isabella felt the dream-like state leave her. All of *reality* came rushing back in. It seemed as if all the others had left the dream-like state as well. They were sinking back into *reality* like helpless victims sinking in quicksand.

Is this reality? Isabella thought. *Or did I just leave reality and return to this dream of life?* She wanted to cry more as the peace she had had seemed to slip away from her. She was desperate to hold on to it, and the more she struggled to possess it, the quicker it left.

"Road." Raphael pointed to the right. In the distance was a well-defined road, with a stream of pilgrims pouring into Santiago, the end-destination of the pilgrimage for many. The pilgrims looked like the blood of the Camino: all coursing to the heart of Santiago, all searching for their purpose, readying themselves to be pumped back out into the world once more to serve it.

Raphael and Benedict turned and rushed past Isabella into the forest. As they disappeared, Benedict let out a howl that rang through the air. The pilgrims on the road below stopped and looked around in terror. Isabella smiled. What had once seemed so terrifying was now the sound of protection and friendship.

"Well, shall we?" Andy asked as he turned toward the road and descended the steep hill.

The group followed, zigzagging back and forth to avoid loose gravel. Before long, they reached the Camino below and joined the other pilgrims. It was strange to be amongst people again, even fellow pilgrims. It felt overwhelming to be around so many other humans. The weight of society pressed hard on Isabella as they entered the town. They were greeted by so many smiling faces, wishing them a *Buen Camino,* but it almost seemed that she had forgotten how to act in society.

They came to a plaza with a stone fountain in the middle and turned right, following the procession of the other pilgrims. After a few moments, the cathedral came into view. It was immense, dwarfing all other cathedrals they had encountered along the way. Isabella stopped and stared up in reverence. Her heart leaping inside her chest. "This truly is a house for a saint," she said. Its edifice seemed to stretch on forever. There were towers and pillars, all ornately decorated, the gray stone catching the light just right, sometimes reflecting the sun in a way that made the cathedral appear to glow.

They continued with the other pilgrims along the side of the cathedral, down a flight of covered stairs, and into a grand plaza. The plaza was twice the size of the church and all the buildings that surrounded it were large and beautifully decorated. To their right was a hospital for the pilgrims. Straight ahead was another church, a graveyard, and what appeared to be an armory. To the left, the building was impressive, but too far away to make out what it contained.

They followed the church around and stood at the front entrance. Almost in disbelief, Andy uttered the words, "Well, I guess this is it."

Gerhart, unable to control his joy, wrapped his massive arms around the whole company, sweeping them in a giant hug. "We made it!!! We made it!!!" he exclaimed, squeezing the others tightly. Everyone laughed in relief; it was the sound of a thousand-pound weight being lifted off their shoulders. Andy hooked Clair by the arm and they did a little jig around the square. Isabella felt tears welling up in her eyes again. The sense of relief was so great, tears were the only form of expression that did it justice.

The giant bells rang out, calling the pilgrims to the mass dedicated to their arrival. Isabella felt the resonance from the bells pulse through her body. The sound shook loose any doubt or worry that clung to her being.

Etienne put his hand on Andy's shoulder. "I think it is time for us to enter." Andy and Clair stopped dancing, and together the pilgrims entered the Cathedral of Santiago de Compostella, the place they had walked so many hundreds of miles to reach.

Upon entering the cathedral, Etienne was met with a chorus of different languages that reverberated off the walls and up into the rafters high above. The entire cathedral was filled with pilgrims. They were all hugging, most of them weeping, with wide grins on their faces. The energy was overwhelming. Etienne felt a tightness in his chest, emotion wanting to escape and spill all over the hard granite floor. The smell of incense filled the air and his lungs swelled as he breathed it in. He had never been as affected by a single moment in his life as he was on entering the cathedral. He bowed deeply in reverence and made the sign of the cross. He clutched Isabella's hand tightly and placed his arm around Andy's shoulder for support. Together they walked toward the altar and the front of the cathedral.

Row upon row of pews were filled with pilgrims, a few of which he recognized from passing them on their journey. Just outside the pews were giant columns, massive both in girth and height. Seeing all of the pews full, they moved to the outside corridor between the columns and the wall. Reaching the first column, Etienne couldn't contain his emotions any longer. He dropped to his knees and wept bitterly.

All the years of grief and hardship poured out of his body. His tears filled the cracks between the granite slabs. He felt as if he were vomiting pure emotion, releasing it from his body; he saw all the faces of those he had killed; he saw his parents before they died; he saw Tristan's face as he stood before the king; he saw Isabella and felt the purgatory of being separated from her. All of this came pouring out of him. He clenched his hands to his stomach and bent forward, placing his head on the cold ground. There was so much release. There was so much he had been holding behind the guise of strength for so long. He just couldn't do it any longer.

Isabella touched his back. He looked up at her with tears streaming down his face. Joining him on the ground, she placed her arms around him and held him tenderly. Tears streamed down her face as well, and together they cried in a loving embrace. Etienne's whole being melted into her arms. He had no words as he gulped for air and sobbed. It wasn't long before Gerhart, sobbing his own tears, placed a large hand on Etienne's shoulder in comfort.

Etienne and Isabella rose, and Etienne put his arm around Gerhart. Soon, Andy, Clair, and Mariano joined in. All with tears staining their cheeks, all letting go of the sorrows of the past and the many hardships and miles that lay behind them. Together, they had made it, and now they could fully let go. There was nothing left to be stripped from them.

The bell for the mass rang again and all the pilgrims stood. Etienne and the others cleared the tears from their eyes, looking at each other with love and appreciation. The mass began, and after a moment, Etienne felt two hands wrap around his bicep and squeeze. Then he heard a familiar voice.

"Sister Caroline!"

Etienne turned his head to see Sister Fransie chastising Sister Caroline, who had her hands firmly around his arm.

"But Sister Fransie, this is the one from Santa Anna," she said, practically ripping Etienne's clothes off to show the scar on his shoulder. "I would know him anywhere." She smiled broadly at Etienne.

Etienne couldn't help but return the smile.

"Why so it is… So it is. Come, pilgrims, sit with us. We can make room," Sister Fransie said as she moved over on the pew.

Sister Caroline grasped at Etienne's bicep again, but Isabella intercepted her hand, saying, "I will sit next to you, Sister." Sister Caroline looked disappointed but made no protests. Soon, all the pilgrims sat holding each other's hands. They were all connected, all one family of remarkable individuals.

After the readings, a young priest stood with great confidence for a man of his age and marched to the pulpit. The moment he opened his mouth, the sweet sound of his voice filled every corner of the church. "Brothers and sisters, pilgrims from all corners of the earth, welcome to Santiago de Compostela. Today, by arriving in Santiago, you have answered the call from our reading.

"Philippians 3:13-14 'Brothers, I do not consider that I have made it my own. But one thing I do: forgetting what lies behind and straining forward to what lies ahead, I press on toward the goal for the prize of the upward call of God in Christ Jesus.' Today you have answered that call by arriving in Santiago de Compostela.

"Along the Camino each day, no matter the difficulty, you strained forward to reach this point. Many of you carried great burdens onto this pilgrimage, but you had to leave those burdens along the way to make it here today. You had to press forward no matter the peril, and today you are rewarded by praying at the feet of Saint James. Your act of penance erasing your past sins. You are born again into this world.

"You have changed, physically, spiritually, and mentally. Each of you is no longer the person you were when you left home. Upon your return, do not be surprised if others do not recognize you, and do not be afraid if you no longer fit into the life you left behind. God has shaped you for a new life on this road. He has shaped you perfectly for the tasks and the life that lies before you.

"I am reminded of Philippians 4:12-13: 'I know what it is to be in need, and I know what it is to have plenty. I have learned the secret of being content in any and every situation, whether well fed or hungry, whether living in plenty or in want. I can do all this through him who gives me strength.'

"Some of you left your homes in need. Some of you left palaces filled with plenty. Along the road, some of you were left destitute and others of you have found great wealth. Wealth in spirit. Wealth in companionship. Wealth in love. Our Lord Jesus gives us the strength to endure all of these trials, whether it be the trials of wealth or of poverty. He is always there for you to lean into; always waiting to carry you in the palm of his hand.

"As you leave here today, know that you will always be a pilgrim in this life. Santiago de Compostela is not the end of your Camino, but just the beginning. As you scatter from here like the stars in the sky, take these words from Ephesians 4:31-32 to heart.

"'Let all bitterness and wrath and anger and clamor and slander be put away from you, along with all malice. Be kind to one another, tenderhearted, forgiving one another, as God in Christ forgave you.'

"Just as God has forgiven you your sins today by reaching Santiago, so should you forgive those who have sinned against you, for we all are one people on one road in this life, always heading toward God. Buen Camino, my brothers and sisters."

The young priest humbly stepped down from the pulpit and made his way back to his seat. The congregation sat in silence, contemplating his words of wisdom. Etienne took these words to heart. He looked over at Isabella, and felt only love. After hearing these words, Etienne's heart was moved to forgive her for her betrayal, lies, and most importantly, for leaving him to go back to France. *I must forgive her.*

At this, he embraced her and his eyes filled with tears. He had no water left in his body, but this release, this forgiveness would not stop. He looked at those who had become so dear to him, and they all smiled, tears streaming down their faces anew—knowing every step they had traveled together, and also knowing that everything would change in a few days.

Five priests lit the giant incense burner and hoisted it into the air with a large rope. The harder the priests pulled the more the burner swung back and forth. At first it only moved slightly, then it created long arcs that stretched the length of the cathedral. Andy's eyes followed it back and forth. He kept waiting for the incense burner to spill out on someone. The smell of incense covered the stench of all the pilgrims. Andy felt God's forgiveness falling on them with the smoke. Andy couldn't help but smile with glee at the giant incense pot, swinging back and forth. He couldn't control himself and he giggled.

The burner stopped swinging and Andy turned to the nuns. "What are you two doin' here?"

Sister Fransie crossed her arms. "Sister Caroline has developed a bit of a carnal craving. The powers that be thought it best that she be transferred to a cloistered convent of only nuns. We are sailing on the Templar ship from Finisterre in two days, for our new assignment in Paris."

"And what are you doing with her? Did you get reassigned as well?" asked Andy.

Sister Fransie looked at Sister Caroline dearly. "She is my best friend. It would take more than a reassignment to take her from my side. Plus, someone had to keep an eye on her."

"Who are you?" Sister Caroline asked, wrapping her arms around Gerhart's massive bicep.

"If ya donna' take your hand off-a him, there will be blood in this church," Clair said, staring down Sister Caroline.

Reluctantly Sister Caroline let go. "I see you finally learned how to speak the common tongue. Miracles are possible."

Clair moved toward Sister Caroline, but before she reached her, Gerhart swept her off the ground into his arms and gave her a massive kiss. Setting her down, he said, "You know I only have eyes for you." He knelt on one knee, which made him the same height as Clair and became very awkward even for himself. He began babbling, "Clair... Um... Ahh... Would you..."

"What do ya wan', ya big man?"

Gerhart reached into his pocket and pulled out something. He opened his large hand to reveal a shiny golden ring. "Would you marry me?" he said. He scrunched up his face, as if the next words Clair would say would slap him.

Clair tapped him on his shoulders and he opened his eyes. She took his face between her hands. "I would like nothin' more. Ya 'ave my 'art." With this, she planted a big kiss on his lips sending him backward.

"Now let's go find a priest!" she said, pulling Gerhart off his knees. As he reached his feet, Clair dragged him toward one of the side chapels.

Gerhart looked dumbfounded with a large smile on his face. "I wasn't thinking right now," he said, as Clair pulled at his arm.

"No time like the present," Mariano said jokingly. Everyone laughed and followed Clair, who was a woman on a mission.

Going from chapel to chapel, Etienne noticed Andy staring up at all the large pillars. Etienne followed Andy's gaze and saw that each pillar was covered in the same code as the Keystone Church.

Andy looked up at the closest pillar in amazement and mumbled, "This will take ages to decode." Etienne knew Andy's mind had accepted the challenge that lay before him.

Unaware of his surroundings, Andy tripped over a set of stairs. Etienne extended a strong arm and caught him before he hit the floor. Andy regained his balance. "Ach, thanks, laddie." He pointed at the pillars. "Did ya see—"

"Not here. Not in front of Isabella." Andy fell silent, looking at him curiously as they ascended the stairs together to the chapel.

Before they reached the top landing, Etienne heard an elderly voice saying, "Do you Carisa take Peter for your lawful husband, to have and to hold, from this day forward, for better, for worse, for richer, for poorer, in sickness and in health, until death do you part?"

As his eyes caught up with his ears, Etienne saw two pilgrims, hand in hand, with an elderly balding priest standing between them. He had the vague feeling that he knew them, but he didn't know from where.

Carisa looked up at Peter with large eyes full of love and sweetness. "I do," she said, smiling at him like an angel. Etienne looked over at Isabella. Feeling his gaze, she turned her head and their eyes met. He froze, held captive in her stare. She smiled softly at him. Etienne felt his heart ache. He turned and looked back at the couple that was now sharing their first kiss as man and wife. When they faced him, Etienne was hit with a wave of recognition. They were the pilgrims whose prayers Santiago had shown him. Etienne bowed his head and gave thanks to God.

"All ri', all ri'. 'Tis our turn now," Clair said, dragging Gerhart to the altar. As they reached the priest, Carisa and Peter stepped slightly to the side.

"What is going on here?" the priest asked. Etienne had to laugh at the flustered look on the priest's face. Clair had that effect on people sometimes.

"'Tis our turn now," Clair said, stopping directly in front of the elderly man.

"This is very... very unorthodox." The priest looked pleadingly at the others in the room.

"I think it's beautiful," Carisa said, smiling at Clair and Gerhart. "What better thing than to share our wedding day with fellow pilgrims." Etienne was still astounded that the pilgrims from his vision were standing right in front of them.

"Umm... Ahhh... it is very spontaneous; these things need to be thought through and..."

Gerhart leaned forward, towering over the priest. "We have thought it through."

"Aye, and I'll be 'appy to give away my Clair," Andy said from the back of the room.

"You've been trying ta give me away for years," Clair said.

Etienne chuckled, happy to be his Camino family again.

"Very well," said the priest. "If you will all enter and take a seat, we can begin." They followed directions and entered the small side chapel. Each took their respective seats except for Gerhart, who stood next to the priest. Clair made her way to the back of the room, hooking her arm with Andy's. After a moment's pause, Clair and Andy marched down the aisle. All in the chapel smiled at them as they passed. When they reached the altar, Andy leaned in and gave Clair a kiss on the cheek. "I love ya." He then turned to Gerhart and said, "If ya hurt her... I will... well, just be good ta her." Gerhart held up his arms.

The priest cleared his throat. "What are your names?"

"I'm Gerhart and this is Clair." Etienne had the thought that if Clair took Gerhart's full "title," she would be Clair the Destroyer. Etienne smiled—the name definitely fit her.

"Very well," said the priest. "Gerhart and Clair, have you come here to enter marriage without coercion, freely, and wholeheartedly? Are you prepared, as you follow the path of marriage, to love and honor each other for as long as you both shall live? Are you prepared to accept children lovingly from God and to bring them up according to the law of Christ and his Church?"

Clair laughed so hard, she doubled over. She put her hand on Gerhart and composed herself. "Me 'ave children at my age," she said, gasping for air.

The priest did not look amused. "You must answer the questions in the affirmative in order for us to continue."

As Clair composed herself, Gerhart responded, "I have, and I am."

Clearing tears from her eyes, Clair said, "Aye."

"I will take that as a yes," said the priest. "Since it is your intention to enter the covenant of Holy Matrimony, join your right hands, and declare your consent before God and his Church."

Gerhart took Clair's hand in his. "I, Gerhart, take you, Clair, to be my wife. I promise to protect you and destroy any who would hurt you. I promise that I will carry you if you ever become ill. I will be true to you in good times and bad. If another man tries to steal you away, God help him. I will bear your temper, like all the swords that have tried to kill me. I will love you and honor you, all the days of my life."

Clair looked up at Gerhart lovingly. "I, Clair, take ya, Gerhart, ta be m'usband. I promise ta be faithful ta ya in good times an' in bad, in sickness an in 'ealth, ta love ya and ta honor ya all the days of my life. When ye're stupid and fat, I'll be there ta make fun of ya."

The priest cleared his throat again. "Well, those are the most interesting vows I have heard. Actually, I am not sure that I understood what you said, but I will assume it was full of love. Now if I can have the rings."

Etienne's heart turned heavy. He remembered the vows Isabella and he had exchanged under the stars on the mountain top. He had promised to be her husband until death. They hadn't exchanged rings, just vows. *I guess that doesn't matter now.* Etienne fought the urge to look in Isabella's direction.

Clair took her ring off and put it into the priest's hand. He looked up at Gerhart. "And where is the groom's ring?"

Before Gerhart could answer, Andy took off his golden ring with a Celtic design. "Here it is!" he shouted, holding it up in the air. Etienne admired Andy's love for Clair.

"No Andy, ya canna," Clair protested.

"Nonsense," Andy said, "You are my sister and I would do anything for ya." Andy dropped his ring into the priest's open hand.

Clair wrapped her arms around him and said, "I luv' ya."

"Now if I can continue," said the priest, clearing his throat again. He placed his hand over the rings. "Father, bless these rings and let them be a token of Clair and Gerhart's love for one another. Just as the circle continues without end, may it be the same with their love for each other."

"Gerhart, take this ring, place it on Clair's finger, and repeat after me. 'Clair receive this ring as a sign of my love and fidelity. In the name of the Father, and of the Son, and of the Holy Spirit.'"

Gerhart took the ring and placed it on Clair's finger and repeated. "Clair take this ring as a sign of my love... In the name of God. Amen."

"Close enough," said the priest. He then turned to Clair saying. "Take this ring and repeat after me. 'Gerhart, receive this ring as a sign of my love and fidelity. In the name of the Father, and of the Son, and of the Holy Spirit.'"

Clair took the ring from his hand and said, "This ring 'tis yours and belongs ta no one else." She placed the ring on his finger, then jumped up and wrapped her arms and legs around him, planting her lips firmly on his.

The priest placed his hand on his forehead and shook his head. "I now declare you man and wife," he said quietly. Everyone erupted in a cheer. As Clair descended from Gerhart, the priest said in a sarcastic tone, "Does anyone else want to get married."

Etienne felt his stomach turn. He looked over at Isabella to see her staring at him, giving him the same pained expression he was feeling. They had made their vows only in front of God and Brother Xavier. There were no other witnesses. Etienne didn't know if that even counted. His eyes locked with Isabella, and he opened his mouth to speak, but their gaze was broken by Andy, dancing up and down the aisle. "C'mon," he implored, pulling Etienne from his seat, and together with the others, they danced up and down the small chapel.

CHAPTER 36

GOOD FORTUNE OR BAD

The sun sunk low in the sky, casting shadows of the mighty pillars across the cathedral. Etienne stood next to Andy on the balcony and observed the clergy lighting the candles of each chandelier. The tiny points of light changed the feeling inside the giant hall. Etienne thought it gave the enormous space an almost cozy feeling. Etienne wanted to hold onto this feeling for as long as it lasted. In two days' time, Isabella would be on the Templar ship back to France. He may never see her again. What would he do when she was gone? Would he try to find his uncle to learn who he truly is?

"I canna' believe we made it," Andy said.

"It's only by the grace of God that we're here. There is no other explanation," replied Etienne, as he put his full weight on the wooden rail.

"Aye." Andy joined him on the railing. After a pause, he turned his head from left to right. "'Tis a shame we have to leave in the morning. It is so beautiful here."

"I agree, but if we don't leave, Isabella will miss her ship in Finisterra." Etienne focused his gaze straight ahead. He hoped that Isabella would miss her ship.

"Is that such a bad thing, laddie?" asked Andy, "Maybe it would be a good thing if she missed it." He placed his hand on Etienne's shoulder.

Etienne shrugged it off and walked away. "I'm sorry, Andy. I can't talk about this right now."

On the ground floor pilgrims were milling around. Some laughed and hugged, and some were deep in prayer at the pews. Etienne craved solitude to quiet the voices and feelings inside of him. Andy's comment had struck a nerve, which was still radiating through his body. His best refuge was a candle lit passage that led below the alter. The candlelight danced on each gray step leading down.

Etienne crossed the threshold of the opening and descended the steps.

"Amen," said a woman's voice as he reached the last few steps. Etienne entered the small passage at the bottom of the steps and recognized the woman was Carisa, the woman who'd been married that afternoon. She was kneeling, deep in prayer with her head pressed hard against her clasped hands.

The room was very small and was actually more of an underground passageway from one side of the altar to the other. He walked quietly behind her, trying not to disturb her.

Just as he reached the set of stairs at the other end of the passage, Carisa said, "Stay, I am done talking with him." She hadn't changed positions; her hands were still pressed hard to her forehead, eyes closed.

"Talking to whom?" asked Etienne.

"Santiago." She turned to look at him. "He has been waiting for you." Carisa walked to the stairs opposite Etienne. He stood in disbelief as she walked up the stairs. Had she really said Santiago was waiting to speak to him? Within moments she disappeared, leaving him alone in the small chamber. He walked to where Carisa had been kneeling and saw nothing but a stone wall staring back at him.

At least I can be alone here. Etienne knelt and bowed his head and prayed.

"Why?" Etienne asked as soon as his eyes were closed. Within seconds, he felt himself falling deeper and deeper into an abyss of darkness. Then there was light all around him and Santiago stood before him, with a golden halo about his head.

"Why?" said Santiago laughing. Etienne averted his eyes to the ground. As Santiago laughed, the glow around him increased in intensity. "My son, did you not learn anything from our first meeting?"

"I have learned so much from you. Thank you for your guidance and help on this journey. I fear without your help, we would have never made it this far."

"Raise your eyes, my son," Santiago said. Slowly Etienne lifted his gaze; the glow had diminished enough for him to look at the saint.

Santiago continued, "Why? You ask why? Why did God put the love in your heart for Isabella, if you can't ever be together? Why did God take your parents? Why? People are always asking this. It is so hard for them to accept that God— and this world, with all that transpires—is perfect.

"Let me tell you an old story from the East. There once was a farmer whose horse ran away. All the other villagers said, 'What bad fortune to have your horse run away.' The farmer turned to the villagers and said, 'Good fortune or bad fortune, we will see.' The next day the horse returned with five wild horses. All the villagers said, 'What great fortune your horse has returned and brought five others.' The farmer replied, "Good fortune or bad fortune, we shall see.' The next day the farmer's son was training the wild horses. One of them threw the boy off, breaking his arm. All the villagers said, 'These horses are a curse. What bad fortune. Your son could have been killed.' The farmer replied once again, 'Good fortune or bad fortune, we will see.' The next day an army came to the village and demanded that all able-bodied men come fight in the war. The villagers said to the farmer, 'What great fortune that your son has a broken arm. Now he won't have to fight in the war.' The farmer replied, 'Good fortune or bad fortune, we shall see.'"

Santiago looked squarely at Etienne. "All are gifts from God, some of which are in disguise. Thus, it is with all of your whys. Had your parents lived, you would have never met Isabella. Had you never met Isabella, you would have never fully stepped into the life God has provided for you. Is it all good fortune or bad fortune? We shall see." Before he could respond, Etienne was shot back into his body and found all but one of the candles that lit the small corridor were extinguished.

CHAPTER 37

OLVEIROA

A large hand startled Isabella awake, followed by another covering her mouth. Her tired eyes shot open. Gerhart was smiling at her with a big puppy grin. He removed his hand from her mouth and put his large finger to his lips. Isabella smiled gently at him and looked past his shoulder; all her companions were already up, gathering their things.

Gerhart left her bedside and Isabella slipped on her traveling clothes under the covers. She quietly packed her meager belongings, trying not to disturb the other pilgrims sleeping soundly. They had spent the night on the second level of the cathedral, with all the pilgrims who had arrived in Santiago over the past few days. There were clusters of pilgrims who had created Camino families gathered together about the balcony.

The only light in the cathedral was one lonely chandelier. Its candles shone brightly, sending shadows dancing on the walls. Isabella could barely make out the forms of her traveling companions, but it didn't matter. After spending so much time together, she would recognize them in complete darkness. She smiled gently and felt a wave of sadness wash over her. She stopped in place. *In two days' time, I may never see any of you again.*

A few moments passed and a chill ran through her body, bringing her back to the present. She quickly continued to pack. They had no time to waste; they had to make a three-day journey in two days. Isabella didn't want to consider missing that ship. If she did, she probably would choose to never return to France. She shook her head. She had to return to marry Edward. With their two nations united, Isabella hoped her father would give up the quest he had sent her on. In her experience, the search for the treasure only brought death. Another chill ran through Isabella's body.

Outside the cathedral the stars were shining merrily in the sky. The moon had set, leaving the little diamonds to show off their brilliance. The Milky Way streamed overhead, a dense path of stars running through the sky, mirroring the Camino. Each star like a pilgrim on the road to Santiago. The only sound the small company made as they navigated the winding streets was the sound of their staffs hitting the cobblestones. The sound sent a rhythmic echo that reverberated off the tall stone buildings. At the edge of the city, Isabella saw a torch and two figures some distance off. They were heading in the same direction as them, heading toward the end of the world, heading toward Finisterre.

The pilgrims pressed on through the day, their bodies strong and durable from the miles they had traveled.

"I think back to the person I was before this Camino, Clair. That Isabella would have thought a walk like today's to be impossible. I would have demanded a horse and a carriage. But now, now I am strong, and I almost feel like laughing at that spoiled child I was. I have found so much strength on this road. I have also found more joy on my Camino, even with all of its strife, than I ever found in my father's castle."

"Aye, lassie. Ya grew up."

"I am worried, Clair. I am worried that when I return home, I will lose who I have become on this journey." Isabella paused for a moment. "I will lose all of you."

"Ahh, lassie," Clair said, wrapping her arm around Isabella's waist. "Ya rememba' thos' stars this mornin'?" Isabella nodded her head. "Well, no matter 'ow far apart we are, if ya miss us, jus' look up at them stars and know we are under them, thinkin' of ya. We will always be with ya, no matter 'ow far apart. Love knows no distance." Isabella wrapped her arms around Clair and held her in an embrace.

"Ha ha, we are here," Andy shouted, from the road ahead. "Thank the Lord. Not sure 'ow much more walking I coulda done."

Isabella and Clair reached Andy and saw the village of Olveiroa close by. They continued on the road, following the stone wall that ran to the village. As they got closer, large stone storehouses stood, raised off the wall by sturdy legs. The storehouses had crosses on both sides of the slate roofs, and ventilation slats lining each wall. This allowed the wind to pass with ease, but protected the produce inside from moisture and vermin.

Andy peered into a storehouse. "Looks like they 'ad a good harvest this year."

Clair passed by him and grabbed him by the ear. "C'mon."

Isabella passed the main church and saw Gerhart, Etienne, and Mariano already at an albergue. Gerhart raised his arms in the air. "Ahh, there you are."

Isabella was happy they were all together again. Over the day, Etienne had broken off from the group and traveled ahead. He would rest and wait for the others to appear, then take off once they were in sight. Isabella knew he was keeping his distance to protect himself. She understood why he was doing it. As Isabella reached the group, she smiled at him kindly and his eyes softened.

The smell of food wafted from the inn, and Gerhart's stomach made a loud growl. Everyone looked at him. "What?" he asked, shrugging.

"We better find where that smell is coming from, and quickly. Otherwise Gerhart might eat us," said Mariano.

They all laughed and followed the smell to the dining area. Upon entering, they saw Carisa and Peter well into a meal. Carisa smiled widely and beckoned them to come join. Without hesitation, the pilgrims took a seat at the long table.

"Please, join us," Carisa said, taking the lid off the large pot that sat in front of her. As she removed the lid, the smell was so intoxicating, Gerhart couldn't control himself. He took a large bowl that lay in front of him and dipped it into the pot, removing a healthy portion of stew.

Clair elbowed him in the ribs and put her other hand on her forehead. "Ach."

Carisa smiled with a ladle in her hand. "All is well. We were just as hungry when we arrived. Who is next?"

Soon, all the bowls had steaming stew inside. Isabella blew gently on her first bite. As the hot fluid entered her mouth, she felt her whole body being warmed and nourished.

After the meal Etienne said, "It must have been you we saw leaving Santiago this morning. I thought we were the only ones in a rush to get to Finisterre."

"My wife and I have a ship to catch," Peter said. Etienne noticed Carisa looked at Peter lovingly when he said the word wife. Gerhart put his massive arm around Clair and pulled her in tight for a hug, his eyes full of love.

It was almost too much for Etienne to take. Without thinking, he said, "I saw you." Everyone looked confused by the statement.

"What do you mean, you saw us?" asked Peter inquisitively.

"I saw you sick in bed in Leon, praying for good health."

Peter's brow furrowed in confusion. "Did we meet in Leon?"

"No," Etienne said. "Santiago showed me. He also showed me Carisa praying for the love of her life. Did you know your prayer wasn't answered, so you could meet her?"

Everyone had a look of confusion on their face except Carisa. "You speak the truth."

"I have never been happier about an illness in my life," said Peter. "Carisa has been teaching me about the perfect tongue of the universe. Perhaps Santiago showed you these things so she can teach you how to speak this language as well."

Looking perplexed, Andy said, "Can someone explain what's going on?"

Carisa smiled at him and said, "The universe and God speak in a perfect tongue—a perfect language. Knowing this language, you can manifest anything in your life through prayer. The *word* has creation power. John 1:1 says, 'In the beginning was the word. And the word was with God and the word was God.' The creation power of the universe is sent into action with the word. Words are energy. Mankind can access this power, however, most have yet to remember how to speak this language."

Gerhart reached for his glass and tipped it over. The contents spilled on the table. Gerhart looked embarrassed. Isabella cleaned up the mess and said, "Don't worry. This will be clean in a moment."

Peter and Carisa smiled at each other like confidants. To Etienne, it looked like they knew something the others didn't.

"What?" asked Isabella.

"You just gave us a perfect example of how modern people speak unconsciously." said Carisa, "By saying, '*Don't worry,*' you are creating '*worry.*'"

"How else should I have said this?" Isabella asked, dropping the rag and putting her hands on her hips.

"All is well," responded Carisa. "When you use words like *worry, can't, must, and want,* the universe's delivery system is confused and we manifest that which is less than ideal in our life. Every word we speak has creation power. Conscious thoughts create empowering words that move the building blocks of the universe to manifest more accurately what is truly desired. So, say exactly what you mean."

"I am even more confused now than I was before," said Andy, taking another bite of stew.

"Another example of this is, by saying 'I *can't wait,*' you are telling the universe, '*I wait.*' In perfect tongue, you say, 'I am ready.' In the first case, you remain waiting, in the second, God can deliver what you are ready for," said Carisa.

"So, I saw the delivery system of God?" Etienne asked.

"It does appear so," said Carisa. "Isaiah said, 'So is my word that goes out from my mouth: It will not return to me empty but will accomplish what I desire and achieve the purpose for which I sent it.' You saw the word sent."

"Ach, I think I get it now." Andy waved his hands excitedly. "So, you are sayin' tha' just by using my words and speaking this perfect language, I can make anything come into existence?"

"That is correct," said Carisa.

"Let's give it a try."

Carisa quickly corrected him, "Let us do this."

"Right," Andy said skeptically. He cleared his throat. "I am ready to have a woman fall into my lap."

The door to the inn flew open and Sister Caroline dramatically entered the dining room.

"I cannot take one more step," she said as she stumbled, sending her flying into Andy's lap.

Andy looked down at Sister Caroline draped across him. With a look of confusion, he said, "Why, hello." Everyone erupted in laughter.

Sister Fransie entered the room. Seeing the scene, she exclaimed, "Sister Caroline!" Everyone erupted in laughter again.

Etienne put his hand on Andy's shoulder. "Well, the Bible does say, 'Ask, and it will be given to you; seek and you will find; knock and the door will be opened to you.'"

Andy looked down at Sister Caroline still in his lap. "I guess I should have been more specific," Andy said, and the whole room erupted with laughter once more.

CHAPTER 38

LAST NIGHT

Unable to sleep, Etienne sat in meditation in front of the embers from the fire. The room that had been filled with so much laughter earlier in the evening now seemed so empty. *This is it. This is my last night with Isabella. Will my life feel as empty as this room once she is gone?* He couldn't quiet his heart; it was speaking too loudly for him to focus his mind. *Ask and you shall receive,* he thought. *God, give me more time with Isabella,* he prayed, with all sincerity, from his heart.

Etienne sat for a few more minutes until the embers were barely glowing. Feeling the cold set in, he rose to get more wood from outside. On opening the door, he wrapped his cloak tightly around him, creating a cushion of heat about his body. He quickly gathered some wood from the pile under the windowsill. Turning back to the door, he looked up at the sky. The stars were shining brilliantly, each one reminding him of the night he had spent on the mountaintop with Isabella.

He reached for the door handle and it turned. Wood went flying in all directions as he stumbled backwards. The door was now open, revealing Isabella.

Trying to control her laughter, she said, "I guess I am not the only one who can't sleep." Etienne cracked a smile and they laughed. "Let me give you a hand." Isabella reached down and helped him up. Together they collected the logs and made their way indoors.

Etienne placed the new logs on the embers and blew, sending sparks in all directions. Each time he blew on the fire, his face was illuminated. Isabella sat quietly examining his every detail. She wanted his face etched into her memory forever. She wanted to remember every line, the color of his eyes, his strong jawline, everything, just like this. Etienne blew hard one last time and the logs burst into flames.

He moved away from the fire and sat by Isabella. She gently laced her arm through his and she felt his whole body relax. Isabella was at peace; she felt whole. The fire crackled, and the room filled with a merry warmth.

"Isabella, I wish it could be like this forever. I wish we were normal people and could have a simple life together."

Etienne had been so distant. This was the last thing she expected to hear from him. She nuzzled her head onto his shoulder. "Me too." After a moment, she continued, "I understand you being so distant. I understand you cutting off to protect yourself and what you have vowed to guard."

"I am sorry," Etienne said.

"I'm the one who should apologize. I have treated you horribly and put your life in danger. I also let you love me and returned your love, knowing I had a duty. Etienne, I have to go back and marry Edward. If I don't, my father will continue his search for the treasure. I'm doing it for you, for all of you. I want you all to be safe. Your safety is more important to me now than my selfish desire to be free." Isabella bit her lip. She didn't know what else to say. She didn't see any other options. "If I don't return they will certainly come looking for me and the treasure."

Etienne clasped her hand and looked at her with his soulful eyes. "I forgave you in Santiago. Just because you are gone, it doesn't mean I have to stop loving you. You always have been and always will be the love of my life."

Isabella reached up and kissed his lips, placing her hand on his coarse cheek. Her kiss said more than any words could have. Returning her head to his shoulder, she said, "Hold me like this night will never end. Hold me as your wife and as if this is our simple home." Together they sat, locked in a loving embrace, until their bodies found rest.

CHAPTER 39

FINISTERRE

Isabella and Etienne were awoken by the shrill cries of Sister Caroline, "Oh! We have overslept! We will never make it. What are we going to do?" She entered the dining room and continued to run around in a frenzy. "Wake up! Wake up!" she called, running around the albergue.

A surge of adrenalin entered Isabella's body and she jumped up. She ran to the window; the east was already glowing a radiant orange. Isabella couldn't miss that ship—she had to make it.

"How could this have happened?" asked Sister Fransie desperately, as every-one gathered in the dining room dressed in their sleeping clothes.

"There musta' been something in tha' stew," Andy rubbed his eyes groggily.

"What do we do now?" asked Isabella. "There won't be another transport back to France for quite some time. Etienne looked around the room and saw every-one had strain on their face except for Carisa and Peter, who both wore a small smile.

Standing up, Etienne turned to them in an almost threatening manner. "May-be Andy is right. Why don't you look concerned? Did you put something in that stew?" Carisa and Peter continued to smile.

"Well?" Etienne took an imposing step forward.

"The only extra ingredient in the stew was love," said Carisa in a kind voice. "Did you learn anything from our conversation last night? We shall set an in-tention in prayer and all who intend to be on that ship will set sail today. Who wishes to set sail on our ship today?" Sister Fransie, and Sister Caroline raised their hands. Isabella looked at Etienne and slowly raised hers as well. "Very good," Carisa said, "Sister Fransie, Sister Caroline, Isabella, Peter and myself are on the ship leaving Finisterre today. The ship shall depart shortly after we board. For my sake, in Jesus' name we pray."

Peter responded, "I second that."

Carisa smiled at him lovingly, "So let it be. Amen."

Andy scratched his head and asked, "What do ya mean you second that?"

"'Where two or more are gathered in my name, I am there,'" responded Peter.

Flustered, Sister Caroline interrupted, "All right, all right, enough of this, we must leave immediately."

Within minutes, all were dressed and on the road traveling west to Finisterre. They traveled together as one group. One Camino family. All from different parts of the world, but bound together by the Camino, with one common purpose.

Wanting to distract her mind from the impending separation, Isabella asked, "Andy, do you know anything about Finisterre?"

Andy puffed up his chest and said, "Actually, I do. This route ta Finisterre predates Christianity. Pagans would flock ta the end of the world, to the Coast of Death, or 'Costa da Morte,' as they called it. They believed the sun would die every day 'ere, bringin' the worlds of the living and dead closer together. It is also rumored tha' Finisterre was the 'ome of, Ara Solis, a magical place which had an altar dedicated ta the dying sun."

Isabella loved hearing Andy's historical rants. She was sad this might be the last time she would hear one. She had learned more from him than any of the scholars in her father's palace. Wanting him to continue she said, "Andy, I will miss all of your stories."

Andy winked and said, "I will continue then. The cult of the dying sun is why 'St. James' or 'Santiago' came ta preach 'ere, after our Lord Jesus Christ's death." Andy made the sign of the cross. "Santiago came ta Finisterre ta bring the true light ta the edge of the world. He converted many-a-pagan in his time 'ere. He then returned ta Judea, where he was executed by Herod Agrippa. Fearing that his remains would be destroyed, his disciples brought 'em back ta 'ere in secret. They were lost, until by a miracle, a bright light led a farmer ta his tomb. His identity was confirmed by the church, and Santiago de Compostela was founded—"

"There it is, there is the ocean," Gerhart shouted.

Isabella took her attention off Andy and looked ahead to see the vast expanse of the ocean stretching out in front of them. The deep blue was a welcome sight, and so different from the colors of land they had seen for so many days.

"Would ya look a tha'," said Clair. "'Tis beautiful!"

As they came closer, the town of Finisterre appeared, and there in the harbor was a large wooden ship, flying the Templar banner. Isabella felt both relief and dread. She slowed her pace. "There is our ship."

Reaching the edge of the town, Etienne stopped.

"What is it?" Isabella asked, she felt a tether on her heart that pulled as he stopped.

"This is as far as Andy and I should go." Etienne wore a stony face, but behind that mask Isabella knew he was crumbling just like she was.

"What do you mean?" She knew exactly what he meant, but she didn't want to believe it.

"Yeah, what do ya mean?" Andy repeated.

"We are wanted by the Templars. They see both of us as deserters, an act punishable by death."

"You didn't desert them." Isabella put her hand on Etienne's chest. "You came to save me."

Etienne gave his head a curt shake. "Sorry, this is as far as we can go."

"Very well," said Sister Fransie, "We shall continue on. May God bless your journey. Buen Camino, my friends." The nuns hooked arms and continued toward the ship.

"As shall we," said Carisa. She looked directly at Etienne. "We shall meet again." She took Peter's hand, and they continued after the nuns who walked arm-in-arm.

Isabella's eyes were fixed on Etienne. She didn't know what to say. She felt a force holding her to him. Every fiber of her person wanted to stay.

"Come on boys," said Clair, "Let 'em be."

"Just a moment, Clair," said Andy. "Isabella, I'm goin' ta miss ya—"

Before he could finish, Isabella put both her hands on his cheeks and kissed the top of his head. "I will miss you too."

Andy stepped back like a drunk man, his face was beet red. Clair grabbed him by the arm. "C'mon." Gerhart, Mariano, and Andy stepped away from the two.

Etienne reached out and Isabella took his hand. The moment their flesh met, electricity shot through her body.

"You are my heart," Etienne said. Isabella saw a torrent of emotion behind his eyes. "I will protect you and your heart until the day I die. I will see you again." No longer able to control herself, she threw her arms around him. A floodgate of tears streamed down her face. She felt his arms come around her to hold her head against his chest. She listened to the rhythm of his heart one last time, then let go and ran toward the ship. Against her will, she looked back to see Etienne rooted where he stood, love in his eyes.

Isabella reached Clair, Mariano, and Gerhart. As she joined them, they caught her in their loving embrace. Together, they walked the last few yards—the last few paces of their Camino.

Sister Fransie, Sister Caroline, Peter, and Carisa awaited them at the foot of the ramp leading to the giant vessel, along with several Knights Templar.

"Well, I'll be!" exclaimed one of the Templars. "I thought we had lost you to the Hounds of Hell. I didn't think we would see any of you again."

Clair clenched her fist into a tight ball and let it fly like a cannonball from her arm. Her fist found its mark, sending the Templar to the ground. Everyone stood in shock.

"Ya son of a—" she began as she moved toward him for another blow. Before she could connect, Gerhart restrained her. With the other arm, he lifted the Templar and held him a foot off the ground.

"You better take care of our Isabella. If not, you will wish that the Hounds of Hell had eaten you." He threw the man to the ground, discarding him like a rag doll.

"Come," Carisa said as she and Peter made their way up the ramp. Sister Caroline and Sister Fransie were quick to follow. Isabella looked at each one of her companions—her friends for so many miles. As her eyes locked with each one, she knew their story wasn't over, she knew that God would bring their paths together once more. They embraced one last time, and Isabella set foot on the ramp. The moment she made contact, a mighty wind rose in the air. The bells of the ship rang out, reverberating through her body. It signaled the end of one chapter in her life and the beginning of the next.

When she stepped onboard, the boat creaked and moaned like a giant beast begging to be released. The anchor was raised, and the sails were lowered, sending the ship out of the harbor. Isabella looked back at the dock to see her friends one last time. They stood there waiting vigilantly for her to disappear out of sight. Just above them to the east, the first stars shone in the evening sky. She thought of Clair's words, and it brought a sad joy to her heart. One star shone brighter than the others, and it made her think of Etienne. Under her breath, she said to the wind, "God willing, we shall see each other again, my love."

THE END

EPILOGUE

Etienne waited patiently on the edge of town with Andy and watched Isabella's ship sail out from the port.

"Are ya alrigh, laddie?" Andy asked.

No! I am not alright. I have lost her again. The only person who I have ever loved. I can still feel her here in my arms. I have nothing now that she is gone. She was my purpose. Now what? Etienne thought.

But he said, "I will be."

He could tell by the look in Andy's eyes that he didn't believe him. "We are all 'ere for ya. We are all goin' ta miss her." He patted Etienne gently on the back. "Ach, what's this?" Andy said, pulling a scroll out from behind Etienne's sheath.

Frowning, Etienne took the scroll from Andy. As he opened it, a small shard of wood fell to the ground. Etienne picked it up "This better not be what I think it is."

"Oh... ah. I dinna... I'm sorry." Andy looked at the ground with an ashamed look on his face.

Etienne placed a hand on his shoulder. "It's ok, the shard of the True Cross is back with us now. I will hold onto it this time." Etienne looked back down at the scroll. "It's from Isabella." He began to read...

My dearest love,

I wish with every fiber of my being I was still with you. I know my arms will regret not holding you for one more day, one more year, a lifetime, but I am bound to my duty.

I wanted to tell you this in the garden but I didn't know how, so I wrote you this letter. I have one last request of you: you must find the secret treasure of the Templars before my father does. I see now that he is an evil man and will bring so much death into this world if he possesses it.

My father knows everything Ronan told you in Leon. Tristan listened to your whole conversation in the cathedral and sent word to him. By now, my father knows how to decode the cathedrals, plus what I know about the doors. I'm sure he is already making preparations to find the treasure. With this knowledge, he no longer needs the Templars alive. He will set into action his plan to rid the world of your order.

I fear that my marriage to Edward may not be enough to stop my father from pursuing the treasure. But, if I do not go back, then he would undoubtedly start a war with the Templars. By showing him I am loyal to France, I will still have his trust and may still be able to dissolve his mission.

If I fail, you must find the treasure before he does and get it to safety. Also, there is a traitor in the Templars working for my father. Trust only Andy. I am telling you this because I love you and want to protect you from any danger.

Yours always,

Isabella

P.S. Don't be too mad at Andy. I took this from him when he was in the initiation ceremony. I was going to give it to my father, but my quest is done. Accept this as a token of my sincerity and changed heart. I will love you always.

APPENDIX

1. **Cathedral of Santiago de Compostela** is the culminating spot for the Camino de Santiago. The Cathedral of Santiago was constructed to hold the remains of Saint James the Greater, an apostle of Jesus. The city of Santiago de Compostela was built up around the cathedral, and is now the capital of the Galicia region in the northwest of Spain.

2. **Grand Master Arnold of Torroja** was the ninth Grand Master of the Knights Templar. He was over seventy years old when he became Grand Master in 1181 and served until his death in 1184. Before becoming a Templar, he was a Knight of the Crown of Aragon in Spain.

3. **The Knights Templar** were a Catholic military order that operated from 1119 to 1312. The order was among the wealthiest and most powerful orders in Christendom. They were renowned fighters and never left a battle until their flag left. They also were arguably the first organization to be a multinational corporation, with over a thousand commanderies and fortifications across Europe and the Holy Land. They also served as the first banking system for pilgrims. The Templar legacy is shrouded in speculation, secrecy, and legend. Part of the Templar leadership was imprisoned in Paris in 1307. However, a majority of the Templars and their wealth disappeared and has yet to be found. The order was officially disbanded by Pope Clement V in 1312.

4. **Grand Master Odo de St. Armand (1110-1179)** was the eighth Grand Master of the Knights Templar serving between 1171-1179. He is most famous for winning the Battle of Montgisard (1177).

5. **The Battle of Montgisard** was on November 25th 1177 between the King-
    dom of Jerusalem and the Ayyubids. In this battle, eighty Knights Templar
    helped 2,500 - 4,000 infantry, and 375 other knights, defeat the feared lead-
    er Saladin, and his army of over 26,000 soldiers.

6. **The Arc of San Anton** was founded in 1146 under the patronage of King
    Alfonso VI. It was formerly the main Preceptory of the Antonian monks in
    Spain. This order was dedicated to the care of pilgrims along the Camino
    de Santiago and to cure those who suffered from the "Fire of San Anton,"
    a disease that spread during the Middle Ages because of an undetected
    fungus that grew on grains. They helped pilgrims and were conferred with
    the Cross of Tau, a sign of protection against evil. It was also one of the five
    Knights Templar Commanderies associated with the town of Castrojeriz.

7. **The Camino de Santiago** was one of the most important pilgrimages in the
    Middle Ages, along with the Roman and Jerusalem pilgrimages. In English
    it is known as the "Way of Saint James." It is a system of pilgrimages that
    spread across Europe, leading to the remains of the apostle Saint James
    the Greater, which are housed in the Cathedral of Santiago de Compostela.
    Pilgrims would walk thousands of miles on the Camino to receive a plenary
    indulgence for the forgiveness of their sins. Today the Camino de Santiago
    is still incredibly popular, attracting over 250,000 pilgrims a year.

8. **The Moors**, a name that was first applied to the Maghrebine Berbers from
    North West Africa, was latter applied to the Muslim inhabitants of the Ibe-
    rian Peninsula, Sicily, and Malta during the Middle Ages. In 711 the Moors
    first crossed over from Africa to the Iberian Peninsula (Spain), conquering
    and ruling most of it until the Christian Reconquista. The attempts by the
    Christians to reclaim Spain began shortly after the Moorish invasion. But
    in 1212 the tides turned and the northern Christian Kingdoms pushed back
    the Moors. In this time they were aided by Christian military orders like the
    Knights Templars and Knights Hospitaller. By 1252 the Moors were pushed
    down to the Kingdom of Granada, where they ruled until 1492.

9. **Princess Isabella of France** was born to King Philip IV and Joan I of Na-
    varre sometime between 1290-1295, and died in 1358. She was their young-
    est child and only daughter. Her nickname was the She-Wolf of France. She
    was notable for her intelligence, beauty, and diplomatic skills. She married
    Edward II of England in 1308 and ruled as Queen of England until 1327.

10. **King Philip the IV of France** was born in 1268 and died in 1314. His nicknames were Philip the Fair, and the Iron King. He reigned as king of France from 1285-1314, and was married to Joan I of Navarre. Philip waged many wars and expanded the power and territory of France. He borrowed heavily from the Templars for these wars and became very indebted to them. In 1307, Philip arrested the Templars, which in turn cleared his debt and eased his fears of them creating a state within France.

11. **Deus Vult (God Wills It)** was the battle cry of the Knights Templar in the first Crusade (1096-1099).

12. **Santiago** (*also called St. Jacob or St. James the Greater*) was born around 3 AD and died 44 AD. Saint James was one of the 12 apostles of Jesus, along with his brother John. They were the sons of Zebedee. James was the first apostle to be martyred. St. James is the patron saint of Spain. According to the 12th century Historia Compostelana, St. James preached the gospel in Spain as well as the Holy Land. After he was martyred by King Herod, his disciples brought his body back to Galicia, Spain.

13. **Solomon's Temple** was the Holy Temple in Jerusalem before its destruction by Nebuchadnezzar. It is said to have stood from 1000-586 BCE. It was constructed under King Solomon and was said to hold many great treasures.

14. **Saladin (1137-1193)** was the founder of the Ayyubid Dynasty, and was the first sultan of Egypt and Syria. He was a Sunni Muslim of Kurdish ethnicity and led the Muslim military campaign against the Crusaders.

15. **The Fire of San Anton** was a disease that spread during the Middle Ages because of an undetected fungus that grew on grains. People would travel to the Arc of San Anton in the hope of being cured. It was later discovered that the grian in this region didn't have the fungus that caused the disease.

16. **Prince Koreyasu (1264-1326)** was the seventh shōgun of the Kamakura shogunate of Japan. He was the nominal ruler controlled by the Hōjō clan regents. Later in life he became a monk.

17. **The Codex Calixtinus** is a 12th century manuscript attributed to Pope Callixtus II about St. James and the Camino de Santiago. It includes sermons, reports of miracles, music, route descriptions of the Camino, and works of art to see along the way. It can be seen today in the museum of Santiago de Compostela.

18. **The Order of Assassins** was a military order that began in the mountains of Syria and Persia. The order was founded in 1090 and lasted to 1295. However, there are rumors that they never fully disbanded. In their time the order of assassins killed hundreds of key Muslim and Christian leaders, possibly avoiding the deaths of many by killing one person. Our modern word "assassin" comes from this medieval order, which was originally labeled with the Arabic word "_hasisin_" (pronounced "hashishin" in English).

19. **Jacques de Molay** was born in 1243 and died March 18^{th,} 1314. He was the 23rd and final Grand Master of the Knights Templar. He led the Templars from 1289 to 1312. His main goal as Grand Master was to rally support for another crusade in the Holy Land.

20. **Cernunnos** is a mysterious horned Gaelic deity. He is supposed to be the god of nature, beasts, and wild places.

21. **Pilier des Nautes,** or the "pillar of the boatmen," was erected by the guild of the boatmen in Paris in the 1st century AD. By the 4th century it had been repurposed into the wall of the Isle de la Cite. It was originally dedicated to Jupiter, but it has a carving of Cernunnos as well.

22. **Baphomet** is a deity that the Knights Templar were accused of worshipping. The name appeared in the Templar trials in 1307, and was subsequently incorporated into occult and mystical traditions. It first came into popular English usage in the 19th century during debate and speculation on the reasons for the suppression of the Templars.

23. **Bishop Gonzalo Osorio** served as a Bishop to both Leon and Burgos, Spain, between the years 1301 and his death in 1327.

24. **A *Green Man*** is a carving or other image of a face surrounded by vines or completely composed of leaves and vines. Many images have vines coming out of the nose, ears, and mouth. They are found on both secular and ecclesiastic buildings across the world. The symbol is usually associated with a nature deity and is the sign of rebirth.

25. **The Order of Knights of the Hospital of Saint John of Jerusalem (*AKA: Hospitallers*)**: The Hospitallers were a Catholic military order formed in the 11th century. Originally, they were associated with an Amalfitan Hospital in Jerusalem. During the first crusade in 1099, they received their own papal charter and were charged with the care and defense of pilgrims. After the Templars were disbanded, they were charged with the care of many of the Templar properties. In 1530 they took up residency in Malta and became known as the Knights of Malta.

26. **Pope Clement V** was born Raymond Bertrand de Got in 1264 and died in 1314. He was Pope from June 1305 – 1314. He is known for suppressing the Knights Templar and for moving the Papacy from Rome to Avignon, which started the Avignon Papacy. When elected Pope, he was neither a cardinal nor Italian; this caused many to speculate that he was tied with King Philip IV.

27. **The Alchemist:** Alchemy is an ancient branch of philosophy practiced throughout Europe, Africa, and Asia. An Alchemist attempts to purify metals, turning base metals into pure metals (ex: lead into gold). They also work on purifying the soul in the process, and creating the Philosopher's Stone.

28. **Cardinal Leonardo Patrasso (1230-1311)** was made a cardinal in 1300 and served most of his career in Rome.

29. **Cardinal Giovanni Boccamazza (Died 1309)** was an Italian cardinal from Roman nobility.

30. **Sir William Wallace (1270-1305)** was one of the main leaders in the First War for Scottish Independence. Wallace defeated the English army at the Battle of Stirling Bridge, September 1297. He became a legend and is remembered in novels and movies.

SUGGESTED READING LIST

There are many experiences, books, and conversations
with friends (both new and old) all over the world, that have
inspired the philosophies and ideas in my life. As I wrote
this novel, and walked the Camino, some of the books that have
inspired me are listed below. I highly recommend reading
these books if you found the concepts in this story
interesting or meaningful to you.

Buen Camino,

~ B.J.S.

1. *THE BIBLE*

2. *LOVING WHAT IS,* **by Byron Katie**
   "The Work" is a system of four questions and a "turnaround" that Katie
   created to help you question your thoughts, which can ultimately
   help you escape from damaging or painful patterns of belief and thinking.

   To learn more about "The Work," read *Loving What Is,* or go to
   www.thework.com, to discover how to use this process to confront and
   overcome your own thoughts.I have personally gotten some really
   life-changing results from engaging in "The Work," and I know many
   others who have as well. I highly recommend it.

3. *THE POWER OF NOW, by Eckhart Tolle*
   This book is amazing and really helps you to be in the present moment. It is
   perfect for those who want to explore meditation. https://eckharttolle.com/

4. *ASK AND YOU SHALL RECEIVE,* **by Receive Joy**
   The concept of the "perfect tongue of the universe," and the philosophy
   of manifesting through spoken prayer, is inspired by this book.
   https://receivejoy.com/

ACKNOWLEDGMENTS

I like to say God has a sense of humor. When I was young, I was obese and I became a dancer; I have dyslexia, and now I am an author. You can never tell what you will be called to in this life. I would like to thank God for inspiring this novel and helping me to achieve a task that I thought was impossible.

Writing this novel has been an exciting and humbling journey. It forced me to face a lot of my fears and to turn something that was my weakness into a strength. It has been a long road, but I have been fortunate enough to have had many companions along the way.

"Every Camino is like a lifetime: some people walk with you for a day, others a few cities, still others come in and out at the perfect moment. But, there are a rare few, who will walk with you until the end of the world."

My journey as an author has paralleled my journey on the Camino. Many people influenced and helped this novel along the way, but I feel blessed to have found a partner willing to walk to the end of the world with me. My wife, Chelsea, has not only helped me with every aspect of the novel, but she also walked over 500 miles on the Camino with me until we reached Finisterra— the end of the world.

Chelsea has been with me since I wrote the first draft. I thought it was perfect, but she kindly let me know it needed a little work. Here we are, three years and many versions later, she is still my constant companion and support. I hope everyone has the opportunity to feel as loved and supported by their partner.

I would like to thank all of the pilgrims who walked countless hours with me and inspired the characters in this novel. I would like to thank all of the mentors that led me down the path of becoming an author. I would like to thank all of my beta readers and editors. You took this novel from an ordinary book into an amazing novel.

To get this novel out into the world, there were numerous individuals who mentored and encouraged me along the way. They were generous with their time and helped to give feedback, or edit. Some of these people include: Shira Hoffman, Robin Sullivan, Andrea Gill, Janet Jones, Sylvia Lehmann, Ethan Okura, Rebecca Kinnie, Doriana Galliano, Michele Fong, Amy Luna, and many others.

There was also a whole slew of people who believed in me enough to support my Kickstarter campaign. Thanks to their generosity we have funded all the costs of editing, creating an audio book, printing, and distributing the first set of novels! To thank those individuals who financially supported the novel, I'd like to give a special shout out here! Oh, and of course a big thanks to my supportive family who planted adventure and spirituality into my heart.

KICKSTARTER BACKERS

Al Greig, Alan Martin and Olivia Harris, Alan Tracey, Amanda, Andrea Knott, Andrea M Smith, Angela Renae Amarillas, Angela T. Beck, Anna Takkula, Anne Marie Talon, Anonymous, April Rosetta, Arioch Morningstar, Aunt Kathy, Barb and Anna - Camino 2019, Ben Ernsten-Birns, Beth Allen DuBois, Brittany Garcia-Kindl, Bro. James William Gregg, Bryan Spellman, C. Corbin Talley, Carl Seese, Carol Lloyd, Carrie Hedden, Catrina Ankarlo, Celia Frost, Channie Wright, Charles Russell, Christopher Ingram, CJ Crooks, Clare Green, Claudia Kroon, Colleen Vaughn, Collin M. Johnson, Cris & Ryan Sand, Crystal Sutherland, Cynthia R. Millman, Daniel Broome, Daphne Mennell, David and Valerie Rokov, David Fuerstenau, David Hrovat, David Lars Chamberlain, Dean Schroeder Reimer, Debbie Attwood, Debbie Davis, Delia Armstrong, Devin, Diane, Donna M. Patterson, Edwin L Weader, Elaine "Lainey" Silver, Elizabeth Fulham Rovira, Emanuele the Barrow-Man, Emily Jane Milne, Eric and Sandy Faw, Erin and Chris McCabe, Eron Wyngarde, Ethan and Akari Okura, Florent Rigaud, Frances Rack, Francesco Tehrani, Franck., Gary & Diane Spurgeon, Genie Goldberger, Gerhard Lukas, Gerri McCullough, Ginny Heatwole, Hadi Nosseir, Hannah Middlebrook, Hannah Plush, Harry & Anju Taylor, Hazel Squire, Heather Hubbard, Howlin' Whale, Ian and Kathryn Gaines, Ian Caldwell, Irene Carrasco, Jackie Mckenzie, James Pesch , Jamie and Aimee

Doyle, Jan Jedersberger, Janet Goss, Jason Wulf, Jeff and Carol Goss, Jeff
Kellem, Jenni D Strand, Jennifer Kay Sherman, Jennifer L. Pierce,
Jennifer Sanchez, Jenny Masterman, Jessica Laikeman, Jimmy Caruso, John
A Hawke, John Idlor, Jordan Bles, Jordan New, Joshua Lieberman, Karen
Hodges, Karma, Kellam Family, Kelly Vourlos, Kevin & Michelle Skillen,
Kimberli Hudson, Korben, Brock, and Finn Byars, Kristine Ochu, Lark
Cunningham, Larry & Barbara McCann, Laura, Laura Sinnott, Laura Smith
Martineau, Leen Lesire, Lesa Hanson, Levi Edwards, Lilly Johnson,
Lindsay Clipner, Liz Gable, Lois Schall, Lorraine Coulson, Lorreta and
David French, Lou Pierce, Malina Dravis-Tucker, Malinda, Mariano Ele,
Mark VanOtterloo, Marko, Mary Dale my awesome sister, MaryAnne
Howard, Matt Wolf, Michael J. Sullivan, Michael Jackson, Michelle Domanico,
Mike & Michelle Giffin, Misty Dawn Chesney, Nancy W Martin, Niels
and Ari Bogardus, Pat Gangwer, Paul & Alaina Pfeiffer, Paula Ulrich,
Peppe, Rafeal Cr, Renira Rutherford, Reno Suhr, Rhoni Blankenhorn,
Richard and Andine, Roby Young, Rod Simpson, Ron and Melody Domanico,
Rosie Vincent, Ruby Rutherford, Ruth Ritchey Moore, Sadie and Dominic,
Sandra McDowell, Sara Tawney-Miller, Sarah Drzazgowski (Burt) UK,
Scott Cohen, Shawna Kinkead, Sheri Herum, Shirley A Dominguez, Silvana
Yaroschuk, Skip and Sue Spellman, Sophie Thévenet, Stacey, Stephanie
Lynn Shapiro-Hakun, Steve & Sue, Sue Williams, Susanne Nunn, Susie Karasic,
Sylvie; Carisa, The absolute legend known as Ness, Thorbjørn Wejdling
and Maia Linnea Wejdling, Timothy Lyons, Tony Pierce, Travis Kotzebue,
Tyler Goss and Abigail Shelly, Varisht Gosain, Vivienne Lenk,
Wade Danielson, Yliander Ainslie